Choderlos de Laclos

LES LIAISONS DANGEREUSES

TRANSLATED AND WITH AN INTRODUCTION
BY P. W. K. STONE

PENGUIN BOOKS

Penguin Books Ltd, Harmondsworth, Middlesex
U.S.A.: Penguin Books Inc., 3300 Clipper Mill Road, Baltimore 11, Md
AUSTRALIA: Penguin Books Pty Ltd, 762 Whitehorse Road,
Mitcham, Victoria

—

This translation first published 1961

—

Copyright © P. W. K. Stone, 1961

—

Made and printed in Great Britain
by Hazell Watson & Viney Ltd
Aylesbury and Slough

The drawing on the cover is by
Cecil Keeling

THE PENGUIN CLASSICS
EDITED BY E. V. RIEU
L116

WITHDRAWN
FROM
MIC-SPCT

CONTENTS

INTRODUCTION

Les Liaisons Dangereuses was first published in Paris in 1782. Society regarded the event as an outrage. The first edition sold out within a few days and subsequent editions were rapidly exhausted.

All Paris read and discussed the book. We hear, inevitably, of how young ladies would retire with it behind locked doors. Many years later a bound copy, title and author's name discreetly absent from its cover, was found in the library of Marie-Antoinette herself.

The author, Pierre-Ambroise-François Choderlos de Laclos, an obscure officer of artillery on leave from a garrison in the provinces, shared personally in the notoriety. Only his initials had appeared on the title page of the first edition, but his identity was soon established, and a character supplied him to suit the impression his book had made. 'Because he has portrayed monsters,' as a contemporary put it, 'people will have it that he is one himself.' It is recorded, for instance, of a certain Marquise de Coigny – who was not apparently remarkable for the strictness of her own principles – that she told the footman at her door: 'You know the tall, thin, sallow gentleman in a black suit who often comes to see me. I am no longer at home to him. If we were left alone together I should be terrified.'

Long after the scandal had died down, the book continued to be held in bad odour; but it continued to be read, until eventually the government decided to take a hand in its fate. In 1824 a decree of the *cour royale de Paris* condemned it to be destroyed as 'dangerous'. This verdict remained the official one throughout the later nineteenth century. The book was spoken of only to be deplored: 'a picture of the most odious immorality, that should never have been revealed even supposing it had been true', 'a work of revolting immorality', 'a book to be admired and execrated'. It is interesting that one of its few supporters should have been Baudelaire – but the article he planned in its defence was never written. Reactions in our own century have been less emotional, and the book has risen enormously in critical and popular esteem, but the idea of 'danger' still recurs in critical commentary. Jean Giraudoux, for instance, writes: 'Even today *Les Liaisons* remains the one French novel that gives us an impression of danger: it seems to require a label on its cover reserving it for external use only.'

The 'impression of danger' is understandable, even if a common-sense view of the matter suggests that the danger can hardly now be more than a hypothetical one. The depiction of immorality *per se* has probably never disturbed anyone but the extremely puritanical. What did, however, disturb contemporary readers of this book was that it depicted a particularly heartless form of immorality in the most elaborate detail and, worse, they could not be sure that the picture was not intended for a sympathetic one.

It is, in fact, still open to question whether the two principal characters – the Marquise de Merteuil and the Vicomte de Valmont – are meant to be the villains of the piece or, on the contrary, a sort of Satanic hero and heroine. The author once claimed, in a letter to a critic, that he had intended the horrors of vice to be apparent beneath their superficial attractions; but opinion is still divided as to whether or not he achieved the desired effect. It is these two characters, at all events, who, from the beginning, have been the source of most of the trouble.

The Marquise de Merteuil and the Vicomte de Valmont are what might be called professional profligates – professional in the sense that, with nothing else to occupy their time, they make of sexual intrigue a business from which they derive both profit and honour. Pleasure for them, however, is incidental. Success is all. They are not troubled by scruples because they consider themselves superior to morality. They devote themselves with utter ruthlessness to exploiting the susceptibilities of others for their own ends. Their own susceptibilities are out of harm's way – if they ever had feelings, they have got rid of them. Only their vanity remains to be touched. They are certainly monsters. And yet they are charming monsters: intelligent, urbane, amusing. One cannot help admiring them. They are taken in by nothing, and they are afraid of nothing.

This ambiguity readers have found sufficiently unsettling. What makes matters worse is that Laclos does not, at the end of his story, dispose of these two frightful and fascinating personages in a suitably damning way. When all is over, too much glamour still attaches to their careers of viciousness and crime. A single unequivocal comment from him might have helped, but, hiding behind his fictional role of 'editor', he makes none but detached and ironical remarks of dubious implication.

He portrays his virtuous characters, it is true, with equal care and equal understanding. The Présidente de Tourvel, at least, who is very little more than a butt for the Marquise's sarcasms at the beginning of the book, he transforms into a figure of considerable dignity and courage, to whom in the end it is impossible to refuse our sympathies. It may even be that he meant her, and the other representatives of virtue in the book, to set its moral tone, but the curious uncertainty of emphasis remains.

The representatives of virtue, besides, are by no means unexceptionable as such, and here is another more obscure but perhaps deeper reason for all the disquiet. We tend to expect of a novel, and the eighteenth century admitted no exceptions, that it should show us virtue triumphant. In this one virtue is defeated on every front. What Laclos, by the direction he gives his story, seems to be insisting on is that virtue, by itself, is no guarantee of success, and that even for the successful practice of virtue other qualities are necessary. His villains are armed with intelligence and a shrewd insight into human motives, and, in a world of personal relationships where there can be no appeal to justice, they carry all before them. He tries, no doubt as a concession to popular prejudice, to make their ultimate fate look like just retribution, but it is quite obviously no more than very bad luck.

There is, then, this shadow of an uncomfortable truth lurking behind the polished façade of the novel, and it is not impossible that a mere suspicion of its presence has accounted for much of the uneasiness felt about the book.

There were, of course, more obvious and superficial reasons for the scandal occasioned by its first appearance. One of these was that it was regarded as a *roman à clef*. 'Keys' identifying the chief characters circulated busily, to be greeted, one may imagine, with much throwing up of hands. Laclos is reported to have said himself that he drew his characters from life. But indications he gave as to their true identities were vague, and, in the absence of any other conclusive evidence, the matter has never been satisfactorily settled. Stendhal claimed that, as a small boy in Grenoble (a town in which Laclos spent part of his army life), he had met the original Madame de Merteuil, by then an old lady, lame and ugly, who petted him and gave him pickled walnuts. But his claim has never been verified.

If the more frivolous of Laclos' contemporaries took a scandalous interest in the identity of his models, the more serious-minded were horrified at the picture he had painted of contemporary manners. This was an age when 'sensibility' was much admired. Novels were expected to offer their readers a flattering reflection of themselves engaged in elegant, refined, and tearfully sentimental love affairs. This one being honest to the point of cynicism about a great deal that was commonly concealed behind elegance, refinement, and sentiment, it is not surprising that it was found to be a viciously distorted caricature of the truth.

Laclos' picture of the times is not, certainly, a comprehensive one. He confines himself to a small group of aristocrats, and concentrates exclusively on their personal relationships. But what he reveals within this narrow compass is sufficiently convincing.

It is common knowledge that the aristocracy in France at this time, on the eve of the Revolution, were excessively wealthy and excessively idle. If their private lives were corrupt, they had every encouragement. The conventions demanded only lip-service. Society expected women to keep up an appearance of 'reputation', men of 'honour', but this need be no more than a test of calculated hypocrisy, though the penalty for failure was severe. Marriage was regarded as an expedient, love as a sort of comic and undignified disaster, the spiritual equivalent of slipping on a banana-skin. Valmont and the Marquise are only extreme exponents of an accepted point of view.

Laclos, however, reserves most of his irony for the 'good' characters who, in their attempts to uphold the conventions, are not much less hypocritical than the others. One cannot ever be sure that his intentions are seriously satirical. His very sub-title, with its promise of 'edification', is mock-solemn. But, in two respects at least, the conventions themselves appear to arouse his critical interest, if not his genuine indignation.

Young women in his day were given very little grounding in the facts of life. They were kept immured in their convents until they were ready for marriage and then were plunged into the great world, dangerously unprotected in their ignorance against the wiles of the Valmonts and Merteuils. The marriage, moreover, would have been arranged solely on a basis of mutual advantage to the families concerned. The *mariage de raison* was an almost universally accepted institution – and almost the only obligations it imposed were economic ones. Society was thus wilfully encouraging the depredations of the immoral, not only by refusing women the safeguard of a proper education, but by denying them the protection of a marriage for love – and then turning a blind eye to the consequences.

Laclos might almost be offering us these considerations, among others of the kind, to explain the tragedy the book portrays. His characters' lives are, of course, governed by the conditions of their time. But, whereas those conditions have vanished, there is no reason to suppose that the Merteuils and Valmonts, as a breed, are extinct, nor indeed that they would now find victims in short supply. The story, in fact, has lost none of the force and psychological truth without which, even a hundred and eighty years ago, it would have made no impression at all.

The book, however, will proclaim its own merits. One aspect of it only requires more comment. It is a novel in letters – a form in which had appeared two of the most celebrated novels of the eighteenth century, Richardson's *Clarissa*, and Rousseau's *La Nouvelle Héloïse*, but which today is liable to savour – and especially for the reader who has had a taste of the above-mentioned great but very solid books – of the laboured and artificial. Laclos, however, was writing more than twenty years after Rousseau and thirty after Richardson, and, while they served him for models in many respects, he was also able to learn from their shortcomings. The chief of these was that their letters were too often mere reports of events, motivated by nothing more convincing than a perpetual urge in their characters to write. This is true of very few of the letters in this book. For the most part they do not only tell the story: they are a part of the story. Each one is an incident in the plot. One gives rise to another, and all are written with some definite purpose of the writer's in view. Thus the artificiality of the method is scarcely perceptible, and none of its advantages is lost, above all the effect of immediacy which letters can be relied upon to make. Laclos commands greater variety, too, than his predecessors. He keeps more than one correspondence alive at a time and, moving from one to another, is constantly providing the reader with a fresh point of view on events. Above all, he is careful not to allow any one of his characters to go on for too long. (Clarissa, it has been calculated, must at certain points in her career have scratched away with her pen for a good eight hours a day.)

Laclos was a student of tactics, and a great deal of the narrative interest of his book springs from the ingenious use to which he puts this preoccupation of his. The novel has been described as a study in the 'strategy' of love. He does in fact make it a fancy of his hero-villains that there is a science of love not different in essentials from the science of warfare, and they do a good deal of their think-ing along military lines. Campaigns are meticulously planned. Advantage, as in war, is the only consideration, 'glory' the final reward. The diabolical cleverness of these 'campaigns' is enthral-ling, but they cast a curious light, too, on the imagination that was capable of conceiving them. It seems, indeed, that one aspect of Laclos' temperament was distinctly Machiavellian: so much so that a more ingratiating one which reveals itself in letters to his family is sometimes dismissed as a sham. But very little is known definitely about his personal life, and of his early career up to the writing of his book scarcely more than a few dates remain on which to base a judgement.

He was born in Amiens on 18 October 1741 into a respectably pedigreed, but undistinguished family. At the age of eighteen he entered upon a military career in the artillery, and spent the next twenty or so years in one provincial garrison town or another. He received successive promotions, and attained the rank of *capitaine-commandant* without ever having seen battle.

Meanwhile he cut some figure in provincial society, and occupied part of his spare time in writing light verse. A few of his pieces were published in the *Almanach des Muses*, a periodical devoted to literature of this kind. In 1777 a comic opera, *Ernestine*, for which he had written the libretto, was produced in Paris. A contemporary reports that, at the first performance, 'both words and music were booed from beginning to end'.

In 1779 he was sent to the island of Aix, near La Rochelle, to supervise the construction of a fort. It was here that *Les Liaisons Dangereuses* was conceived and written. His immediate personal motives for writing the book are interesting. A famous *roué* of the time, the Comte Alexandre de Tilly, recalls in his *Memoirs* the confession Laclos once made to him: '... having written a few elegies on the dead, who will make nothing of them, and a few epistles in verse which, fortunately for myself and the rest of the world, will never be printed; having prepared myself for a profession which could bring me no great advancement or consideration, I resolved to write a book which would make a new departure, which would create some stir in the world and continue to do so after I had gone from it.'

In 1781 Laclos obtained leave of absence to supervise the printing and publishing of his book in Paris. It appeared the following year. The stir it created did him no great harm, but it did him no good. He had overstayed his leave and was promptly ordered back to his regiment.

The rest of his career is better documented, but of less interest here. Of his other writings, a treatise on the education of women and another on the tactician Vauban are still of interest to students.

In 1786 he married a lady of Bordeaux, Solanges Duperre, two years after the birth of their first child. In spite of the irregular beginning, he appears to have made a model husband and father. Letters he wrote his wife and family in later years show that his domestic attachments were strong, and it is not difficult behind other productions of his pen to imagine the conventional pillar of decency.

The obverse side of this curious character, the bent for chicanery and intrigue that betrays itself in the novel, was given fuller scope when in 1788, having left the army, he entered political life in the service of the Duke of Orleans. There is no room here, however, to explore some of the obscurer secret passages and back-alleys of history. Laclos never achieved eminence in politics, but he was important enough to be twice imprisoned – and lucky enough to be twice released – during the Reign of Terror.

In 1800 he returned to the army as one of Napoleon's generals.

He served under Marmont with the army of the Rhine, and in Italy where, on 5 September 1803, at Taranto, he died.

His fame now rests on his novel. Oddly enough, its fate, after the initial success, ceased to interest him. Towards the end of his life he proposed writing another to show that true happiness could be achieved only in family life. Admirers of this book will probably not regret that so worthy an intention remained unfulfilled.

LES LIAISONS DANGEREUSES

OR LETTERS COLLECTED IN ONE
SECTION OF SOCIETY AND
PUBLISHED FOR THE
EDIFICATION
OF OTHERS
BY
MONSIEUR C—— DE L——

*

J'ai vu les mœurs de mon temps,
et j'ai publié ces Lettres.

J.-J. ROUSSEAU
Preface to *La Nouvelle Héloïse*

PUBLISHER'S NOTE

WE think it our duty to warn the public that, in spite of the title of this work and of what the editor says about it in his preface, we cannot guarantee its authenticity as a collection of letters: we have in fact, very good reason to believe that it is only a novel.

What is more, it seems to us that the author, in spite of his evident attempts at verisimilitude, has himself destroyed every semblance of truth – and most clumsily – by setting the events he describes in the present. In fact, several of the characters he puts on his stage are persons of such vicious habits that it is impossible to suppose they can have lived in our age: this age of philosophy, in which the light of reason, illumining every heart, has turned us all, as everyone knows, into honourable men and modest and retiring women.

Our opinion, therefore, is that if the adventures recorded in this book have any foundation in truth, they must have happened in other places or at other times: and we consider the author – who has evidently been beguiled by hopes of attracting more interest for his story into locating it in his own time and country – we consider him very much to blame for venturing to represent, under the guise of our costume and our customs, a way of life so altogether alien to us.

To keep the over-credulous reader, as far as we can, at least from being taken unawares in this connexion, we shall support our opinion with an argument which we offer him with confidence, since it appears to us to be incontrovertible and unchallengeable: this is that, though like causes will always produce like effects, we never see girls nowadays who have dowries of sixty thousand *livres* taking the veil, any more than we see young and pretty married women dying of grief.

EDITOR'S PREFACE

THIS work, or rather this collection of letters, which the public will perhaps find too voluminous in any case, contains nevertheless only a very small portion of the correspondence from which it was drawn. Commissioned by the persons into whose possession the letters had fallen (and whom, I knew, intended to have them published) to set them in order, I asked nothing for my pains but permission to delete what seemed to me to serve no purpose. I have tried, in fact, to retain only those letters which appeared necessary either to an understanding of events or to the development of the characters. If to this trifling task is added that of arranging in order such letters as I allowed to remain (an order which almost invariably follows that of the dates), and finally a few brief and sparsely scattered notes, which, for the most part, have no other object than that of indicating the sources of quotations, or of explaining the abridgements I have permitted myself to make, my whole contribution to this work is accounted for. My mission extended no further.[1]

I had proposed more considerable alterations, almost all of them relating to purity of diction and style, which will often be found very much at fault. I should also have liked permission to abridge certain of the letters which are too long: several of them discuss successively, but with scarcely any transition between, subjects which have nothing whatever in common with each other. This course of action was not approved: it would not, of course, have been sufficient by itself to give the work any merit, but would at least have removed some of its faults.

It was objected that the intention was to publish the letters themselves, and not simply a literary work modelled on the letters;

1. I must indicate here, too, that I have suppressed or changed the names of all the persons concerned in these letters; and that, if among the names I have invented, are found any that belong to living persons, they represent merely accidental errors on my part, from which no necessary consequence is to be drawn.

that it would have been as much counter to probability as to truth if the eight or ten persons participating in this correspondence had written with equal correctness. And upon my representing that, far from there being any question of correctness, there was not a single one of these persons who had not committed the grossest errors, which could not fail to meet with criticism, it was replied that every reasonable reader would surely expect to find mistakes in a collection of letters that had passed between private individuals, since of all those published hitherto by various authors of reputation (including certain Academicians) not one could be found totally beyond reproach in this respect. These arguments did not convince me, and I found them, as I still find them, easier to put forward than accept: but the final say was not mine and I submitted. I reserved only the right to protest, to declare, as I now do, my difference of view.

As for any merit that might attach to this work, it is perhaps not for me to offer an opinion which neither can nor should influence that of anyone else. Those, however, who, before they begin to read a book, would be glad to know what, more or less, they are to expect, would do well to read on: others would do better to proceed immediately to the text itself. They know enough about it already.

What I must say to begin with is that, if it was my conviction (as I admit it was) that these letters ought to be published, I am still very far from expecting any success for them – and let not this frankness on my part be taken for the false modesty of an author; for I must declare, with the same candour, that, if this collection had not seemed to me worthy of being offered to the public, I should have had nothing to do with it. Let us try to reconcile these apparent contradictions.

The merit of a work derives from its usefulness or from the pleasure it gives, or even from both when it has both to offer. But success, which is not always a proof of merit, depends more often on the choice of a subject than on its execution, on a certain combination of subjects rather than on the way in which they have been treated. Now since this collection contains, as its title announces, the letters of a whole section of society, a diversity of interests is represented which are not all those of the reader. Moreover, since nearly all the sentiments expressed are either pretended or dissembled, they can excite only the interest of curiosity, an interest always much inferior to that of feeling; one, above all, which, inclining the reader less to indulgence, leaves errors of detail more open to criticism, since it is they that continually frustrate the one desire he wishes to satisfy.

These faults are perhaps partly redeemed by a quality inherent in the very nature of the work: the variety of its styles, a merit which a single author would find it difficult to achieve, but which here appears of itself, sparing the reader the tedium, at least, of uniformity. Some people might also take into account the fairly large number of either original or little-known observations, to be found dispersed throughout the work. These, too, I think, constitute all that may be hoped for from the book in the way of pleasure, and even so only upon the most lenient appraisal.

The usefulness of the work, which will perhaps be even more strongly contested, seems to me nevertheless easier to establish. I think, at any rate, that it is rendering a service to public morals to reveal the methods employed by those who are wicked in corrupting those who are good, and I believe these letters may effectively contribute something to this end. In them will also be found proof and example of two important truths which one might almost think go unrecognized in view of the fact that they are so rarely remembered in practice: one, that any woman who consents to receive an unprincipled man into her circle of friends must end his victim; the other, that any mother is, to say the least, imprudent who allows anyone but herself to win her daughter's confidence. Young people of either sex might also learn that the friendship which unprincipled persons offer them so glibly is always a dangerous trap, as fatal to their happiness as to their virtue. On the other hand, the abuse of knowledge, which so often follows close upon benefit from it, seems to me in their case too much to be feared; far from recommending this book to young people, it seems to me very important to keep it from them. The time at which it may cease to be dangerous and become useful has been very well determined, for her own sex, by a good mother who is not only intelligent but sensible as well: 'Having read this correspondence in manuscript,' she told me, 'I should consider it a true service to my daughter to give her the book on her wedding day.' If mothers in every family thought like this I should never cease to congratulate myself upon having published it.

But, putting aside such agreeable fancies, it still seems to me that this collection can please very few. Libertines of either sex will find it in their interest to decry a book which may do them harm; and since they are never without cunning, they will perhaps be clever enough to attract the puritans to their side, who will be alarmed by the picture of wickedness that is here fearlessly presented.

Would-be free-thinkers will not be interested in a devout woman, who, because she is devout, they will regard as a ninny, while the devout will be angry at seeing virtue fall, and will complain that religion does not appear to enough effect.

From another point of view, readers of fastidious taste will be disgusted at the excessively simple and incorrect style of many of these letters; whereas the general run of readers, misled by the idea that everything that is printed is the result of deliberation, will think they detect in others the laboured manner of an author who appears in person behind the characters through whom he speaks.

Finally, it will be said in general that nothing is of any value out of its proper place; and that if ordinarily letters in the social world are deprived of all grace by an over-cautious style in their authors, the smallest negligence in such as these becomes a fault, is made insupportable by being committed to print.

I admit in all sincerity that these criticisms may be well-founded: I believe, too, that I could reply to them, even without exceeding the permissible length of a preface. But it must be apparent that if it were necessary to answer for everything, the book itself could answer for nothing: and if I had judged that to be the case, I should have suppressed both book and preface.

PART ONE

LETTER 1: *Cécile de Volanges to Sophie Carnay at the Ursuline Convent of —*

You see, my dear Sophie, I am keeping my word. Frills and furbelows do not take up all my time; there will always be some left over for you. Nonetheless, I have seen more frippery in the course of this one day than I did in all the four years we spent together; and I think our fine Tanville[1] is going to be more mortified by my next visit to the convent (when I shall certainly ask to see her) than she could ever have hoped we were by all those visits of hers to us *en grande tenue*. Mamma has consulted me in everything; she treats me much less like a schoolgirl than she used to do. I have my own maid, a bedroom and closet to myself, and I am sitting as I write at the prettiest desk to which I have been given the key so that I can lock away whatever I wish. Mamma has told me that I am to see her every morning when she gets up. I need not have my hair dressed before dinner, since we shall always be alone, and then every day she will tell me at what time she expects me to join her in the afternoon. The rest of the time is at my disposal, and I have my harp, my drawing, and my books – just as at the convent, except that Mother Perpétue is not here to scold me, and, if I choose to be idle, it is entirely my affair. But, as I have not my Sophie to chat and laugh with me, I had just as soon be busy.

It is not yet five o'clock and Mamma is not expecting me till seven: plenty of time if only I had something to tell you! But so far I have been told nothing, and if it were not that preparations are plainly being made and numbers of women employed on my behalf, I should be inclined to think that no one had ever dreamed of marrying me and that the idea was just another of our dear Joséphine's absurdities. Still, Mamma has so often told me that a young lady ought to stay at her convent till she is married that, since she has taken me out, Joséphine must certainly be right.

1. A fellow-pupil.

23

A carriage has just come to the door and Mamma has sent to tell me to come to her room at once. Supposing it is he? I am not dressed. My hands are trembling and my heart beating fast. I asked the maid whether she knew who was with my mother. 'Indeed,' she said, 'it is Monsieur C —' And she laughed! Oh, it must be he! I shall come back without fail and tell you what has happened. That is his name, at any rate. I must not keep them waiting. For the moment, goodbye!

How you will laugh at your poor Cécile! I was so ashamed of myself! But you would have been caught just as I was. As I came into Mamma's room I saw, standing by her, a gentleman dressed in black. I greeted him as best I could and stood there, quite unable to move. You can imagine how I scrutinized him!

'Madame,' he said to my mother as he bowed to me. 'What a charming young lady; I am more than ever sensible of the extent of your kindness.'

The meaning of this was so plain that I was seized with trembling and my knees gave way; I found a chair and sat down, very flushed and very disconcerted. I had hardly done this when the man was at my feet. Upon which I lost my head; I was, as Mamma said, utterly panic-stricken. I jumped up uttering a piercing shriek . . . just as I did that day there was a thunderstorm, do you remember? Mamma burst out laughing and said: 'Come now, what is the matter? Sit down and give your foot to Monsieur.' In short, my dear, the gentleman was a shoemaker. I cannot tell you how ashamed I was: luckily no one but Mamma was there. I think I shall have to find another shoemaker when I am married.

How worldly-wise we are – you must admit! Good-bye. It is nearly six o'clock and my maid says I must dress. Good-bye, my dear Sophie; I love you as much as I ever did at the convent.

P.S. I don't know by whom to send this letter, so I shall wait till Joséphine comes.

Paris
1 August 17—

LETTER 2: *The Marquise de Merteuil to the Vicomte de Valmont at the Château de —*

COME back, my dear Vicomte, come back: what are you doing, what can you possibly do at the house of an old aunt whose property is all entailed on you? Leave at once: I need you. I have had an excellent idea and I want to put its execution in your hands. These few words should be enough; only too honoured by this mark of my consideration, you should come, eagerly, and take my orders on your knees. But you abuse my kindness, even now that you no longer exploit it. Remember that, since the alternative to this excessive indulgence is my eternal hatred, your happiness demands that indulgence prevail. Well, I am willing to inform you of my plans, but swear first that, as my faithful cavalier, you will undertake no other enterprise till you have accomplished this one. It is worthy of a hero; you will serve Love and Revenge; and in the end it will be yet another *rouerie*[1] to include in your memoirs – for one day I shall have your memoirs published, and I take it upon myself to write them. But let us leave that for the moment and return to what is on my mind.

Madame de Volanges is marrying her daughter: it is still a secret, but yesterday it was imparted to me. And whom do you think she has chosen for son-in-law? The Comte de Gercourt! Who would have thought that I should ever become Gercourt's cousin? It has put me in a fury. ... Well! Have you guessed? Oh, dull-witted creature! Have you forgiven him, then, for the affair of the Intendante?[2] As for me, have I not even more reason to complain of him, monster that you are?[3] Still – I am calm. The hope of vengeance soothes my soul.

1. The words *roué* and *rouerie*, which in good society are now happily falling into discredit, were very much in vogue at the time these letters were written.
2. [The wife of an Intendant, the administrator of a province. *Translator's note.*]
3. To understand this passage it must be known that the Comte de Gercourt had left the Marquise de Merteuil for the Intendante de — who, in her turn, had given up the Vicomte de Valmont for him. It was after this that the attachment between the Marquise and the Vicomte began. As the latter affair took place long before the events with which the present letters are concerned, the entire correspondence relating to it has been suppressed.

You have been irritated as often as I at the importance Gercourt attaches to the kind of wife he wishes to have, and at the stupid presumption that makes him believe he will escape his inevitable fate. You know his absurd predilection for convent girls, and his even more ridiculous prejudice in favour of modest blondes. In fact I am quite certain that, in spite of the sixty thousand *livres* a year the little Volanges will bring him, he would never have considered this marriage if she had been dark or had never been inside a convent. Well, let us prove to him that he is only a fool. It will certainly be proved one day: I am not anxious about that. But the delightful thing would be his beginning in that role. How amusing it would be, the morning after, to hear him boast! – for he will certainly boast. Then, if you had succeeded in educating the girl, it would be nobody's fault if he did not become, with the best of them, the laughing-stock of Paris.

For the rest, the heroine of this new romance deserves your fullest attention. She is really pretty: only fifteen years of age, a rose-bud. Gauche, of course, to a degree, and quite without style, but you men are not discouraged by that. What is more, a certain languor in her looks that really promises well. Add to these recommendations the consideration that it is I who make them, and you have only to thank me and obey.

You will receive this letter tomorrow morning. I insist upon your being at my house at seven o'clock in the evening. I shall receive no one till eight, not even the reigning favourite: he has not the head for affairs of such moment. With me, you will observe, love is not blind. At eight I shall give you your liberty, and at ten you will return to sup with the beautiful creature: both mother and daughter will be taking supper with me. Good-bye. It is past noon. I shall have done with you before long.

Paris
4 August 17—

LETTER 3: *Cécile de Volanges to Sophie Carnay*

I KNOW nothing yet, my dear. Mamma had a great many people to supper yesterday. In spite of my interest in examining them, the men especially, I was terribly bored. Everybody, men and women alike, looked at me a great deal and then whispered in each other's ears; and it was obvious they were whispering about me, which made me blush. I could not help it. I wish I had been able to. I noticed that when the other women were looked at they did not blush. Or else it is the rouge they use that prevents it being seen when they colour with embarrassment, because it must be very difficult not to blush when a man stares at you.

What made me feel most ill at ease was that I did not know what they were thinking of me. I think I heard the word 'pretty' once or twice; 'gauche' I heard very distinctly, and that must really be true about me because the woman who said it is a relation and friend of my mother's. She seems to have decided of a sudden to be my friend as well, and was the only person who spoke to me a little the whole evening. We are to have supper with her tomorrow.

After supper I also heard a man, who I am sure was talking about me, saying to another: 'That one must be left to ripen. Next winter we shall see.' Perhaps it is to him I am to be married; but in that case it will not be for another four months! I should so much like to know how things stand.

Here is Joséphine, and she tells me she is in a hurry. But I must tell you first about one of my *gaucheries*. Oh, I am afraid my mother's friend was right!

After supper they began to play cards, and I sat down beside Mamma. I don't know how it happened, but I fell asleep almost immediately. A great burst of laughter woke me up. I don't know whether they were laughing at me, but I believe they must have been. Mamma, to my great relief, gave me permission to retire. Imagine, it was past eleven o'clock! Good-bye, my dear Sophie; I hope you will always love your Cécile. I assure you the world is not nearly as amusing as we used to imagine it was.

Paris
4 August 17—

LETTER 4: *The Vicomte de Valmont to the Marquise de Merteuil in Paris*

YOUR orders are charming; your manner of giving them still more delightful; you would make tyranny itself adored. This is not, as you know, the first time I have regretted that I am no longer your slave. *Monster* though you say I am, I can never remember without pleasure a time when you favoured me with sweeter names. I often wish, too, that I might earn them again, and that, in the end, I might give, with you, an example to the world of perfect constancy. But larger concerns demand our attention. Conquest is our destiny: we must follow it. Perhaps at the end of the course we shall meet again, for, if I may say this without offending you, my dear Marquise, you follow close at my heels: indeed, it seems to me that on our mission of love, since we decided to separate for the general good and have been preaching the faith in our respective spheres, you have made more conversions than I. I know your zeal, your fiery fervour. And if our God judges us by our deeds, you will one day be the patron of some great city, while I shall be, at most, a village saint. Does my idiom astonish you? But for a week I have not heard or used any other, and it is because I must master it that I am obliged to disobey you.

Don't be angry; listen. I am going to tell you, the confidante of all my inmost secrets, the most ambitious plan I have yet conceived. What is it you suggest? That I should seduce a young girl who has seen nothing and knows nothing, who, so to speak, would fall undefended. She would be beside herself at the first compliment and would perhaps sooner be swayed by curiosity than by love. Twenty other men could do it as well as I. Not so the enterprise that claims my attention: its success will ensure me not only pleasure but glory. The god of love himself cannot decide between myrtle and laurel for my crown and he will have to unite them to honour my triumph. Even you, my love, will be struck with holy awe, and will say with enthusiasm: 'There goes a man after my own heart.'

You know the Présidente[1] de Tourvel: you know her piety, her

1. [The wife of a *Président*, the presiding magistrate of a court of justice. *Intendants* and *Présidents* belonged to the *noblesse de robe*, the magisterial nobility, as opposed to the *noblesse de race*, the old feudal nobility. *Translator's note*.]

conjugal devotion, her austere principles. That is where I have launched my attack. There is an enemy worthy of me. That is the goal I aspire to attain.

> And though at last I fail to carry off the prize,
> I shall have ventured on a glorious enterprise.

One may quote bad poetry if it is by a great poet.[1]

You probably know that the Président is in Burgundy attending to an important case. (I hope to make him lose a still more important one.) It is here that his inconsolable spouse is to spend the whole of her distressing grass-widowhood. Mass every day, a few visits to the poor of the district, morning and evening prayers, solitary walks, pious conversations with my old aunt, and sometimes a dreary game of whist, are her only distractions. But I am preparing more effective ones. My guardian angel brought me here, for her happiness and for mine. Fool that I was, I begrudged twenty-four hours sacrificed to respect for the conventions. What a penance it would be now, to be obliged to return to Paris! Fortunately it requires four to play whist and as there is no one here besides the local *curé*, who makes a third, my immortal aunt has implored me to stay a few days. As you have guessed, I consented. You cannot imagine the fuss she has made of me ever since, and how edified she is by my regular attendance at prayers and at Mass. She has no suspicion of the nature of the divinity I go to worship.

Here I am, then: for the past four days the victim of an overpowering passion. You know how strong my desires are, how they thrive on obstacles; what you do not know is the extent to which solitude can increase their force. I have only one idea: I think of it all day and dream of it at night. It has become necessary for me to have this woman, so as to save myself from the ridicule of being in love with her: for to what lengths will a man not be driven by thwarted desire? O sweet delight that for my happiness, for my very peace of mind, I crave! How lucky we are that women defend themselves so poorly! We should, otherwise, be no more to them than timid slaves. At this moment I feel grateful to all women of

---

1. La Fontaine.

easy virtue, a sentiment which brings me naturally to your feet. Prostrate there, I beg your forgiveness, and finish this too long letter. Good-bye, my dearest love: no ill-feeling.

Château de —
5 August 17—

LETTER 5: *The Marquise de Merteuil to the Vicomte de Valmont*

Do you know, Vicomte, that your letter is most extraordinarily insolent and that I might very well be angry? It proves clearly, however, that you are out of your mind; and that, if nothing else, spares you my indignation. Ever your generous and sympathetic friend, I shall forget my injuries so as to devote my whole attention to you in your danger. However tedious it may be to reason with you, I yield to your present need.

You – have the Présidente de Tourvel! But what a ridiculous fantasy this is! How characteristic of your perverse heart that longs only for what appears to be out of reach. Come, what is there to this woman? Regular features, if you like, but so inexpressive; a passable figure, but no grace and always so ludicrously ill-dressed, with those bundles of kerchiefs on a bodice that reaches to her chin! I tell you as a friend: you will not need two women of that sort to lose you your reputation. Have you forgotten the day when she took the collection at Saint-Roch and you thanked me so delightedly for having afforded you the spectacle? I can see her still, on the arm of that great spindleshanks with long hair, ready to collapse at every step, forever burying someone's head in five yards of pannier, and blushing at every genuflection. Would you have believed then you would one day want this woman? Come now, Vicomte, you must blush yourself and return to your senses. I shall keep the secret, I promise.

After all, consider the disagreeable things in store for you! What sort of rival have you to contend with? A husband! Does not the very idea humiliate you? If you fail, what dishonour! And so little glory if you succeed! I shall go further: you must give up all hope of pleasure. Can there ever be any with prudes? I mean those who are truly so. At the very heart of rapture they remain aloof, offering you only half-delights. That absolute self-abandon, that ecstasy of the senses, when pleasure is purified in its own excess, all that is best in love is quite unknown to them. I prophesy to you: at the very best, your Présidente will think she is doing everything for you by treating you as she treats her husband, and, remember, even the tenderest conjugal *tête-à-tête* takes place across a distance. In your case things are still worse. Your prude is devout, and with that sort of simple piety that condemns a woman to eternal childishness. You will perhaps surmount this obstacle, but do not flatter yourself that you will destroy it. You may conquer her love of God: you will never overcome her fear of the devil. And when you hold your mistress in your arms, and you feel her heart beat, it will be beating in fear and not for love. Had you met this woman earlier you might perhaps have been able to make something of her, but she is twenty-two, and she has been married for nearly two years. Believe me, Vicomte, when a woman has become so *encrusted* with prejudice, she is best left to her fate. She will never be anything better than a nobody.

Yet it is on account of this fine creature that you refuse to obey me; for her that you bury yourself in that mausoleum of your aunt's, renouncing the most delightful adventure in the world and the one most calculated to do you honour. Is it then your fate that Gercourt shall always maintain some advantage over you? Do you know, with the best will in the world – I am tempted at this moment to believe you do not deserve your reputation. What is more, I am tempted to withdraw the confidence I have placed in you. I should never get used to telling my secrets to the lover of Madame de Tourvel.

I want you to know, nonetheless, that the little Volanges has already turned one head. Young Danceny dotes on her. He has sung with her; and, in fact, she sings better than is proper in a convent girl. They must have practised a great many duets now, and I daresay she would be willing enough to try something in unison, but Danceny is a child: he will waste all his time flirting and achieve nothing. The little creature, for her part, is as diffident; and, in any event, it will all be much less amusing than you could have made it. I am in a bad humour, therefore, and I am sure to quarrel with the Chevalier when he arrives. He would be well advised to be kind: at this moment it would cost me nothing to break with him. I am sure that if I had the good sense to leave him now he would be in despair, and nothing amuses me so much as a lover's despair. He would call me 'false', a word that has always given me pleasure. There is none more welcome to a woman's ear, excepting 'cruel', which, however, one must take more pains to deserve. Seriously, I am going to consider breaking with him. See what you have brought about! I lay it on your conscience! Goodbye. Recommend me to the prayers of your Présidente.

Paris
7 August 17 —

LETTER 6: *The Vicomte de Valmont to the Marquise de Merteuil*

So there is, after all, no woman who will not abuse the power she has been able to acquire! You, too, you that I so often called my indulgent friend, are at length no longer so. You do not even hesitate to attack me in the object of my affections. How dare you paint such a picture of Madame de Tourvel? . . . Any man would have paid with his life for such insolent presumption. Any other woman but you would have deserved severe punishment at least. Never, I beg you, put me to such harsh tests again: I shall not be able to answer for the consequences. In the name of our friendship wait, at least, till I have had this woman before you insult her. Did you not know that only pleasure has the right to take the bandage from love's eyes?

But what am I saying? What need has Madame de Tourvel of illusions? To be adorable she has only to be herself. You accuse her of being ill-dressed. I agree. Clothes don't become her. Everything that hides her, disfigures. It is in the freedom of dishabille that she is truly ravishing. Thanks to the present overpowering heat she wears only a simple linen gown which reveals her supple, rounded figure. A single muslin kerchief covers her breasts, and my covert but searching glances have already grasped their enchanting contours. Her face, you say, is inexpressive. But what is it to express at

moments when nothing touches her heart? No, she is not of course
one of your coquettes with their deceptive looks that are sometimes
seductive, but always false. She does not know how to disguise an
empty phrase with a studied smile; and, although she has the most
beautiful teeth in the world, she laughs only when she is amused.
If you could see, when she is playful, what a picture she makes of
frank and simple gaiety, how, when she is beside some unfortunate
she is anxious to help, her eyes shine with innocent joy and com-
passionate kindness! If you could see, especially at the slightest
word of praise or flattery, how her divine features colour with that
touching embarrassment which springs from an entirely artless
modesty! . . . She is chaste and devout: you therefore judge her
cold and lifeless. I think very differently. What an astonishing sensibility she must have, if her feelings extend even to her husband, if she
can continue to love a man whom she never sees! What more certain
proof could you wish for? I have, however, discovered yet another.

I contrived one of our walks so that we came to a ditch that had
to be cleared. Although she is very agile, she is even more timid;
as you may imagine, a prude is always afraid she may *fall*.[1] She
was obliged to entrust herself to me. I have held the modest woman
in my arms. Our preparations and the transhipment of my old aunt
kept our playful devotee in fits of laughter; but, when I took her up,
I contrived it awkwardly, so that our arms intertwined, and, during
the short space of time that I held her against my breast, I felt her
heart beat faster. That delightful blush came again to her face, and
her modest embarrassment was proof enough to me that *it was love
and not fear that had caused her agitation*. My aunt, however, made
the same mistake as you, and began to say: 'The child is afraid';
but the 'child's' charming honesty will not allow a lie, and she
replied simply: 'Oh, no! But . . .' That one word was an illumination. Since that moment cruel anxiety has given way to the sweetness of hope. I shall have this woman. I shall free her from a husband
who profanes her. I shall carry her off from the very God that she
adores. How enchanting to be in turn the cause and the cure of her
remorse! Far be it from me to destroy the prejudices that possess
her. They will add to my gratification and to my glory. Let her

1. Evidence of the deplorable taste for punning which was then beginning
to grow and has since become so widespread.

believe in virtue, but let her sacrifice it for my sake; let her be afraid of her sins, but let them not check her; and, when she is shaken by a thousand terrors, may it only be in my arms that she is able to overcome them and forget them. Then, if she wishes, let her say: 'I adore you'; she alone, of all women, will be worthy to utter those words. And I shall indeed be the god of her choice.

Let us be frank. Since our intimacies are as cold as they are shallow, what we call happiness is scarcely even a pleasure. But shall I tell you something? I thought my heart had withered away, and, finding nothing left to me but my senses, I lamented my premature old age. Madame de Tourvel has restored the charming illusions of my youth. When I am with her I have no need of pleasure to be happy. The one thing that alarms me is the amount of time I must give up to this adventure, for I dare not leave anything to chance. It is no use reminding myself of bold schemes that have succeeded before: I cannot bring myself to put them into practice. I cannot be really happy unless she gives herself to me; and that is no trifling matter.

I am sure that you would admire my prudence. I have not yet uttered the word 'love', but we have already arrived at 'confidence' and 'interest'. So as to deceive her as little as possible, and in order, especially, to forestall any rumours which might reach her ears, I have myself described, as if in self-accusation, some of my better-known exploits. You would laugh to see how openly she preaches at me. She wishes, she says, to convert me. She has no suspicion as yet of how much the attempt will cost her. She has no idea that in 'pleading', as she puts it, 'for the unlucky women I have ruined', she is speaking in advance on her own behalf. This occurred to me yesterday in the middle of one of her sermons and I could not resist the pleasure of interrupting her to assure her that she spoke exactly like a prophet. Good-bye, my dearest love. As you see, I am not lost beyond recall.

P.S. By the way, has your poor Chevalier killed himself in despair? If the truth were known, you are a hundred times more depraved than I am: you would put me to shame if I had any pride.

Château de —
9 August 17 —

LETTER 7: *Cécile Volanges to Sophie Carnay*[1]

IF I have told you nothing on the subject of my marriage it is because I know no more now than I did at the beginning. I am growing used to thinking no more about it and I find life in other ways agreeable enough. I work a great deal at my singing and at my harp: I seem to like it more now that I no longer have a music-master, or rather the fact is I have a better one. The Chevalier Danceny, the gentleman I mentioned to you, with whom I sang at Madame de Merteuil's, is kind enough to come here every day and sing with me for whole hours at a time. He is extremely amiable. He sings like an angel and composes the prettiest tunes for which he writes the words as well. It is such a pity he is a Knight of Malta![2] It seems to me that, if he married, he would make his wife very happy . . . He is extremely civil. He never seems to be paying compliments, and yet everything he says is flattering. Although he is forever finding fault with me, as much about music as anything else, there is so much enthusiasm and good humour in his criticisms that it is impossible not to be grateful for them. When he is only so much as looking at you he seems to be saying something agreeable. And, to crown all, he is very obliging. For instance, yesterday he was invited to a great concert, but he preferred to spend the whole evening at our house. I was very glad of that because, when he is not here, nobody speaks to me and that is boring, whereas when he is here we sing and talk to each other. He always has something to tell me. Besides Madame de Merteuil, he is the only person here who is at all agreeable. But good-bye, my dear: I promised to learn

1. So as not to try the patience of the reader, a large part of the daily correspondence between these young ladies has been suppressed. Only those letters appear which are necessary to an understanding of the course of events. For the same reason all Sophie Carnay's letters, and several written by others who figure in this history, have been omitted.

2. [It was often arranged for the younger sons of the nobility, who were precluded from inheriting property or office, to be provided for as *Chevaliers* in the semi-military, semi-monastic Order of Malta. Not all its members were bound by the vow of celibacy, as Cécile Volanges appears to think. *Translator's note.*]

an arietta with a very difficult accompaniment for today, and I don't want to break my word. I shall go back to work until he comes.

7 August 17 —

LETTER 8: *The Présidente de Tourvel to Madame de Volanges*

No one, Madame, could be more sensible than I am of the confidence you place in me, and no one could take more of an interest in your daughter's establishment. It is indeed with all my heart that I wish her that happiness which I have no doubt she deserves, and which I am certain may safely be entrusted to your prudence. I do not know Monsieur le Comte de Gercourt, but, since you have honoured him with your choice, I cannot but think most highly of him. I shall say no more, Madame, than that I wish this marriage as much success as attends my own, which is equally the result of your good offices, and for which I am every day more grateful to you. May your daughter's happiness be your recompense for the happiness you have brought me, and may the best of friends become the most fortunate of mothers!

I am truly sorry that I cannot offer you these sincere wishes in person, and that I cannot make your daughter's acquaintance as soon as I should like. Since your own kindness to me has been truly maternal, I have some right to expect from her the tender affection of a sister. Please be so kind, Madame, as to ask her for it on my behalf for as long as I am without the opportunity to win it for myself.

I expect to remain in the country all the time Monsieur de Tourvel is away, and I have taken this occasion of enjoying and benefiting from my acquaintance with the worthy Madame de Rosemonde. She is still charming: her great age has taken nothing from her: her memory and her gaiety are unimpaired. Her body, it is true, is eighty-four years old, but her spirit is only twenty.

Our life of retirement has been much enlivened by her nephew, the Vicomte de Valmont, who has consented to spare us a few days of his time. I used to know him only by a reputation which left me with little desire to know him better: but I think he is worth more than people think. Here, where he is not distracted by the bustle of the great world, he shows a surprising aptitude for talking seriously, and admits his faults with rare candour. He confides freely in me, and I lecture him with the utmost severity. You, who know him, will agree that this would be a fine conversion to make, but I have no doubt that, in spite of his promises, a week in Paris will make him forget all my sermons. His stay here will at least to some extent restrict his customary activities: it seems to me, from what I know of them, that he could not do better than do nothing at all. He knows that I am writing to you and has asked me to present his most respectful compliments. Please receive my own with your accustomed kindness, and never doubt the sincerity with which I have the honour to be, etc.

Château de —
9 August 17—

LETTER 9: *Madame de Volanges to the Présidente de Tourvel*

I HAVE never, my dear young friend, doubted the sincerity either of your friendship or of the interest which you take in all that concerns me. But it is not to explain this (which I hope is henceforth taken for granted between us) that I am replying to your letter: the fact is I do not think I can avoid saying a few words to you concerning the Vicomte de Valmont.

I did not expect, I will admit, that I should ever find his name in one of your letters. What, after all, could there be in common between you and him? You do not know what sort of man he is; where could you have learnt to recognize a profligate's soul? You tell me of his *rare candour*: oh, yes! In a Valmont candour must indeed be very rare. Even more treacherous and dangerous than he is charming and fascinating, he has never, since his early youth, taken a single step or spoken a single word without some dishonourable or criminal intention. My dear, you know me; you know that, of all the virtues I aspire to, tolerance is the one I value most. So, were Valmont the victim of impetuous passions, if, like so many thousand others, he had been led astray by the errors of the time, then, while I should still not approve his conduct, I should pity him, waiting in silence for a time when some happy change of heart would recover him the esteem of decent people. But Valmont is not a man of that sort: his conduct is the outcome of his principles. He knows exactly how far a man may carry villainy without danger to himself, and, so that he can be cruel and vicious with impunity, he chooses women for his victims. I shall not stop to count the number he has seduced: but how many has he not ruined?

These scandalous stories do not reach you in your modest and secluded world. I could tell you some that would make you shudder, but your sight, pure as your soul, would be defiled by such pictures; besides, since you are sure that Valmont will never hold any danger for you, you have no need to arm yourself against him. There is only one thing I must tell you: every single one of the women he has pursued, whether successfully or not, has had reason to regret it. The Marquise de Merteuil is the only exception to the rule – she alone has been able to resist and even to master his wickedness. It is this episode in her life that does her most credit in my view: it has, in fact, been enough to excuse her fully in the eyes of all for certain indiscretions she was found guilty of at the beginning of her widowhood.[1]

Be that as it may, my dear friend, age, experience, and above all friendship give me the right to point out to you that society has begun to notice Valmont's absence, and that, if it is known that he has spent some time alone with his aunt and you, your reputation lies in his hands – the greatest misfortune that could ever befall a woman. I advise you, therefore, to persuade his aunt not to keep him any longer; and if he persists in staying I do not think you should hesitate to leave yourself. But why should he stay? What, after all, he is doing in the country? If you were to observe his movements I am certain you would find that he has only taken up a convenient headquarters for some villainy he is contemplating in

1. Madame de Volanges' mistake shows that, like all other rogues, Valmont never betrayed his accomplices.

the neighbourhood. Since, however, it would be impossible to prevent it, let us be content with ensuring our own safety.

Good-bye, my dear. My daughter's marriage has been somewhat delayed. The Comte de Gercourt, whom we were daily expecting, writes to say that his regiment is sailing for Corsica, and, since there are still military operations in progress, he cannot obtain leave of absence before the winter. It is most inconvenient; I can now hope, however, that we shall have the pleasure of seeing you at the wedding and I should have been disappointed had it taken place without you. Good-bye. Without compliments and without reserve, I am wholly yours.

P.S. Remember me to Madame de Rosemonde whom I shall always love as much as she deserves to be loved.

11 August 17—

LETTER 10: *The Marquise de Merteuil to the Vicomte de Valmont*

ARE you sulking, Vicomte? Or are you dead? Or, which would come to very much the same, do you live now only for your Présidente? This woman who has given you back the illusions of youth will very soon be giving you back its ridiculous prejudices. I see you are already as timid as a slave: you might as well be in love. You renounce your *bold schemes that have succeeded before*, so that you now lead a life devoid of principles, leaving everything to chance, or rather to the whim of the moment. Don't you remember that love, like medicine, *is only the art of encouraging nature?* You see how I can fight you with your own weapons. But I take no pride in that; for in fact I am beating a man who is down. 'She must give herself to me', you say. Oh yes, without any doubt, she will—like the others, but with this difference: she will do it with a bad grace. But, so that she will give herself to you in the end, the proper method is to begin by taking her. How truly characteristic that absurd paradox is of the fatuity of love! I say love because you are in love. To say otherwise would be to deceive you; it would be to hide your malady from you. Tell me then, languishing lover: the women you have had – do you imagine you violated them? Don't you know that however willing, however eager we are to give ourselves, we must nevertheless have an excuse? And is there any more convenient than an appearance of yielding to force? As for me, I shall admit that one of the things that most flatters me is a lively and well-executed attack, when everything happens in quick but orderly succession; which never puts us in the painfully embarrassing position of having to cover up some blunder of which, on the contrary, we ought to be taking advantage; which keeps up an appearance of taking by storm even what we are quite prepared to surrender, and adroitly flatters our two favourite passions: the pride of defence and the pleasure of defeat. This talent, which is less common than you would think, has always given me pleasure, even when it has not prevailed with me, and it has sometimes happened that I have given myself simply by way of reward. So, in our ancient tournaments, did Beauty present the prize for valour and skill.

But you – you are no longer yourself: you behave as if you were afraid of succeeding. When did you take to making journeys in small stages along side-roads? If you want to reach your destination, my good man – post-horses and the highway! But let us leave this subject which puts me in so much the worse humour in that it deprives me of the pleasure of seeing you. Write to me, at least, more often than you do and keep me informed of your progress. Did you know that for two weeks now you have been engrossed in this silly adventure, neglecting the rest of the world?

Speaking of neglect, you remind me of those people who invariably send to inquire after their sick friends but never trouble about a reply. At the close of your last letter you asked me whether the Chevalier was dead. I did not answer your question, but that in no way increased your anxiety. Have you forgotten that my lover is your bosom friend? But rest assured, he is not dead; were he so it would be from a surfeit of joy. The poor man, how tender-hearted he is, how perfectly suited to being a lover! Such intensity of feeling: it makes my head swim. Seriously, the perfect happiness he finds in being attached to me has really attached me to him.

How happy I made him the very day that I wrote to you saying

I was going to consider breaking with him! As a matter of fact, I was thinking, when he was announced, of how best to throw him into despair. For some reason, or for none at all, it seemed to me that he had never looked so handsome. I gave him, however, a sulky welcome. He hoped to spend two hours with me before the time my doors are opened to everybody. I told him that I would be going out; he asked me where I was going and I refused to tell him. He insisted. 'Away from you,' I said acidly. Fortunately for him he was quite paralysed by this reply: one word, and a scene would inevitably have followed severing our relations forever, just as I had planned. Surprised by his silence, I glanced at him, for no other reason, I assure you, than to see how he looked. There, on that charming face, was the melancholy, at once profound and most tender, that was once before, as even you allowed, so difficult to resist. The same cause produced the same effect: I was vanquished a second time. From that moment on I could think only of how to avoid leaving him with the impression that I had slighted him. 'I am going out on some business,' I said a little more gently, 'business indeed, which concerns you. But don't ask questions now. I shall be taking supper at home; come back here and I shall tell you everything.' Whereupon he found his tongue, but I did not allow him to use it. 'I am in a great hurry,' I continued. 'Go now; I shall see you this evening.' He kissed my hand and left.

Immediately, as compensation, perhaps as much for myself as for him, I decided to introduce him to my *petite maison*[1] of which till then he had no suspicion. I called my faithful Victoire. I was ill with migraine; for the benefit of the servants I retired to bed. As soon as we were alone the *one and only* dressed herself as a footman, while I changed into chambermaid's clothes. Then she fetched a *fiacre* to the garden gate and we drove off. On arriving at my temple of love I chose the most elegant negligee I could find: a delicious one of my own creation. It reveals nothing and suggests everything. I promise you the pattern for your Présidente when you have made her worthy of wearing it.

After these preparations, while Victoire busied herself with

1. [Fashionable society in the eighteenth century kept its clandestine rendez-vous on its own property, in suburban villas known as *petites maisons*, which were maintained specially for the purpose. *Translator's note*.]

other details, I read a chapter of *Le Sopha*,[1] a letter from *Héloïse*,[2] and two of La Fontaine's tales, so as to establish in my mind the different nuances of tone I wished to adopt. Meanwhile my Chevalier, as eager as ever, arrives at my door. The footman refuses to admit him, informing him that I am ill: first incident. At the same time he is handed a letter from me, but not, as I am always careful in these matters, written by me. He opens it and finds, in Victoire's handwriting, these words: 'At nine o'clock precisely, on the boulevard, outside the cafés.' Once there, a little footman he has never seen before, or thinks he has never seen before, for it is in fact Victoire, comes up to say he must send back his carriage and follow on foot. This whole romantic episode has excited his imagination to a degree, and an excited imagination never does any harm. At length he arrives and is quite spellbound with surprise and passion. To allow him time to recover we walk for a while in the shrubbery; then I take him back to the house. First he sees a table laid for two; next – a bed prepared. We pass through to my boudoir, decked out for the occasion in its full splendour. There, half deliberately, half impulsively, I put my arms around him and sink to his knees. 'Oh, my dear!' I say, 'I am sorry that I distressed you by a show of bad humour: it was but for the sake of arranging this surprise. I am sorry that I could for an instant have veiled my heart from your gaze. Forgive me, and let my love make amends for my sin.' You can imagine the effect produced by this sentimental speech. The happy Chevalier having raised me up, my pardon was solemnized on the same ottoman where you and I so gaily celebrated our final parting, and in the same manner.

Since we had six hours to spend together, and I was determined he should find the whole of the time uniformly delicious, I curbed his transports and modified my own demonstrations of tenderness to a friendly coquetry. I think I have never been at so much pains to please, nor ever felt more satisfied with my success. After supper, now childish, now reasonable, now playful, now sentimental, at times even abandoned, I amused myself imagining him a sultan in the midst of his harem while I played in turn a succession of his

1. [By Crébillon *fils*, a writer of witty and licentious novels. *Translator's note.*]

2. [Rousseau's *La Nouvelle Héloïse*. *Translator's note.*]

favourites, so that, each time he paid his respects, it was a different mistress, although the same woman, that received them.

At daybreak it was time to part, and, in spite of all he could say or do to prove to the contrary, he had by then as much need to go as little desire to do so. As we left, by way of a last adieu, I took the key from the door of our happy abode and, putting it in his hands, said: 'I acquired this only for you: it is proper that you should have it in your keeping. The temple must be at the high priest's disposal.' I thus skilfully forestalled whatever reflections he might otherwise have made on the propriety – always doubtful – of keeping a *petite maison*.

I know him well enough to be sure that he will not use it for anyone but me; and, if I am moved to go there without him myself, I have, of course, a duplicate key. He was determined at all costs to fix the day for our next meeting there, but I like him too much to exhaust him so quickly. One can allow oneself too much only of those one intends shortly to be rid of. He does not know this, but, fortunately for him, I know it for both of us.

I see it is already three o'clock in the morning and I have written volumes when I meant to write no more than a word. So strong is the charm of a trustworthy friend; for which reason you are still the man I like best. To be honest, however, my Chevalier pleases me more.

———

12 August 17——

LETTER 11: *Madame de Tourvel to Madame de Volanges*

THE gravity of your letter would have disturbed me, Madame, had I not luckily found more cause here for assurance than you are able to give me for alarm. The redoubtable Monsieur de Valmont, terror of our sex, put off his murderous weapons, it seems, before he came into this house. Far from being the victim of his schemes, I am not even the object of his pretensions; what is more, the worldly charm that even his enemies allow him, has here given way almost entirely to the amiability of a child. It is apparently the country air that has accomplished the miracle. I can only assure you that although he is constantly with me and seems even to enjoy my company, not a word has passed his lips that so much as hints at love – not one of those phrases which other men, without having, like him, anything to justify their using them, would never have denied themselves. Never is one obliged to assume with him that reserve, without which these days no self-respecting woman can keep the men in her circle at their proper distance. And he would never think of exploiting the gaiety he inspires. He is perhaps something of a flatterer, but his delicacy would disarm modesty itself. In short, had I a brother in Monsieur de Valmont I could not be better pleased. There are women, no doubt, who would wish him to show them more conspicuous marks of his favour. I shall confess I like him so much the more for his good judgement in distinguishing me from their kind.

This is certainly a very different picture from the one you paint of him; yet you will see, when you set the portraits in their respective periods, that they have something in common. He admits to having been very much in the wrong. Rumour has undoubtedly made him appear even more so. But I have met few men who speak of respectable women with greater esteem – I had almost said enthusiasm. You tell me that in this respect, at least, he is not dissembling. His relations with Madame de Merteuil are the proof of it. He speaks often of her; never without so many compliments and such a tone of true affection that, until I received your letter, I was sure that what he called their friendship must really be love. I was wrong to have judged so rashly, the more so in that he has often spoken expressly in her justification. I fear I regarded as polite deception what was in fact the plainest sincerity. I am not sure; but it seems to me that the man is not an irredeemable libertine who is capable of so devoted a friendship for so admirable a woman. For the rest, I do not know whether he is behaving well here because, as you suggest, he is planning something in the neighbourhood. There are certainly several handsome women in these parts. He is seldom out, however, except in the mornings, when, he says, he goes hunting. He rarely returns, it is true, with any game – but that is because, he assures us, he is not a good shot. At all events, what he does out of doors is no concern of mine. I should only wish to make sure about it so as to have one reason the more for bowing to your opinion, or for converting you to mine.

As for your suggestion that I contrive to cut short the stay that Monsieur de Valmont proposes making here, it seems to me that it will be very difficult to ask his aunt to send her own nephew from her house; the more so because he is a great favourite of hers. I promise you, however – but only out of deference to you, and not because I think it necessary – that I shall make this request at the first opportunity, either to her or to Monsieur de Valmont himself. As for me, Monsieur de Tourvel is aware that I intend to stay here until his return. He would be astonished, and with good reason, were I to change my mind upon so little provocation.

Forgive me, Madame, these long explanations. I felt it necessary in the cause of truth to make some statement on Monsieur de Valmont's behalf, particularly since, where you are concerned, he appears to be very much in need of an advocate. I am by no means any the less aware of the friendly sentiments which prompt your advice. To them, again, I owe the charming compliment you pay me apropos of your daughter's wedding, for which I thank you most sincerely. But I would, with all my heart, sacrifice every pleasure I anticipate in spending that time with you to my wish that Mademoiselle de Volanges could the sooner be made happy – that is to say if she can ever be happier than she is with a mother so worthy of her respect and affection. Be so kind as to believe I share these sentiments with her in expressing my attachment to you.

I have the honour to be, etc.

———

13 August 17—

LETTER 12: *Cécile Volanges to the Marquise de Merteuil*

MAMMA is not well, Madame. She is confined to the house and I must keep her company, so that I am, after all, not to have the honour of accompanying you to the Opera. But it is not so much the Opera, I assure you, that I shall miss, as the pleasure of being with you. Please believe this. I do like you so much! Would you be so kind as to tell the Chevalier Danceny that I do not have the songbook he spoke of, and that I shall be very pleased if he will bring it to me tomorrow? If he comes today he will be told we are not at home; it is only that Mamma does not wish to receive anyone. I hope she will be better tomorrow.

I have the honour to be, etc.

13 August 17—

LETTER 13: *The Marquise de Merteuil to Cécile Volanges*

I AM very much distressed, my dear, not only because I shall be deprived of the pleasure of seeing you but because of the reason you give. I hope we shall find another opportunity. I shall convey your message to the Chevalier Danceny, who will certainly be very sorry to hear of your mother's illness. If she will receive me tomorrow I shall come and keep her company. She and I will challenge the Chevalier de Belleroche[1] to piquet, and, to enhance our pleasure in taking his money from him, we shall listen to you singing duets with your charming teacher; I shall suggest it to him. If this is agreeable to you and to your mother, I can answer for myself and the two Chevaliers. Good-bye, my dear: my compliments to dear Madame de Volanges. My fondest embrace for you.

13 August 17—

LETTER 14: *Cécile Volanges to Sophie Carnay*

I DID not write to you yesterday, my dear Sophie, but it was no idle pleasure, I promise you, that prevented me. Mamma was ill and I was with her the whole day. When I returned to my room in the evening I had not the heart to do anything, and went immediately to bed so as to convince myself that the day was really over – I

1. The Chevalier mentioned in Madame de Merteuil's previous letters.

have never known such a long one. It is not that I do not love Mamma – I don't know what it is. I was to have gone to the Opera with Madame de Merteuil; the Chevalier Danceny was to have been there. As you know, I have more regard for these two people than for anyone else in the world. When the time came, and I should have been with them, my heart felt as though it would break. I was suddenly weary of everything and wept and wept quite helplessly. Luckily Mamma was in bed, so that she did not notice anything. I am sure the Chevalier Danceny suffered too: but he will have had the theatre and the audience to distract him: quite a different matter.

Fortunately Mamma is better today and Madame de Merteuil is coming to see us with the Chevalier Danceny and another gentleman. But she always arrives late, and, oh, it is very tiresome to be alone for so long. It is only eleven o'clock now. I have to practise the harp, of course, and then my *toilette* will take up some time: I want my hair to look particularly well today. Mother Perpétue was right, I think. One turns coquette directly one enters society. I have never wanted so much to be pretty as during the last few days; and I find I am not so pretty as I used to think. Of course, among women who paint one is at a great disadvantage. Madame de Merteuil, for example. It is quite clear that all the men prefer her to me: but I am not very much put out by that because I know she has a great affection for me. What is more she gives me her word that the Chevalier Danceny thinks I am prettier than she. How kind of her to tell me! She seems even to be pleased about it. I really cannot conceive why. Because she likes me so much? And he! – oh, I'm delighted with him! It seems to me, too, that I have only to look at him to grow prettier. I should look at him all the time if I were not so afraid of meeting his eyes. Whenever that happens I am quite out of countenance. It is almost painful. But no matter.

Good-bye, my dear. I am going to begin my *toilette*. I love you now as always.

Paris
14 August 17—

LETTER 15: *The Vicomte de Valmont to the Marquise de Merteuil*

IT is very obliging of you not to leave me to my dismal fate. The life I lead here is truly tedious in its tasteless uniformity and the superfluity of leisure it affords. Your letter, and the charming extract from your journal, tempted me twenty times to invent a pretext of business in town and fly to your feet, there to beg you for an infidelity to your Chevalier in my favour. After all, he does not deserve the happiness he enjoys. Do you know that you have made me jealous of him? And what is this of a final parting? I renounce the vows we made in that moment of delirium. If they were intended to be kept, we cannot have been worthy of making them. Ah, let me one day revenge in your arms the annoyance your Chevalier's happiness has caused me! I cannot deny that I am angry when I think, that, without the help of intelligence, without taking the smallest pains, obeying without question the instincts of his heart, he has found a happiness I am not able to achieve. Oh, I shall spoil it for him! Promise me that I shall! As for you, are you not ashamed? You put yourself to the trouble of deceiving him, and he is, notwithstanding, happier than you are. You imagine him to be at your mercy: it is you who are at his. He sleeps soundly while you watch over his pleasures. Would a slave do more?

The fact is, my love, that as long as you distribute your favours in more than one quarter I am not in the least jealous: your lovers remind me of Alexander's successors, unable to maintain between them that mighty empire where once I reigned alone. But that you should give yourself entirely to one of them! That there should exist in one other man a challenge to my power! I will not tolerate it; you need have no hope that I will. Take me back, or at least take a second lover. Do not betray for the sake of a single whim the inviolable friendship to which we are sworn.

It is quite enough, in all conscience, that I endure the torments of love. Notice that I take your view; I admit my mistake. After all, if to be unable to live without possessing the object of one's desire, if to sacrifice one's time, pleasures, one's whole life to attaining it, is to be in love, then I am certainly in love. But I have made scant progress. I might have nothing at all to report on this subject, were it not for an incident that has given me much food for thought, and on which I am not as yet sure whether to set hopes or fears.

You know my manservant, that master of intrigue, that pattern comedy valet. As you may well imagine he has been instructed to make love to the chambermaid and to ply the rest of the household with drink. The fellow has better luck than I: he has already succeeded. He has just discovered that Madame de Tourvel has charged one of her servants with obtaining news of my activities, if necessary by following me on my excursions of a morning, as far as it is possible for him to do so without being observed. What is this woman about? How like the most timid of people to take risks that even we should be very loath to run! I swear . . . But before planning my revenge on this feminine chicanery let us think of a means of turning it to our advantage. Until now my suspicious goings-abroad have been without object: they must be given one. This matter requires all my attention, and I take my leave of you the better to consider it. Good-bye, my love.

Still Château de —
15 August 17 —

LETTER 16: *Cécile Volanges to Sophie Carnay*

OH, Sophie! News at last! I should not perhaps tell it to you, but I must positively tell somebody. I cannot help it. This Chevalier Danceny . . . I am in such a state that I cannot write: I don't know where to begin. Since I wrote telling you of the charming evening[1] Mamma and I spent with him and Madame de Merteuil, I have said no more about him. I did not wish to say any more to anybody, although I thought of him all the time. He began, after this, to look so dejected – so *very* dejected – that it hurt me to see it. And when I asked him why, he denied it, but it was quite plainly so. Well, yesterday it was even more obvious than before. It did not prevent

1. This letter has not been discovered. There is reason to believe that the meeting referred to is the one suggested by Madame de Merteuil in her note, and mentioned in Cécile de Volanges' preceding letter.

his usual kindness in singing with me; but every time he looked at me my heart ached. When we had finished singing he put my harp away in its case, and, bringing me the key, asked me whether I would play it again as soon as I was alone that evening. I suspected nothing at all, and had no desire, in any case, to play the harp that evening. He was so pressing, however, that I said I would. He certainly had his reasons for asking. In short, when I had returned to my room and my maid had left me, I took out my harp: between the strings was a letter, folded but unsealed – from him. Oh, if you knew what he asks me to do! Since reading his letter I have been so happy that I have been unable to think of anything else. I re-read it four times in succession, then locked it away in my writing-desk. I knew it by heart, and as I lay in bed went over it in my mind so often that it banished all thought of sleep. As soon as I closed my eyes there he was repeating it all in his own voice. It was very late when I went to sleep, and still very early when I awoke. I immediately looked for the letter to read it again at my leisure. I took it into my bed, and then I kissed it as if . . . It was perhaps wrong to kiss a letter like that, but I could not help it.

But now, my dear Sophie, though I am very happy, I am also in great difficulties. There is no doubt that I must not reply to this letter. I know quite well that I ought not to, but he asks me to. And if I don't reply he is sure to start moping again. Still, it is most unfortunate for him. What do you think I should do? But you are no better able to tell than I. Perhaps I shall ask Madame de Merteuil, who is always so kind. I should be very happy to oblige him, but I don't wish to do anything that is wrong. How often have we been urged to cultivate a good heart! Yet we are forbidden to follow its dictates where a man is in question. That cannot be right, either. Is not a man a neighbour to be loved as much as any woman, and even more so? After all, have we not fathers as well as mothers, brothers as well as sisters – and husbands besides? However, if I were to do something which was not right, maybe even Monsieur Danceny himself would think less of me. Oh heavens, I had much rather he were a little dispirited now! Besides, after all, there is still time. Simply because he wrote yesterday I am not bound to reply today. Besides I shall see Madame de Merteuil this evening, and if I have the courage I shall tell her everything. If I do only what she tells me to do, I shall have nothing to be ashamed of. And then perhaps she will tell me after all to send him some little reply to console him! Oh, how I suffer!

Good-bye, my dear. Tell me, in any case, what you think.

———

19 August 17—

LETTER 17: *The Chevalier Danceny to Cécile Volanges*

BEFORE I give way, Mademoiselle, to the pleasure, or shall I say to the imperative necessity, of writing to you, I shall begin by begging you to hear me out. I feel that, for daring to declare my sentiments, I shall need your indulgence: if I were merely justifying them I should not ask for it. What, after all, am I about to do but show you what you have yourself accomplished? What can I tell you that my looks, my gestures, my embarrassments, and even my silences have not already told you? Why should you find fault with a feeling that you yourself have inspired? What comes from you is surely worthy of being restored to you: though ardent like my being, it is pure like yours. Is it a crime in me to admire your charming person, your brilliant accomplishments, your enchanting graces, and that touching candour which puts your already precious virtues beyond price? No, assuredly not. But even the innocent can be most unhappy: and that is the fate in store for me if you refuse to accept my homage, the first this heart has offered. Were it not for you I should be now, not happy, but at best content. Since I saw you peace of mind has forsaken me and my happiness hangs in the balance.

Meanwhile you are surprised at my despondency, and you ask me what causes it. I might have thought sometimes that you were distressed by it. Ah! write one word and you will restore me to felicity. Pause only to consider, before you write anything, that one word may also be my ruin. I appoint you, then, the mistress of my fate. You alone can deliver me up to eternal misery or everlasting bliss. But in what better hands could I leave matters of such moment?

I shall finish, as I began, by begging your indulgence. I have asked you to hear me out; I shall go further and ask you to reply. To refuse would be to persuade me that you are offended; and my heart is answerable as much for my respect as for my love.

P.S. Your reply can reach me in the same way that this letter was conveyed to you. The method is both safe and convenient, it seems to me.

———

18 August 17—

LETTER 18: *Cécile Volanges to Sophie Carnay*

COME, Sophie! You are not scolding me in advance for what I am going to do? I was concerned enough before: here you are making it worse. It is quite clear, you say, that I must not reply. It is all very well for you to say so from a distance. You don't know the precise circumstances: you could not possibly, unless you were here. I am sure that if you were in my place you would do as I am going to do. Of course, in theory, one ought not to reply. You will see from my letter of yesterday that I did not want to in any case. But I don't think anyone has ever before been in my special situation.

And then to have to make this decision by myself! Madame de Merteuil, whom I expected to see last evening, did not come. Everything conspires against me: it is only through her that I know him. It has almost always been in her company that I have seen him or spoken to him. It is not that I bear her any grudge, but she has deserted me in the hour of my most need. Oh, I am really to be pitied!

As you can imagine, he was here again yesterday as usual. I was so confused that I dared not look at him, and he could not speak to me because Mamma was present. I was sure it would make him wretched to find that I had not written to him. I did not know what kind of face to put upon it. A moment later he asked me whether I should like him to fetch my harp. My heart beat so furiously that it was all I could do to answer yes. It was much worse when he returned. I glanced at him only for a single instant. He did not look at me at all, but one would have thought from his expression that he was ill. It was really most painful. He began to tune my harp and then, bringing it to me, said: 'Oh, Mademoiselle . . .' He said no more than those two words, but in such a tone of voice that I was quite overcome. I ran my fingers over the strings without knowing what I was doing. Mamma asked whether we would sing. He excused himself, saying he was not feeling well, so that I, who had no excuse, was obliged to sing by myself. I wished I had been born dumb: I purposely chose a song I did not know. I should not have been able to sing even the ones I did know, and I was afraid of someone noticing. Luckily another visitor arrived, and as soon as I heard the carriage I stopped and asked him to put away my harp. I was very much afraid he would take his departure at the same time, but he came back.

While Mamma talked to the lady who had come to see her I thought I might risk another glance at him. My eyes met his and I found I could not look away again. A moment later I saw the tears well up in his eyes, and he had to turn his head to one side to hide them. At that moment it was more than I could bear; I knew that I too was going to cry. I left the room, and there and then wrote in pencil on a slip of paper: 'Please do not look so sad. I promise you I shall reply.' Surely you are not going to tell me that this was wrong: besides I could not help it. I slipped the piece of paper between the strings of my harp, where his letter had been, and returned to the drawing-room. I felt more at ease, but I longed for Mamma's visitor to be gone. Fortunately she was merely paying a call, and left soon after. As soon as she was out of the room, I said that I should like to play my harp again, and asked him to fetch it. It was obvious from his expression that he suspected nothing. But when he returned, oh, how happy he looked! As he placed the harp in front of me he stood so that Mamma could not see, and, taking my hand, he squeezed it . . . in such a particular way! – it was only for an instant, but I cannot tell you how agreeable it was. I withdrew it, of course; so that I have nothing on my conscience.

You see, my dear Sophie, that I cannot now avoid writing to him. I have promised him. Besides I am not going to cause him further distress, which would be even more painful to me than to him. If it were wrong I would not do it. But what wrong can there be in writing a letter, especially when it is to spare someone unhappiness? What troubles me is that I shall not be able to write it very well, but he will know that is not my fault. Besides, I am sure he will be pleased to have it, if only because it is mine.

Good-bye, my dear. If you consider I am doing wrong, tell me: but I don't think I am. The nearer the time comes to write to him, the more anxious I feel. But I must write, since I have promised to. Good-bye.

———

20 August 17 —

LETTER 19: *Cécile Volanges to the Chevalier Danceny*

You were so sad yesterday, Monsieur, and I was so sorry to see it that I allowed myself to promise you a reply to the letter you wrote me. I feel today, none the less, that I ought not to have done so: but, since I promised, I do not wish to break my word; and that, if anything, is proof of the friendship I bear you. Now that you know this, I hope you will not ask me to write to you again; I hope, too, that you will not tell anyone that I have written to you at all, because of course I should be taken to task for it, and this might very well be most unpleasant. Above all, I hope you will not think ill of me yourself, since that would distress me more than anything else. I assure you that I would not be doing as much to please anyone else. I should like you in turn to do me a favour. Please do not look so sad; it deprives me of all the pleasure I might have in seeing you. You see, Monsieur, I speak very frankly. I cannot hope for more than that our friendship should last forever. But, I beg you, write to me no more.

I have the honour to be,

Cécile Volanges

———

20 August 17 —

LETTER 20: *The Marquise de Merteuil to the Vicomte de Valmont*

AH, you blackguard! You flatter me to keep me from laughing at you! Well, I shall have mercy; your letter is so full of reckless absurdities, that I must perforce excuse the circumspection your Présidente imposes upon you. I do not think my Chevalier would be as indulgent as I: he would be just the man to frown upon the renewal of our little contract, and to find nothing amusing at all in your ridiculous proposal. As for me, it made me laugh a great deal, and I was really sorry to be obliged to laugh alone. Had you been here, heaven knows to what this hilarity might have brought me; but I have had time to reflect and to recover my gravity. I am giving you no permanent refusal, but am deferring my decision; I am right to do so. My vanity would, perhaps, be too much involved. Once one becomes interested in the game, there is no knowing where one will stop. I am the sort of woman who would cast you in chains all over again; who would make you forget your Présidente. And what a scandal if I, unworthy creature, were to fill you with a disgust for virtue! That danger may be averted, but here are my conditions.

As soon as you have seduced your Fair Devotee, as soon as you can furnish me with proof that you have done so, come to me and I shall be yours. Remember, however, that in important affairs of this kind, proof, to be valid, must be in writing. If we keep to this arrangement I shall, on the one hand, be your reward and not your consolation, and I prefer it that way; on the other, you will add spice to your success by making it a step towards your infidelity. Come then, bring me the token of your triumph with all possible speed: like those worthy knights of old who came to lay the brilliant spoils of their victories at their ladies' feet. Seriously, I am very curious to know what a prudish woman will find to write in such circumstances, what disguise she will contrive to throw over her sentences when she has none left to cover her person. It is for you to judge whether I am setting too high a price upon myself; I warn you, however, that no reduction can be made. Meanwhile, my dear Vicomte, you will suffer me to remain faithful to my Chevalier, making him happy for my own entertainment, in spite of the slight annoyance this causes you.

Nevertheless, were my morals less strict, he would at this moment have a dangerous rival: I mean the little Volanges. I dote on the child: it is a real infatuation. I may be deceived, but I see her becoming a woman of the highest fashion. I watch her little heart opening to the world and it is an enchanting spectacle. She is already frantically in love with her Danceny, but is still quite unaware of the fact. He, too, is very much in love, but, with the timidity of his years, dares not make it too obvious. Both of them are rapt in admiration of me. The girl especially has a great desire to tell me her secret; during the last few days it has really oppressed her, and it would have been doing her a great kindness to help her a little. But I have to remember that she is still a child. I don't wish to compromise myself. Danceny has spoken in plainer terms. But, as far as he is concerned, I have already made my decision; I turned a deaf ear. As for the girl, I have often been tempted to make her my pupil; for Gercourt's benefit. Considering that he will be in Corsica till October he leaves me time enough, and I have a mind to make good use of it, so as to present him at the end with a woman of experience in place of his innocent convent girl. How can this man have the arrogance to sleep in peace, as long as a woman who has every reason to hate him remains unavenged? I assure you, were the girl here at this moment, there is no knowing what I would not tell her.

Good-bye, Vicomte. Good night and good luck: but for God's sake, make some progress. Think, should you not succeed with this woman, of the others who must blush for having succeeded with you.

———

20 August 17—

LETTER 21: *The Vicomte de Valmont to the Marquise de Merteuil*

I HAVE at last, my love, taken a step forward, and a considerable one, which, if it has not brought me to my destination, reassures me at least that I am on the right road and dispels all my fears of losing the way. I have at last made a declaration of love, which, although it was received in obstinate silence, yet roused a response of the most unambiguous and flattering kind. But I must not anticipate. Let us go back to the beginning.

You remember that my movements were to be watched. Well: I decided to make a public example of this scandalous proceeding, and I did so, as follows. I instructed my manservant to find some unfortunate creature in the neighbourhood, who was particularly in need of help. This was not difficult. Yesterday afternoon he brought me news of a family whose furniture was to be seized this morning in lieu of taxes they could not pay. Having made sure there was no female member of the household whose face and figure might cast suspicion on my actions, I announced at supper that I would be going hunting the following morning. Here I must give my Présidente her due. She undoubtedly regretted to some extent the orders she had given, and, without being able to conquer her curiosity, she did try, at least, to obstruct my plans. It would be extremely hot; I should risk making myself ill; I should kill nothing and tire myself to no purpose – during which conversation her eyes, which expressed more perhaps than she wanted them to, told me plainly enough that she wished me to take these bad arguments for good ones. I was proof against this, as you can imagine, and withstood with equal success a little diatribe against hunting and hunters, as also a little cloud of ill humour which for the rest of the evening darkened that heavenly face. I was afraid for a moment she might have countermanded her orders; that her delicacy might ruin everything. But I had not reckoned on feminine curiosity: I was mistaken. That very evening my servant brought me my reassurance and I went satisfied to bed.

I rose at daybreak and left the house. I had not gone twenty yards when I caught sight of the spy behind me. Walking across country in the direction of the village which was my destination, I chose my path with no other purpose in mind than to make it as difficult as possible for the idiot to follow me. He dared not leave the roads, and was forced at times to run at full tilt over three times the distance that I covered myself. But in giving him this exercise, I began to feel extremely hot, and at length sat down at the foot of a tree. Will you believe that he had the insolence to slip behind a bush not twenty feet away from me and sit down too? I was tempted for a moment to fire at him: that, though it would only have been small shot, would have taught him a severe enough lesson on the dangers of curiosity. Fortunately for him I remembered that he was not only useful but necessary to my plans; which consideration saved his life.

Now I arrive at the village. There is a hubbub. I come forward; I ask questions. I am acquainted with the facts. I summon the tax-collector, and yielding to my generous compassion pay him fifty-six *livres*, for the lack of which sum five persons were to be reduced to living on straw and despair. You cannot imagine the shower of blessings this simple little action brought down upon me from those present, the tears of gratitude that flowed from the eyes of the old paterfamilias, the softening of that patriarchal countenance which only a moment before had been disfigured by a wild and hideous despair. While I contemplated the spectacle, another peasant, a younger man, leading a woman and two children by the hand, rushed towards me and said: 'Let us fall at the feet of this image of God', and in an instant the family were on their knees around me. I shall confess to some weakness. My eyes were moist with tears and I felt within me an unwonted but delicious emotion. I was astonished at the pleasure to be derived from doing good, and I am now tempted to think that what we call virtuous people have less claim to merit than we are led to believe. Be that as it may, I thought it common justice to repay these poor people for the pleasure they had given me, and I gave them ten *louis* I happened to have on me. Whereupon there was more giving of thanks, but without the same pathos. Necessity had produced the sublime, the true effect. The rest was merely a simple expression of surprise and gratitude for superfluous gifts.

However, in the midst of these voluble benedictions, I appeared not unlike the hero in the last act of a drama. And you will not forget that my faithful spy was among the crowd. My aim achieved, I extricated myself and returned to the house. All things considered, I am pleased with my strategem. I have no doubt the woman is worth all this trouble, which one day will in itself constitute a claim on her. Having, in a sense, paid for her in advance, I shall have the right – my conscience clear – to dispose of her as I please.

I had almost forgotten to tell you that, so as to leave no stone unturned, I asked the worthy peasantry to intercede with God for the success of my plans. You will see whether their prayers have not already in part been answered . . . . But I am told that supper is served, and it will be too late to send this letter if I leave it to be finished tonight. So the rest must follow by the next post. I am sorry, because the rest is more interesting. Good-bye, my love. You have already stolen a moment of my pleasure in seeing her.

20 August 17—

LETTER 22: *Madame de Tourvel to Madame de Volanges*

You will, I have no doubt, be very pleased, Madame, to know something about Monsieur de Valmont which cannot, it seems to me, be reconciled with the representations of his character made to you. How painful it is to think ill of anyone, how distressing to find only vices in those who might have all the qualities necessary to make their virtue loved. In short, I know that you are so much inclined to be indulgent, that I can only oblige you by giving you reason to reverse an over-harsh judgement. Monsieur de Valmont, it seems to me, has grounds for expecting so much favour – I had almost said justice; and here are my reasons for thinking so.

This morning he made one of those expeditions which might have led one to suppose he is hatching some plot in the neighbourhood – the idea, indeed, that occurred to you; the idea I myself seized upon, perhaps too eagerly, for which I am very much to blame. Fortunately for him, and still more fortunately for us, since it has saved us from committing an injustice, one of my servants chanced to take the same road as he,[1] and it was in this way that my curiosity, reprehensible perhaps, but timely, was satisfied. It was reported that Monsieur de Valmont having discovered in the village of — an unfortunate family whose furniture was to be sold because they lacked the means to pay their taxes, not only hastened to pay their debts, but gave them in addition a not inconsiderable sum of money. My servant was witness to this virtuous act; he has told me,

1. So Madame de Tourvel dares not say she ordered him to do so !

moreover, that the peasants, in the course of their conversation amongst themselves and with him, said that a servant (whom they pointed out and whom my own servant believes to be one of Monsieur de Valmont's) had been sent yesterday to inquire into the circumstances of other villagers who might be in need of assistance. If this is so, there is no question here of a mere fugitive pity, aroused by circumstance, but of the solicitude of true charity, of a calculated plan for doing good, of rare virtue in a fine soul. But, whether it was the outcome of chance or plan, it was still a decent and praiseworthy deed; the mere account of it moved me to tears. Furthermore – and still in the interests of justice – when I spoke to him – he had not himself breathed a word – he began by disclaiming it, and, even when he had admitted to it, seemed to take so little account of it that his modesty doubled his merit in my eyes.

Now tell me, my respected friend, is Monsieur de Valmont really an irreclaimable libertine? If he is so indeed, and can yet behave in this way, what is there left for respectable people to do? Are the wicked to share the sacred pleasures of charity with the good? Would God allow a virtuous family to receive help at the hands of a rascal; help for which they will return thanks to Divine Providence? And would He willingly hear their pure tongues speak blessings on a reprobate? No. I prefer to believe that though error endures, it is not perpetual, and I cannot think of anyone as an enemy of virtue who does good. Monsieur de Valmont is perhaps only another example of the danger of ill-considered intimacies. I leave you with this idea, which pleases me. If, on the one hand, it seems to justify him in your eyes, it will, on the other, make that tender friendship doubly precious which binds me to you for as long as I live.

I have the honour to be, etc.

P.S. Madame de Rosemonde and I are just about to visit the worthy and unfortunate family ourselves so as to add our belated alms to Monsieur de Valmont's. We are taking him with us. We shall at least be affording the good people the pleasure of seeing their benefactor once again; this is all, it seems, he has left us to do.

20 *August* 17—

LETTER 23: *The Vicomte de Valmont to the Marquise de Merteuil*

WE had reached the point of my return to the house. I shall take up my story from there.

I had time only for a brief *toilette* before presenting myself in the drawing-room. My beauty was working a piece of tapestry while the local *curé* read the gazette aloud to my old aunt. I sat down by the frame. Looks that were more than usually gentle, almost caressing, very soon led me to guess that the servant had already reported the result of his mission. In short, the curious creature was no longer able to keep the secret she had prised from me, and without hesitating to interrupt the venerable priest who was reading the news as though it had been a sermon, said: 'I, too, have my news to tell you', and immediately recounted the details of my adventure, with a precision that did great credit to the intelligence of her informer. I leave you to imagine my modest protestations: but who can stop a woman who, without suspecting it, is singing the praises of the man she loves? So I let her continue. One might have thought she was preaching a panegyric on a saint's behalf. Meanwhile I took note, not unhopefully, of all the promise of love in her animated looks, in the freedom of her gestures, and most of all in the sound of her voice, so noticeably changed that it betrayed all the emotion in her heart. She had scarcely finished speaking when Madame de Rosemonde said: 'Come here, nephew, so that I may embrace you.' I realized immediately that our pretty preacher could hardly avoid being embraced in her turn. She made to escape, but was soon in my arms. Far from having the strength to resist, she was scarcely able to sustain herself on her feet. The more I know of this woman, the more desirable she becomes. She hastily returned to the frame and looked for all the world as if she were busy again with her tapestry. But to me it was quite plain that her trembling hands would not allow her to continue.

After lunch the ladies insisted upon visiting the poor creatures to whose relief I had so piously contributed; I made one of the party. I shall spare you the boredom of this second scene of gratitude and approbation. A certain delicious memory makes my heart impatient for the moment of our return to the house. On the way home the fair Présidente, more pensive than ever, said not a word. I, preoccupied as I was with finding some means of turning the effects of the recent incident to account, was equally silent. Only Madame de Rosemonde spoke, and our replies to her were few and brief. We must have bored her: I had intended we should, and my plan succeeded. On leaving the carriage she went directly to her rooms, leaving us *tête à tête* in a dimly lit salon: in the soft obscurity that encourages timid love!

I was not put to the trouble of leading the conversation into the course I wished it to take. Our beauty's missionary enthusiasm was more to the purpose than any tact of mine could have been. 'When someone is so worthy of doing good', she said, fixing her gentle gaze upon me, 'why is it that he spends his life behaving badly?' 'I deserve', I replied, 'neither the compliment nor the reproof; and I cannot think that, with all your intelligence, you have yet arrived at an understanding of me. But I shall not refuse you my confidence, of which you are more than worthy, even though I am thereby injured in your esteem. The key to my conduct you will find in the unfortunate pliability of my character. Living amongst people without morals, I imitated their vices; perhaps I took pride, too, in outdoing them. Impressed in the same way here by your virtuous example, I have, without hope of emulating it, tried at least to follow it. And perhaps the action, on which you now congratulate me will lose all its value in your eyes when you know its real motive.' (Notice, my love, how near I came to the truth.) 'It is not to me', I continued, 'that those unfortunates owe the help I gave them. What you see as praiseworthy conduct was, for me, simply an attempt to please. I was, since I must tell you everything, only the humble agent of the goddess I adore.' (Here she made as if to interrupt me, but I gave her no time.) 'At this very moment', I added, 'it is only because I am weak that my secret escapes my lips. I promised myself to keep it from you: I took pleasure in paying the most innocent homage to your virtues, and to your charms, without your knowing it. But with the very paragon of honesty before my eyes I am incapable of deception, and I would not be guilty in your eyes of the least dissimulation. Do not imagine you are being insulted by improper expectations on my part. I shall be unhappy, I know, but I shall welcome my sufferings. They will prove the strength of my love. And it is at your feet, upon your breast that they will be appeased; there that I shall recover strength to suffer anew; there that I shall find goodness and compassion, and think myself consoled because you have pitied me. O you that I adore, hear me, pity me, help me!' By this time I was on my knees, clasping her hands in mine. Suddenly, however, she withdrew them and, covering her eyes in an attitude of despair, cried out: 'Oh, wretched woman!' then burst into tears. I had been so carried away that luckily I too was able to weep. Taking her hands once more in mine, I bathed them in tears. This was a very necessary precaution. She was so preoccupied with her own grief that she would not have noticed mine had I not discovered this means of bringing it to her attention. It afforded, moreover, another advantage: that of observing at my leisure her charming face as, more beautiful than ever, it proffered the powerful enticement of tears. My blood was on fire, and I was so little in control of myself that I was tempted to make the most of the occasion.

How weak we must be, how strong the dominion of circumstance, if even I, without a thought for my plans, could risk losing all the charm of a prolonged struggle, all the fascination of a laboriously administered defeat, by concluding a premature victory; if, distracted by the most puerile of desires, I could be willing that the conqueror of Madame de Tourvel should take nothing for the fruit of his labours but the tasteless distinction of having added one more name to the roll. Ah, let her surrender, but let her fight! Let her be too weak to prevail, but strong enough to resist; let her savour the knowledge of her weakness at her leisure, but let her be unwilling to admit defeat. Leave the humble poacher to kill the stag where he has surprised it in its hiding-place; the true hunter will bring it to bay. Do you not think my scheme sublime? None the less, I should, perhaps, be regretting at this moment that I failed to follow it, had not chance come to the rescue of my prudence.

We heard a noise. Someone was approaching the salon. Madame de Tourvel, alarmed, rose hurriedly, and seizing a candlestick left the room. I was obliged to let her go. But it was only a servant. As soon as I was certain of this, I followed her. I had taken scarcely a dozen steps when I heard her, on recognizing me, or perhaps out of some vague feeling of alarm, quicken her pace, fling herself rather than walk into her room, and lock the door behind her. I went after her; but the key was inside the door. I took care not to knock, since that would have provided occasion for too easy a resistance. I hit, instead, upon the simple and happy idea of looking through the key-hole; whereupon I actually saw the adorable woman on her knees, bathed in tears and rapt in fervent prayer. What God did she hope to invoke? Is there one strong enough to prevail against love? She will look in vain for help elsewhere, when it is I alone who can guide her destiny.

Having decided I had done enough for one day, I too retired to my room and set about writing to you. I hoped to see her again at supper; but she sent word that she felt indisposed and had taken to her bed. Madame de Rosemonde thought of going up to see her; but our wicked invalid excused herself, saying that a headache did not permit her to receive anyone. You may be sure we did not sit long after supper, and that I, too, was attacked by a headache. Having returned to my room, I wrote a long letter bemoaning my harsh fate and, with the intention of delivering it to her this morning, went to bed. I slept badly, as you will deduce from the date to this letter. When I rose, I re-read my little missive. It struck me that I had been too little critical of myself, that I had displayed more fire than tenderness, more bad humour than low spirits. I shall have to rewrite it: but I shall have to wait till I am calmer.

I see it is daybreak. I hope that with the fresh breezes of dawn will come sleep. I am going back to bed. I promise you that, however much I am under the sway of this woman, I shall never be so preoccupied with her that I want time to think a great deal of you. Good-bye, my love.

———

21 August 17 — , at four
o'clock in the morning

LETTER 24: *The Vicomte de Valmont to Madame de Tourvel*

AH, for pity's sake, Madame, vouchsafe to calm my troubled heart, to tell me what cause I have for hope or fear! With extremes of joy and anguish in prospect, this doubt is most cruel torment. Why did I tell you anything? Why did I not withstand the imperious charm that delivered up my thoughts to you? Content to worship you in silence, I was able at least to enjoy my love; that innocent sentiment, untroubled as yet by the image of your grief, was enough to make me happy. But since I have seen you in tears, the source of my happiness has become a fount of despair. Since I heard you say: 'Oh, wretched woman!', Madame, those cruel words have re-echoed without cease in my heart. Why must it be that the gentlest of sentiments excites only your fear? Of what is there to be afraid? Oh, not of losing your heart! That was not made for love: I have been deceived. Mine, which you never cease to vilify, is the one that feels; there is not so much as an impulse of pity in yours. Were this not true, you would not have refused a word of consolation to the wretch who had told you of his sufferings; you would not have shielded yourself from his gaze when he has no other pleasure in life but that of looking at you; you would not have made cruel game of his distress, sending him word that you were ill without allowing him to satisfy his solicitude; you would have realized that the same night which brought you twelve hours of sleep, would turn for him into a whole century of suffering.

Why, tell me, do I deserve to be treated with such crushing severity? I am not afraid to let you pass judgement upon me: what, then, have I done? What, except yield to a natural feeling, inspired by beauty, sanctioned by virtue, and kept at all times within the bounds of respect, its innocent expression prompted not by hope but by trust? Will you now betray that trust, which you yourself seemed willing to receive, and to which I gave myself unreservedly? No, I cannot think so. This would be to suppose you capable of wrong, and my feelings revolt at the mere idea. I disown my reproaches. They came to my pen, not to my heart. Ah, let me think you perfect! There is no other pleasure left me. Prove to me that you are so, by giving me your generous care. Where is the starving pauper you have saved, who was more in need of your help than I am? Do not leave me in the delirium into which you have thrown me: lend me your reason, since you have deprived me of mine. When you have cured me, enlighten me so that your work will be complete.

I have no wish to deceive you: you will never succeed in conquering my love. But you will teach me to control it. Guide me in what I do, rule me in what I say, and you will at least spare me the terrible misfortune of offending you. Banish, above all, that desperate fear. Tell me that you pardon me, that you pity me; promise me your indulgence. I shall never win as much of your favour as I could wish; I claim only as much as I need; will you refuse me?

Good-bye, Madame. Be so very kind as to receive this tribute of a feeling which in no way mitigates what I owe you of respect.

———

20 August 17 —

LETTER 25: *The Vicomte de Valmont to the Marquise de Merteuil*

HERE is yesterday's bulletin.

At eleven o'clock I paid my respects to Madame de Rosemonde and, under her auspices, was brought to the pseudo-invalid who was still in bed. There were dark rings under her eyes; I hope she slept as badly as I did. I took advantage of Madame de Rosemonde's withdrawing for a moment to another part of the room to deliver my letter. It was rejected. But I left it on the bed, and obligingly went to fetch up a chair for my old aunt who wished to be near 'her dear child'. The letter had to be snatched up and scandal averted. The invalid made the mistake of remarking that she believed she ran a little fever. Madame de Rosemonde, speaking very highly of my medical learning, directed me to take her pulse. So my beauty was obliged to suffer the double annoyance of delivering up her arm to me and of knowing that her little lie would be discovered. I took her hand, holding it in one of mine while with the other I felt up and down the soft skin of her plump and dimpled arm. The malicious creature responded not at all, so, letting her go, I said: 'There is not even the slightest disturbance.' I knew she must be looking daggers at me, so to punish her I avoided her eyes. A moment later she decided to rise, and we left the room. She appeared at dinner, which was a dismal affair; she announced that she would not be going for a walk, as much as to tell me I should have no opportunity of speaking to her. It occurred to me that this was precisely the time for a sigh and a grief-stricken glance. She must have been expecting it, for this was the one occasion during the day when I succeeded in meeting her eyes. Prudent as she is, she is, like any other woman, not above a few little tricks. I found an opportunity to ask her 'whether she had had the kindness to let me know my fate' and I was not a little surprised to hear her reply: 'Yes, Monsieur, I have written to you.' I was most anxious to have the letter. But, whether this was another trick, or lack of address or courage on her part, it was not till the evening, as she retired to her room, that she delivered it to me. I send it to you with the draft of my reply. Read and judge. Notice the arrant hypocrisy with which she declares she is not in love, when I am certain that she is; she does not hesitate to lie to me now, yet will complain when I lie to her later. Even the cleverest man, my love, could not hope to keep pace with the truest of women. Nevertheless I shall have to pretend to believe all this drivel and to wear myself out in despairing, because it pleases Madame to play at being cruel. How shall I keep myself from paying out this villainy? Ah, patience! . . . But good-bye. I have still a great deal to write.

By the way, please return the monster's letter. It may well happen that in the course of things she will decide to put a price upon such stuff, and one must be prepared.

I have said nothing about the little Volanges. We shall talk about her at the first opportunity.

Château de —
22 August 17—

LETTER 26: *Madame de Tourvel to the Vicomte de Valmont*

You would certainly, Monsieur, receive no letter from me were it not for the fact that my stupid conduct last evening obliges me now to make some explanation to you. Yes, I cried, I own it: perhaps, too, the three words you are at such pains to quote did escape my lips; tears, words: you noticed everything. Everything, therefore, must be accounted for.

Accustomed to inspiring none but honourable feelings, to being addressed only in such terms as I can listen to without blushing, to enjoying, as a result, a security which I have the temerity to believe I deserve, I have never learnt to disguise or to repress the emotions that I feel. Astonishment and embarrassment at your behaviour; a fear which I cannot define, prompted by a situation in which I should never have found myself; revulsion, perhaps, at the thought of being mistaken for one of those women you despise, and of being treated with the same indifference; all these feelings contrived to provoke my tears and to cause me to say – with good reason, it seems to me – that I was wretched. That remark, which so impressed you, would certainly have been inadequate, had it, with my tears, been prompted by any other motive: had I, instead of disliking an avowal of sentiments which could only offend me, thought myself in danger of sharing them.

No, Monsieur, I am in no such danger. If I were, I should put a hundred leagues between myself and you; I should remove to a desert to mourn the misfortune of having known you. Perhaps, even though I am certain that I do not love you, that I shall never love you, I should have done better, in following the advice of my friends, never to have allowed you near me.

I thought – and I was wrong only in this – I thought that you would respect a decent woman who asked no more than decency of you; who was concerned to see justice done you; who, indeed, had already begun to speak in your defence when you insulted her by your preposterous attentions. You do not know me; no, Monsieur, you do not know me, or else you would not have tried to make a right of two wrongs: you would not, because you had made me an address to which I should never have listened, have thought yourself entitled to write me a letter I should never have received. And you ask me to 'guide you in what you do, rule you in what you say!' Well, then Monsieur, say nothing and forget everything. That is the advice it becomes me to give and you to follow. You will then, after all, have the right to my indulgence; it will remain only for you to win the right to my gratitude. . . . But no, I shall ask nothing of someone who has shown me no respect; I shall give no mark of confidence to someone who has abused my innocence. You oblige me to fear you, perhaps to hate you. I did not wish to do so. I wished to see you as no more than the nephew of my most respected friend. I answered public accusations of you in a spirit of friendship. You have ruined everything, and I cannot even foresee that you will wish to make amends.

I confine myself, Monsieur, to saying that your feelings are offensive, their avowal insulting, and, above all, that, far from bringing me one day to share them, unless you commit them to the silence I think I have the right to expect and even to demand, you will oblige me never to see you again. I attach to this letter, which I hope you will be kind enough to return, the one you wrote me: it would very much distress me to think any trace remained of an incident which ought never to have occurred. I have the honour to be, etc.

———

21 August 17—

LETTER 27: *Cécile Volanges to the Marquise de Merteuil*

HEAVENS, how good you are, Madame! How well you understood that it would be easier for me to write than to speak to you! Especially since what I have to say is very difficult; but you are truly my friend, are you not? Oh, yes, my dear, dear friend! I shall try not to be shy; besides I need you, I need your advice so much. It is most provoking: it seems that everybody can read my thoughts, especially when he is there: I blush every time anyone looks at me. Yesterday when you saw me cry it was because I wanted to speak to you, but could not, for some reason; and, when you asked me what was the matter, I could not keep back the tears. I was quite incapable of saying a word. But for you, Mamma would have noticed, and then what would have become of me? At all events, here is the history of what has happened, during the last four days especially.

That very day, Madame – yes, I am going to tell you everything – it was that very same day that the Chevalier Danceny wrote to me. Oh, I assure you, when I found the letter I had no idea what it was. But, to be quite candid, I cannot say that I read it without pleasure. Do you know, I would rather the rest of my life were spent in misery, than that he had never written it? But I knew quite well that I must not tell him so, and I can assure you that I even gave him to believe that I was offended. But he says that he could not help writing, and I can quite well believe that: I decided not to reply, yet I, too, found I could not help doing it. Oh, I have written to him only once – and that was, partly, to forbid him to write to me again. Nevertheless, he still writes to me and is obviously hurt because I don't reply, which hurts me even more – so much that I no longer know what to do or where to turn, and am really very much to be pitied.

Tell me, I beseech you, Madame, would it be wrong to reply to him from time to time? Only until he can be persuaded not to write to me any more himself, and we can go on as before: for, if this continues, I don't know what will become of me. I may say that after reading his last letter I thought I should never stop crying. I am certain that if I still do not reply, we shall both of us be made exceedingly miserable.

I shall send you his letter with this, or else a copy of it, so that you may judge. You will see that there is no harm in what he asks. If, however, you consider I ought not to reply, I promise you not to do so. But I think you will agree with me that there could be nothing wrong in it.

While I have the opportunity, Madame, forgive me for asking you yet another question. I have repeatedly been told that it is wrong to love someone; but why is this so? What makes me ask is that the Chevalier Danceny maintains that it is not wrong at all, and that practically everybody loves someone. If this is so, I do not see why I should be the sole exception. Or is it that it is only wrong for young girls? I heard Mamma herself say that Madame D — was

Monsieur M——'s lover. She did not speak of it as though it were something terrible; and yet I am sure she would be angry with me if she so much as suspected my friendship with Monsieur Danceny. She treats me as if I were still a child and tells me nothing. I thought, when she withdrew me from the convent, that I was to be married. But it seems now that this is not the case. Not that I care, I assure you; but you, her friend, will perhaps know what there is to know, and if you do know I hope you will tell me.

What a very long letter, Madame! But since I have your permission to write, I have taken the opportunity to tell you everything. I count on your friendship. I have the honour to be, etc.

Paris
23 August 17——

LETTER 28: *The Chevalier Danceny to Cécile Volanges*

CAN it be, Mademoiselle, that you still refuse to reply? Nothing can touch you. Each day takes away with it the hope that it brought. What are these feelings of friendship worth that you grant exist between us, when they are not even strong enough to make you aware of my grief; when they leave you cold and unmoved while I endure the torments of a fire that cannot be extinguished; when, far from giving you confidence in me, they cannot so much as arouse your pity? Can you do nothing to help your friend in his sufferings? A single word, no more, is all he asks, and you deny him even that. And you expect him to be content with so feeble a sentiment, a sentiment of which you are afraid even to reassure him!

You do not wish to be ungrateful, you said yesterday. Oh, believe me, Mademoiselle! To want to repay love with friendship shows no fear of being ungrateful; only a fear of seeming so. However, I must not continue to speak of a feeling which, if it does not interest you, can only be tiresome: I must at least keep it to myself until such time as I can learn to suppress it. I am aware how much suffering this will cost me: I cannot conceal from myself that I shall need all my strength of mind. But I shall try every means, and there is one that will be more painful to me than the rest: that of continually reminding myself that there is no feeling in your heart. I shall even try to see less of you, and I have already begun to think of a suitable pretext.

Am I then to forgo the sweet privilege of seeing you every day? Ah, I shall, at any rate, never cease to regret it! Perpetual torment will be the price of the most tender love; and it will be your will, your doing. Never, I know, will I recapture the happiness I lose today. You alone were made for me: how much pleasure it would give me to make a vow to live only for you! But you would not accept it. Your silence tells me plainly enough that there is no place for me in your heart: it is at once the most cruel way of declaring your indifference and the most certain proof of it. Good-bye, Mademoiselle.

I can no longer flatter myself that you will reply. Love would have hastened to write; friendship would have been glad to do so; even pity would have obliged: but pity, friendship, and love alike are strangers to your heart.

Paris
23 August 17 —

LETTER 29: *Cécile Volanges to Sophie Carnay*

I TOLD you, Sophie: there are, after all, circumstances in which it is quite possible to write. I assure you I very much regret having followed your advice, which has caused both of us, the Chevalier Danceny and myself, a great deal of unhappiness. The proof that I was right is that Madame de Merteuil, a woman who certainly knows about these things, finally came round to my opinion. I told her everything. At first, it is true, she said what you did: but when I had explained everything to her, she agreed that my case is a very special one. She insists only that I show her all my letters, and all those I receive from the Chevalier Danceny, so that she can make sure I say only what is proper. For the moment, then, my mind is at rest. Heavens, how much I like Madame de Merteuil! She is so good! And a most respectable woman. So there is no more to be said.

What letters I shall write to Monsieur Danceny and how delighted he is going to be! Even more so than he expects. Until now I have spoken to him only of my friendship, whereas he has always wanted me to talk of love. I do not really think there is any difference; however, I hesitated to mention the word, although he seems to set great store by it. I have told Madame de Merteuil about this, and she tells me that I did right. One should never admit to love until one can no longer help it. Well, I am sure I shall not be able to help it for very much longer. After all, it all comes to much the same thing, and this will give him more pleasure.

Madame de Merteuil has told me, too, that she will lend me books about all this, to teach me how best to conduct myself and how to write better than I do at present. She tells me all my faults, you know, which proves how much she likes me. She merely advises me to say nothing to Mamma about the books, which might seem to accuse Mamma of having neglected my education, and that might be annoying. Oh, I shan't say a word!

None the less it is most extraordinary that a woman who is scarcely a relation takes more care of me than my own mother! How lucky I am to know her!

She has also asked Mamma whether she may take me the day after tomorrow to her box at the Opera, where, she says, we shall be alone together, and can chat to our hearts' content without fear of being overheard. I shall much prefer that to any opera. We shall also discuss my marriage. She has told me that it is in fact true that I am to be married; but so far we have not been able to discuss it any further. Really, is it not altogether amazing that Mamma still has nothing at all to say on the subject?

Goodbye, my dear Sophie, I am now going to write to the Chevalier Danceny. Oh, how happy I am!

———

24 August 17 —

LETTER 30: *Cécile Volanges to the Chevalier Danceny*

I HAVE at length decided to write to you, Monsieur, and to assure you of my friendship, of my *love*, since otherwise you are unhappy.

You say that I have a cold heart; I assure you that you are mistaken, indeed I hope that you yourself can now no longer doubt that you are. If my not writing to you has given you pain, do you think it has made me any the less unhappy? It was just that I did not on any account wish to do anything wrong: what is more, I should certainly not have spoken of my 'love' had I been able to help it: but your despondency was more than I could bear. I hope that your spirits will now revive and that we shall both be very happy.

I hope to have the pleasure of seeing you this evening and that you will come early; you cannot possibly come earlier than I should like. Mamma is taking supper at home, and she will probably suggest that you stay: I hope you will have no other engagement, as you did the day before yesterday. You left very early. The supper to which you were invited must have been, I suppose, very amusing. Let us not talk about that, however. Now that you know I love you I hope you will see me as often as you can: I am only happy when I am with you, and I should very much like it to be the same with you.

I am very sorry that at this moment you are still out of spirits, but that is not my fault. I shall ask to play the harp as soon as you arrive, so that you will receive my letter immediately. I can do no more.

Good-bye, Monsieur. I love you with all my heart. The more I tell you so, the happier it makes me. I hope you will be happy too.

———

24 August 17 —

LETTER 31: *The Chevalier Danceny to Cécile Volanges*

YES! There can be no doubt we shall be happy. My happiness, since I am loved by you, is certain; and yours, if it last as long as the love you inspire in me, will never end. Can it really be that you love me, that you are no longer afraid to tell me so? The more you tell me so, the happier it makes you! After reading that charming 'I love you', written in your own hand, I seemed to hear the words fall from your pretty lips; I seemed to see your charming eyes gaze into mine, so much the more beautiful for their look of tenderness. I have accepted your vow to live always for me. Ah, will you accept the one I make to devote my whole life to your happiness? Accept it, and be confident that I shall never break it.

What a delightful day we spent yesterday! Oh, why is it not every day that Madame de Merteuil has secrets to tell your mamma? Why must there ever be thoughts of the constraint under which we meet to disturb my delicious recollections? Why can I not forever hold the pretty hand in mine that wrote 'I love you'; cover it with kisses, and so revenge myself on your refusal to grant me greater favours?

Tell me, my dear Cécile, when your mamma returned, when her presence forced us once again to look with indifference at each other, when you could no longer console me by assuring me of your love for your refusal to give me proof of it – did you then feel no regrets? Did you not tell yourself, 'A kiss would have made him happier, and it is I who deprived him of that happiness'? Promise me, my dear, that you will take the next opportunity to be less disobliging: and with the help of that promise I shall find courage to face the difficulties that circumstances have in store for us. The bitterest privation would be sweetened by the knowledge that you shared my sorrow.

Good-bye, my sweet Cécile. I should find it impossible to leave you were it not for the sake of seeing you again. Good-bye. I love you so much! I shall love you more and more every day.

23 August 17 —

LETTER 32: *Madame de Volanges to Madame de Tourvel*

WOULD you then, Madame, have me believe in the blameless virtue of Monsieur de Valmont? I am compelled to say that I cannot bring myself to do so, and that I should have as much difficulty in believing him to be a good man on the strength of the single circumstance you relate, as I should in considering a man of excellent reputation, on the grounds of a single fault, to be vicious. Mankind is never perfect in anything, no more so in wickedness than in virtue. The scoundrel has his good qualities, and the good man his weaknesses. It seems to me all the more necessary to realize this truth for its being both the basis of one's obligation to tolerate the wicked with the good, and a means by which the latter are preserved from pride, the former from losing heart. You will no doubt be of the opinion that at this moment I am not very conscientiously practising the tolerance that I preach. But tolerance I see as no more than dangerous frailty when it brings us to look with equal favour upon virtue and vice.

I shall not allow myself to examine the motives of Monsieur de Valmont's action: I should like to believe they were as laudable as the deed itself. But for all that, is it any the less true that he has spent his life bringing trouble, dishonour, and scandal into innocent families? Listen, if you like, to the voice of the unfortunate he has rescued, but let it not deafen you to the cries of a hundred victims he has sacrificed. Though he should only be, as you say he is, an example of the dangers of intimacy, would he be, for that reason, any the less dangerous an intimate himself? You imagine him likely to undergo a happy reformation. Let us go even further: let us imagine the miracle accomplished. He would still remain under the condemnation of public opinion, and what else should govern your conduct? God alone can absolve us of our sins the moment we repent; He alone can look into our hearts. Men judge of thoughts only by actions: and no man, once he has forfeited the esteem of others, has the right to complain of their inevitable distrust of him, a distrust which makes his loss so difficult to repair. Remember above all, my dear, that esteem may sometimes be lost for no more than our seeming to attach too little importance to it: a severe punishment, but do not call it an unjust one: for not only is there reason to believe that no one would forgo so precious a benefit who had some claim to deserving it, but it is after all the person who is not restrained by any such consideration that is the most likely to do wrong. Such, at any rate, would be the light in which an intimate relationship with Monsieur de Valmont would make you appear, however innocent that relationship might be.

I am so alarmed at the warmth with which you defend him that I hasten to meet objections I foresee you will make. You will cite

Madame de Merteuil who has been forgiven her connexion with the Vicomte. You will ask me why I receive him in my house. You will tell me that, far from being ostracized by respectable people, he is accepted and even sought after in what is called polite society. I think I can answer all these objections.

First, you will agree that Madame de Merteuil is a most admirable woman who has perhaps only one fault: too much confidence in her own resources. She is like the skilful coachman who delights in manoeuvring a carriage between mountainside and precipice, and whose only justification can be success. It is proper to admire her: it would be imprudent to imitate her. She herself would agree. She admits her faults. The more she sees of the world, the stricter become her principles, and I have no hesitation in assuring you that she will think in this matter as I do.

In so far as I am concerned, I have no more excuse than anybody else. Certainly I receive Monsieur de Valmont as he is received everywhere: there you have another of the thousand inconsistencies that rule society. You know as well as I do that one spends one's life noticing them, complaining about them, and submitting to them. Monsieur de Valmont, with an illustrious name, a large fortune, and many agreeable qualities, early realized that to achieve influence in society no more is required than to practise the arts of adulation and ridicule with equal skill. He has more talent for both than anyone. In the one instance he uses it to charm: in the other to intimidate. No one respects him, but everybody flatters him. Such is his position among people who, with more discretion than courage, would rather humour him than cross swords with him.

But no woman, not Madame de Merteuil herself, would dare to shut herself up in the country almost alone with such a man. It has been left to the most circumspect, the most modest of all to set a pattern for such perversity: forgive me that word, I use it in friendship. My dear friend, your integrity itself, as it inspires you with confidence, betrays you. Think of the people who will sit in judgement on you: on the one hand frivolous creatures who will be sceptical of a virtue they find unexampled among themselves; on the other hand the mischief-makers who will pretend to be sceptical of it so as to punish you for having possessed it. Consider that you are doing at this moment what many men would not dare risk doing. I have remarked that even among the young people, who only too readily accept Monsieur de Valmont as their oracle, the more judicious are afraid to appear upon too intimate terms with him; yet you – you have no fears at all! Ah, come back, come back, I beg you. . . . If my arguments cannot persuade you, yield at least to my friendship: that only has made me renew my entreaties and only that can justify them. You find its demands severe, and I wish they did not have to be so; but I would rather you complained of my solicitude than of my negligence.

24 August 17 —

LETTER 33: *The Marquise de Merteuil to the Vicomte de Valmont*

Now that you have begun to recoil from success, my dear Vicomte, now that your intention is to supply the enemy with arms, now that you look forward more to the battle than the victory, I have nothing further to say. Your strategy is a masterpiece of prudence. On any supposition to the contrary it would have been mere imbecility; and, to tell you the truth, I am still afraid you may be deluding yourself.

What I have to find fault with is not the opportunity you lost. On the one hand, I cannot see that it had indeed arrived, on the other I am pretty sure, whatever people say, that an opportunity missed once will present itself again, whereas a too hasty action can never be recalled.

Your real mistake is in allowing yourself to enter into a correspondence. I defy you now to foresee where this will lead you. Are you, by any chance, hoping to prove to this woman by logical demonstration that she is bound to give herself to you? It seems to me that a truth such as this is better grasped by the feelings than by the understanding; and that to persuade her of it you will have to appeal to her heart rather than to her head. But then what use is softening her heart if you are not there to take advantage of it?

When your fine phrases have intoxicated her with love, do you suppose the intoxication will last long enough to be expressed before reflection supervenes? Consider how long it takes to write a letter, how long it is before one dispatches it, and tell me whether any woman, especially a woman of principle such as your Fair Devotee, could possibly sustain for that length of time an intention she struggles constantly to suppress. Such tactics might succeed with children who, when they write, 'I love you', do not know that they are saying, 'I am yours'. But it seems to me that Madame de Tourvel's disputatious virtue can better assess the value of words. Moreover, in spite of your having got the better of her in conversation, she is more than your match in letter-writing. Besides, have you no idea what is going to happen? No one willingly yields in a dispute: for the simple reason that it is a dispute. By sheer dint of looking for good arguments, we find them and we state them; and afterwards hold by them, not because they are good ones, but because we do not wish to contradict ourselves.

Another observation, which I am surprised you have not made for yourself: there is nothing more difficult in love than expressing in writing what one does not feel – I mean expressing it with conviction. It is not a question of using the right words: but one does not arrange them in the right way. Or rather one does arrange them, and that is sufficiently damning. Read your letter again. It is so beautifully composed that every phrase betrays you. I should like to believe that your Présidente is innocent enough not to understand this, but what difference will that make when the effect is none the less missed? This is the great defect of all novels. Though the author whips himself up into a passion the reader is left cold. *Héloïse* is the sole exception one might be tempted to make. Despite the author's talent, it is for this reason that I have always thought it true. There is not the same difficulty in conversation. Long practice in using the voice has made it a sensitive instrument; tears that come easily are an added advantage; and in the eyes an expression of desire is not easily distinguished from tenderness. Moreover the most haphazard of speeches can successfully express that excitement and incoherence which is the true eloquence of love. Above all, the presence of the beloved is a check to thought and an incentive to surrender.

Take heed, Vicomte: you have been implored to write no more letters. Seize this opportunity to correct your mistake and await an occasion to speak instead. Do you know, this woman has more intelligence than I credited her with? Her defence is good. Were it not for the length of her letter, and the pretext she gives you in her phrase about gratitude to re-enter the lists, she would have given nothing away.

What seems to be even more auspicious for your success is that she employs too many of her resources at once: I can see she will exhaust them in a verbal defence, and have none left to withstand the material attack.

I return your letters. If you are wise, there will be no more until after the happy day. Were it not so late I would tell you about the little Volanges who is making rapid progress; I am very pleased with her. I believe my work will be done before yours, and I am sure you are glad to hear it. Good-bye for today.

———

24 August 17 —

LETTER 34: *The Vicomte de Valmont to the Marquise de Merteuil*

YOUR letter was splendid, my love, but why exhaust your energies in proving what everyone knows? In love one makes better progress by speaking rather than writing: that, I think, is all you have to say. But really! These are the very elements of the art of seduction. I shall observe only that you make a single exception to the rule, whereas there are two. To the children who follow the wrong course out of timidity, and whose ignorance is their downfall, must be added the women of wit, who are led into it by self-esteem, whose vanity lures them into the trap. For instance, I am quite sure that, the Comtesse de B— who did not hesitate to reply to my first letter was at the time no more in love with me than I with her, but saw her opportunity to discuss a subject that could not fail to redound to her credit.

Be that as it may, the principle, as a lawyer might say, does not apply in the present case. You assume that I have a choice between writing and speaking, but I have no choice. Since the incident of the nineteenth, the monster, put on the defensive, has avoided any possible encounter between us with an ingenuity that has put my own contrivances to shame. We have reached a point where, if this continues, she will force me into a serious attempt at recovering the advantage; for, I assure you, I will not be outdone by her in any way. My letters themselves are a little *casus belli*: not content with leaving them unanswered, she refuses to receive them. For each one I have to invent a new strategem, which does not always succeed.

You remember the simple method by which I delivered the first; the second offered no greater difficulties. She had demanded the return of her letter: I sent her mine in its place and she accepted it without the slightest qualm. But whether out of pique at having been taken in, or mere capriciousness, or – she will at length oblige me to believe it – whether it is indeed virtue, for some reason she has obstinately declined the third. I hope, none the less, that the difficulties her refusal has put her to will teach her a lesson for the future.

I was not very surprised that she did refuse a letter sent her in the ordinary way; to accept it would have been something of a concession, and I expected a more prolonged defence. After this first attempt, which was no more than a preliminary sally, I enclosed the letter in an envelope; then, choosing a time when I knew she would be at her *toilette*, I gave the letter to my manservant to take to her, with instructions to tell her that it was the document she had asked for. I was quite certain she would stop short of the scandalous explanation that must necessarily follow a refusal: and in fact, she took the letter. My ambassador, who is not unobservant and who had been ordered to take note of her expression, perceived only a slight colouring, a sign more of embarrassment than of anger.

I flattered myself, of course, that, whether she kept the letter or whether she decided to return it to me, she would have to meet me alone and give me an opportunity of speaking to her. About an hour later one of her servants entered my room and, on behalf of her mistress, handed me an envelope – of a shape different from mine – and addressed in a handwriting I recognized as the one I was so eagerly hoping to see. I tore it open. . . . Inside I found my own letter, unopened and folded in two. It was, no doubt, fear of my being less scrupulous than she in the matter of scandal that prompted this diabolical ruse.

You know me: I need hardly describe my fury. However, I had to recover my sang-froid so as to contrive new schemes. This is the only one I could think of.

Every morning letters are fetched from the post about a mile from here: employed for this purpose is a box with a slit in its lid, something like a collecting-box, to which the postmaster holds one key, and Madame de Rosemonde another. Into it, during the day and as occasion arises, we put our letters, which are carried each evening to the post. In the morning incoming letters are brought back. All the servants, foreign and indigenous, take their turn at this service. It was not my man's day, but he took it upon himself to go, explaining that he had affairs of his own in the neighbourhood.

Meanwhile I wrote my letter, addressed it in an assumed handwriting and – not without success – counterfeited a Dijon postmark on the envelope. I chose Dijon because I thought it would be more jolly if, demanding the same rights as the husband, I should write from the same place. It was also that my beloved had been talking all day of her longing to receive letters from Dijon, and I thought it would be a kindness to afford her the pleasure.

My preparations made, it was easy enough to dispatch my letter with the others. Another advantage of the scheme was that I could be present at its reception: the custom here is to assemble for breakfast and to await the letters from the post before dispersing.

At length they arrived. Madame de Rosemonde opened the box. 'From Dijon,' she said, handing the letter to Madame de Tourvel. 'It is not my husband's handwriting,' returned the latter in an anxious voice, and broke the seal hurriedly. The first glance told her everything. Her expression changed so noticeably that Madame de Rosemonde asked whether anything was the matter, and I, too, approaching her asked: 'Is the news so very bad?' Our shy devotee dared not lift her eyes, said not a word, and to mask her embarrassment pretended to glance through the letter which she was scarcely in any condition to read. I was enjoying her distress, and did not hesitate to provoke it a little further. 'Your composure now', I said, 'makes me hope that the letter has caused you more surprise than pain.' Anger then afforded the inspiration that prudence had failed to provide. 'It contains', she replied, 'nothing that does not offend me, and I am astonished that the author dared write to me at all.' 'Who was it then?' put in Madame de Rosemonde. 'There is no signature,' replied the beautiful Fury, 'but letter and writer inspire me with equal contempt. You will oblige me by saying no more about it.' As she spoke, she tore the offending missive to pieces, put the pieces in her pocket, rose, and left the room.

Angry or not, she still has the letter, and I believe I can trust to her curiosity for a complete perusal of it.

To give you every detail of the day's proceedings would be going too far, but with this abbreviated account I send you the drafts of my two letters: you will then know as much as I. If you wish to keep up with this correspondence you must train yourself to decipher my drafts, because nothing in the world will reconcile me to the tedium of copying them out a second time. Good-bye, my love.

25 August 17—

LETTER 35: *The Vicomte de Valmont to Madame de Tourvel*

I MUST obey you, Madame; it is essential to prove to you that, with all the faults you are pleased to ascribe to me, I have yet enough delicacy to forbear reproaching you, and enough courage to impose the most painful of sacrifices upon myself. You command me to say nothing and to forget everything. Ah, well! I shall compel my love to be silent, and I shall forget, if that is possible, the cruelty with which you greeted it. Certainly the mere desire to please you gives me no right to do so, and I am ready to admit that my need of your indulgence is no title to its possession. But you regard my love in the light of an insult. You forget that, if it were a crime, you yourself would be not only its motive but its justification. You forget, too, that, having learnt to open my heart to you, even when such confidences were not to my advantage, it was no longer possible for me to hide the feelings that had taken possession of me. You took the proof of my honesty for a mark of audacity. As reward for the most tender, the most respectful, the truest love, you cast me away from you. To crown all, you tell me of your hatred ... who else in the world would not complain of such treatment? I alone submit. I suffer in silence. You persecute and I adore. The extraordinary spell you cast over me makes you absolute mistress of my feelings, and if my love alone is recalcitrant, if that alone you cannot destroy, it is because my love is your own handiwork and not mine.

I am by no means asking you to return my feelings; I have never flattered myself that you might do so. I do not even expect your pity, for which the interest you showed in me might once have led me to hope. But I confess I consider myself entitled to justice.

You have told me, Madame, that certain of your friends have tried to lower me in your estimation. Had you taken their advice you would never have allowed me near you: those were your words. Who, if you please, are these officious friends? People of such strict principles, of such uncompromising probity, will surely not object to being identified; surely they cannot wish to hide in an obscurity where they may easily be confused with mere scandal-mongers. Let me hear not only their accusations but their names. After all, Madame, I have a right to both since it is on their authority that you judge me. No criminal may be condemned unless his crime is specified and his accusers named. I ask no other favour: and I shall undertake in advance to clear myself, to compel these people to retract.

If I have perhaps been too scornful of empty acclaim in a society I make little account of, it is not the same with your esteem, which, now that I have devoted my life to winning it, cannot with impunity be snatched from me. It has become so much the more precious to me in that to it, I am sure, I owe the request you were afraid to make: which, you say, might have given me *the right to your gratitude*. Ah! Far from claiming your gratitude, I shall think mine due to you if you will allow me an opportunity to please you. Begin now to do me justice. Leave me no longer in ignorance of what you wish me to do. If I could guess, I should spare you the trouble of telling me. Add the pleasure of obliging you to my delight in seeing you, and I shall think myself fortunate in your kindness.

What is there to stop you? Not, I hope, a fear of being refused? I do not think I could forgive you that. I refuse you nothing by not returning your letter. I wish, even more than you do, that it were no longer necessary to me: but I have become so used to thinking of you as kind-hearted, that only in the letter can I find you as you wish to appear. Whenever I resolve to declare my feelings, I read there that rather than tolerate them you would put a hundred leagues between yourself and me; whenever I feel that everything about you increases and excuses my love, there I learn that my love insults you; and whenever, looking at you, I am tempted to think my love the summit of happiness, I have to return to your letter to find that it is nothing but frightful torture. As you may imagine, nothing would make me happier than to return this terrible document: to ask for it again would be to release me from my obligation to believe what it says. You are in no doubt, I hope, that I would be most anxious to let you have it.

———

21 August 17 —

LETTER 36: *The Vicomte de Valmont to Madame de Tourvel (postmarked Dijon)*

EVERY day increases your severity, Madame; you seem – dare I say it? – to be less afraid of being unjust than of being too kind. Having condemned me without a hearing, you must have realized it would be easier not to read my arguments than to reply to them. You obdurately refuse to receive my letters; you return them with contempt. You oblige me at last to have recourse to deceit, at the very moment when my one and only wish is to convince you of my honesty. But the absolute necessity you have imposed upon me of defending myself, I am sure, will excuse the means I employ. Besides which, the sincerity of my feelings convinces me that I have only to make you understand them in order to make them acceptable to you: I thought, therefore, I might allow myself this little subterfuge. I venture to think, too, that you will forgive me for it, and that you will scarcely be surprised to find that love is more adept at coming forward than indifference at brushing it aside.

Permit me then, Madame, to lay my heart entirely open to you. It belongs to you and it is only right that you should know what is there. On my first arrival at this house, I was very far from imagining the fate that awaited me. I was not aware that you were here, and I must add with my accustomed sincerity that, had I known, my peace of mind would in no way have been disturbed. Not that I failed to pay your beauty the homage which no one could withhold from it. But till that time I had known only desire, to which I yielded only when it was encouraged by hope. I had never felt the torments of love.

You were present when Madame de Rosemonde urged me to make a longer stay. I had already spent one day in your company. Nevertheless I consented, or at least believed that I was consenting, only because of that very natural and legitimate pleasure one takes in showing regard for a relation one respects. The sort of life you lead here is of course very different from the one I am accustomed to. I found no difficulty in conforming to it; and without attempting to discover the origin of the change I felt to be working in me, I put it down once more entirely to that pliability of character which I think I have already mentioned to you.

Unfortunately (and why, alas, must it be a misfortune?), I soon found, when I knew you better, that your enchanting face, which alone had interested me, was the least of your attractions. The angelic purity of your soul astonished me, fascinated me. Beauty I had admired: virtue I worshipped. Without the smallest pretensions to obtaining your regard, I applied myself to deserving it. While begging your forgiveness for the past, I was ambitious for your approval in the future. I sought it in your words, I watched for it in your looks – those poisoned looks that are so much the more deadly for being given without intent and received without suspicion.

At last I knew the meaning of love. But how little I thought of lamenting my condition! Having resolved to impose perpetual silence upon my feelings, I could give myself up to enjoying them with as little apprehension as reserve. Every day increased their strength. My pleasure in seeing you was soon transformed into a necessity. You had only to be absent for a moment for my heart to shrink with disappointment; at the first sound of your return it would palpitate with joy. I lived only in you and for you. I call upon you, however, to judge: did I at any time, whether in jest during some foolish game, or in earnest when the conversation was serious, speak a single word that might have betrayed my secret?

At length the day arrived on which my unhappy fate was to be sealed: and by some extraordinary chance an honourable deed was to provide the occasion. Yes, Madame, it was among the unfortunates I had succoured, when you displayed that sensibility which adds beauty to beauty and worth to virtue itself, it was then that you accomplished the confusion of a heart already distracted by too much love. Perhaps you noticed my silent preoccupation during our return? Alas! I was trying to repress inclinations that were becoming too strong for me.

It was when the unequal battle had weakened my powers of resistance that an accident, which I could not have foreseen, brought me face to face with you, alone. Whereupon I gave way, I admit. My overfraught heart could no longer contain its protestations, its tears. But was that, after all, a crime? And if it was, have I not been enough punished by the frightful torments to which I am condemned?

Consumed by a hopeless love, I implore your pity and receive nothing but your hatred. With no other happiness left me but that of seeing you, my eyes seek you out in spite of myself, and when they meet your glance I tremble. My whole life is spent in the cruel condition to which you have reduced me, the days in concealing my torments, the nights in suffering them: whereas you live in peace and quiet with no thought of torture but to cause it and commend yourself for doing so. It is you, all the same, who make the accusations, I the excuses.

There, at all events, Madame, there is a faithful account of what you call my crimes, which might perhaps more justly be called my misfortunes. A pure and sincere love, a respect which has never faltered, an absolute submission to your will: these are the feelings you have inspired in me. I would have no reluctance in offering them in homage to God Himself. O fairest of His creation, follow the example of His charity! Think of my cruel sufferings. Consider, especially, that you have put my despair and my supreme felicity on either scale, and that the first word you utter will irremediably turn the balance.

———

23 August 17 —

LETTER 37: *The Présidente de Tourvel to Madame de Volanges*

I YIELD, Madame, to your friendly counsel. I am already accustomed to defer to your opinion in everything: I am now persuaded that it is always founded in reason. I shall even admit that Monsieur de Valmont must, after all, be infinitely dangerous if he can at one and the same time pretend to be what he appears to be here and continue to be the man that you have described. Be that as it may: since you insist, I shall send him away. At all events I shall do my best: things which in theory are perfectly simple are often difficult in practice.

A request to his aunt still seems to me impracticable: it would be as disagreeable to her as it would be to him. Nor could I without some reluctance take the step of going away myself. Apart from the reasons I have already given you concerning Monsieur de Tourvel, if my departure were to annoy Monsieur de Valmont, which is possible, would it not be quite easy for him to follow me to Paris? And would not his return there, for which I will be, or at least will seem to be, responsible, appear in an even worse light than a meeting at the country house of someone who is known to be his relation and my friend?

I have no alternative but to obtain from Monsieur de Valmont himself an assurance of his willingness to leave. I know this will be difficult. However, as he seems to be most anxious to prove to me that he has more sense of honour than is generally supposed, I am not without hope of succeeding. I shall not, in any case, be sorry of an opportunity to test him, to discover whether what he has so often told me is true: that the really virtuous women have never had, and will never have, any reason to complain of his behaviour. If he leaves, as I wish him to do, it will certainly be out of regard for me: for I am sure he intends to spend a large part of the autumn here. If he refuses and insists on staying, there will be nothing to prevent my leaving instead, and I promise you I shall do so.

This, I think, Madame, is all that your friendship demands of me; I look forward to satisfying that demand, to proving that, however *warmly* I might have spoken in Monsieur de Valmont's defence, I am none the less prepared, not only to listen to, but to follow the advice of my friends.

I have the honour to be, etc.

———

25 August 17 —

LETTER 38: *The Marquise de Merteuil to the Vicomte de Valmont*

YOUR enormous packet has this moment arrived, my dear Vicomte. If it is correctly dated I should have received it twenty-four hours ago. In any case, were I to spend time reading it I should have none left to reply to it, so I prefer merely to acknowledge it: we shall talk of other things. Not that I have anything to tell you on my own account. Paris in autumn contains scarcely a single male being that is recognizably human, so that for the last month I have been killingly circumspect. Anyone else but my Chevalier would long ago have been thoroughly bored by so much proof of my fidelity. With nothing else to occupy me, I have amused myself with the little Volanges, and it is about her that I want to talk to you.

Do you know that you have missed more than you think in not taking charge of the child? She is truly delicious! She has neither character nor principles: imagine how easy and agreeable her company will one day be. I don't think she will ever be conspicuous for her sentiments: but everything about her speaks of the most lively sensations. She has neither wit nor guile, but a certain natural duplicity – if I may use such a phrase – at which even I am sometimes astonished, and which will succeed so much the better because her face is the very image of candour and ingenuousness. She is by nature very demonstrative, and this amuses me very much sometimes: she loses her little head with incredible ease and is so much the more diverting because she knows nothing, absolutely nothing, of all that she wants so much to know about. Her fits of impatience are altogether comic: she laughs, she gets angry, she cries, and then she begs me to teach her with a sincerity which is truly enchanting. In fact I am almost jealous of the man for whom such pleasures are in store.

I don't know whether I told you that for the last four or five days I have had the honour of being her confidante. As you can imagine, I was severe at first: but as soon as I saw that she believed me convinced by her doubtful arguments, I pretended to take them for good ones. She is firmly persuaded that she owes this success to her eloquence: the precaution was necessary to avoid compromising myself. I allowed her to write, and to say 'I love you'. The same day, without her suspecting, I arranged a *tête-à-tête* for her with Danceny. But would you believe that he is still so dull as not to have obtained so much as a kiss? And yet the boy writes such very pretty verses! Lord, how stupid clever people can be – this one to the point of embarrassing me. After all I cannot lead him by the nose!

It is now that you could be extremely useful to me. You are intimate enough with Danceny to obtain his confidence, and once you had that we could proceed at a great pace. Finish off your Présidente, then; after all I cannot have Gercourt escape. For the rest, I told the little creature about him yesterday and described him so well that had she now been his wife for ten years she could not hate him more. I also, however, expatiated a great deal on the subject of marital fidelity: nothing could have equalled my firmness on this point. Thus I have on the one hand established a reputation for virtue which too much complaisance might have destroyed: on the other I have increased the feelings of hatred with which I intend her husband shall be gratified. Lastly I hope that, for my having persuaded her that she may surrender to love only during the short time that remains before her marriage, she will decide so much the more quickly not to waste any of that time.

Good-bye, Vicomte; I am going to begin my *toilette*, during which I shall read your compilation.

27 August 17—

LETTER 39: *Cécile Volanges to Sophie Carnay*

I AM so anxious and sad, my dear Sophie. I have been crying almost the whole night: not that for the present I am anything but extremely happy, but I see that it cannot last.

I was at the Opera yesterday with Madame de Merteuil; we talked a great deal about my marriage, and nothing that I learned was in the least encouraging. I am to marry the Comte de Gercourt, and it is to happen in October. He is rich, a man of fashion, and Colonel of the — Regiment. So far so good. But he is old: thirty-six, can you imagine? Madame de Merteuil says, besides, that he is stern and gloomy and she is afraid I might not be very happy with him. I saw, in fact, that she was quite certain I would not be happy, and that she did not wish to say so for fear of distressing me. She spoke of nothing almost the whole evening but the duties a woman owes to her husband. She admits that Monsieur de Gercourt is not in the least agreeable, but says I must love him all the same. She told me too that, once I am married, I shall have to stop loving the Chevalier Danceny: as if that were possible! Oh, I promise you, I shall love him forever! I should prefer, you know, not to be married at all. Let this Monsieur de Gercourt make the best he can of it; I did not, after all, ask for him. He is at present in Corsica — very far from here. I wish he would stay there for the next ten years. If I were not afraid of being sent back to the convent I should tell Mamma that I don't want him for a husband; but the convent would be still worse. I am in a terrible dilemma. I feel that I have never loved Monsieur Danceny as much as I do at this moment; and when I think that I have no more than a month of freedom left me, the tears come immediately to my eyes. Madame de Merteuil's friendship is my only consolation. She has such a good heart. She shares all my troubles as if they were her own. Besides, she is so agreeable that when I am with her I can almost forget them. What is more, she is a great help to me. The little that I know I have learned from her. And she is so good that I can tell her all my thoughts without feeling the least embarrassment. She scolds me a little sometimes, when she thinks I am in the wrong, but so gently, and then I put my arms around her and kiss her until she is no longer angry. She, at least, is one person I can love as much as I like without doing wrong, and that is a great happiness. I have agreed however not to display so much affection in company, especially when Mamma is there, in case she suspects anything concerning the Chevalier Danceny. I assure you that if I could live forever in the way I do now I should be very happy. If only this dreadful Monsieur de Gercourt... But I shall say no more about him or I shall be unhappy again. I shall write to the Chevalier Danceny instead, telling him only of my love and not of my troubles, because I don't wish to distress him.

Good-bye, my dear friend. You were wrong, you see, to complain: I could never be so *busy*, as you say, as to have no time left to think of you and write to you.[1]

———

27 August 17—

LETTER 40: *The Vicomte de Valmont to the Marquise de Merteuil*

IT is not enough for the monster to leave my letters unanswered or even to refuse to receive them. She wants to deny me the very sight of her. She insists on my leaving. What will come as more of a surprise to you is that I have submitted to these harsh demands. You are going to disapprove. However, I thought I had better not miss an opportunity of accepting an order: for I have always thought that, on the one hand, an order issued is a responsibility assumed, and on the other, that the illusion of authority we tempt women to entertain is one of the pitfalls they find it most difficult to avoid. Moreover, this one's skill in eluding a *tête-à-tête* with me

1. Letters between Cécile Volanges and the Chevalier Danceny continue to be omitted since they are of little interest and throw no light on events.

has put me in a dangerous situation, from which I have thought it necessary to withdraw at all costs. Constantly in her company, with no opportunity of bringing my love to her notice, I have had good reason to fear that she would at length become accustomed to seeing me without a qualm: and you know how difficult it would be to recover from such a setback.

For the rest, you may be quite sure that I have not surrendered unconditionally. I have in fact taken care to lay down a condition which it will be impossible to observe: as much for the sake of remaining at liberty to keep my word or break it, as for the sake of entering upon a dispute, either by word of mouth or in writing, at a time when my beauty is more than usually pleased with me, and wants me to be pleased with her: what is more, I should be very stupid if I found no way of obtaining compensation for my waiving this claim, totally unsupported though it is.

Having given you in this long preamble an analysis of my motives, I shall now begin the history of the last two days. By way of documentation I enclose the letter from my beauty and my reply to it. You will agree that there are few historians as meticulous as I.

You remember the effect of my letter from 'Dijon' two mornings ago. The remainder of the day proved exceedingly stormy. Our pretty prude did not appear at all before lunch. When she did, she complained of a bad headache: which excuse was designed to conceal one of the most violent fits of ill temper to which woman has ever been subject. A complete change had come over her features: in place of the sweet expression which you know, a look of defiance gave new beauty to her face. I shall certainly put this discovery to good use in the future, exchanging my tender mistress now and again for a rebellious one.

I foresaw that conversation after lunch would be tedious, so to spare myself unnecessary boredom I pleaded letters to write and withdrew to my room. At six I returned to the drawing-room. Madame de Rosemonde proposed a drive and her suggestion was approved. But, as we were on the point of stepping into the carriage, our mock invalid, with diabolical malice and perhaps in revenge for my absence earlier on, pleaded in turn an exacerbation of her sufferings, and condemned me without mercy to a *tête-à-tête* with my aunt. I shall never know whether my curses upon this she-devil were fulfilled, but we found on our return that she had gone to bed.

Next morning at breakfast she was no longer the same woman. Her natural sweetness had returned, and I came to the conclusion that I had been forgiven. Immediately after breakfast the dear lady rose with a languid air and made for the park. I followed her, of course. 'What, I wonder, can have persuaded you to take a walk?' I asked as we met. 'I spent a long time writing this morning', she replied, 'and I am a little fatigued.' 'I am not, surely, so fortunate', continued I, 'as to be responsible myself for your fatigue?' 'I have indeed written to you,' she returned, 'but I am not sure whether I shall give you the letter. It contains a request, and you have given me no reason to hope that it might be granted.' 'Oh, I swear, if it is at all possible . . .' 'Nothing could be easier,' she interrupted, 'and even though you ought perhaps to grant it as my rightful due, I shall not object to receiving it as a favour.' As she spoke she handed me the letter, and as I took it I seized her hand. The latter she withdrew immediately, but not angrily – with less spirit, indeed, than embarrassment. 'It is warmer than I thought it would be,' she said. 'I must go indoors.' And she hurried back towards the house. All my efforts to persuade her to continue the walk were in vain, and I was obliged to remind myself that we were fully visible and that I must confine myself to verbal entreaties. She walked back without a word, and I saw clearly that the sole object of this pretence of a walk had been the delivery of her letter. As soon as we reached the house she went up to her room, while I retired to mine to read the epistle which you, too, would do well to read – and my reply to it – before proceeding further. . . .

LETTER 41: *The Présidente de Tourvel to the Vicomte de Valmont*

IT seems to me, Monsieur, that your behaviour towards me has no other motive than that of adding each day to the sum of my complaints against you. Your obstinacy in treating me to sentiments which it is equally against my desire and my duty to acknowledge;

your unhesitating abuse of my good faith and my modesty in sending me your letters; above all, the means – scarcely a proof of delicacy in you, I venture to say – which you employed in sending me my last, without so much as considering that the surprise by itself might compromise me; everything you have done gives me reason to call you to account in terms as outspoken as they are just. Instead, however, of recalling my grievances I shall confine myself to making a request of you, a request as simple as it is fair: when I obtain it from you I promise that everything else will be forgotten.

You yourself have told me, Monsieur, that I need fear no refusal from you; and even though, with that inconsistency characteristic of you, you followed this same injunction with the one refusal you were able to make me,[1] I should like to believe none the less that today you will keep your solemn promise of a few days ago.

I want you, then, to be so good as to go away from me, to leave this house, where a longer stay on your part could only further expose me to the criticism of a society which is always prepared to think ill of others, and which, thanks to you, is only too ready to fix its attention upon the women who count you among their acquaintance.

My friends have for a long time warned me of this danger, yet, as long as your behaviour towards me gave me reason to believe that you would distinguish between me and that multitude of women who have had cause to revile you, I disregarded and even disputed my friends' advice. Now that you treat me in the same way as the others, now that I can no longer ignore the truth, I owe it to society, to my friends, and to myself to take this course and no other. I might, perhaps, add here that you will gain nothing by refusing my request since I have decided to leave myself if you persist in staying: I do not, on the other hand, mean to belittle the obligation I shall owe you if you consent; I am, in fact, quite willing to tell you that in compelling me to leave here you would be upsetting my plans. Prove to me then, Monsieur, that – as you have so often told me – no honourable woman will ever have occasion to complain of you. Prove to me at least that, when you have wronged one, you know how to make amends.

If I thought it necessary to justify my request to you, I could say

1. See Letter 35.

no more than that you have spent your life in making it necessary, yet that it is one I ought never to have found it necessary to make. But let us not recall incidents I wish only to forget; remembering them would compel me to think harshly of you at a moment when I am offering you an opportunity to earn my undivided gratitude. Good-bye, Monsieur; your conduct now will determine the feelings with which, for the rest of my life, I shall subscribe myself your very humble, etc.

25 August 17—

LETTER 42: *The Vicomte de Valmont to the Présidente de Tourvel*

HARD as the conditions are, Madame, which you impose on me, I shall not refuse to accept them. It would be impossible for me, I think, to cross you in a single one of your desires. This question once settled, I venture to hope that you will permit me in my turn to make some requests of you. They will be much easier to comply with than yours; I wish, nevertheless, to obtain your consent only through an absolute submission to your will.

The first, which I hope will find an advocate in your sense of justice, is that you will be so good as to give me the names of your friends, my accusers. They have, it seems to me, done me as much harm as entitles me to their acquaintance. The second, an appeal to your indulgence, is that you will be kind enough to permit my paying you now and then the homage of a love which, more than ever before, deserves your pity.

Consider, Madame, that I am anxious to obey you even at the expense of my own happiness – I shall go further and say, even when I am convinced that you urge my departure only to spare yourself what we always find painful: the sight of a victim to our injustice.

You must agree, Madame: you are less afraid of society, which is too used to respecting you to pass sentence against you, than of being plagued by a man whom you find it easier to punish than condemn. You send me away from you exactly as one averts one's eyes from the unfortunate one has no intention of assisting.

But when absence has redoubled my sufferings, who but you will listen to my lamentations? Where else shall I find the consolation that is soon to become so necessary to me? Will you deny it me, when it is you alone who have caused my miseries?

You will not, of course, be surprised to learn that I am most anxious, before leaving, to make my justification to you in person of the feelings you have inspired in me; nor that, unless I receive my commands at your own lips, I find I lack the courage to carry them out.

For these two reasons, I beg you for a moment's interview. It is useless to imagine that letters would do as well. One writes volumes, and only half explains what a quarter of an hour's conversation would make quite clear. There will be quite time enough for the meeting; for, eager as I am to obey you, I have already told Madame de Rosemonde, as you know, that I intend to spend a part of the autumn with her, and I must at least wait to receive a letter before offering her a pretext of business which obliges me to leave.

Good-bye, Madame. Never has it cost me more to write that word than it does now, when it calls up the thought of our separation. If you could conceive how much it makes me suffer, I daresay you would be a little grateful for my willingness to please you. Look more kindly, at least, upon the assurance and homage of my most tender and respectful love.

26 August 17 —

LETTER 40 (CONTINUED): *The Vicomte de Valmont to the Marquise de Merteuil*

Now, my love, let us consider. You know as well as I do that the scrupulous, the honourable Madame de Tourvel cannot grant me the first of my requests; she cannot, in giving me the names of my accusers, betray the confidence of her friends; so that in making that the condition of all I promise, I am committed to nothing. But you understand, too, that her denial of this request will give me a right to obtaining the others. Thus I shall have the advantage, when I go away, of a correspondence with her that she herself has authorized. I attach little importance to the interview I asked for: almost my sole object in doing so was to prepare her to consent to others when they become really necessary.

The only thing I have left to do before my departure is to discover who these people are that are engaged in disparaging me to her. Her pedant of a husband is, I presume, one of them: I hope so. Apart from the fact that conjugal protection is a spur to desire, from the moment my beauty agrees to write to me I shall be sure of having nothing further to fear from him, since she will already be under the necessity of deceiving him.

But if she happens to have a friend intimate enough with her to be in her confidence, and if that friend happens to be against me, it will be necessary to stir up a quarrel between them. I think I can do it. The first essential, however, is to acquaint myself with the facts.

I was on the point of making a discovery yesterday; but this woman never does anything in the normal way. We were in her room when it was announced that dinner was served. She had only just completed her *toilette*, and as she hurried off, making excuses, I noticed she had left the key in her writing desk. I knew that the one in the door of her room was never removed. During dinner, as I turned this over in my mind, I heard her maid come down. I made my decision immediately: inventing a bleeding nose, I left the room. I flew to the desk – to find all the drawers open and not the smallest sign of a letter anywhere. Yet at this time of the year there are no fires in which they could have been burnt. What does she do with the letters she receives? She receives them often enough! I missed nothing; everything was open, and I looked everywhere; all I acquired was the conviction that the precious treasure must be buried in her pockets.

How remove it from there? I have been trying since yesterday, but without success, to think of a means; I am still determined to find one. I wish I had been trained in the arts of the pickpocket. Ought they not, after all, to have figured in the education of a man of intrigue? How amusing it would be to steal a rival's letter or his miniature, or to filch from the pockets of a prude the wherewithal to unmask her hypocrisy! Our parents think of nothing; as for me, I think of everything, but to no purpose. I can only recognize my incompetence without being able to remedy it.

At all events, I returned to table very disgruntled. My ill temper, however, was a little mollified by noting the interest my feigned indisposition appeared to have aroused in my beauty. I did not, of course, fail to inform her that for some time, and to the great detriment of my health, I have been subject to the most violent fits. Convinced as she is that she is responsible for them, ought she not in all conscience to apply herself to their cure? But, albeit religious, she is not very charitable. She refuses to give alms of any kind in the name of love. Being refused them, it seems to me, is more than enough to justify stealing them. But good-bye. Even as I chatter to you I can think of nothing but those cursed letters.

27 August 17 —

LETTER 43: *The Présidente de Tourvel to the Vicomte de Valmont*

WHY, Monsieur, do you seek to lessen my gratitude? Why resolve to comply only by halves with my wishes, to bargain, as it were, over a perfectly fair proposal? Is it not enough that I know how much I ask you? What you ask of me is not only too much, it is impossible. If, in fact, friends of mine have spoken to me of you, they could have done so only in my own interest. They may have been mistaken: their intentions were none the less honest. Do you suggest that I recognize this proof of their attachment by betraying their trust? I have already done wrong to tell you of them at all, a fact of which you make me amply aware at this moment. What with anyone else would have been simple candour was recklessness where you were concerned; and I should be guilty of much worse were I to concede to your request. I appeal to you, to your honour. Do you really think me capable of such a thing? Should you ever have made such a proposal? Of course not. I am sure that, when you have thought more about it, you will press your demands no further.

Your proposal that I write to you is scarcely less difficult to assent to; and, if you are just, it is not me you will blame for this. I have no wish whatever to offend you, but with the reputation you have acquired, which, at your own admission, you have at least in part deserved, what woman could admit to being in correspondence with you? What woman of honour, besides, would resolve on doing what she knows she will be obliged to conceal?

Yet if I were confident that your letters would be of a kind I could find no fault with, that I could always justify myself in my own eyes for having received them, then, perhaps, because I want to prove to you that I am guided by reason and not by hatred, I might be persuaded to overlook other considerations, however serious, and to go much further than I ought in allowing you to write to me from time to time. If you do, in fact, wish this to happen as much as you say you do, you will willingly submit to the single condition I have imposed; and if you are able to feel some gratitude for what I do at this moment for your sake, you will defer your departure no longer.

Permit me to observe *à propos* that, though you received a letter this morning, you did not take advantage of the opportunity to announce your departure to Madame de Rosemonde as you promised you would. I hope that henceforth nothing will prevent you from keeping your promise; above all that you will not expect, in return, any promise from me concerning the interview you ask for, to which I have positively no intention of consenting. I hope, too, that in place of the orders you fancy are necessary to you, you will be content with my pleas, which I now renew. Good-bye, Monsieur

———

27 August 17 —

LETTER 44: *The Vicomte de Valmont to the Marquise de Merteuil*

SHARE my joy, love; I am beloved; I have triumphed over that intransigent heart. She continues to pretend, but in vain; fortune and skill have sprung her secret. Now, thanks to my unflagging endeavours, I know everything that can be of interest to me. Since last night – happy night! – I have been in my element again; my whole life has begun anew. I have penetrated a twofold mystery, uncovered both love and infamy: the one I shall enjoy, the other revenge. I shall fly from pleasure to pleasure. At the mere thought of it I am carried away to a point where I have some difficulty in recalling my prudence, and I shall probably find it no less difficult to give a semblance of order to the story I have to tell you. Let me try all the same.

Yesterday, after writing my letter to you, I received one from the Heavenly Devotee herself. I send it to you; you will observe that, as gracefully as she can, she gives me permission to write to her. But she is more concerned about my departure from here; and I decided that to defer it much longer would be to damage my cause.

Meanwhile I was still tormented by a desire to know who could have written to her about me and still uncertain what I should do to find out. I thought I might prevail upon the maid. I would have her bring me her mistress's pockets, which she could without difficulty remove in the evening and as easily replace in the morning without arousing the smallest suspicion. I offered her ten *louis* for this trifling service. But she proved to be either too scrupulous or too frightened, at all events a broken reed, and neither my eloquence nor my money could move her. I was still cajoling when the bell rang for supper and I had to leave her, considering myself lucky enough to have obtained a promise of secrecy – upon which, needless to say, I could scarcely rely.

I have never been in worse humour. I felt I had compromised myself; I spent the entire evening regretting my rash experiment.

Still uneasy, I retired to my room and spoke to my valet who I thought must, in his role of successful lover, have some credit with the girl. My plan was that he should either persuade her to do as I had asked, or, at the least, ensure that she would be discreet.

But he, who is ordinarily confident about everything, seemed to doubt whether any negotiation of this kind would succeed, and passed an astonishingly profound comment on the subject.

'Monsieur knows better than I do', he said, 'that to lie with a girl is only to make her do what she likes doing. It's often a far cry from that to making her do what we want her to do.'

The good sense Maraud shows quite frightens me at times.[1]

'I am the less able to answer for this one', he continued, 'because I have reason to believe that she has another lover, and that I owe my own success with her only to the fact that there is not enough to do in the country. Were it not for my eagerness to serve Monsieur, I would have had her only once.' (This fellow is a real treasure!) 'As for her keeping your secret,' he went on, 'what use will it be making her give her promise, when she has nothing to lose by breaking it? To refer to the subject again will only give her an idea that it is important, and so make her even readier to make use of it for currying favour with her mistress.'

My perplexities increased with the justice of these reflections. Fortunately the odd creature was in a mood to chatter: and, as I needed him, I let him go on. In the course of relating his adventures with the girl he revealed the fact that, since the room she occupies is separated from her mistress's only by a thin partition through which they are afraid suspicious noises might be heard, it is in his room that they meet each night. My plan was formed upon the instant: I told him of it, and we executed it with brilliant success.

I waited till two o'clock in the morning at which time I proceeded, as agreed upon, to the scene of the lovers' rendezvous, taking a candle with me, forearmed with the excuse that I had rung several times without success. My accomplice, who can play a part to perfection, staged a little drama of surprise, despair, and excuses which I brought to a close by sending him to fetch some hot water I pretended to need. Meanwhile our fastidious chambermaid was so much the more abashed because the ridiculous man, determined to outdo me in ingenuity, had coaxed her into a state of undress which the season might have explained, but could not excuse.

Knowing that the more I could humiliate the wench the more

1. Piron: *Métromanie.*

tractable she would be, I forbade her to change either her position or her costume, and, having ordered my valet to wait for me in my room, I sat down beside her on the bed, which was in great disarray, and began to speak. It was necessary to maintain the power over her that circumstances had given me: so I preserved a composure that would have done credit to the self-restraint of a Scipio. Without taking the smallest liberty with her, which nevertheless the occasion and her preparedness might have given her the right to expect, I talked business as calmly as I would have done to any solicitor.

My conditions were that I should guard her secret faithfully provided that the next morning, at about the same hour, she would bring me her mistress's pockets. 'For the rest,' I added, 'I promised you ten *louis* yesterday; my promise holds good today. I do not wish to take advantage of your situation.' Everything was consented to, as you may imagine, whereupon I retired to bed, leaving the happy couple to make up for lost time.

My own time I spent sleeping; and when I woke, because I needed an excuse for leaving my beauty's letter unanswered until I had examined her papers (which I could not do until the night following), I decided to go hunting, and indeed spent almost all day at it.

On my return I was coldly received. I have a suspicion that a little pique was felt at my want of zeal in making the most of the time that was left me: particularly after so much more amiable a letter had been written me than any heretofore. I came to this conclusion because, Madame de Rosemonde having put forward a few protests at my long absence, my beauty returned somewhat sharply: 'Ah, let us not take Monsieur de Valmont to task for enjoying the one pleasure this place is able to afford him.' I complained of the injustice of this, and took the opportunity to assure the ladies that I enjoyed their company so much that for its sake I was about to sacrifice the satisfaction of writing a most interesting letter. I added that, having been unable to sleep for several nights, I had meant to try whether fatigue would help me. My looks, of course, clearly indicated both the subject of my letter and the cause of my sleeplessness. I took care the whole evening to preserve an air of gentle melancholy, which appeared to succeed quite well; behind it I concealed my impatience for the moment when the secret so obstinately kept from me would be revealed. At length we separated, and some time later came the trusty maid, bringing me the reward of my discretion.

Master, now, of the treasure, I proceeded to examine it, but with the prudence you know is customary to me: for it was important to leave everything in its proper place. I chanced first upon two of the husband's letters: indigestible compounds of legal jargon and conjugal rhetoric, which I was so long-suffering as to read entire, and in which I found not a single word relating to me. I replaced them with some annoyance; which, however, left me when I discovered that in my hand I held the pieces – carefully put together again – of the famous letter from Dijon. Fortunately I took it into my head to glance through it. Imagine my joy on finding traces, very distinct traces of my Adorable Devotee's tears. I must admit that, surrendering to a very callow impulse, I kissed the letter with a rapture I had ceased to believe I could feel. I returned happily to the investigation. I found all my own letters together, arranged in order of date. I was still more agreeably surprised to find the first one of all among them: the one I thought she had been so ungrateful as to return unread. It had been faithfully copied in her own hand, and the uncertain scrawl bore witness to the agreeable disturbance in her heart as she carried out her task.

Till now my thoughts had been entirely given up to love; but the next moment I was possessed by fury. Who do you think it is that has plotted my ruin in the eyes of the woman I adore? What Fury, do you suppose, would be vicious enough to plan such villainy? You know her: she is your friend, your relation. It is Madame de Volanges. You cannot imagine the tissue of unspeakable lies that diabolical shrew has fabricated around me. It is she and only she who has bereft this angelic woman of her peace of mind. It is thanks to her representations, thanks to her pernicious advice, that I find myself obliged to leave. It is to her, after all, that I am to be sacrificed. Oh yes, certainly her daughter must be seduced. But that will not be enough: she must be ruined too. Since this cursed woman is of an age that must protect her own person from my onslaughts, it is through the object of her affections that I shall have to attack her.

So she wants me to return to Paris! She insists upon it! So be it.

I shall return. But she shall groan for it. I am sorry that Danceny has to be the hero of the piece. He has a fundamental honesty which will be in our way. However: he is in love, and I see him often, and perhaps we can turn that to some advantage. I have forgotten in my annoyance that I owe you an account of what happened today. Let us continue. This morning I saw my sensitive prude once more. Never to my mind had she looked more beautiful. Inevitably so. A woman reaches the height of her beauty – and only at this time can she inspire that intoxication of the soul which is so often talked of and so rarely experienced – when we are sure of her love, but not of her favours. And that was precisely my situation. Perhaps, too, the thought that I should soon be deprived of the pleasure of seeing her added to her attractions. The post arriving, your letter of the twenty-seventh was delivered to me. Even as I read it I was in two minds whether or not to keep my word. But when my beauty's eyes met mine, I knew that it would be impossible to refuse her anything.

So I announced my departure. A moment later Madame de Rose-monde left the room and we were alone. I was still four yards away from the timorous creature when rising to her feet with a look of alarm she cried: 'Leave me alone, Monsieur; in heaven's name, leave me alone.' So earnest a plea, such a betrayal of emotion, served only to increase my excitement. In an instant I was beside her holding the hands she had clasped together in the most touching gesture. I was just beginning my tender protestations when some hostile demon brought Madame de Rosemonde in again. My timid devotee, who after all has some grounds for her fears, took the opportunity to withdraw.

I immediately offered her my arm, and was accepted. This mark of favour so long withheld from me augured well, and as I renewed my protestations I attempted to squeeze her hand in mine. At first she tried to remove it, but upon more earnest entreaty gave in with a good enough grace: without, however, returning the pressure or making any reply. As we arrived at the door of her room I made to kiss her hand before leaving her. Resistance was at first unequivocal, but at a 'remember that I am going away' uttered in my most tender tones, it became clumsy and ineffective. The kiss had scarcely been planted upon it when the hand recovered strength enough to escape and our beauty went into her room where her maid awaited her. Here ends my story.

Since you will, I presume, be at the Maréchale de —'s tomorrow where I shall certainly come to look for you, and since I am quite sure we shall have more than one subject to discuss at our first meeting – notably the little Volanges, who is never far from my thoughts – I have decided to send this letter ahead of me. Long as it already is, I shall not seal it until it is time for the post. In my present circumstances everything may depend on a moment's opportunity, and I leave you now to go and lie in wait for it.

P.S. *Eight o'clock in the evening*

Nothing new: not a single moment's liberty: pains taken indeed to prevent it. At least, however, a show of regret: as far, that is, as decency permitted. Another circumstance which may not prove to be without interest: I am charged with an invitation from Madame de Rosemonde to Madame de Volanges to spend some time with her in the country.

Good-bye, my love, till we meet tomorrow, or the day after at the latest.

———

28 August 17 —

LETTER 45: *The Présidente de Tourvel to Madame de Volanges*

MONSIEUR de Valmont left this morning, Madame; you have seemed to me to be so anxious for his departure that I think it only proper to inform you of it. Madame de Rosemonde misses her nephew very much, and it must be admitted that, in spite of all, his company was agreeable. She spent the whole morning talking to me about him, with that sensibility which you know is characteristic of her. She could not say enough to his credit. I thought I owed her the consideration of listening without contradicting, the more so in that on several counts it must be allowed that she is right. I felt, too, that I was guilty of being the cause of their separation and that I could not expect to compensate for the pleasure of which I had deprived her. You know that I do not naturally possess a great fund of spirits: the kind of life we shall be leading here is not calculated to increase it.

If it were not that your advice has always ruled me in my conduct, I might wonder now whether I have acted a little thoughtlessly I was really disturbed by my dear friend's disappointment, touched indeed to the point where I could willingly have mingled my tears with hers.

We live now in hopes that you will accept Madame de Rose-monde's invitation, which Monsieur de Valmont brings you, to spend some time here with her. I need not tell you, I suppose, what a pleasure it will be for me to see you; and, after all, you owe us some reparation. I shall be delighted to have an earlier opportunity than I expected of making Mademoiselle de Volanges' acquaintance, and to be in a position to persuade you more with each day of the sincere respect, etc.

29 August 17—

LETTER 46: *The Chevalier Danceny to Cécile Volanges*

WHAT can have happened, my darling Cécile? What can have prompted you to change so suddenly and so cruelly? What has become of your promises never to change? Promises you repeated only yesterday, and with so much pleasure! Who has made you forget them today? I have searched my conscience, and the blame is not mine: it would be too dreadful to have to look for it in you. Oh, I am certain you are not frivolous or deceitful: in the very midst of despair my heart shall be free of insulting suspicions. But by what mischance are you altered? No, cruel girl, you are no longer the same. The sweet Cécile, the Cécile that I adore, the Cécile who made me those promises would never have avoided my eyes, would never have thwarted the happy chance that placed me by her side; or if some circumstance I cannot guess at had obliged her to treat me with such severity, she would at least have not thought it beneath her to tell me of it.

Ah, my Cécile, you don't know, you will never know how much you have made me suffer today, how I suffer still at this moment. Do you imagine that I can live without your love? Yet, when I begged a word from you, one single word to banish my doubts, you made no reply, but pretended instead to be afraid we might be overheard – a danger which did not then exist, but which you immediately created by your choice of a place among the company. And when, having to leave you, I asked at what time I could see you tomorrow, you pretended to be uncertain, and it was Madame de Volanges who was obliged to tell me. So that tomorrow the moment which returns me to your side, the moment I have always looked forward to so much, will bring me nothing but anxiety, and the pleasure of seeing you give way to a fear of being troublesome.

I feel it already: it stops my pen. I dare no longer speak to you of my love. Those words that I never tired of repeating when I could in turn hear them repeated to me: 'I love you', that sweet phrase which made up all my happiness, has, if you have changed, no longer any more to offer me than a prospect of perpetual despair. Yet I cannot believe that such a talisman of love has lost all its power, and I venture to try again what it can do.[1] Yes, my Cécile; I love you. Those words are my happiness: say them with me again. Remember that you have accustomed me to hearing them, and that in depriving me you condemn me to a torture which, like my love, will only cease with my life.

———

29 August 17—

LETTER 47: *The Vicomte de Valmont to the Marquise de Merteuil*

I SHALL not be seeing you today, my love, and here are my reasons, which I beg you will indulgently accept.

Yesterday, instead of returning here directly, I stopped at the

1. Those who have never on occasion been brought to realize the value of a word or a phrase that has been hallowed by love will find no meaning in these words.

Comtesse de —'s, which was not far out of my way, and stayed there for dinner. I did not arrive in Paris until nearly seven o'clock, when I made my way to the Opera where I hoped you might be.

After the performance, I went to revisit my acquaintance of the green-room. There I found my old friend Émilie surrounded by a host of admirers of both sexes for whom she was that very evening to provide supper at P—. I had no sooner joined the company when the invitation was, by general acclaim, extended to me, and in particular by a short and corpulent little man, who jabbered it out in Dutchman's French. He I perceived to be the real hero of the occasion. I accepted.

On the way I learned that the house we were bound for represented the price fixed upon for Émilie's favours to this grotesque creature, and that the evening's supper was in fact to be a sort of wedding feast. The little man could not contain his delight at the prospect of the happiness he was soon to enjoy. He looked so pleased with himself that I was tempted to disturb his complacency: which, as it happens, is what I did.

My only difficulty lay in prevailing upon Émilie: the burgomaster's riches had made her a little scrupulous. After some hesitation, however, she gave her approval to my plan for glutting the little beer-barrel with wine, so putting him *hors de combat* for the rest of the night.

The high opinion we had formed of Dutch drinkers led us to employ every known method in our attempts: which succeeded so well that at dessert he no longer had strength enough to hold up his glass. Nevertheless the obliging Émilie and I continued to vie with each other in filling it up. He collapsed at length under the table in a drunken stupor such as cannot but last for a week. We decided then to send him back to Paris, and as we had not kept his carriage, I had him packed into mine and remained behind in his place. Whereupon I received the compliments of the company, who retired soon after leaving me in possession of the field. So much amusement, and perhaps my long retirement, has made me find Émilie so desirable that I have promised to stay with her until the Dutchman returns to life.

This kindness I confer in exchange for one she has just done me. I have been using her for a desk upon which to write to my fair devotee – to whom I find it amusing I should send a letter written in bed, in the arms, almost, of a trollop (broken off, too, while I committed a downright infidelity), in which I give her an exact account of my situation and my conduct. Émilie, who read it, split her sides laughing: I hope you will laugh too.

As my letter must be franked in Paris, I am sending it to you; I leave it open. Be so good as to read it, to seal it, and to have it taken to the post. Please do not on any account use your own seal or one bearing any amorous device whatever; a head, no more. Good-bye, my love.

P.S. I have re-opened this. I have persuaded Émilie to go to the Italiens[1] and I shall take this opportunity of coming to see you. I shall be at your house by six at the latest, and, if you are agreeable, we shall call together on Madame de Volanges at seven. I can no longer decently defer the invitation I have to make her on behalf of Madame de Rosemonde; besides I shall be very glad to see the little Volanges.

Good-bye, my fairest of the fair. I intend to greet you with such rapture that the Chevalier will be jealous.

P —

30 August 17 —

LETTER 48: *The Vicomte de Valmont to Madame de Tourvel*

I COME, Madame, after a stormy night during which I never closed an eye, after suffering without cease now the turmoil of a consuming passion, now the utter exhaustion of every faculty of my being, I come to you to seek the peace I need, but which as yet I cannot hope to enjoy. Indeed my situation, as I write, makes me more than ever aware of the irresistible power of love. I have scarcely enough

1. [The Comédie-Italienne and the Comédie-Française were the two principal theatres of the time in Paris. The designation of the company performing at the former was Les Italiens, the official title of the latter Théâtre français: people spoke of going 'to the Italiens' or 'to the Français'. *Translator's note.*]

command of myself to put my ideas into order. I foresee already that I shall not be able to finish this letter without breaking off. Surely then I can hope that one day you may share the agitation I feel at this moment? I venture to think meanwhile that were you to understand it better you would not be entirely insensible to it. Believe me, Madame: a cold composure – that torpor of the soul, that semblance of death – can never make for happiness, to which only the active passions can lead. In spite of the torments you make me suffer I think I can assure you without any hesitation that I am at this moment happier than you. You try to no purpose to crush me with your devastating severities. They will never prevent me from giving myself wholly to love and, in the delirium it affords, forgetting the despair into which you have cast me. And that is how I shall take my revenge for the exile to which you have condemned me. Never have I taken more pleasure in writing to you; never have I felt in doing it so sweet and yet so lively an emotion. Everything seems to enhance my rapture; the air I breathe is all ecstasy; the very table on which I write, never before put to such use, has become in my eyes an altar consecrated to love. How much dearer will it be to me now that I have traced upon it a vow to love you forever! Forgive, I beg you, these unruly feelings. I should perhaps not yield so far to transports which you cannot share. But I must leave you for a moment to calm an excitement which mounts with every moment, and which is fast becoming more than I can control.

I return to you, Madame, and certainly with as much eagerness as ever before. But my feelings of happiness have flown, leaving in their place a sense of cruel privation. To what purpose do I speak to you of my feelings when I cannot find the means to persuade you of their sincerity? After so many repeated efforts, confidence and strength alike have deserted me. If I seek to recall the pleasures of love it is only to feel their loss more deeply. I see no help but in your indulgence, and I am too sensible at this moment of how much indulgence will be necessary to hope that I may secure it. My love, none the less, has never been more respectful, never less capable of giving offence; it is a love, I venture to say, that the strictest virtue would have no reason to fear. But I am afraid of occupying you too long with my sufferings. Since I am sure that she who causes them does not share them, I must at least forbear from abusing her kindness. I should surely be doing so were this doleful history to take up more of your time – of which I shall ask only as much as is necessary to beg you to reply, and to beseech you never to doubt the truth of my feelings.

Written at P —, dated Paris
30 August 17 —

LETTER 49: *Cécile Volanges to the Chevalier Danceny*

WHILE I am neither frivolous nor deceitful, Monsieur, it is enough I should be shown my conduct in its true light in order to feel I must change it. I have promised God this sacrifice until such time as I can offer Him in addition the feelings I have for you, which I find all the more sinful on account of the religious order to which you belong. I am quite aware that this will cause me pain, and I shall not even conceal from you that for two days I have cried every time I have thought of you. But I hope God will be good enough to give me the strength to forget you, since I pray for it night and day. I expect, too, of your friendship and your honour that you will make no attempt to weaken the good resolutions I have been led to make, and which I am trying to keep. Consequently, I ask you to be so kind as to write no more, particularly since I should not, I warn you, make any reply and since you would compel me to inform Mamma of everything that has happened – and that would deprive me forever of the pleasure of seeing you.

I preserve for you, none the less, the deepest attachment it is possible to feel without doing wrong, and it is with all my heart that I wish you every kind of happiness. I know that very soon you will no longer love me so much, and very soon, perhaps, will love someone else more. But that will be one more penance for my error in giving you a heart which I owe only to God, and to my husband when I have one. I hope that the Divine Mercy will pity my weakness and inflict no more suffering upon me than I am able to endure.

Good-bye, Monsieur. I can give you my complete assurance that were I permitted to love anyone, it would never be anyone but you. But that is all I can say, and it is perhaps more than I ought to say.

———

31 August 17 —

LETTER 50: *Madame de Tourvel to the Vicomte de Valmont*

Is it thus, then, Monsieur, that you fulfil the conditions upon which I agreed to receive your letters from time to time? How can I find no fault with them when they speak only of sentiments I should still be reluctant to acknowledge even if I could do so without violence to my whole sense of duty?

For the rest, were I in need of new arguments to support such a salutary reluctance, I think I should be able to find them in your last letter. After all, what do you do in the very moment of your setting forth, as you think, an apology for love but show me the effect of its terrible ravages? Who would wish for a happiness bought at the expense of reason, its pleasures short-lived, succeeded at best by regrets when they are not by remorse?

You yourself, in whom the ill-effects of this dangerous derangement must have been weakened by your being inured to it, were you not compelled to admit that it had become more than you could control? And were you not the first to complain of the disturbance it caused you? What frightful destruction, then, would it wreak upon an innocent and sensitive soul, so much the more at its mercy for the greatness of the sacrifices it would be required to make?

You think, Monsieur, or you pretend to think, that love makes for happiness. As for me, I am so convinced that it would make me miserable that I could wish never again to hear it spoken of. It seems to me that the mere mention of it is unsettling, and it is as much my inclination as my duty to beg you henceforth to be silent upon the subject.

After all, you should find it easy to grant me this request. Now that you have returned to Paris, you will find opportunity enough to forget a feeling which perhaps was only the outcome of your habitual preoccupation with such things, and owed its strength only to your lack of other interests in the country. Are you not now in the same place where once you were able to look upon me with indifference? Can you now take a step without coming face to face with evidence of your inconstancy? Are you not surrounded by women worthy of your attentions? I have none of that vanity which is the reproach of my sex, still less of that false modesty which is only a refinement of pride, and it is in all honesty that I tell you here that I am very little versed in the arts of pleasing. Were I mistress of them all I should not think them sufficient to prevail upon you for very long. Asking you to forget me is therefore no more than asking you to do what you have done before, and what you would unquestionably do again in a little while even though I were to beg you not to.

I have never lost sight of this truth which in itself would be a strong enough motive for my not wishing to listen to you. I have a thousand others; but to avoid entering upon a tedious discussion I confine myself to begging, as I have already done, that you will no longer treat me to sentiments I have no business to hear, still less to reply to.

1 September 17 —

PART TWO

LETTER 51: *The Marquise de Merteuil to the Vicomte de Valmont*

TRULY, Vicomte, you are intolerable. You treat me as casually as though I were your mistress. I shall be angry, you know: as it is I am in no very good humour. Really! You are to see Danceny tomorrow morning; you know how important it is that I should see you before that interview; and without further ado you allow me to wait a whole day for you while you run off heaven only knows where. You are responsible for my arriving *indecently* late at Madame de Volanges, and for all the old ladies finding me *extraordinary*. I was obliged to spend the entire evening flattering them to appease them. Old ladies must never be crossed: in their hands lie the reputations of the young ones.

It is now one o'clock in the morning. Instead of going to bed, which I yearn to do, I have to write you a long letter which for very boredom is going to make me twice as sleepy as I am now. Consider yourself lucky that I haven't the time for further strictures upon you. Don't, however, conclude thereby that I forgive you: it is simply that I am in a hurry. Listen then; I shall be quick.

If you are at all clever, Danceny will confide in you tomorrow. The time is ripe for disclosures: he is unhappy. The girl has been to confession; she has given everything away, like a child, and has since been tortured to such a degree by fear of the devil that she has decided to break with him completely. It was quite clear from the earnestness with which she spoke to me of all her little scruples, that she has quite lost her head. She showed me the letter in which she dismisses him: a real sermon. She babbled to me for an hour without uttering a single word of common sense. My position was none the less difficult; as you may imagine, I could not risk being frank in the face of such befuddlement.

Through all this chatter, however, I noticed that she is, in spite of everything, in love with her Danceny. I noticed, too, that the little creature is amusingly enough a victim to one of those tricks that love never fails to play. Tortured by the desire to think of her lover and afraid she will be damned for doing so, she has hit upon the idea of praying to God to banish him from her thoughts. As she repeats the prayer every instant of the day, this serves her for a means of thinking about him constantly.

For someone more experienced than Danceny this little contre-temps would perhaps be more favourable than otherwise. But that young man is such a Céladon[1] that, if we don't help him, he will need so much time to surmount the smallest obstacles that he will leave us none to accomplish our ends.

You are quite right. It is a pity – and I am as sorry as you are – that he should be the hero of this escapade. But what do you expect? What is done is done, and it is all your fault. I asked to see his reply; it was pitiable.[2] He offers her interminable arguments to prove that an involuntary feeling cannot be a crime: as if it did not cease to be involuntary the moment one ceases to resist it! The idea is so simple that it had occurred even to the girl. His complaints of unhappiness are moving enough: but his grief is so tender and seems to be so strong and so sincere that it seems to me impossible that any woman, given the opportunity of driving a man to this pitch of despair at so little peril to herself, would be tempted to forgo the pleasure. He explains finally that he is not a monk as the girl thinks, and here, without doubt, he speaks to most effect. Were one to go so far as to yield to monastic embraces, it is most assuredly not to Messieurs the Chevaliers de Malte that one would give preference.

Be that as it may, instead of wasting my time in argument that might have compromised me – perhaps, too, without convincing her – I gave my approval to her decision to break with him. I insisted, however, that in circumstances such as these, it was more proper to justify oneself in speech than in writing, and that it was also customary to give back whatever letters and other trifles one might have received. This seemed to accord with the little creature's views, and I persuaded her to give Danceny a rendezvous. Then and there we devised a plan, my part in which is to persuade her

1. [A sentimental lover. Céladon is the hero of d'Urfé's *L'Astrée*, a popular novel of the previous century. *Translator's Note.*]
2. This letter has not been discovered.

mother to go out without her: tomorrow afternoon is appointed for the fateful occasion. Danceny knows already; but, for God's sake, if you can find an opportunity, rouse that lovesick swain from his languour, and tell him, since he must always be told about everything, that the only way to conquer scruples in others is to leave them with nothing to lose.

For the rest, so as to avoid any repetition of this ridiculous episode, I have taken care to raise a few doubts in the girl's mind as to the discretion shown by confessors. She is now, I can assure you, paid back for frightening me by the dread she herself is in that her confessor will go and tell her mother everything. I hope that when I have had another word or two to say to her upon the subject, she will no longer feel impelled to give account of her stupidities to the first comer.[1]

Good-bye Vicomte; take hold of Danceny and push. How shameful if we should fail to do as we liked with two children! If they should prove to be more difficult than we thought at first, let us, to rouse our determination, consider: you, that we are dealing with Madame de Volanges' daughter, I, that she is destined to be Gercourt's wife. Good-bye.

———

2 September 17 —

LETTER 52: *The Vicomte de Valmont to Madame de Tourvel*

You forbid me, Madame, to speak to you of my love; but how shall I find the courage to obey? Wholly absorbed in a feeling which should have been tender had you not made it cruel; sentenced by you to languish in exile; living only on privation and regret; a prey to tortures which are so much the more grievous for reminding me of your indifference; must I then lose the one consolation remain-

1. The behaviour of Madame de Merteuil must long ago have led the reader to guess that she held religion in small respect. This whole paragraph should perhaps have been omitted; on the other hand it was thought that, where effects are represented, their causes ought not to be ignored.

ing to me? What other can I have but that of opening my heart to you from time to time, a heart that you have filled with bitterness and unrest? Will you turn your eyes away from the tears you have caused to flow? Will you not acknowledge the homage of sacrifices you have yourself exacted? Would it not be more worthy of you, of your tender and honourable heart, to pity an unfortunate man, who is so only because of you, than to inflict further sufferings upon him by a prohibition that is as harsh as it is unjust?

You pretend to be afraid of love, and do not wish to see that it is you alone who are the cause of the behaviour for which you hold love to blame. Ah, certainly it is a painful feeling when it is not shared by the one who inspires it. But let it be reciprocated, and where else can happiness be looked for? Tender affection, mutual confidence – and a confidence without reserve – griefs assuaged and pleasures multiplied, sweet hopes, delicious memories, where else but in love can these be found? You slander its name, you who have only to cease from resisting it in order to taste all the joys it has to offer you. As for me, I forget all my sufferings to speak in its defence.

You oblige me to speak in my own defence too; for while I devote my life to worshipping you, you spend yours in finding fault with me. You already imagine me to be fickle and deceitful and, holding against me those few indiscretions I myself confessed to being guilty of, you are pleased to confound what I was then with what I am now. Not content with having committed me to the torment of living so far away from you, you add to it with your cruel mockery of pleasures to which you know well enough you have made me insensible. You trust neither my promises nor my vows. Well, I have one guarantee left to offer you, one at least which you cannot suspect: yourself. I ask you only to examine yourself honestly: if you do not believe in my love, if you doubt for a single moment that you are sole empress of my heart, if you are not sure that you can depend entirely on my feelings – till now, after all, only too changeable – then I shall take the consequences of my error. I shall cry out in pain, but I shall make no appeal. If, on the contrary, you are forced in justice to both of us to admit to yourself that you neither have nor ever will have a rival, oblige me, I beseech you, by tilting no longer at windmills: leave me at least the consolation of knowing you do not doubt a feeling which, after all, will only cease and can only cease with my life. Permit me, Madame, to ask you for a positive reply to this part of my letter.

If, meanwhile, I speak no more of that period of my life which, it seems, does me such cruel injury in your eyes, it is not because I lack arguments to summon, if need be, to my defence.

What, after all, was I guilty of but a failure to struggle against the whirlpool into which I had been cast? I came into society young and inexperienced; I was passed, so to speak, from hand to hand by a series of women all of whom, in their readiness to succumb, seemed in a hurry to anticipate what they felt would inevitably be an unfavourable opinion of themselves. Was it for me to set an example of resistance, when no resistance was offered me? Should I have punished myself for momentary aberrations to which very often I had been encouraged, by promising a fidelity which would certainly have been unnecessary, and could only have been regarded as ridiculous? Pah! What else but breaking it off immediately can excuse a shameful connexion?

Yet I think I may say that this disorder of the senses – perhaps, too, it was inflamed vanity – never touched my heart. My heart was made for love: intrigue might serve for distraction, it was never my whole concern. I was surrounded by seductive but contemptible creatures; none of them could reach my soul. I was offered pleasure: I sought virtue. At length, because I happened to be fastidious and sensitive, I began to think myself inconstant.

When I met you my eyes were opened: I soon realized that love depends for its charm on qualities of the soul: only they can provoke it to an excess which only they can excuse. And finally I found that it was as impossible for me to keep from loving you as it would be to love anyone but you.

You see, Madame, to what sort of heart you are afraid to yield, the heart whose fate it is for you to determine. Whatever the destiny you hold in store for it, you will never alter the feelings by which it is bound to you. They are as unchanging as the virtues that gave them being.

3 September 17 —

LETTER 53: *The Vicomte de Valmont to the Marquise de Merteuil*

I HAVE seen Danceny, but have had nothing but half-confidences from him. He was especially persistent in refusing to reveal the little Volanges' name. He spoke of her merely as a good and even rather devout young woman. Apart from this, his account of the whole episode was truthful enough, particularly as it concerned the final incident. I stirred him up as much as I could, and teased him a great deal about his delicate scruples. But it seems he is proud of them, so that I cannot take any responsibility for him. For the rest, I shall have more to tell you the day after tomorrow. Tomorrow I take him to Versailles, and on our way there shall make it my business to examine him further.

I have hopes, too, that the rendezvous which was to have taken place today may have passed off to our satisfaction. Nothing perhaps remains for us to do but extract a confession and collect the evidence. This you will find easier to do than I. The girl is more confiding, or, which comes to the same thing, more talkative, than her discreet admirer. Nevertheless I, too, shall do my best.

Good-bye, my love. I am in a great hurry. I shall not see you this evening, nor shall I tomorrow. If you, on your part, have discovered anything new, write me a line against my return. I shall certainly be back in Paris for the night.

———

3 September 17 —, evening

LETTER 54: *The Marquise de Merteuil to the Vicomte de Valmont*

OH yes, of course! There is so much to be discovered from Danceny! If he has told you so himself he was boasting. I have never known anyone so incompetent in love, and I regret more and more the kindness we have shown him. Do you know, I thought I might have been compromised on his account? And to think it would have

120

been to absolutely no purpose! Oh, I promise you, I shall have my revenge.

When I arrived yesterday to fetch Madame de Volanges, she no longer wanted to go out; she felt unwell and it required all my eloquence to persuade her. I could picture Danceny arriving before we had left; the situation would have been all the more awkward for Madame de Volanges having told him the previous evening that she would not be at home. Her daughter and I were on tenterhooks. At length we left, and the little creature, as she said good-bye, clasped my hand with so much warmth that, in spite of her believing in all honesty that she was still resolved upon parting with her lover, I could have predicted an evening of prodigies.

This was not the last of my anxieties. Scarcely half an hour after we had arrived at Madame de —'s, Madame de Volanges was indeed taken ill, and seriously ill; quite understandably she wanted to return home. For my part, I was the less willing to do so for being afraid that, if we should surprise the young couple, as there was every reason to suppose we would, my representations to the mother in persuading her to leave the house would fall under suspicion. I took the course of playing upon her fears for her health, which fortunately it is never difficult to do; and for an hour and a half refused to take her home, pretending that I was reluctant to subject her to the dangerous jolting of the carriage. We did not, in the end, arrive back before the appointed time. The embarrassed expression that greeted our return gave me hopes, I must say, that my efforts had not been in vain.

My wish to be informed of everything that had passed kept me with Madame de Volanges, who immediately took to her bed. We left her very early, after supper at her bedside, excusing ourselves on the grounds that she needed rest, and made our way to her daughter's room. The latter has done everything I expected her to do: scruples have vanished, new vows of eternal love been sworn, etc., etc.; she has, in short, obliged us with a very good grace. Oh, I could say a word or two to that young man! Reconciliations take us nowhere.

The girl, however, assures me that he asked for more, but that she was able to defend herself. I would stake anything that she is either boasting or making excuses for him: I am in fact virtually certain of it. At all events, an impulse took me to find out how far I could believe in her capacity to defend herself, and I, a mere woman, was able step by step to rouse her to a pitch where . . . In short, you may believe me when I say that never has anyone been more susceptible to an assault upon the senses. She is really charming, the dear little thing! She deserves a better lover. She will at least have a good friend, for I am sincerely attached to her. I have promised to undertake her education, and I believe I shall keep my word. I have often felt I needed to take a woman into my confidence, and I should prefer this one to another. But I can do nothing about it as long as she is not . . . what she must become. Yet another reason for bearing Danceny a grudge.

Good-bye, Vicomte: don't come to see me tomorrow, unless you come in the morning. I have yielded to my Chevalier's entreaties for an evening at the *petite maison*.

———

4 September 17 —

LETTER 55: *Cécile Volanges to Sophie Carnay*

You were right, my dear Sophie; you are better at making prophecies than giving advice. Danceny, as you predicted, has triumphed over my confessor, over you, and over myself: and here we are exactly where we were before. Oh, I don't regret it: and if you are going to scold, it will be because you don't know what pleasure there is in loving someone like Danceny. It is easy enough for you to declare what must be done: there is nothing to stop you doing it. But if you had felt how much pain there is in the grief of someone we love, how their happiness becomes our own, and how difficult it is to say no when we want only to say yes, you would no longer be surprised at anything. I, who have felt all this, and felt it really deeply, still cannot understand why. Do you think, for example, that I can see Danceny cry without crying myself? I assure you I find it impossible; and when he is happy, I am happy too. It is no use your saying anything; what people say cannot change the way things are, and I am quite sure that this is how they must be.

I should like to see you in my place. . . . No, that is not what I meant to say, I certainly would not change places with anyone. But I wish that you, too, were in love with someone: not only because you would understand me better and scold me less, but also because you would be happier, or rather because only then would you begin to know what it is to be happy.

Our games, our amusements, all that, you know, was only child's play; nothing is left of it when it is over. But love, oh, love! . . . a word, a look, just knowing that he is there – now that is happiness. When I see Danceny I want nothing more; when I don't see him he is all I want. I don't know how to explain it, but I might say that whatever pleases me is a part of him. When he is not with me, I think of him, and when I can think of him without being distracted in any way, for instance when I am alone, I am happier still; I close my eyes, and all at once I seem to see him; I remember what he has said and seem to hear him saying it; that makes me sigh, and then I feel a sort of fire, an agitation . . . I cannot keep still. It is a sort of torture, a torture which gives inexpressible pleasure.

I think, too, that once one is in love something of that feeling enters into friendship as well. My friendship for you, of course, has not changed: it is still just as it used to be at the convent. What I mean is my feeling for Madame de Merteuil. It seems to me that I love her more as I love Danceny than as I love you, and sometimes I wish she were he. This is perhaps because our friendship is not a childhood one as is yours and mine, or else because I often see both of them together which confuses my feelings. At all events, it cannot be denied that between them they make me very happy. And, after all, I don't think there is anything very wrong in what I am doing. I ask no more than to stay as I am: it is only the idea of my marriage that gives me any anxiety. For if Monsieur de Gercourt is at all like what he is said to be, and I don't doubt he is, I don't know what is to become of me. Good-bye my dear Sophie: I still love you most dearly.

―――

4 September 17 —

123

LETTER 56: *Madame de Tourvel to the Vicomte de Valmont*

WHAT would be the use to you, Monsieur, of the reply you ask for? If I believed in your feelings would I not have even more reason to be afraid of them? Moreover, quite apart from attacking or defending their sincerity, is it not enough for me, should it not be enough for you, to know that I neither wish, nor have any right, to return them?

Let us suppose that you do really love me (and it is only so as to avoid returning in future to this subject that I allow such a supposition) would the obstacles that lie between us be any the less insurmountable? And could I even then do anything else than wish you might soon overcome your love; above all, by hastening to deprive you of all hope, do everything in my power to help you overcome it? You yourself admit that love is 'a painful feeling when it is not shared by the one who inspires it'. Now, you know quite well that it is impossible for me to share it; even were such a misfortune to befall me, I should suffer for it while you yourself would be none the happier. I hope you respect me enough not to doubt that for an instant. No more then, I beg you; give up your attempts to disturb a heart which is so much in need of peace. Do not oblige me to regret having known you.

Cherished and esteemed by a husband whom I love and respect, my duties and my pleasures find in him their common source. I am happy: I have a right to be so. If livelier pleasures exist, I have no desire for them: I do not wish to know them. Can any pleasure be sweeter than that of living at peace with oneself, passing one's days in serenity, sleeping untroubled, waking without remorse? What you call happiness is nothing but a tumult in the mind, a tempest of passion, frightful to behold even for the spectator on the shore. Come, how could I face such storms? How dare to embark upon a sea strewn with so many thousand wrecks? And with whom? No, Monsieur, I shall hold my ground: I cherish the ties that keep me there. I would not break them, if I could, and if I had none I should hasten to make them.

Why do you dog my footsteps? Why do you so obstinately pursue me? Your letters, which were to have come seldom, arrive in rapid succession. They were to have been discreet and they speak of nothing but your insane love. I am more beset by the thought of you than I ever was by your person. Repulsed under one guise you reappear in another. Things you are asked not to say you say again, but in a different way. You are ready to entangle me in specious arguments, but refuse to answer mine. I do not wish to reply to any more of your letters. I shall not reply to them. . . . How you treat the women you have seduced! With what contempt you speak of them! I can believe that some of them deserve it, but were they all so despicable? Ah, of course – since they betrayed their duty in surrendering to unlawful love. At that moment they lost everything, even the respect of the man for whom they made their sacrifice. The punishment is just, but the mere thought of it makes one shudder. What is it to me, after all? Why should I care about them or about you? What right have you to disturb my peace of mind? Leave me alone, see me no more, write to me no more, I beg of you; I insist. This letter is the last you will receive from me.

—

5 September 17 —

LETTER 57: *The Vicomte de Valmont to the Marquise de Merteuil*

I FOUND your letter awaiting my return yesterday. Your annoyance quite delighted me. You could not be more sensitive to the wrong Danceny has done had he done it to you personally. No doubt it is in revenge that you are getting his mistress into the way of committing small infidelities to him. What a very wicked creature you are! Yes, you are charming, and I am not surprised that you have better success with her than Danceny.

I can now at last read that fine romantic hero like a book: he has no further secrets from me. I assured him so often that honourable love was the supreme good, that one true feeling was worth ten intrigues, that I myself was at that moment in love and afraid to own it, and he found my way of thinking so conformable to his own, that enchanted by my frankness, he told me everything, and swore himself to a friendship without reserve. But this scarcely carries our plans any further.

To begin with, it seems to me that to his mind a young girl deserves to be treated with far more consideration than a woman, seeing that she has so much more to lose. He thinks, above all, that a man can have no excuse for putting a girl to the necessity of either marrying him or living dishonoured when the girl is infinitely richer than the man, as is the case with him. The mother's confidence, the girl's honesty, everything frightens and inhibits him. The difficulty is not to defeat his arguments, however true they are. With a little skill and the help of his own passion they can soon be destroyed: the more easily in that they lend themselves to ridicule, and that against them can be pitted the authority of custom. What is in the way of our securing any hold upon him is that he feels happy as he is. After all, if our first loves appear on the whole to be innocent, and, as they say, more pure; if at any rate they make much slower progress, it is not, as is generally thought, because of delicacy or modesty, but because the heart, surprised by a new feeling, pauses, so to speak, at every step in order to enjoy the delight it feels, and because this delight in an untutored heart is so intense as to preoccupy it to the exclusion of all other pleasures. This is so true that even when a libertine falls in love, if a libertine ever does, he becomes from that moment less anxious to enjoy his mistress. In the end there is, between Danceny's behaviour towards the little Volanges and mine towards my prudish Madame de Tourvel, only a difference of degree.

More obstacles than he has encountered so far will be necessary to stir our young man's blood; more mystery especially, for it is mystery that inspires to daring. I am very near believing that you have in fact done us a disservice in serving him so well. Had we been concerned with an *experienced* man who felt nothing but desire, your line of proceeding would have been excellent; but you might have guessed that to a man who is young, upright, and in love, his mistress's favours would be of no more importance than as they furnished proof of her love, so that the more certain he were of being loved, the less enterprising he would be. What is there now to be done? I don't know; but I have little hope that the girl will succumb before her marriage. We shall have nothing for our pains. I am sorry, but I can see no help for it.

While I hold forth here you find better occupation with your Chevalier. Which reminds me that you are promised to an infidelity in my favour. I have, as you might say, your promissory note, and I mean to see that it is honoured. I admit that payment is not yet due, but it would be generous of you not to wait, and for my part I shall be keeping an account of the interest. What say you, my love? Are you not weary of your constancy? Is your Chevalier so extraordinary a man? Oh, give me but the opportunity and I shall compel you to admit that if you have found any merit in him it is because you have forgotten me.

Good-bye, my love. I embrace you as ardently as I desire you. I defy the Chevalier's kisses to burn like these.

———

5 September 17—

LETTER 58: *The Vicomte de Valmont to Madame de Tourvel*

How, pray, Madame, have I deserved to be the object both of your reproaches and of your anger? An attachment of the deepest, yet most respectful kind, a most perfect submission to the least of your wishes: there in two phrases is the history of my conduct and my feelings. Crushed by the misery of unhappy love, no other consolation was open to me but that of seeing you: you commanded me to forgo it and I obeyed without a murmur. In return for this sacrifice you permitted me to write to you: now you would deprive me of that one remaining pleasure. Shall I allow it to be snatched from me without attempting to resist? No, indeed not. Come, how could it fail to be precious to me? I have no other left, and I owe it to you.

My letters, you say are too frequent! Consider, then, if you please: my exile has lasted ten days, and not a single moment of that time have you been out of my thoughts: yet you have received only two letters from me. 'They speak of nothing but my love!'

Naturally! What can I say, if I do not say what I think? The utmost I can do is to give no more than partial expression to my thoughts, and, believe me, I have only allowed you to know what I was unable to conceal. You threaten me finally with a refusal to reply to my letters. So, not content with your harsh treatment of a man who prefers you above anything and who respects you even more than he loves you, to that you would add contempt. And why this menacing, this wrath? What is the necessity for it? Are you not sure you will be obeyed even when your commands are unjust? Can I possibly, do you think, cross you in a single one of your desires? Have I not already proved that I cannot? Will you then abuse the power you have over me? Having made me unhappy, having perpetrated an injustice, will you now find it easy to enjoy the peace you declare is so necessary to you? Will you never say to yourself: 'He put his fate in my hands, and I condemned him to misery; he implored my help, and I looked upon him without pity'? Can you conceive to what extremities I may be reduced in my despair? No.

To estimate my sufferings you would have to know how much I loved you, and you are ignorant of my heart.

To what are you sacrificing me? Chimerical fears. And who arouses them? A man who adores you; a man who will never cease to be absolutely in your power. What have you to fear, what can you have to fear from a feeling of which you will always be mistress, which is yours to command at your pleasure? But your imagination creates monsters, and the terror they inspire you attribute to love. A little confidence and these phantoms will disappear.

A wise man once said that discovering the cause of our fears nearly always serves to get rid of them.[1] It is to love especially that this truth applies. Love, and your fears will vanish. In place of the things that terrify you, you will discover delicious feelings, a tender and submissive lover; and all your days, given over to happiness, will leave you with no other regret than that you wasted so many of them in indifference. I myself, now that I have been retrieved

1. Probably Rousseau in *Émile*, but the quotation is inaccurate, and Valmont's application of it here quite wrong. Besides, would Madame de Tourvel have read *Émile*?

from errors, and live only for love, regret that time of my life which I believed I was devoting to pleasure; and I feel that it is now you alone who can make me happy. But, I beg of you, let not my pleasure in writing to you be any longer marred by the fear of giving you offence. I have no wish to disobey you: but on my knees I crave the happiness you wish to take from me, the sole happiness I have left; I cry out to you; hear my prayers and witness my tears. Ah, Madame, can you refuse?

7 September 17 —

LETTER 59: *The Vicomte de Valmont to the Marquise de Merteuil*

TELL me, if you know, what this drivel of Danceny's signifies? What has happened, and what has he lost? Perhaps the lady has taken offence at his everlasting respect? In all fairness to her, offence has been taken on far less provocation. What shall I say to him this evening when I meet him, as he asked me, and as I agreed on an impulse, to do? I shall most certainly not waste my time listening to his whinings, if listening is going to do us no good. Lovers' complaints are not entertaining outside the Opera. Tell me then what this is about and what I have to do; or else I shall decamp, to escape the boredom I forsee. May I have a word with you this morning? If you are *busy*, write me a line at least, giving me my cues.

By the way, where were you yesterday? I never succeed in seeing you these days. Really, why go to the trouble of keeping me in Paris in September? Make up your mind, nevertheless, for I have just received the most pressing invitation from the Comtesse de B— to visit her in the country. As she so drolly informs me, her husband owns the finest woods[1] in the world 'which he is careful to preserve for the entertainment of his friends'. Now, as you know, I have more than a little interest in those woods, and I shall go back

1. [There is a pun in the French text. *Bois* means 'horns' as well as 'woods'. *Translator's note.*]

to enjoy them if I am of no use to you here. Good-bye. Remember that Danceny will be with me at four o'clock.

———

8 September 17 —

LETTER 60: *The Chevalier Danceny to the Vicomte de Valmont (enclosed with the preceding letter)*

OH, Monsieur! I am desperate; I have lost everything. I dare not confide the secret of my grief to paper, yet I feel I must pour it out to a faithful and trustworthy friend. When may I see you to ask your consolation and advice? I was so happy the day I opened my heart to you. How different now! My whole life has changed. Even so, what I suffer on my own account is the least part of my torment. What I cannot endure is my anxiety on behalf of a much more precious person. You are more fortunate than I: you will be able to see her, and I expect of your friendship that you will not refuse me this favour. But I must speak to you first; I must tell you everything. You must pity me, help me: you are my only hope. You are a man of feeling, you understand love, and you are the only person I have to confide in. Do not refuse me your aid.

Good-bye, Monsieur. The thought that there still remains to me a friend such as you is the only solace to my grief. Let me know, I beg you, at what time I may find you at home. If not this morning, I should like it to be early this afternoon.

———

8 September 17 —

LETTER 61: *Cécile Volanges to Sophie Carnay*

MY dear Sophie, take pity on your Cécile, your poor Cécile: she is very unhappy! Mamma knows everything. I cannot conceive how she was able to suspect anything, none the less she has discovered it all. Last evening I thought her more than a little ill-humoured, but did not pay much attention to that. While she was at cards I even chatted gaily to Madame de Merteuil, who had taken supper with us. We spoke a great deal of Danceny. I don't think, all the same, we could have been overheard. Madame de Merteuil left, and I retired to my room.

I was undressing when Mamma came in and dismissed my maid. She asked me for the key to my writing-desk. The tone in which she made this request made me tremble so violently that I was scarcely able to stand. I pretended not to be able to find the key; but in the end I had to obey. The first drawer she opened was the very one which contained the Chevalier Danceny's letters. I was in such a state that, when she asked me what they were, I could think of no better reply than 'Nothing'. But when I saw her begin to read the first one, I had just time enough to reach an armchair before I felt so unwell that I lost consciousness. As soon as I recovered, my mother, who had recalled the maid, withdrew, telling me to go to bed. She took all Danceny's letters with her. I shiver every time I think that I shall have to face her again. I have done nothing but cry all night long.

It is now daybreak, and I am writing to you in the hopes that Joséphine will come. If I can speak to her alone I shall ask her to deliver a note that I am about to write to Madame de Merteuil. If not, I shall enclose it with this, and you will perhaps be kind enough to send it as coming from you. It is only from her that I can hope to receive any comfort. At least we shall be able to talk about him, for I cannot expect to see him again. I am so very unhappy! She will perhaps be so kind as to take charge of a letter for Danceny. I dare not trust Joséphine with it, much less my maid; it may perhaps have been she, the maid, who told my mother that I had letters in my writing-desk.

I'll not write at greater length to you because I must have time to write to Madame de Merteuil[1] and also to Danceny, so that my letter will be ready if she is willing to deliver it. After that I shall go back to bed so that my maid will see me there when she comes into

1. The letter from Cécile Volanges to the Marquise has been omitted as containing no more than the facts presented above with fewer details. Her letter to the Chevalier Danceny has not been discovered. The reason for this will appear in Letter 63, from Madame de Merteuil to the Vicomte.

the room. I shall say I am ill so as to avoid going to see Mamma. This will not be far from the truth: there is no doubt that I am more unwell than I would be even if I had a fever. My eyes are burning from having cried so much and I cannot breathe freely for a feeling of weight upon my stomach. When I think that I shall never see Danceny again I could die. Good-bye, Sophie. Tears choke me, and I can say no more.

7 September 17 —

LETTER 62: *Madame de Volanges to the Chevalier Danceny*

SINCE you have abused, Monsieur, not only a mother's trust, but the innocence of her child, you would not of course be astonished were you henceforth to be refused admittance to a house where the most sincere demonstrations of friendship have been repaid only by your violation of every propriety. But I had rather ask you not to come to my house again, than give orders at my door, which, because the footmen would not fail to talk, would compromise us all equally. I have the right to expect you will not compel me to have recourse to such measures. I warn you, too, that if you make the slightest attempt to encourage the folly into which you have precipitated my daughter, an austere and perpetual seclusion shall be her protection against your advances. It is for you to decide, Monsieur, whether you will bring down calamity upon her with as little compunction as you assailed her honour. As for me, my decision is made, and I have told her of it.

With this you will find a packet containing your letters to my daughter. I trust you will let me have in exchange her letters to you, and that you will join me in obliterating every trace of an incident which I should never be able to think of without indignation, my daughter without shame, and you without remorse. I have the honour to be, etc.

7 September 17 —

LETTER 63: *The Marquise de Merteuil to the Vicomte de Valmont*

YES, indeed; I can explain Danceny's note. The crisis which prompted him to write was my work, and, I am inclined to believe, one of my finest triumphs. I have lost no time since you last wrote. Like the Athenian architect I said to myself: 'What he says, I shall do.'

Is it obstacles, then, that this fine romantic hero wants? Has his felicity put him to sleep? Oh, let him rely on me! I shall give him work to do; and I shall be much mistaken if his slumbers continue to be peaceful. It was essential to teach him the value of time, and I flatter myself that he now regrets the time he has lost. You say, too, that he needed more mystery. Well, he shall have no lack of that either! There is this much of good in me: once I have been made aware of my faults, I know no rest until I have mended them. Here, then, is what I have done.

I read your letter on my return home the day before yesterday morning: I found it most illuminating. Convinced that you had correctly diagnosed the source of the trouble, the search for a remedy was my only concern. I began, however, by going to bed. My indefatigable Chevalier had not allowed me a wink of sleep, and I thought I needed it. But not at all. Possessed by the idea of Danceny, the desire to arouse him from his apathy or to punish him for it, I was unable to close an eye, and it was not until I had satisfactorily made my plans that I was able to rest for an hour or two.

The same evening I went to see Madame de Volanges and, as I had planned, told her in confidence of my conviction that a dangerous intimacy had sprung up between her daughter and Danceny. The woman, who has shown so much insight in her attacks upon you, was so blind in this case that she began by saying that I was undoubtedly mistaken; that her daughter was a mere child, etc., etc. I couldn't tell her everything I knew; but I instanced certain looks, certain remarks at which I said *my sense of propriety and my friendship for her had taken alarm*. I spoke in short almost as well as one of the elect could have done; and, so as to deal a decisive blow, went so far as to say that I believed I had seen a letter exchange hands. 'That reminds me', I added, 'that one day in my presence she opened a drawer in her writing-desk which I saw to be full of papers, clearly put there for safe-keeping. Do you know of anyone with whom she is in frequent correspondence?' Here Madame de Volanges' expression changed and I saw a tear or two gather in her eyes. 'Thank you, my dear friend,' she said, clasping my hand. 'I shall find out.'

After this conversation, too short to have aroused suspicion, I paid my respects to the young lady. Soon afterwards I left her to ask the mother to avoid compromising me with her daughter. She agreed the more willingly for my having pointed out how fortunate it would be were her daughter to trust me enough to confide in me, since I should then be in a position to give her *my good advice*. I am certain she will keep her promise because I am convinced she will not willingly forgo her daughter's respect for her perspicacity. I am, therefore, enabled to keep on terms of friendship with the girl without that appearance of insincerity in the eyes of Madame de Volanges, which is what I wished to avoid. An added advantage is that in future I shall be able to spend as much time as I wish as secretly as I wish with the young lady: the mother will never object.

I made the most of this advantage that very evening. Our pastimes over, I ensconced the little thing in a corner and introduced the topic of Danceny, upon which she talked without stopping. I amused myself exciting her in anticipation of the pleasure she was to have in seeing him the next day; there is no sort of inanity I did not make her utter. It was only proper to recompense her in the world of dreams for what I had taken from her in the real one. And then all this will have made her feel the blow more deeply, and I am convinced that the more she suffers, the more eager she will be to make up for it at the first opportunity. Besides, it is as well to accustom to great disasters someone one has destined to great enterprises.

After all, can she not afford to pay with a few tears for the pleasure of having her Danceny, when she so dotes on him? Well, I promise she shall have him, and even sooner than she would have done without this brouhaha. It is a bad dream and the awakening will be delicious. All things considered, it seems to me that she owes me her gratitude. And, if I have been a little malicious, well, one must amuse oneself.

It is to fools we owe the minor joys of life[1]

I left at length very pleased with myself. Either, I said to myself, Danceny will be inspired by obstacles to redouble his efforts, in which event I shall help him to the limit of my capacity; or, if he is only the fool I have sometimes been tempted to think he is, he will, succumbing to despair, accept defeat. Now, in this case I shall at least have had my revenge upon him as far as was possible, and shall incidentally have increased not only the mother's esteem for me but the daughter's friendship and the confidence of both. As for Gercourt, always first in my concerns, I shall think I have been very unlucky or very clumsy, with his wife under my tutelage as she is and as she will be increasingly, if I do not find a hundred ways of making of him what I intend he shall become. I retired to bed in this agreeable frame of mind: I slept well, and awoke very late.

On rising I found two letters had arrived, one from the mother, and one from the daughter. I couldn't help laughing at their both employing the same phrase: 'It is to you alone that I can look for consolation.' It is, after all, amusing to have to provide consolation both for and against, to be the sole representative of two directly contrary interests! There I was, like God, acknowledging the conflicting claims of blind humanity, changing not a syllable of my inexorable decrees. I have since, however, exchanged this august role for that of ministering angel, and, according to the rules, have been to visit my friends in their affliction.

I began with the mother. I found her sunk in such melancholy that you may already consider yourself in some part revenged for the inconvenience she has caused you with your prudish beauty. Everything has passed off to perfection. My one anxiety was that Madame de Volanges might take advantage of this opportunity to win the confidence of her daughter. It could quite easily have been done: one has only to speak gently to the girl as a friend, to give reasonable advice an appearance and tone of indulgent tenderness. Fortunately she adopted a line of severity, and in short has conducted the affair so badly that I have only to sit back and applaud.

1. Gresset: *Le Méchant*, a comedy.

True, she was about to ruin our plan by deciding to return her daughter to the convent, but I have parried this blow, and have committed her to reserving it in threat against Danceny's continuing the pursuit. This was necessary to compel them both to that circumspection which I believe is essential to success.

Thereupon I went to see the daughter. You would not believe how grief enhances her beauty! If ever she takes to coquetry I guarantee she will find a great many occasions to weep: as yet, her tears are innocent. . . . Struck by this new charm which I had not hitherto suspected and which I was very pleased to have discovered, my consolations at first were of the kind that caused more pain than they relieved: in this way I was able to bring her to the point of utter suffocation. She had stopped crying and for a moment I feared she would throw a fit. I suggested she go to bed and she agreed. I served her for maid. She had not yet performed her *toilette*, and soon her dishevelled hair had escaped over her shoulders and naked bosom. I took her in my arms, and as she gave herself to my embrace the tears began once more to flow freely. Lord! How beautiful she was! If the Magdalene was at all like this her penitence must have been much more dangerous than her sin.

When my woebegone beauty had taken to her bed I set about consoling her in earnest. First I calmed her fears concerning the convent. I aroused hopes of her seeing Danceny in secret, and, sitting down on her bed, I began: 'If he were here –', then, with embroideries upon this theme, led her on from one distraction to another until she could no longer remember the reason for her distress. We would have parted upon perfect terms had she not tried to consign a letter for Danceny to my charge. I firmly refused to accept it – for the following reasons, which I am sure you will approve.

In the first place it would have compromised me with Danceny; and if this was the only reason I was able to give the girl, there were many others that you might have given me. Would it not have been risking the fruit of my labours to provide our young couple with so immediate and so easy a means of relieving their sufferings? Besides, I shall not be sorry if they are obliged to implicate a few domestics in this business: for, if it is to succeed, as I hope it will, it must be made public immediately after the marriage, and there could be few more reliable means of spreading the news. If by some miracle the servants don't talk, we can do so, you and I, and it will then be more convenient if we can attribute our indiscretion to them.

It is for you, then, to put the idea into Danceny's head today. Since I cannot rely on the little Volanges' maid, whom she herself seems to distrust, suggest that he try mine, my faithful Victoire. I shall see to it that the experiment succeeds. I am so much the more pleased with the idea in that their taking a servant into their confidence will serve not their purpose but ours: for I have not yet finished my story.

While protesting against taking charge of the girl's letter, I was afraid that she might at any moment suggest my putting it in the post, which I could scarcely have refused to do. Fortunately, through confusion or ignorance on her part, or perhaps because she was less concerned about the letter than about the reply, which she could not have received through the post, she did not make the suggestion. But so as to prevent any possibility of the idea occurring to her, or at least of her being able to make use of it, I took immediate precautions. Returning to the mother, I persuaded her to remove her daughter for some time, to take her into the country. ... And where? Does your heart leap for joy? ... To your aunt's, to old Rosemonde's. She is to be given notice of it today. There! You can now make an unimpeachable return to your devotee who will no longer have grounds for objecting to a scandalous *tête-à-tête*. Thanks to my pains, Madame de Volanges will herself redeem the wrong she has done you.

But be careful: don't take so lively an interest in your own affairs that you lose sight of this one: remember that it is of concern to me. I want you to appoint yourself go-between and adviser to our youthful pair. Tell Danceny, then, about this trip and offer him your services. Let there be no difficulty in your way but that of presenting your credentials to the young lady, and remove that obstacle immediately by suggesting that my maid convey them. There can be no doubt that he will accept the suggestion, and for your pains you will have the confidence of an unfledged heart, which is always interesting. Poor little girl! How she will blush when she gives you her first letter! Truly the role of confidant, against which there is so much prejudice nowadays, seems to me to be a very charming relaxation for one who is otherwise occupied, as you will be.

On you will depend the dénouement of this intrigue. Choose your moment with care for the final reunion. A hundred opportunities will offer themselves in the country, and Danceny will certainly be ready to appear there at a signal from you. Nightfall, a disguise, a window . . . how can I possibly tell? But if in the end the girl returns as she was when she went I shall hold you to blame. If you should think she needs encouragement from me send me your instructions. I think I have taught her so severe a lesson on the danger of keeping letters that I may venture now to write to her myself; and I still intend to keep her for my pupil.

I think I have forgotten to tell you that suspicion in the affair of the betrayed correspondence fell at first upon her maid, and that I have deflected it upon her confessor, so killing two birds with one stone.

Good-bye, Vicomte. I have been a long time writing to you and in consequence I am late for my lunch. Vanity and friendship have been dictating my letter, and they are both chatterboxes. For the rest, you will receive it at three o'clock, and that is all that is necessary.

Complain of me now if you dare; and go back if you are tempted, to enjoy the Comte de B—'s woods. You say that he keeps them for the entertainment of his friends! Is he then *everybody's* friend? But good-bye, I am hungry!

9 September 17 —

LETTER 64: *The Chevalier Danceny to Madame de Volanges (draft enclosed with Letter 66, from the Vicomte to the Marquise)*

WITHOUT attempting to justify my conduct, Madame, and without complaining of yours, I still cannot but deplore an incident which has caused unhappiness to three people, all of whom deserved a better fate. Since I am even more painfully conscious of being the cause of the calamity than of being its victim I have, since yesterday, tried several times to do myself the honour of replying to you, without being able to summon the necessary strength of mind. I have, however, so many things to tell you that I must absolutely make an effort to master my feelings; and if this letter has little coherence or plan, you will be well enough aware how painful my situation is to allow me some indulgence.

Permit me first of all to protest against the first sentence of your letter. I have abused, may I be so bold as to say, neither your trust nor the innocence of Mademoiselle Volanges; I have respected both in my every action. So much it was within my power to do; and when you hold me responsible, too, for an involuntary feeling, I am not afraid to add that the feeling your daughter has inspired in me is one which might displease you but could never give you offence. In this matter, which touches me more nearly than I can say, I wish for no other judgement than yours and no other witness than my letters.

You forbid me to appear in future at your house, and of course I shall comply with whatever commands you see fit to give me in this connexion: but will not my sudden and complete absence offer as much occasion for the gossip you are anxious to avoid as the order to exclude me which, for that very reason, you are reluctant to issue to the servants at your door? I shall insist the more upon this point because it is of more concern to Mademoiselle de Volanges than to me. I beg, therefore, you will weigh every consideration with care and will not allow your principles to impair your prudence. Convinced that it is your daughter's interest alone that will dictate your decisions, I shall await your further orders.

Meanwhile, in the event of your permitting me, Madame, to pay my respects to you from time to time, I engage (and you may rely upon my promise) never to take advantage of these occasions for any attempt to speak to Mademoiselle de Volanges in private, or to put letters into her hands. My fear of anything which might compromise her reputation reconciles me to this sacrifice, and the pleasure of seeing her sometimes will recompense me for it.

The paragraph above is also all I have to say in reply to your remarks on the fate you have in store for Mademoiselle de Volanges, which you say will depend upon my conduct. It would be deceitful in me to promise you more. The base seducer will adapt his schemes to circumstances, calculating afresh upon each new turn of events, but I am inspired by a love that allows me only two feelings: courage and confidence.

Do you think I can consent to being forgotten by Mademoiselle de Volanges, to forgetting her myself? No, no, never! I shall be faithful to her: she has accepted that promise, which I here renew. Forgive me, Madame, I forget myself. I must continue.

I have one other matter left to discuss with you: the letters you have asked for. It really distresses me to add a refusal to the wrongs you already hold me guilty of: but hear my reasons, I beg you, and so that you may appreciate them, be so good as to remind yourself that my only consolation for the misfortune of having forfeited your friendship is a hope of retaining your respect.

Mademoiselle de Volanges' letters, always so precious to me, have now become much more so. They are all that I have left of value: they alone can preserve for me a feeling that is the whole charm of my life. Believe me, however: I should not hesitate for an instant to sacrifice them for your sake; regret at losing them would yield to the desire of proving my most respectful deference to you; but considerations of great moment restrain me, and I am certain that you yourself would not disapprove of them.

It is true that you know Mademoiselle de Volanges' secret; but, if you will permit me to say so, I know upon good authority that you discovered it by means of surprise and not because of her confidence in you. I have no wish to impugn a proceeding which is, perhaps, justified by maternal solicitude. I respect your rights, but they do not extend so far as to relieve me of my duties, and our most sacred duty is never to betray the confidence that is placed in us. I should fail in it were I to expose to another's eye the secrets of a heart which meant to reveal itself only to mine. If your daughter wishes to confide these secrets to you, she will do so; her letters are not to the purpose. If, on the contrary, she wishes to keep her secrets to herself, you will not, of course, expect me to disclose them to you.

As to the obscurity in which you wish to bury this affair, rest assured, Madame, that in everything that concerns Mademoiselle de Volanges I can rival even a mother's solicitude. So as to set your mind completely at rest I have taken every precaution. That precious box which until now bore the inscription: 'Papers to be burnt', now bears the inscription: 'Papers belonging to Madame de Volanges'. The steps I have taken will also prove that my refusal bears no relation to any fear of your finding in these letters a single sentiment to give you, personally, any grounds for complaint.

This is a very long letter, Madame. It is not yet long enough if it is to leave you in the smallest doubt that my sentiments are honourable, that I most sincerely regret having displeased you, and that it is with profound respect that I have the honour to be, etc.

———

9 September 17 —

LETTER 65: *The Chevalier Danceny to Cécile Volanges (sent unsealed to the Marquise de Merteuil with Letter 66 from the Vicomte)*

OH, my dear Cécile, what is to become of us? Where is the God who will save us from the disasters that threaten? May love give us courage at least to endure them! How shall I describe my despair at seeing my letters returned to me, at reading Madame de Volanges' note? Who can have betrayed us? Whom do you suspect? Have you, perhaps, been a little indiscreet? What are you doing at present? What has been said to you? I should like to know everything, and I know nothing. Perhaps you yourself know no more than I do?

I am sending you your mamma's note, and a copy of my reply. I hope you will approve of what I say to her. I want your approval, too, of the steps I have taken since the fatal incident; they are all directed to the same end, that of hearing your news and sending you mine, and that, too, perhaps – who knows? – of seeing you again, under less constraint than ever before.

Can you imagine, Cécile, the pleasure it will be to meet again, to be able to pledge ourselves once more to everlasting love, and to feel in our hearts and see in each other's eyes that our vows will never be broken? Where are the cares that so sweet a moment could not make us forget? Well, I have hopes the moment will come, hopes I owe to the same expedients I have asked you to approve. But what am I saying? I owe them rather to the kind offices of a most solicitous friend; and I have no more to ask of you than that you will permit him to be your friend as well.

I should not perhaps have divulged your secrets to him without your permission, but unhappiness and necessity must be my excuse. It was love that persuaded me to it, and it is love that demands your indulgence, that asks your pardon for a confidence it was necessary to make, for had I not done so we should, perhaps, have been separated for ever.[1] The friend I refer to is known to you; he is a friend, too, of the woman who is most dear to you. I mean the Vicomte de Valmont.

My purpose in approaching him was at first to ask him whether he could induce Madame de Merteuil to convey a letter to you. He did not think this plan would meet with any success, but, in default of the mistress, he said he could answer for the maid, who is under some obligation to him. It will be she who delivers this letter to you and you may give your reply into her hands.

Her assistance will scarcely be of much use to us if, as Monsieur de Valmont thinks, you are to leave for the country forthwith. But in that case it is he himself who is willing to help us. The lady with whom you are going to stay is a relation of his. He will make this his excuse for going there at the same time as you; and our correspondence will then pass through his hands. He even assures me that, if you are willing to do as he instructs, he can arrange a means of our meeting there without risk of compromising you in any way.

Now, my dear Cécile, if you love me, if you pity my unhappiness, if, as I hope you do, you share my regret that we are apart, will you refuse to put your trust in a man who offers himself as our guardian angel? Were it not for him I should be reduced to despair at not being able so much as to alleviate the sufferings I cause you. They will come to an end, I hope: but, my sweet Cécile, promise me that you will not give in too much to them, that you will not allow them to cast you down. The mere thought of your pain is insupportable torment to me. I would give my life to make you

1. Monsieur Danceny's admissions are not altogether honest. He had already confided in Monsieur de Valmont before the 'fatal incident' (see Letter 57).

happy! You know that. Let the certain knowledge that I adore you bring comfort to your heart. As for mine, it needs only your assurance that you pardon love for the evils it makes you suffer.

Good-bye, my dear Cécile; good-bye, my dearest heart.

———

9 September 17 —

LETTER 66: *The Vicomte de Valmont to the Marquise de Merteuil*

You will see, my love, from the two letters enclosed with this, that I have entirely fulfilled your commands. Although both letters carry today's date they were written yesterday, at my house and under my very eyes: the letter to the girl says all we require. One can only bow down before the depth of your insight, if that is to be measured by the success of your undertakings. Danceny is ready for anything; and I am sure that as soon as he is given an opportunity you will find him beyond reproach. If our fair ingénue proves tractable, everything will be over a short time after her arrival in the country; I have a hundred schemes in readiness. Thanks to you I am now out of all question *Danceny's friend*; he has only to turn *Prince*.[1]

He is still very young, our Danceny! Would you believe that I was quite unable to make him promise the mother to renounce his love? As if it were so very difficult to make a promise one has no intention of keeping! 'I should be lying,' he never stopped saying. Are not such scruples edifying, especially since he means to seduce the girl? How very like a man! Our intentions make blackguards of us all; our weakness in carrying them out we call probity.

It is your concern to prevent Madame de Volanges from taking

1. Reference to a passage in one of Monsieur de Voltaire's poems.

[The passage, which occurs in Voltaire's *La Pucelle*, describes how Agnès Sorel, the mistress of Charles VII, was taken captive by the English, and consoled herself in the arms of Monrose, page to an English nobleman. Valmont sees himself as Monrose, Cécile as Agnès, Danceny as the King. *Translator's note.*]

offence at the little lapses our young man has allowed himself in his letter; keep us away from the convent; try, too, to effect a withdrawal of her demand for the girl's letters. Apart from anything else, he certainly will not give them back; he is determined not to, and I think he is right: love and reason for once agree. I have read the letters. I have drained boredom to the dregs. But they may be useful. Let me explain.

However prudent we may be in this affair, there is always the possibility of a scandal – which would prevent the marriage, would it not, and ruin all our Gercourt plans? Should this happen, I, who have a revenge of my own to take upon the mother, reserve the right to accomplish the daughter's dishonour. A carefully chosen selection of these letters would show that the little Volanges had made all the advances and indeed thrown herself at his head. Some of the letters could even be made to compromise the mother and at least cast a *slur* upon her of unpardonable negligence. I am quite aware that our scrupulous Danceny would rebel to begin with; but since he would be under attack himself, I think it might be carried through. It is a thousand to one that events will take this turn; but one must be prepared for everything.

Good-bye, my love. It would be very kind of you to come to supper tomorrow at the Maréchale de —'s; I was not able to refuse.

I need not, I imagine, advise you to keep my intended visit to the country a secret from Madame de Volanges. She would immediately decide to stay in town, whereas once she has arrived at Madame de Rosemonde's she can hardly leave again the next day. If she will only give us a week, I can answer for everything.

9 September 17 —

LETTER 67: *Madame de Tourvel to the Vicomte de Valmont*

I DID not intend to reply to you, Monsieur, and perhaps my present embarrassment is in itself a proof that in fact I ought not to be doing so. I do not wish, however, to leave you with a single cause for complaint against me; and I propose to convince you that I have done everything for you that I could.

I permitted you to write to me, you will say. That is so, but, since you remind me of this permission, do you suppose that I do not at the same time remember the conditions upon which it was given you? If I had observed them as absolutely as you have ignored them, would you have received a single reply from me? This, nevertheless, is the third. While you do everything in your power to oblige me to discontinue this correspondence, it is I who am put to finding some way of sustaining it. There is a way, but there is only one; and if you refuse to take it, you will, whatever you might say, be proving to me the small importance you attach to the matter.

Desist, then, from speaking a language I neither can nor wish to hear; abjure those feelings that offend and alarm me, which perhaps you will cherish less when you consider that they themselves are the obstacle that keeps us apart. Surely they are not the only feelings you know? Is love, because it excludes friendship, to fall even lower in my estimation? Are you yourself to do so because you do not want a woman from whom you have begged demonstrations of kindness to be your friend? I cannot believe it; I should be revolted by so humiliating an idea; it would estrange me from you forever.

In offering you my friendship, Monsieur, I am giving you all that is mine, all that it is in my power to give. What more could you wish? To call forth from me the kindest of feelings, and the one that best accords with my nature, you have only to give me your promise – and the only promise I exact from you is that you will rest content with friendship. I shall forget everything that has been said, and I shall rely upon you to justify my decision.

As you see, I speak with a frankness which proves my confidence in you. It is entirely for you to strengthen that confidence. But I warn you that the first word of love will destroy it for ever, and give me back my fears; it will, I warn you particularly, mark the beginning of a perpetual silence between us.

If, as you say, you have been 'retrieved from error', should you not prefer to be the object of a good woman's friendship than the subject of a guilty one's remorse? Good-bye, Monsieur; you will appreciate that, having spoken as I have, I can say nothing further until I receive your reply.

———

9 September 17 —

LETTER 68: *The Vicomte de Valmont to Madame de Tourvel*

HOW, Madame, shall I reply to your last letter? How dare I tell the truth, when sincerity may be my ruin with you? No matter, I must: I must have courage. I tell myself over and over that it is better I should deserve you than win you, and that even if you must for-ever deny me the happiness I long for without cease, I must at least prove to you that I am worthy of it.

What a pity that I have been, as you say, 'retrieved from error'! With what transports of joy I should once have read the very letter to which I now reply in fear and trembling! You speak with *frankness*, you avow *confidence*, lastly you offer me your *friendship:* what blessings, Madame, and how I regret I cannot turn them to profit! Why am I no longer the man I was?

If I were that man, after all, if I felt nothing for you but vulgar appetite, the transitory desire fostered by a life of intrigue and pleasure which nevertheless goes nowadays by the name of love, I should hasten to take advantage of everything I could acquire. With little scruple in my choice of means, provided they led to success, I should encourage your frankness so as to divine your secrets, welcome your confidence with the intention of betraying it, accept your friendship in the hope of perverting it. . . . Come now, Madame, does this picture terrify you? . . . Well! It would, none the less, be a faithful likeness of me were I to tell you that I agree to being no more than your friend. . . .

How could I agree to sharing with others a feeling that sprang from your heart? If ever I tell you that I do, have no more faith in me. From that moment I shall be trying to deceive you; I may still desire you but I shall beyond question no longer love you.

It is not that frankness, confidence, and friendship have no value in my eyes. . . . But love! true love, such as you inspire, though it contains all those feelings, though it increases their force, cannot admit, as they do, that composure, that coldness of heart which will suffer comparisons to be made, and even preferences to be shown. No, Madame, I shall on no condition be your friend: I shall love you with the most tender, the most passionate, yet the most respectful love. You may deprive it of hope, but you will never destroy it.

By what right do you presume to dispose of a heart whose homage you refuse to accept? What refinement of cruelty is this you practise in begrudging me even the happiness of loving you? That happiness is mine: it exists independently of you, and I know how to protect it. If it is the source of my misfortunes, it is also their solace.

No, no, and again no. Persist in your cruel rebuffs, but leave me my love. You are pleased to make me unhappy. Well, so be it! You may try to wear out my courage; but I can at least oblige you to decide my fate. And perhaps one day you will treat me more justly. Not that I hope ever to change your feelings: but while you remain unmoved, you will perhaps think differently. You will say to yourself: I judged him wrong.

It might more truly be said that you do yourself an injustice. It is as impossible to know you without loving you as it is to love you without loving you faithfully, and in spite of the modesty behind which you shelter, you should find it more natural to pity yourself than to be surprised at the feelings you inspire. As for me, my only merit is that I have been capable of appreciating yours, and I do not wish to lose it. Far from accepting your insidious proposals, I renew at your feet my vow to love you forever.

———

10 September 17 —

LETTER 69: *Cécile Volanges to the Chevalier Danceny*
(*note written in pencil and copied by Danceny*)

You ask me what I do: I love you and I weep. My mother no longer speaks to me. She has deprived me of paper, pen, and ink. I am writing to you on a piece of paper torn from your letter. I must, of course, approve of everything you have done; I love you too much not to take every opportunity of receiving your news and sending you mine. I did not like Monsieur de Valmont, and I did not think he was so much your friend, but I shall try to get used to him, and shall like him for your sake. I do not know who it was that betrayed us; it can only have been my maid or my father confessor. I am very unhappy: tomorrow we leave for the country, I do not know for how long. My God! Never to see you again! I have no more space. Good-bye; try to read this. These pencilled words will perhaps fade one day; never so the feelings engraved upon my heart.

———

10 September 17 —

LETTER 70: *The Vicomte de Valmont to the Marquise de Merteuil*

I HAVE an important warning to give you, my dear. As you know I was at supper yesterday with the Maréchale de —; you were the topic of conversation, to which I contributed not the good opinions I have of you, but the good opinions I don't have of you. Everyone appeared to be of my mind, and the conversation languished as it always does when one has nothing but compliments for one's neighbour, until suddenly a voice was raised in contradiction: it was Prévan's.

'God forbid', he said, rising from his chair, 'that I should cast doubt upon Madame de Merteuil's virtue, but I venture to believe she owes it rather to her levity than to her principles. It is perhaps even more difficult to pursue her than to please her, and since in running after one woman one can scarcely fail on the way to en-counter several others, since, all things considered, these others are likely to be worth as much as she if not more, some of her admirers are diverted by new inclinations and others stop short out of fatigue, so that she is perhaps the woman in all Paris who has least often been put to the trouble of defending herself. As for me,' he added (encouraged by smiles from some of the women) 'I shall not believe in Madame de Merteuil's virtue until I have ridden six horses to death in paying court to her.'

This bad joke was a success – as slanderous jokes always are – to judge from the laughter it provoked. Prévan returned to his place and the conversation took a different turn. But the two Comtesses de B—, near whom our sceptic was seated, engaged him in a private conversation of their own, which fortunately I was so placed as to be able to hear.

A challenge to win your favours was accepted; word of honour to conceal none of the facts was given, and of all the promises that may be made in the course of this enterprise, there will certainly be none more religiously observed than this one. But now you are forewarned, and you know the proverb.

It remains for me to say that Prévan, whom you do not know, is infinitely agreeable, and cleverer still. If you have sometimes heard me say otherwise, it is only because I don't like him, because it suits me to obstruct his designs, and because I am not unaware that my opinion is of some weight with two dozen or so of our most fashionable ladies. In fact I did, by this means, succeed for a long time in preventing his appearance in what we call the great world; he performed prodigies without the smallest increase of reputation. The scandal, however, of his triple affair fixed the eyes of society upon him and having given him the confidence he lacked before, has turned him into someone to be reckoned with. He is, at any rate, the only man today whom I should not care to have cross my path; and, whatever you do in your own interest, you would be rendering me a great service if, in passing, you were to bring down a little ridicule upon him. I leave him in good hands; I hope that when I come back I shall find him a ruined man.

I promise you, in return, that I shall bring your pupil's affairs to a prosperous conclusion, and that I shall take as much interest in her as in my beautiful prude.

The latter has just sent me an offer of capitulation. Her entire letter declares a longing to be deceived. It would be impossible to have presented me with a more convenient and more straightforward means of doing so. She wants to be *my friend*. But I, who like to try new and difficult schemes, have no intention of letting her off so easily. I certainly have not gone to so much trouble on her behalf only to make an end of it with some commonplace seduction.

My plan, on the contrary, is to make her perfectly aware of the value and extent of each one of the sacrifices she makes me; not to proceed so fast with her that remorse is unable to catch up; it is to show her virtue breathing its last in long-protracted agonies; to keep that sombre spectacle ceaselessly before her eyes; and not to grant her the happiness of taking me in her arms until I have obliged her to drop all pretence of being unwilling to do so. After all, I am not worth much if I am not worth the trouble of asking for. And could I take any lesser revenge upon a haughty woman who, it seems, is ashamed even to admit she is in love?

I have therefore declined her precious friendship and insisted upon my claim to the title of lover. Since I am under no illusions as to the real importance of securing this title (though it might appear at first to be a mere quibbling about words), I took great pains with my letter and attempted to reproduce in it that disorder which alone can portray feeling. I was, at all events, as unreasonable as I was capable of being: for there is no showing tenderness without talking nonsense. It is for this reason, it seems to me, that women are better writers of love-letters than men.

I finished mine with flattery; this, too, the fruit of deep reflection. When a woman's heart has been severely tried for any length of time it needs rest; and I have noticed that flattery is in every case the softest pillow to proffer.

Good-bye, my love. I leave tomorrow. If you have messages to give me for the Comtesse de —, I shall stop at her house, at least for dinner. I am sorry I must leave without seeing you. Send me your lofty commands and help me with your sage advice in this crucial time.

Above all, defend yourself from Prévan; and may I one day repay you for your sacrifice! Good-bye.

———

22 September 17 —

LETTER 71: *The Vicomte de Valmont to the Marquise de Merteuil*

IF my idiot of a valet hasn't left my portfolio in Paris! My beauty's letters, Danceny's to the little Volanges are all left behind, and I need them. He is about to turn back to redeem his stupidity, and while he saddles his horse I shall tell you the story of my last night's adventure. I hope you will give me credit for not wasting my time.

The adventure amounted to nothing very much in itself: I merely disinterred an old affair of mine with the Vicomtesse de M—. But the details interested me. I should, in any case, be very glad of an opportunity to show you that, if I have a talent for bringing women to ruin, I have no less a talent, when I wish, for saving them from it. It is always either the most difficult or the most amusing line of action that I invariably pursue, and I am never ashamed of a good deed as long as it entertains me or tries my capacities.

Well, I found the Vicomtesse here, and as she added her entreaties to the general importuning that I spend the night in this house – 'Well, I agree,' I said, 'on condition that I spend it with you.' 'Impossible', she replied. 'Vressac is here.' Till then I had thought only of paying her a compliment, but the word 'impossible', as always, disgusted me. I felt humiliated at being sacrificed to Vressac, and I decided not to allow it: so I insisted.

Circumstances were not favourable. Vressac has been so stupid as to give offence to the Vicomte, so that the Vicomtesse can no longer receive him at home: this visit to the good Comtesse was arranged between them in an attempt to snatch a few nights from the husband. The Vicomte was at first a little ill-humoured at finding Vressac here, but since his keenness as a sportsman exceeds his jealousy as a husband, he decided to stay. The Comtesse, who has changed not at all since you knew her, put the wife in a room off the main corridor with the husband on one side and the lover on the other, and left them to settle matters between them. Their evil fate decreed that I should be lodged directly opposite.

That same day, that is to say yesterday, Vressac, who as you can imagine flatters the Vicomte, went hunting with him although he has little taste for the sport, expecting to be consoled that night in the arms of the wife for the boredom the husband had inflicted upon him during the day. But I decided that he would need rest after his exertions, and set about persuading his mistress to allow him time to take some.

I succeeded, and was given a promise that she would pick a quarrel over the hunting party, to which, needless to say, he had only submitted for her sake. She could scarcely have chosen a weaker pretext: but no woman is more gifted than the Vicomtesse with that talent, common to all women, for putting bad temper to work where reason will serve, and for being never so difficult to pacify as when she is in the wrong. This was, besides, not the time for arguments, and, as I wanted only the one night, I agreed to their being reconciled the next day.

Well, Vressac was duly greeted with sulks. He asked for an explanation: a quarrel ensued. He made some attempt to justify himself, but the husband, who was present, served as an excuse to cut short the conversation. At length he tried taking advantage of a moment when the husband was elsewhere to ask whether he would be expected that evening: it was then that the Vicomtesse rose to sublimity. She railed at the audacity of men, who, because they have felt a woman's kindness, imagine they have the right to exploit it even when they have done her an injury; and having thus shrewdly changed the subject she spoke with so much delicacy and feeling that Vressac stood dumb and confused, and even I was tempted to believe her right: for, you see, as the friend of both I made a third in their conversation.

In the end she declared roundly that she could not think of imposing the fatigues of love upon him after those of the chase, and that she would not be guilty of spoiling a day of such agreeable pleasures. The husband returned. Vressac, overwhelmed and no longer at liberty to make a reply, addressed himself to me, and having cleared himself at great length, begged me to speak to the Vicomtesse, which I promised to do. I did, of course, speak to her, but it was to thank her and to arrange a time and place for our rendezvous.

She told me that, as her bedroom lay between her husband's and her lover's, she had judged it more prudent to go to Vressac's room than to receive him in hers, and she thought, too, that since my room was opposite hers, it would be safer to come to me. She would do so, she said, as soon as her maid had left her: I had only to leave my door ajar and wait.

Everything happened as arranged. She arrived in my room at about one o'clock in the morning,

> . . . In simple robe attir'd,
> As of some goddess roused but lately from her sleep.[1]

Since I have no vanity, I shall not linger over the night's events: but you know me, and I was not dissatisfied with myself.

At daybreak it was time to part. This is where it begins to be interesting. The silly creature thought she had left her door open: we found it locked with the key inside. You cannot imagine the expression of despair upon the Vicomtesse's face as she said to me: 'Oh, I am lost!' I must admit that it would have been amusing to leave her in this situation, but how could I have allowed a woman to be ruined for me who had not been ruined by me? And why should I, like the generality of men, have allowed myself to be overpowered by circumstance? I had therefore to think of a way out. What would you have done, my love? This was my scheme, and it succeeded.

I soon realized that the door in question could be broken open, provided a great deal of noise were not amiss. Accordingly, and not without difficulty, I obtained the Vicomtesse's consent to giving loud shrieks of alarm such as 'Thief! Murder!' etc., etc.; and it was agreed that, at the first shriek, I should break open the door, whereupon she would run to her bed. You will never believe how long it took to persuade her, even after she had given her consent. She had, however, to give way in the end. The door gave way at my first kick.

The Vicomtesse did well to waste no time. At that very instant the Vicomte and Vressac appeared in the corridor, and the maid, too, flew to her mistress's chamber.

I alone preserved my composure, taking advantage of that circumstance to extinguish the night-light, which was still burning, and to knock it over on to the floor. You can imagine how ridiculous all this pretence of panic terror would have been with a lamp alight

1. Racine: *Britannicus*, a tragedy.

in her room. Next I upbraided husband and lover for the heaviness of their slumbers, assuring them that the cries which had fetched me running, and my efforts to break open the door, had lasted at least five minutes.

The Vicomtesse, who had recovered her courage in bed, supported me quite well, swearing by all the gods that there had been a thief in the room; she was able to aver with more sincerity that she had never been so frightened in all her life. We had looked everywhere and found nothing, when I pointed out the overturned night-light and observed that doubtless a rat had been responsible both for the accident and for the alarm. My verdict met with unanimous assent, and after some of the usual well-worn pleasantries about rats, the Vicomte was the first to return to his room and bed, begging his wife to keep rats of more sober habit in future.

Vressac, left alone with us, drew near the Vicomtesse to tell her tenderly that this had been Love's revenge; to which she replied, looking at me, 'A revenge taken in anger, then, for it has been a cruel one. But', she added, 'I am exhausted and I want to sleep.'

I was in generous mood: consequently, before we separated, I pleaded Vressac's cause and brought about a reconciliation. The two lovers embraced, and I was in turn embraced by both of them. I was no longer interested in the Vicomtesse's kisses, but I will confess that Vressac's gave me pleasure. We left the room together and when I had received his much-protracted thanks, returned to our respective beds.

If you find this story amusing, I shall not insist that you keep it secret. Since it has provided me with entertainment, it is only fair to give the public its turn. I refer at present only to the story, but perhaps one day we shall be able to say as much for its heroine.

Good-bye. My valet has been waiting for an hour. One moment more while I kiss you and, above all, urge you to beware of Prévan.

Château de —
13 September 17 —

LETTER 72: *The Chevalier Danceny to Cécile Volanges* (*not delivered until the fourteenth*)

OH, my dear Cécile, how I envy Valmont! Tomorrow he will be seeing you. It is he who will deliver this letter to you, while I, repining afar, drag out my painful existence in longing and misery. My dear, my darling, pity me for my misfortunes; pity me, rather, for yours: it is in face of those that my courage deserts me.

How terrible it is to be the cause of your affliction! Were it not for me, you would be happy and at peace. Do you forgive me? Say, ah, say that you do! Tell me, too, that you love me and that you will love me always. I need to be told again and again. Not that I doubt it, but it seems that the more sure I am, the sweeter it is to hear you say those words. You do love me, don't you? Yes, you love me with all your heart. I have not forgotten that those words were the last I heard you utter. How I have cherished them in my heart! How deeply they are engraved upon it! With what rapture did my heart reply!

Alas, little did I suspect in that moment of happiness what a frightful fate was in store for us. Let us try, my dear Cécile, to find a means of making it easier. If I can trust my friend in this matter, no more is necessary than that you place that confidence in him which he deserves.

I was distressed, I shall admit, at the unfavourable opinion you seem to have of him. I detected your mother's prejudices there: it was to conform to them that I so long neglected this truly amiable man, who now does everything for me, who, after all, is trying to reunite us when your mother has separated us. I beseech you, my dear, to look a little more kindly upon him. Consider that he is my friend, that he wishes to be yours, and that it is in his power to give me back the happiness of seeing you. If these considerations do not weigh with you, my dear Cécile, you do not love me as much as I love you, you no longer love me as much as once you did. Oh, if ever you were to love me less . . . But no, my Cécile's heart is mine; and it is mine for life. And if I have cause to lament an unhappy love, her constancy will at least spare me the torments of a love betrayed.

Good-bye, my dear heart. Remember that I suffer and that it is only you that can make me happy, perfectly happy. Accept the vow my heart makes you and the tenderest kisses love can bestow.

Paris
11 September 17 —

LETTER 73: *The Vicomte de Valmont to Cécile Volanges (attached to the preceding letter)*

THE friend who puts himself at your service, having learnt that you are without writing materials, has made suitable provision. You will find in the large cupboard on the left, in the antechamber to the room you occupy, a stock of paper, pens, and ink, which he will replenish whenever you wish, and which, in his opinion, you would do well to leave in that place unless you find a safer.

He asks you not to be offended if he appears to pay you no attention, to treat you as a mere child in the presence of company. This way of proceeding seems to him to be necessary so as to inspire in others the confidence essential to his purpose, and so that he may the more effectively work for the happiness of his friend and yours. He will try to make opportunities to speak to you when he has something to tell you, or to deliver to you; and he hopes to succeed if you are willing to do your utmost to help him.

He advises you, too, to return your letters to him, one by one, as you receive them, so as to run less risk of compromising yourself.

He will end here by assuring you that if you wish to put your trust in him he will do everything in his power to alleviate the persecution an over-cruel mother inflicts upon two persons, one of whom is already his best friend, while the other appears to him to deserve the most affectionate interest.

Château de —
14 September 17 —

LETTER 74: *The Marquise de Merteuil to the Vicomte de Valmont*

SINCE when, my dear man, have you taken to being so easily frightened? Is Prévan really so very formidable? How modest and simple, then, must I be who have often met this arrogant conqueror and scarcely ever looked at him! It required a letter such as yours to bring him to my notice, and yesterday I repaired my oversight. He was at the Opera, almost opposite me, and I gave him my full attention. He is, at any rate, handsome, very handsome; such fine, delicate features! I am sure they improve, too, upon closer inspection. And you say he intends to have me! It will most certainly be an honour and a pleasure. Seriously, I have a mind to it, and I tell you here in confidence that I have taken the preliminary steps. I don't know whether they will succeed, but this is how it is.

He was standing not two yards away from me as we left the Opera, when, in a very loud voice, I told the Marquise de — I would meet her at supper on Friday at the Maréchale's. This, I think, is the only house at which I am likely to see him. I have no doubt that he heard me. . . . What if the ungrateful fellow has no intention of coming? Tell me, tell me, do you think he will come? Do you know that if he is not there I shall be in a bad humour the whole evening? He will have no difficulty, you see, in *pursuing* me; and, what will surprise you more, even less in *pleasing* me. He wants, does he, to ride six horses to death in paying court to me? Oh, let me spare their lives. I should never have patience enough to wait so long. It is not, you know, in accordance with my principles to let a man pine away for me once I have made up my mind, and in this case I have already done so.

Well, well: is it not a satisfaction to you to talk seriously to me? What a great success your *important warning* has been! But what do you expect? I have been vegetating for so long! For more than six weeks I have allowed myself not a single frivolity. The occasion presents itself; how can I refuse? Is not the person in question worth the pains, and, in whatever sense you take the word, could any pains be more agreeable?

You yourself are obliged to give him his due, and you do more

157

than praise him: you are jealous of him. Well, I am going to set up as judge between you: but first I must know the facts, and I intend to find them out. I shall be a judge of great integrity, and you will both be weighed in the same balance. As far as you are concerned, the case is already documented and fully prepared. Is it not fair that I should now concern myself with your rival? Well then, comply with a good grace; and, to begin with, tell me please about the 'triple affair' he has figured in. You speak as though I had never heard of anything else, and I know not the first thing about it. It must evidently have happened during my stay in Geneva and your jealousy prevented you writing to me about it. Repair this omission as soon as possible: remember that *nothing that concerns him is without interest for me*. There must still have been talk about it when I returned, but I was busy with other things, and I rarely listen to talk of this kind when it is more than two days old.

You may feel a little aggrieved at what I ask, but is this not the least return I can expect for the trouble I have given myself on your account? Was it not I who brought you back to your Présidente, when your stupidity had taken you from her? Was it not I again who provided you with a means of avenging the bitter attacks made upon you by Madame de Volanges? You have so often complained of the time you waste going about in search of adventure! Now you have it under your nose. Love, hatred, you have only to choose: it is all there with you under the same roof. You can enjoy life, caressing with one hand and killing with the other.

It is to me yet again that you owe your adventure with the Vicomtesse. I am happy enough about that, but, as you say, one must talk. For though circumstances might, as I see it, have inclined you for the moment to prefer humbug to scandal, it must all the same be admitted that this woman does not deserve such considerate treatment.

Besides, I bear her a grudge. The Chevalier de Belleroche finds her prettier than I could wish, and there are many other reasons why I should be very glad of a pretext to break with her. Now there is none more convenient than that of having to say to oneself: I cannot possibly meet that woman again.

Good-bye, Vicomte. Remember that, in a position such as yours, time is precious. My time I intend to devote to the greater happiness of Prévan.

Paris
15 September 17 —

LETTER 75: *Cécile Volanges to Sophie Carnay*

(*In this letter Cécile Volanges gives an account in the minutest detail of her part in the events described in Letters 59 and those following, with which the reader is already familiar. This account has been omitted to avoid repetition. Towards the end of the letter she speaks of the Vicomte de Valmont as follows:*)

... I ASSURE you he is the most extraordinary man. Mamma speaks very ill of him, but the Chevalier Danceny very well, and I think it is he who is right. I have never met such a clever man. When he delivered Danceny's letter to me it was in full view of everyone and nobody saw anything. True, I was very frightened because I was not expecting anything; but from now on I shall be prepared. I already understand perfectly what he wants me to do when I give him my reply. It is quite easy to come to an understanding with him: he has a look which says whatever he wishes to say. I don't know how he does it. He says in the note I have already mentioned that he will appear not to pay me any attention in Mamma's presence, and in fact one would imagine that he never gives me a thought. Yet every time I look in his direction I can be sure of meeting his eyes immediately.

A good friend of Mamma's is here, whom I have not met before, and who also seems not to like Monsieur de Valmont very much, although he pays her a great deal of attention. I am so afraid he will tire soon of the life we lead here and return to Paris: that would be a great disappointment. He must really have a good heart to have come here especially to render a service to his friend and to me! I should very much like to show my gratitude, but I don't know how to find a way of speaking to him; and if the opportunity did arise I should be so shy that I should probably not know what to say.

It is only to Madame de Merteuil that I can speak freely about my love. Perhaps, even with you, to whom I tell everything, if we were to talk about it I should be embarrassed. With Danceny himself I have often, in spite of myself, felt a certain constraint which prevented my telling him all my thoughts. I am very sorry for it now, and I should give anything in the world for a moment's opportunity to tell him once, just once, how much I love him. Monsieur de Valmont has promised that if I follow his instructions he will arrange a meeting. I shall certainly do whatever he says; but I cannot imagine how it will be possible.

Good-bye, my dear friend. I have no more space.[1]

Château de —
14 September 17 —

LETTER 76: *The Vicomte de Valmont to the Marquise de Merteuil*

EITHER your letter is a joke which I don't understand, or your mind, when you wrote it, was very seriously deranged. If I knew you less well, my love, I should really be very frightened, and, whatever you may say, I am never frightened too easily.

No matter how often I read your letter I am no further towards understanding it: for, taking it to mean what ostensibly it says, there is no possibility of understanding it. What, then, can it be taken to mean?

Is it only that it was unnecessary to take so many precautions against so unalarming an enemy? In that case you might well be wrong. Prévan is really very charming: more so than you think. He has, too, a very useful talent for attracting a great deal of attention to his feelings, a flair for speaking of them in company, in everybody's hearing, making use, for the purpose, of the first opportunity that offers of addressing the lady concerned. Few women can escape the trap of replying: since they all have preten-

1. Mademoiselle de Volanges shortly afterwards changed her confidante, as will be seen in the following letters; those she continued to write to her friend at the convent will not be included in this collection, since they contain nothing of further interest to the reader.

sions to *savoir-faire*, they cannot let slip an opportunity of displaying it. Now, as you will know, any woman who permits herself to speak of love will end by acknowledging it, or at least by behaving as though she did. This method, which he has really perfected, frequently gives him the added advantage of being able to call upon the women themselves to bear witness to their defeat: and that I can vouch for as having seen it happen.

I was never in the secret except at second hand, for I was never intimate with Prévan. At any rate, there were six of us present when the Comtesse de P —, quite persuaded of her own worldly guile – and in fact, for all that she explicitly said, she might have been making general conversation – recounted to us in the minutest detail the history of her surrender to Prévan and all that had passed between them. She delivered her recital with so much composure that she was not at all disconcerted even when the six of us fell simultaneously into fits of laughter. I shall always remember that when one of us, by way of excuse, pretended to doubt the truth of what she had said, or rather what she appeared to have been saying, she replied with perfect gravity that she was quite certain none of us was as well acquainted with the facts as she, and that she would not even hesitate to put the matter to Prévan, to ask him whether a single word of her story were untrue.

I concluded that the man was a menace to society in general: for you in particular, Marquise, is it not enough that he is 'handsome, very handsome', as you say yourself? Or that he may launch against you one of those attacks you are pleased sometimes to reward for no other reason than that they are well executed? Or that you might find it amusing to surrender for one reason or another? Or . . . how can I tell? How can I guess at those hundreds upon hundreds of whims that rule the mind of a woman, by virtue of which alone you remain typical of your sex? Now that you are warned of the danger, I have no doubt that you will easily avoid it. Yet it was necessary to warn you. I return, then, to my text: what did your letter mean?

If it was a joke about Prévan, apart from the fact that it was very long, it was thrown away upon me: it is in public that he needs to be subjected to some well-aimed ridicule, and I renew my plea to you on this point.

Ah, I think I have found the clue to the mystery! Your letter is a prophecy, not of what you are going to do, but of what he is going to think you are ready to do at the moment of the catastrophe you are preparing for him. I don't disapprove of the plan; it requires very great caution however. You know as well as I that, in the public view, there is absolutely no difference between being a man's mistress and receiving his attentions; unless the man is a fool, which Prévan is not by a very long way. If he can only bring about the necessary appearances, he will begin boasting, and all will be over. The fools will believe him, the malicious will pretend to believe him: what resource will be left to you? Come, it frightens me. Not that I doubt your skill: but it is always the good swimmers who drown.

I don't think I am more stupid than the next man. I know a hundred, a thousand ways of robbing a woman of her reputation; but whenever I have tried to think how she might save herself I have never been able to conceive of a single possibility. You yourself, my love, whose strategy is masterly, have triumphed a hundred times, I consider, more through good luck than good judgement.

But perhaps, after all, I am looking for an explanation where none is to be found. I wonder I can have spent the last hour taking seriously what was certainly meant on your part as a joke. You wanted to make fun of me. Oh, well, laugh! But be quick about it, and then let us speak of other things. Other things! – I am wrong: it is always the same thing: women to be possessed or to be ruined, and frequently both.

Here, as you have so acutely observed, I have opportunities for practice in both fields; not, however, equal opportunities. Revenge, I can see, will prosper sooner than love. I can answer for the little Volanges, who would already have yielded but for want of an occasion, and that I can undertake to provide. But it is not the same with Madame de Tourvel. That woman is devastating: I don't understand her. I have a hundred proofs of her love, but at the same time a thousand of her aversion, and, to tell you the truth, I am afraid she may escape me.

Her first reaction to my return left me feeling more hopeful. As you may imagine, I wished to see it for myself, and, so as to be sure of witnessing spontaneous emotions, I sent no one ahead to announce me, timing my journey so as to arrive while everyone was at table. In fact I dropped from the clouds, like a god in an opera who comes down to unravel the plot.

Having made enough noise at my entrance to fix the attention of the whole company upon me, I was able at a glance to perceive the joy of my old aunt, the vexation of Madame de Volanges, and the confusion and pleasure of her daughter. My beauty was sitting with her back to the door, and, as she was for the moment occupied in cutting something on her plate, did not so much as turn her head. Then I said something to Madame de Rosemonde and at the first word the sensitive creature, having recognized my voice, let out a little cry in which I was certain I detected more love than surprise or alarm. I had by then come far enough forward to be able to see her face, upon which the tumult in her soul, the struggle of thought with feeling, displayed itself in twenty different ways. I sat down beside her at table: she had absolutely no further consciousness of what she was doing or saying. She attempted to continue eating, but without success. At length, in less than a quarter of an hour, her embarrassment and pleasure proving too much for her, she could think of nothing better than to ask permission to leave the table, whereupon she escaped into the park under the pretext of wanting to take the air. Madame de Volanges offered to accompany her: our tender prude refused, only too glad, no doubt, of an excuse to be alone, so that she could give herself up without constraint to the sweet emotions of her heart!

I cut dinner as short as I could. Scarcely had dessert been served when the infernal Volanges, impelled apparently by an urge to thwart me, rose from her place to set out in search of our charming invalid: but I had anticipated this move and forestalled it. I pretended to take her withdrawal as the signal for a general departure, and having myself risen from the table, the little Volanges and the local *curé* let themselves be swayed by our example, so that Madame de Rosemonde found herself alone at table with the old Commandeur de T——. They, too, decided to leave, so that all of us went together to join my beauty, whom we found in the grove near the house. As she wanted not to walk but to be alone, she was just as happy to come back with us as to have us stay with her.

As soon as I was sure that Madame de Volanges would have no opportunity of speaking to her alone, I bethought me of your commands and busied myself in your pupil's interest. Immediately after coffee I went up to my room, and through all the other rooms as well, reconnoitring the territory. I made my arrangements for the safety of the little creature's correspondence, and having performed this preliminary good deed, wrote her a line to tell her about it and to ask for her confidence. I attached my note to Danceny's letter, then returned to the drawing-room. There I found my beauty stretched on a chaise-longue in the most delicious attitude of abandon.

This prospect, in rousing my desires, at the same time animated my expression; I was aware how much it showed of eagerness and tenderness, so placed myself where I could use it to best advantage. The first consequence of this was that my heavenly prude lowered her large bashful eyes. For a time I considered that angelic face; then, my glance wandering over her person, I amused myself imagining the shapes and contours beneath her light but all too reticent garment. I looked down her from head to foot and then up again. . . . My love, that sweet gaze was fixed upon me! It was immediately lowered, but so as to encourage its return I looked away. Thus was established between us that tacit agreement, the first treaty ratified by timid lovers, which, to satisfy a mutual need of seeing and being seen, allows glances to succeed each other until the moment when they can safely meet.

Deciding that this new pleasure would occupy my beauty's whole attention, I turned my consideration to our safety; but having assured myself that the conversation was lively enough to prevent our being noticed, I attempted to persuade her eyes to speak in plainer terms. To this end I first took one or two of her glances by surprise; but with as much reserve as could give modesty no alarm; and to put the bashful creature more at her ease I pretended to be as embarrassed as she was. By degrees our eyes, growing accustomed to meeting, met for longer, and at last looked away no more; and I saw in hers that languid softness which is the happy signal of love and desire. But it was only for a moment. She soon came to herself, and, not without some embarrassment, changed her expression and demeanour.

Not wishing to leave her in any doubt that I had noticed these various emotions, I rose briskly and feigning alarm asked her whether she felt ill. She was immediately surrounded by the whole company. I allowed them all to move in front of me and, as the little Volanges who had been working at her tapestry near a window needed time to put down her work, I seized the opportunity to deliver Danceny's letter.

I was at some distance from her and threw it in her lap. She had really no idea what to do with it. You would have died laughing at her surprise and embarrassment. I, needless to say, did not laugh: I was afraid that so much floundering would betray us. But with a very peremptory glance and gesture I finally made her understand that she must consign the letter to her pocket.

The remainder of the day was without interest. The sequel to the story will perhaps develop to your satisfaction, at least in so far as your pupil is concerned. But one ought to spend one's time carrying out plans rather than talking about them. Besides, I have written you eight pages and I am tired. So good-bye.

You would be right to suppose, without my telling you, that the girl has replied to Danceny.[1] I have also received a reply to the letter I wrote my beauty the day after arriving here. I send you my letter and hers. You may read them or not as you like. This perpetual harping on the same string, which I already find comes something short of the irresistibly amusing, must be exceedingly insipid to anyone who is not personally concerned.

Once more good-bye. I still love you very much. But I beg you, if you speak again of Prévan, do so in terms that I can understand.

Château de —
17 September 17 —

LETTER 77: *The Vicomte de Valmont to the Présidente de Tourvel*

WHENCE comes, Madame, this cruel determination to be rid of me? How is it that the most tender cordiality on my part is answered on yours by conduct which could scarcely be merited even by a man you had every reason to execrate? How, when love

1. This letter has not been found.

brought me again to your feet, when a lucky accident placed me beside you, could you have pretended an indisposition to the alarm of your friends rather than stay beside me? How many times yesterday did you turn your eyes away from me so as to deny me the favour of your regard? And if for a single instant you showed me less severity, the moment was so brief that I think you must have meant me less to enjoy it than to realize how much I was losing when you took it from me.

Love, I make bold to say, does not deserve such treatment, nor does friendship permit it; yet, of those two sentiments, one to your knowledge I profess, while I have been led to believe, it seems to me, that you would not refuse me the other. You were certainly willing once to offer me a friendship of which no doubt you considered me worthy: what have I done since to forfeit it? Will my trust in you be my undoing, will you punish me for my honesty? Have you not the least suspicion that you might be abusing one or the other? After all is it not to the bosom of a friend that I have disclosed the secrets of my heart? Was it not for her sake alone that I refused to agree to conditions which I might simply have accepted, so that I could the more easily have left them unfulfilled or perhaps turned them to my advantage? Will you, in short, compel me to believe by reason of this undeserved severity that I have only to deceive you to win your more favourable regard?

I do not at all regret a decision which I owed it to you and to myself to make; but what dreadful fate decrees that my every praiseworthy action shall become a source of further unhappiness to me?

It was after I had given you occasion for the only compliment you have hitherto condescended to bestow upon my conduct that I first had cause to groan for the misfortune of having displeased you. It was after I had proved my perfect submission to your will in depriving myself of the happiness of seeing you, solely out of regard for your delicacy, that you wanted to break off all correspondence with me, to deny me my feeble recompense for the sacrifice you had exacted, to take everything from me, even the love which alone could give you the right to ask so much. And now it is after I have spoken to you with a sincerity which even self-interest cannot mitigate that you send me packing like some dangerous seducer whose perfidy you have at last found out.

Will you never tire of being so unjust? Tell me, at least, what new crimes can have provoked you to such unkindness; and do not hesitate to dictate the commands you wish me to obey. Since I undertake to obey them, is it presuming too much to want to know what they are?

———

15 September 17 —

LETTER 78: *The Présidente de Tourvel to the Vicomte de Valmont*

You seem, Monsieur, to be surprised at my conduct; what is more, you are not far from calling me to account for it, as though you had the right to approve or blame. I might tell you that to my mind I have better grounds for surprise and complaint than you; but after the refusal contained in your latest reply, I have decided to wrap myself in an indifference which can give rise to neither remark nor reproach. However, since you ask for explanations and since, heaven be thanked, there is nothing as far as I am concerned to prevent my making them, I am quite willing once again to expose my motives to view.

Anyone reading your letters would think me either unjust or very strange. I do not think I have deserved that anyone should have such an opinion of me: it seems to me, moreover, that you, least of all, have any reason to entertain it. No doubt you reckoned, in obliging me to clear myself, upon forcing me into a repetition of all that has passed between us. You considered, evidently, that you could only gain by this rehearsal. Since, for my part, I consider that I have nothing to lose by it, at least in your eyes, I have no hesitation in committing myself to it. Perhaps it is, after all, the only way of discovering which of us has a right to complain of the other.

To start, Monsieur, with the day of your arrival at this house, I think you will allow that your reputation, if nothing else, justified my treating you with some reserve, and that I might, without fear of being accused of excessive prudery, have confined myself solely to expressions of the coldest courtesy. You would have tolerated this, finding it quite natural that a woman with so little experience of the world had not merit enough to appreciate your own. It would certainly have been the course of prudence; and I shall not conceal from you that I should have found it so much the easier course to follow for the fact that when Madame de Rosemonde came to tell me of your impending arrival, I had to remind myself of my friendship for her, and of hers for you, before I could hide from her how unwelcome the news was to me.

I willingly admit that at first you appeared to me in a more attractive light than I had imagined you would; but you, in turn, will admit that this did not last very long and that you soon tired of a constraint for which, apparently, the favourable opinion it gave me of you was not, in your view, sufficient recompense.

It was then that, taking advantage of my innocence and sincerity, you did not hesitate to importune me with feelings which you can have had no doubt would be offensive to me; and I, while you blackened your crimes by adding to their number, looked only for some excuse to forget them, offering you at the same time an opportunity to redeem them, at least in part. My demands were so just that you yourself could not find it in you to refuse them. Taking my indulgence, however, as your due, you exploited it in asking a favour, which no doubt I should not have granted you, but which, nevertheless, you obtained. Of the conditions upon which it was granted, you observed not a single one; and such has been the nature of your correspondence that each of your letters has reminded me afresh of my duty to leave them all unanswered. At the very moment when your persistence compelled me to send you from me, I tried with, perhaps, reprehensible complaisance the only means which could have brought about our reconciliation: but how much is an honourable feeling worth to you? You despise friendship and in your intoxicated folly, setting shame and misfortune at naught, you look for nothing but pleasure and the victims to sacrifice to it.

Your behaviour is as frivolous as your reproofs of mine are unreasonable. You forget your promises, or rather you make a game of violating them. Having agreed to stay away from me, you return here without having been recalled, without regard for my pleas, my arguments, without consideration enough for me to warn me that you are coming. You make no scruple of exposing me to a surprise, the consequences of which, perfectly natural though they were of course, might have been interpreted to my disadvantage by the people around us. Far from attempting to distract attention from the embarrassment you had caused, or to dispel it, you appeared on the contrary to turn all your efforts to increasing it. You carefully chose a place at table next to mine. When a slight indisposition had obliged me to leave before the others, instead of respecting my solitude, you rallied the rest of the company to come and disturb me. If, when we had returned to the drawing-room, I took a step I found you beside me; if I said a word, it was always you who replied. The most indifferent remark served you as a pretext to introduce into the conversation what I did not wish to hear, what might moreover have compromised me. After all, Monsieur, however clever you are, it seems to me that what I can understand must be plain to everybody else as well.

Having compelled me thus to immobility and silence, you were no less unrelenting in your pursuit; I was unable to raise my eyes without meeting yours. I had perpetually to turn away from you, with the quite incredible consequence that you made me the cynosure of all eyes at a moment when I could have wished to be deprived of my own.

And you complain of my treatment, you are astonished at my anxiety to fly from you! Oh, blame me rather for my kindness; let it astonish you that I did not leave myself as soon as you arrived. I should, perhaps, have done so, and you will oblige me to adopt this desperate but imperative course if you do not once and for all cease your offensive solicitations. No, I have by no means forgotten, I shall never forget what I owe to myself, what I owe to the ties I have formed, which I respect and cherish. And I ask you to believe that if ever I am reduced to making the unhappy choice between sacrificing them and sacrificing myself, I shall make it without an instant's hesitation. Good-bye, Monsieur.

16 September 17 —

LETTER 79: *The Vicomte de Valmont to the Marquise de Merteuil*

I HAD intended to go hunting this morning, but the weather is appalling. I have nothing to read but a new novel which would bore a convent girl to tears. It is at least two hours to breakfast, so in spite of my long letter of yesterday I am going to chatter to you again. I am quite sure I shan't bore you, since I shall be speaking of *the very handsome Prévan.* How can you not have heard of that celebrated affair which separated 'the inseparables'? I am sure it will come back to you before I have said two words about it. Here is the story, however, since you have asked for it.

You remember how all Paris raised its eyebrows when three women, all of them pretty, all endowed with the same talents and a right to equal pretensions, lived on terms of the most intimate friendship with each other from the moment of their entry into society? This was at first put down to their extreme timidity: but they were soon surrounded by a throng of admirers whose homage they shared, and as the objects of so much interest and attention they could scarcely have wanted self-assurance. Yet their friendship only grew stronger. It was as though the success of one were always as much the success of the other two. It was hoped that love, at any rate, might provoke some rivalry, and our gallants set about disputing their respective claims to the honour of representing the apple of discord. I myself would have entered the lists, had not the Comtesse de — at that time risen so high in favour that I could not allow myself an infidelity to her until I had obtained the pleasure I was soliciting.

Meanwhile our three beauties made their choices at the same carnival ball, as though by pre-arrangement: far from stirring up the storm that was looked for, the circumstance only made their friendship more interesting by introducing into it the new charm of shared confidences.

All the unsuccessful claimants now joined with all the jealous women in submitting this scandalous display of loyalty to public censure. Some asserted that in a society of 'inseparables' (as they were called at the time) the basic law demanded that all goods be held in common, even lovers; others were sure that while the three gallants need fear no male rivals they had female rivals to contend with, and even went so far as to say that, having been accepted only for the sake of appearances, they had acquired a title without a function.

These rumours, true or false, did not achieve the intended effect. On the contrary, the three couples realized they would be ruined if they were now to separate: they decided to weather the storm. Society, which tires of everything, soon tired of its ineffective campaign. Following its naturally frivolous inclinations, it turned its attention to other things; then, with its usual inconsequence, reverted to the subject and transformed criticism into praise. Since everything with us is a question of fashion, enthusiasm ran high: it had reached the point of delirium, when Prévan took it upon himself to investigate the phenomenon, to determine once and for all both public opinion and his own.

He accordingly sought out these paragons of perfection. He was readily received into their society, and he took this for a favourable omen. He knew well enough that happy people are not so easy of access. He soon saw, in fact, that their much vaunted contentment was, like the estate of kings, more envied than enviable. The supposed 'inseparables' had begun, he perceived, to look for pleasures outside their circle, to give, indeed, their whole attention to the search for distraction. The bonds of love, and friendship, he concluded, had already been relaxed or broken and it was only those of vanity and custom that retained any strength.

Meanwhile the women, drawn together by necessity, kept up the old appearance of intimacy among themselves. The men, however, being more at liberty to do as they pleased, rediscovered obligations to be fulfilled and business affairs to be attended to; they still complained about them, but no longer neglected them, and gatherings in the evening were rarely complete.

This circumstance was of considerable advantage to the assiduous Prévan who, since he naturally found himself beside the unfriended one of the day, was able, according to circumstances, to offer the same homage to each of the three ladies in turn. He was quick to see that to choose between them would be to ruin everything, that false shame at being the first to commit an infidelity would frighten the one he singled out, that wounded vanity would

make the two others his enemies, and that they would not fail to
bring the highest and strictest of principles to bear against him;
lastly, that jealousy would surely embroil him with a rival from
whom he might still have something to fear. There was so much
that might have gone against him; his threefold plan made everything easy. The women were indulgent, because they were interested parties; the men because they thought they were not.

Prévan, who at that time had only one woman to sacrifice, was
fortunate enough to see her become a celebrity. Her status as a
foreigner and her skill in declining the attentions of a great prince
had attracted the notice of both court and town. Prévan shared in
the glory, and profited by it in the estimation of his new mistresses.
The only difficulty was to keep his three intrigues abreast of one
another, their rate of progress being necessarily determined by the
slowest. In fact I had it from one of his confidants that he had
enormous trouble keeping one of them in check when it came to
maturity a full two weeks before the others.

At last the great day arrived. Prévan, who had obtained avowals
from all three, found that he was already in control of the proceedings, and conducted them as you are going to see. Of the three
husbands, one was away, the other was to leave at dawn the next
day, and the third was in town. The 'inseparables' were to sup with
the grass-widow-to-be; but their new lord had not permitted the
old cavaliers to be invited. That morning he made three packets of
his mistress's letters: in one he enclosed a portrait he had received
from her, in the second an amorous emblem she had painted herself,
in the third a lock of her hair. Each of the friends took her third part
of the sacrifice for a complete surrender, and agreed in return to
write her own disgraced lover a peremptory letter of dismissal.

This was a great deal, but it was not enough. The one whose
husband was in town did not have her nights at her disposal: it was
accordingly arranged that an indisposition would prevent her taking
supper with her friend and that the evening would be Prévan's; the
one whose husband was away accorded him the night; while daybreak, the lover's hour, at which time the third husband was to
leave, was appointed by the last.

Prévan, who leaves nothing to chance, flew at once to his fair
foreigner, threw a fit of bad temper, was repaid in kind, and did not

leave until he had established a quarrel which would assure him twenty-four hours' liberty. His dispositions made, he returned home with the idea of resting; but further business awaited him there.

The letters of dismissal had come as a flood of illumination upon the disgraced lovers. Not one of them could doubt he had been given up for Prévan; and all three, out of pique at having been duped – and that annoyance which nearly always accompanies the minor humiliation of being jilted – resolved without telling each other, but as though in agreement, to demand satisfaction from their successful rival.

The latter therefore found three challenges awaiting his return home. Loyally, he accepted them. But determined to forgo neither pleasure nor glory in the course of this adventure, he fixed a rendez-vous for the next morning, assigning the same time and place – one of the gates to the Bois de Boulogne – to all three.

That evening he accomplished his triple task with complete success; at all events he boasted afterwards that each of his new mistresses had thrice received the pledge and proof of his love. As you may imagine, the story at this point lacks authentication. All that the impartial historian can do is to point out to the incredulous reader that vanity and an inflamed imagination may work miracles; and that, besides, it looked as though the morning that was to succeed so brilliant a night, would obviate any necessity to provide against the future. Be that as it may, more certainty can be attributed to the following facts.

Prévan arrived punctually at the appointed rendezvous to find his three rivals a little surprised at meeting each other there, but perhaps already somewhat comforted to discover companions in misfortune. He approached them with an affable, nonchalant air and made them the following speech, which was faithfully reported to me:

'Gentlemen,' he said, 'you have doubtless guessed, since you are here together, that all three of you have the same grounds for complaint against me. I am ready to give you satisfaction. Let it be decided by lot which of you shall first attempt the revenge to which you all have equal right. I have brought neither seconds nor witnesses with me. I did not need them when I committed the offence; I ask for none while I make the reparation.' Then, in the true gambler's spirit, he added: 'I know that one rarely wins at *le sept et le va*; still, no matter what fate has in store, one has lived long enough if one has had time to win the love of women and the esteem of men.'

As his astonished adversaries gazed at him in silence, and while, perhaps, their consciences were beginning to suggest that an opposition of three to one would not be a fair one, Prévan spoke again. 'I shall not conceal from you', he continued, 'that the night I have just spent has cruelly fatigued me. You would be generous to allow me time to refortify myself. I have given orders for breakfast to be served here; do me the honour of joining me. Let us eat together and, above all, let us not be solemn about it. We may kill each other for trifles, but let them not weigh on our minds.'

The invitation to breakfast was accepted. Never, I am told, had Prévan been more agreeable. He was clever enough to avoid humiliating his rivals, and clever enough to persuade them that they might as easily have met with the same success as he; clever enough, above all, to make them admit that they would never, any more than he had done, have let such an opportunity slip. Once these truths had been admitted, everything fell into place of its own accord. Before breakfast was over it had been asserted a dozen times that women such as these did not deserve that men of honour should fight over them. The idea inspired great cordiality, which the wine increased, so much so that shortly afterwards it was felt that to banish ill-will was not enough: friendship without reserve must be sworn.

Prévan, who was certainly as pleased as anyone was with this turn of events, intended none the less to forfeit no whit of his glory. Accordingly, adapting his plans with great skill to circumstances, he addressed the three injured gentlemen as follows: 'After all, it is not upon me but upon your faithless mistresses that you must take revenge. I can provide the opportunity. I have already begun to harbour, in sympathy with you, a resentment I should soon have to share with you: for if not one of you was able to keep his own mistress to himself, how can I hope to hold all three? Your quarrel has become mine. Please accept an invitation to supper this evening at my house, where I hope your revenge will not long be deferred.' An explanation was requested, but in the tone of superiority which the circumstances entitled him to adopt he replied: 'I think, gentlemen, I have given you sufficient proof of my skill: rely upon me.' All agreed, and having embraced their new friend, separated to await the fulfilment that evening of his promises.

Prévan lost no time; he returned to Paris and, as is customary, visited his new conquests. He extracted promises from all three to come that evening to sup *tête à tête* at his house. Two of them did, it is true, make difficulties: but what, since the night before, had they left to deny him? They were to come at intervals of an hour, the length of time necessary to his plans. These preliminaries accomplished, he withdrew, reported to his accomplices, and the four of them went off joyfully to await their victims.

The first one was heard arriving. Prévan received her alone, and with an air of solicitude conveyed her into the sanctuary whose presiding goddess she believed herself to be. He then made some trifling excuse to disappear, and was immediately replaced by an outraged lover.

As you can imagine, the consternation of a woman not yet accustomed to proceedings of this kind made his victory easy: with every reproach he omitted to make, he conferred a favour, so that the fugitive slave, given up once more to her old master, was obliged to think herself lucky that, by submitting again to the original bondage, she could hope to be forgiven. The peace treaty was ratified in a more secluded spot; the stage, thus left empty, was filled in turn by the other actors in the piece to more or less the same effect, in each case, of course, with the same result.

Each woman, meanwhile, believed herself to be the sole heroine of the drama. At supper, to their further surprise and embarrassment, the three couples came together for the first time; consternation reached its height when Prévan, reappearing in their midst, was cruel enough to make his excuses to the ladies, thus, in betraying their secrets, revealing the full extent to which they had been tricked.

Meanwhile they sat down to table and before long were able to put a face upon it: the men yielded and the women submitted. Hatred consumed every heart: but conversation was none the less *galant*. Gaiety aroused desire, which in turn gave a fresh fillip to gaiety. This astonishing orgy lasted till morning. When they separated the women must have thought themselves forgiven, but the men had been nursing their resentments and broke irrevocably with them the very next day. Not content, moreover, with abandoning their fickle mistresses they crowned their revenge by publicizing the affair. Since then, one of the women has entered a convent, while the two others have languished in exile on their estates.

So much for Prévan's story. It is for you to decide whether you wish to contribute to his glory, to be yoked to his triumphal car. Your letter really made me anxious and I shall wait with impatience for one more sensible and more intelligible in reply to my last.

Good-bye, my love. Distrust all amusing and bizarre ideas; you are so easily led astray by them. Remember that for the role you have elected to play, intelligence is not enough. A single imprudence may bring about irremediable disaster. Allow it, lastly, to a prudent friend to be at times the director of your pleasures.

Good-bye. I love you still, almost as though you were a reasonable being.

———

18 September 17 —

LETTER 80: *The Chevalier Danceny to Cécile Volanges*

CÉCILE, my dear Cécile, when shall we see each other again? How shall I learn to live without you? Where shall I find the strength and courage to do so? Never, no never, shall I accept this horrible separation. Each day increases my misery: and to see no end to it! Valmont, who promised help and consolation, neglects me and has perhaps forgotten me. He is beside his beloved and no longer knows what it is to suffer in isolation. He sent me your last letter, but not a word from himself. Yet it is for him to tell me when I may see you, and by what means. Has he nothing to say? You yourself do not speak of the matter: can it be that you no longer share my longing? Oh, Cécile, Cécile, I am very unhappy! I love you more than ever: but love, which was once all the charm of my life, is becoming its torment.

No, I can no longer live like this. I must see you, I must, if only for a moment. When I wake, I say to myself: 'I shall not see her.' I go to bed thinking: 'I did not see her.' Not a moment's happiness in all the long day. All is want, regret, despair; and these evils spring from what I used to think the source of all my pleasures! If to such mortal sufferings you add my anxiety on your account you will have some idea of my state of mind. I think of you constantly, and never without pain. When I imagine you troubled and unhappy I suffer all your griefs, when I see you comforted and at ease, my own are redoubled. Wherever I turn, I find misery.

Oh, how different it was when you lived where I did! Then all was pleasure. The certainty of seeing you brightened even the moments when you were not with me; the time I had to spend away from you brought me nearer you as it passed. And however I spent it, you were always a part of my concerns. If I fulfilled my duties, it was to make me more worthy of you; if I cultivated my talents, it was in the hope of giving you greater pleasure. Even when the distractions of society carried me far out of your sphere, we were never apart. At the theatre I tried to imagine what would please you; a concert would remind me of your talents and of our delightful times together. In company and in the street I would seize upon the slightest resemblance to you. I compared you with everything, and always to your advantage. Not a moment of the day passed without my paying you some new homage, and every evening I brought my tributes to your feet.

What remains now? Sad regrets, perpetual privation, and the faint hope that Valmont will break his silence and that yours will turn to concern. There are only ten leagues between us, a distance so easily covered, but for me it has become an insurmountable obstacle! And when I beseech my friend and my mistress to help me surmount it, both are cold and indifferent! Far from offering me assistance, they do not even reply.

What has happened to Valmont's sedulous friendship? What especially has become of the tender feelings which once prompted you to so much ingenuity in finding means for us to meet every day? I remember that sometimes, when I was by no means unwilling, I would nevertheless have to sacrifice my wishes to prudence, to duty; what did you not find to say to me then? What were the excuses you did not bring forward against my arguments? And, if you remember, Cécile, my arguments always yielded to your wishes. I take no credit for that: it was not even a sacrifice. What-ever you wished for, I longed to give you. But now it is I who have something to ask. And what is it, after all? To see you for a mo-ment, to renew to you and to hear you renew our vows of everlast-ing love. Does this no longer seem the happiness to you that it would be to me? I put away that desperate thought, which would make my sufferings intolerable. You love me, you will always love me. I believe it, I am sure of it, I want never to doubt it. But my situation is terrible, and I cannot support it much longer. Good-bye, Cécile.

Paris
18 September 17 —

LETTER 81 : *The Marquise de Merteuil to the Vicomte de Valmont*

How pitiful your apprehensions are! How perfectly they prove my superiority over you! And you would like to teach me, to direct me! Oh, my poor Valmont, what a distance there still is between us! No, all the vanity of your sex cannot make up the disparity. Because you yourself would not be able to carry out my plans, you decide that they are impracticable! Weak and conceited creature, how ill it becomes you to appraise my methods or estimate my resources! Truly, Vicomte, your advice has put me out of humour and I cannot conceal it.

That in order to put a face upon your incredible clumsiness in dealing with the Présidente you flaunt, as though in triumph, your having for a moment disconcerted that poor timid women who is in love with you, I shall allow. That you succeeded in obtaining a look, a single look, I grant you with a smile. That conscious, in spite of yourself, of the little merit in your behaviour you hope to distract my attention from it by delighting me with your trans-cendental effort to bring two children together, both of whom are burning to meet and who, let me say in passing, owe the ardour of their desires to me alone: that I am still willing to permit. That, lastly, you consider your brilliant accomplishment authorizes you to tell me in a magisterial tone that 'one ought to spend one's time rather in carrying out plans than in talking about them' – that harmless vanity I can forgive. But that you could imagine that I am in any need of your prudence, that I should go astray were I not to defer to your opinions, that to them I must sacrifice my pleasure, my caprice: really, Vicomte, that is presuming too much upon the confidence I have been willing to place in you!

And where, after all, is the achievement of yours that I have not a thousand times surpassed? You have seduced, even ruined a great many women: but what difficulty did you have in doing so? What obstacles stood in your way? Where is the merit you can truly claim as your own? A handsome figure, which was simply the gift of fortune; the social graces that experience will nearly always confer; wit, it is true, though nonsense would do as well at a pinch; a most praiseworthy assurance, due perhaps, however, solely to the ease of your first successes. That, if I am not mistaken, is the sum of your assets. As to the celebrity you have acquired, you will not, I think, insist that I value very highly a talent for making and seizing opportunities to create scandal.

When it comes to prudence or good judgement – I leave myself out of account, but where is the woman who has not more of them than you? Pooh! Your Présidente has you by the leading-strings, like a child.

Believe me, Vicomte, unnecessary virtues are rarely acquired. Since you risk nothing in your battles, you take no precautions. For you men, defeat means only one victory the less. In this unequal contest we are lucky not to lose, you unlucky when you do not win. Were I to grant you as many talents as we possess, how far we should still surpass you in their exercise by reason of the continual necessity we are under of putting them to use!

I am willing to suppose that you employ as much skill in conquest as we do in defence or surrender, but you will at least agree that, once you have achieved success, skill is immaterial to you. Entirely absorbed in your new pleasure, you give yourself up to it without constraint or reserve: it is of no importance to you how long it lasts.

After all, to talk the jargon of love, promises reciprocally given and received can be made and broken at will by you alone: we are lucky if upon an impulse you prefer secrecy to scandal, if, content with a humiliating submission, you stop short of making yesterday's idol the victim of tomorrow's sacrifice.

But when it is the unfortunate woman who first feels the weight of the chain, what risks she has to run if she tries to escape from it, or even to lighten it! Only in fear and trembling can she attempt to be rid of the man her heart so violently rejects. If he is determined to remain, that which once she granted to love must be given up to fear.

Her arms are open still although her heart refuse.

Her prudence must be skilfully employed in undoing the same bonds which you would simply have broken. At the mercy of her enemy, she is without resource if he is without generosity; and how can generosity be expected of him when, although men are sometimes commended for showing it, they are, notwithstanding, never thought the less of for lacking it?

You will not of course deny truths which are so evident as to be trivial. Since, then, you have seen me controlling events and opinions; turning the formidable male into the plaything of my whims and fancies; depriving some of the will, others of the power to hurt me; since I have been capable, according to the impulse of the moment, of attaching to or banishing from my train

These tyrants that I have unseated and enslaved;[1]

since amidst a great many vicissitudes, I have kept my reputation untarnished; should you not therefore have concluded that I, who was born to revenge my sex and master yours, have been able to discover methods of doing so unknown even to myself?

Oh, keep your warnings and your fears for those giddy women who call themselves women of *feeling*, whose heated imaginations

1. It is not known whether these lines, this one and the one which appears earlier in the letter: *Her arms are open still although her heart refuse*, are quotations from little known works or whether they in fact form part of Madame de Merteuil's prose. What makes the latter supposition more probable is that there are innumerable lapses of the same kind throughout the letters in this collection. Only the Chavalier Danceny's are free from them, perhaps because, being an occasional reader of poetry, his more practised ear helped him to avoid errors of taste.

persuade them that nature has placed their senses in their heads; who, having never thought about it, invariably confuse love with a lover; who, with their stupid delusions, imagine that the man with whom they have found pleasure is pleasure's only source; and, like all the superstitious, accord that faith and respect to the priest which is due to only the divinity.

Keep your fears, too, for those who are more vain than prudent and cannot, when the time comes, bear to consider being abandoned.

Tremble above all for those women whose minds are active while their bodies are idle, whom you call sensitive; who are always so easily and so powerfully moved to love; who feel they must think about it even though they don't enjoy it; who, surrendering themselves completely to the fermentation in their minds, give birth as a result to letters full of tenderness but fraught with danger; and who are not afraid to confide these proofs of their weakness to the person responsible for them: imprudent creatures, who cannot see in the lover of today the enemy of tomorrow.

But I, what have I in common with these empty-headed women? When have you known me break the rules I have laid down for myself or betray my principles? I say 'my principles' intentionally. They are not, like those of other women, found by chance, accepted unthinkingly, and followed out of habit. They are the fruit of profound reflection. I have created them: I might say that I have created myself.

At my entrance into society I was still a girl, condemned by my status to silence and inaction, and I made the most of my opportunities to observe and reflect. I was thought scatter-brained and absent-minded: I paid little attention, in fact, to what everyone was anxious to tell me, but was careful to ponder what they attempted to hide.

This useful curiosity, while it increased my knowledge, taught me to dissemble. Since I was often obliged to conceal the objects of my attention from the eyes of those around me, I tried to be able to turn my own wherever I pleased; from that time I have been able at will to assume the air of detachment you have so often admired. Encouraged by my first success, I tried in the same way to control the different expressions on my face. When I felt annoyed I practised looking serene, even cheerful; in my enthusiasm I went so far as to suffer pain voluntarily so as to achieve a simultaneous expression of pleasure. I laboured with the same care, and even more difficulty, to repress symptoms of unexpected joy. In this way I was able to acquire the power over my features at which I have sometimes seen you so astonished.

I was still very young and almost without serious concerns, but since I had only my thoughts to call my own, I was indignant when anyone was able to force them from me or to surprise me against my will. Provided with my first weapons, I practised using them: not content with being inscrutable, it amused me to assume different disguises, and once sure of my demeanour I attended to my speech. I regulated both according to circumstances, or simply as the whim took me. From that moment on my thoughts were purely for my own benefit, and I revealed only what I found it useful to reveal.

This experiment in self-mastery led me to make a study of facial expression and of character as it is displayed in physical features. Through this I acquired the searching glance which experience has taught me not to trust entirely, but which, on the whole, has seldom deceived me.

I was only fifteen, I already possessed the talents to which most of our politicians owe their reputation, and I had as yet acquired only the elements of the science I intended to master.

As you may guess, I was, like every other young girl, anxious to discover love and its pleasures. But since I had never been at a convent, nor made any close friendship, and since I lived under the eye of a vigilant mother, I had only the vaguest ideas on the subject, which I was quite unable to clarify. Nature herself, with whom since then I have certainly had every reason to be satisfied, had as yet given me no sign. One might almost have said that she was working in secret to the completion of her task. My mind alone was in a ferment: I had no wish to enjoy, I wanted to know, and the desire for knowledge suggested a means of acquiring it.

I realized that the only man I could speak to upon the subject without fear of compromise was my confessor. I made my decision immediately; overcoming a slight sense of shame, I laid claim to a sin I had not committed, accusing myself of having done 'everything that women do'. That was the expression I used, but in using it I had, in fact, no idea what it might convey. My hopes were not altogether disappointed, nor were they altogether fulfilled. My fear of betraying myself prevented my obtaining any explanation, but the good priest made so much of the crime that I concluded the pleasure of committing it must be extreme, and my desire for knowledge gave way to a desire for gratification.

Who knows where this desire might have led me; with my lack of experience at the time a single encounter might perhaps have been my ruin. Fortunately for me my mother announced a few days later that I was to be married. The certainty of learning before long what I wanted to know subdued my curiosity, and I proceeded a virgin into the arms of Monsieur de Merteuil.

I awaited the moment of enlightenment with confidence, and had to remind myself to show embarrassment and fear. The first night, which is generally thought of as 'cruel' or 'sweet', offered me only a further opportunity for experience. I took exact account of pains and pleasures, regarding my various sensations simply as facts to be collected and meditated upon.

My studies soon became a delight. But, faithful to my principles and aware, perhaps by instinct, that no one should be further from my confidence than my husband, I decided, for the very reason that I had become susceptible to pleasure, to appear in his eyes as impassive. This apparent frigidity proved later to be the unshakeable foundation of his blind trust in me. I decided in addition, after careful thought, to indulge the giddy airs my age permitted me: never did he think me more of a child than when I was most flagrantly deceiving him.

Meanwhile, I will admit, I had allowed myself to be caught up in the whirl of society and had surrendered completely to its futile distractions. But after a few months, when Monsieur de Merteuil had carried me off to his gloomy country house, fear of boredom revived my taste for study. Finding myself surrounded by people whose distance in rank from me would keep my relations with them above suspicion, I took the opportunity to enlarge my field of experience. It was here, in particular, that I confirmed the truth that love, which we cry up as the source of our pleasures, is nothing more than an excuse for them.

Monsieur de Merteuil's illness came as an interruption to these agreeable preoccupations. I was obliged to follow him to town where he went for treatment. He died, as you know, a while later, and although, all things considered, he had given me nothing to complain of, I nevertheless fully appreciated the value of the liberty that widowhood was about to confer upon me, and promised myself I should make good use of it.

My mother expected me to enter a convent or to return to living with her. I refused to do either; and my only concession to decency was to return to the house in the country, where I had not a few observations still to make.

These I supplemented with the aid of books: and they were not all of the kind you imagine. I studied our manners in the novelists, our opinions in the philosophers; I went to the strictest moralists to find out what they demanded of us, so as to know for certain what it was possible to do, what it was best to think, and what it was necessary to seem to be. Having reached my conclusions on all three subjects, it was only the last that presented any difficulty in practice, but that I hoped to overcome, and meditated a means of doing so.

My bucolic pleasures, too little varied for an active mind, had begun to bore me. I felt the need of coquetry to reconcile me once more to love; not in order to feel it, of course, but in order to inspire it and pretend to be inspired. In vain had I been told and had I read that it was impossible to feign the feeling; I have already observed that to do so one had only to combine an actor's talents with a writer's wit. I cultivated both, and not without success: but instead of courting the vain applause of the theatre, I decided to use for happiness what so many others sacrificed to vanity.

A year passed while I was thus variously occupied. It was then permissible for me to come out of mourning, and I returned to town with my great designs. The first obstacle I encountered there came as a surprise.

I had, during my long term of solitude and austere retirement, acquired a veneer of prudery that alarmed all our most agreeable gallants. They retreated, and gave me up to a throng of bores, all of whom aspired to my hand. I had no difficulty in refusing them, but several of the refusals were unwelcome to my family, and I lost in domestic bickering time which I had dedicated to more charming pursuits. In order therefore to attract one party and repel the other, I was obliged to advertise an indiscretion or two, taking as much pains to mar my reputation as I had meant to take to preserve it. I succeeded quite easily, as you may imagine. But since I was not influenced by passion, I did only what I judged necessary, measuring out my doses of folly with a prudent hand.

As soon as I had reached my intended goal, I retraced my steps – and laid the honour of my reformation at the feet of certain of those women, who, since they are incapable of any pretensions to charm, fall back upon their merits and their virtues. This stroke of policy accomplished more for me than I had hoped. The grateful duennas set up as my apologists; and their blind enthusiasm for what they called their 'charge' was carried to such a pitch that at the least suggestion of a word against me a whole battalion of prudes would cry 'scandal' and 'slander'. The same proceeding won me, too, the suffrage of our ladies with pretensions, who, convinced that I had renounced the career they pursued themselves, chose me for the object of their commendations every time they wished to prove that it was not everybody that they maligned.

Meanwhile my previous activities had brought me lovers, and so as to steer a middle course between them and my misguided protectresses I played the part of an impressionable but fastidious woman whose excess of delicacy was her defence against passion.

It was then that I began to display upon the great stage the talents I had acquired for myself. My first object was to secure a reputation for being invincible. To succeed in this I contrived that the men who interested me not at all were the only ones whose homage I appeared to accept. I made use of them to win me the honours of successful resistance; meanwhile I could safely yield to the lover of my choice. The timidity I pretended, however, would not permit of his following me into society, so that at all times it was an unhappy lover who caught the attention of my circle of acquaintance.

You know how quickly I come to decisions. It is because I have remarked that it is nearly always preliminary deliberations that betray a woman's secret. In spite of all one can do, one's manner is never quite the same before the event as after. This difference never escapes the attentive observer; and I have found it less dangerous to choose wrong than to be found out in my choice. There is an added advantage to this in that it offers no basis for the likely assumptions by which alone others are able to judge us.

These precautions, together with those of never writing letters and never providing evidence of my defeat, may seem excessive, but to me they never seemed enough. I searched the depths of my heart for clues to the hearts of others. I observed that there is no one without a secret which it is in his interest never to reveal: a truth that antiquity seems to have known better than we do, and of which the story of Samson might be no more than an ingenious allegory. A latter-day Delilah, I have always, as she did, devoted all my powers to springing the important secret. Oh, I have my scissors to the hair of a great many of our modern Samsons! Of them I am no longer afraid; and they are the only men I have sometimes allowed myself to humiliate. With the others I am more pliant: skill in making them unfaithful to me so as to avoid appearing fickle myself, a pretence of friendship, a show of confidence, a few generous gestures, and the flattering idea each one is made to entertain of being my only lover, such contrivances ensure that they will be discreet. In the last resort, when all else has failed, I have always, foreseeing the end, been able in good time to destroy, under ridicule or contempt, whatever credence these dangerous men may have been able to obtain.

I speak now of what you see me doing all the time, and yet you doubt my prudence! Well! Call to mind the time when you first favoured me with your attentions. No homage ever flattered me more. I desired you before I had seen you. Your reputation so impressed me that it seemed that only you could bring me glory. I longed to measure swords with you. This is the only one of my desires that has ever for a moment gained sway over me. Yet, had you wanted to ruin my reputation, with what could you have done it? Mere talk, which had left no trace behind it, whose authenticity your own reputation would have helped to render suspect; and a series of improbable events, a faithful account of which would have sounded like a bad novel? It is true that I have since surrendered all my secrets to you: but you are aware of the interests that unite us, and know quite well whether, of the two of us, it is I who deserve to be taxed with imprudence.[1]

1. In a subsequent letter (152) the reader will learn, not Monsieur de Valmont's secret, but the nature of it more or less, and will appreciate why it was not possible to enter here into fuller explanations upon the subject.

Since I have begun to justify myself, I may as well do it thoroughly. Even at this distance I can hear you say that I am, at any rate, at the mercy of my chambermaid: after all, though she cannot read my feelings, my actions are an open book to her. When you spoke of this once before, I replied merely that I was sure of her; and the proof that this was enough at the time to satisfy you is that you have confided in her since then for your own purposes, letting her into some fairly dangerous secrets. But now that you have lost your head in your annoyance at Prévan, I very much doubt that you will still take me at my word. I shall therefore be more explicit.

First of all, this girl and I were nursed at the same breast, and while you and I do not regard this as establishing a connexion, it is a consideration of some weight with people of her class. Moreover, I know her secret. Better still, she was at one time the victim of some disastrous amour, and would have been lost had I not saved her. Her parents, bristling with outraged honour, wanted her locked away, nothing less. They approached me. One glance told me how useful their wrath could be. I gave it my support and applied for an order of arrest, which I obtained. Then, with a sudden shift of ground from severity to mercy, to which I persuaded the parents too, I turned my credit with the old Minister to advantage, and made them all agree to leave the order in my hands, with the power to cancel it or demand its execution according as I should judge of the girl's future conduct. She knows, then, that her fate is in my keeping; and if the impossible happens and she defies these considerations, is it not obvious that her past, when it is revealed, not to speak of the punishment she must suffer, will deprive whatever she says of all credibility?

Such precautions, which I think of as fundamental, involve, according to time and place, a thousand others which practice and reflection supply at need. An account of them would be tedious, notwithstanding their importance, and I must put you to the trouble of studying the whole of my conduct if you wish to achieve a knowledge of them all.

But to expect that I should have gone to so much trouble only to refrain from seizing my rewards; that, having raised myself by painful effort above other women, I should now consent to creep along as they do between prudence on the one hand and timidity on the other; that above all I should be so afraid of a man as to see no safety anywhere but in flight. No, Vicomte; never. Conquer or perish. As for Prévan, I want him, and I shall have him; he will want to be able to say so, and he shall not say so. There, in two sentences, you have our story. Good-bye.

———

20 September 17 —

LETTER 82: *Cécile Volanges to the Chevalier Danceny*

DEAR God, how your letter has upset me! And to think that I was so impatient to receive it! I hoped to find comfort in it, and now I am sorrier than ever I was before I had it. I cried so much as I read it: but it is not for that I blame you. I have often cried on your account without it distressing me. But this time it is not at all the same.

What do you mean when you say that love has become a torment for you, that you can no longer live like this, or endure your situation any longer? Are you going to stop loving me because it is no longer as pleasant as it used to be? It seems to me that I am no happier than you are, quite the contrary; and yet I love you all the more. If Monsieur de Valmont has not written to you, it is not my fault; I have not been able to ask him, because I have not been alone with him at all, and because we agreed that we would never speak to each other in company. That, too, was for your sake, so that he could the sooner do what you wish. I am not saying that I do not want it too; you surely don't doubt that: but what do you expect me to do? If you think it is easy to know, tell me: I could ask for nothing better.

Do you think it is so very agreeable for me to be grumbled at every day by Mamma, who at one time never said anything to me at all? On the contrary. At the moment it is worse here than it would be at the convent. I have been consoling myself, thinking that it was for you; there were even moments when I found I was very pleased that it was so. But when I discover that you are angry too, without it being in any way my fault, it makes me more unhappy than anything that has ever happened to me before.

Simply to receive your letters creates difficulties, and, if Monsieur de Valmont were not as obliging and as clever as he is, I should not know what to do; writing to you is even more difficult. I dare not do so in the morning since Mamma's room is very near mine and she is likely to come in at any time, but I can sometimes do so in the afternoon, on the pretext of wanting to sing or play the harp. Even so I have to break off at every line so as to be heard practising. Fortunately my maid sometimes falls off to sleep of an evening and I tell her I am quite willing to prepare for bed without her, so that she goes away and leaves me the light. And then I have to hide behind the bed-curtains so that no one will notice the light, and then listen for the slightest noise so that I can hide everything in the bed should anyone come. I wish you could be there to see! You would immediately realize that one must be really in love to be able to do such things. At any rate, it is certainly true that I do all I can, and that I wish I could do more.

Of course I don't refuse to tell you that I love you, and that I shall love you always. Never have I said that more from my heart. Yet you are angry! And once you assured me, before I had said anything at all, that those words would be enough to make you happy. You cannot deny it: it is in your letters. Although I no longer have them, I remember them as well as if I read them over every day. And because we are now separated you no longer feel the same way! But this separation will not last for ever, will it? Dear God, how unhappy I am! And it is you who are to blame! . . .

Speaking of your letters, I hope you have kept the ones that Mamma took away and then returned to you. There will certainly come a time when I am not so persecuted as I am at present and you will give them all back to me. How happy I shall be when I am able to keep them forever without anyone minding! For the moment I return your letters to Monsieur de Valmont as they come, because I should be risking too much otherwise: none the less I never give them back to him without the most painful regrets.

Good-bye, my dear. I love you with all my heart. I shall love you all my life. I hope you are no longer angry now; if I were sure you were not, I should no longer be angry myself. Write to me as soon as you can, for till then I know I shall continue to be sad.

Château de —
21 September 17—

LETTER 83: *The Vicomte de Valmont to the Présidente de Tourvel*

FOR pity's sake, Madame, let us take up the conversation again that was so unfortunately interrupted! That I could succeed in proving to you how different I am from the hateful picture you have painted of me; that I could, above all, enjoy once more the friendly confidence you had begun to show towards me! What a charm you are able to give to virtue! What beauty and what value you confer upon all the decent feelings! Ah, that is the secret of your fascination: the most powerful kind, and the only one which is at the same time both potent and respectable.

Merely to see you, of course, is to desire to please you; to hear you speak in society is for that desire to grow. But he who is so fortunate as to know you better, he to whom it is sometimes given to read your heart, soon yields to a nobler enthusiasm, and, imbued as much with reverence as with love, worships in you the image of all the virtues. I, who am perhaps by nature more than usually apt to love those virtues and be guided by them, was misled by certain misapprehensions into turning away from them. It is you who have recalled me, you who have made me conscious again of all their charm: will you turn this new devotion into a crime? Will you condemn your own handiwork? Will you reproach yourself for taking an interest in it? What is there to fear in so pure a feeling, and what sweetness might there not be in tasting it?

My love frightens you, you find it violent, unbridled! Temper it then with more gentle feelings; do not refuse the power I offer you, which I swear I shall never renounce, and which, I venture to believe, will not be entirely useless to the cause of virtue. What sacrifice would I find too painful were I certain that your heart appreciated its worth? Is there a man so unfortunate that he cannot enjoy the restraint he imposes upon himself; that he does not prefer a word, a look that is willingly granted to all the pleasures he can snatch by force or surprise? And you thought me such a man! You were afraid of me! Ah, if only your happiness depended on me! How I should revenge myself upon you in making you happy! But barren friendship cannot engender so sweet a power; it is only love that can.

That word intimidates you! Why? It means a more tender attachment, perhaps, a closer intimacy, the sharing of thoughts, of the same happiness and the same pain, but what is there in that so foreign to your nature? And love is no more than that – the love, at any rate, which you inspire and which I feel! A love which, more than anything, is disinterested in its judgements, appreciating an action for its merit rather than for its value. It is the inexhaustible treasure of sensitive souls. Everything becomes precious that is fashioned by it or for it.

These truths being so easy to grasp, and so pleasant to confirm in practice, of what are you afraid? How, besides, can you possibly be afraid of a man of feeling whose love allows him no happiness unless it be yours? That is now the only vow I am bound to: I shall sacrifice everything to it, except the feeling by which it is inspired. And even this feeling, if you consent to share it, you will dispose of as you choose. But let us no longer suffer it to separate us, when it ought to bring us together. If the friendship you have offered me is any more than an empty word; if, as you told me yesterday, it is the tenderest feeling known to your heart; let that feeling then arbitrate between us, and I shall not dispute its decision. But if it is to pass judgement upon love, it must allow love a hearing; to refuse would be an injustice, and friendship is never unjust.

A second meeting would not be more difficult to arrange than was the first; chance may again furnish an opportunity; you yourself might indicate a suitable moment. I should like to think that I am wrong; would you not prefer to subdue me than to struggle against me, and can you doubt my docility? If that importunate third party had not arrived to interrupt us, perhaps I should already be entirely converted to your opinion; who knows how far your power may extend?

Shall I tell you? Sometimes your unconquerable supremacy, to which I yield without daring to consider its scope, your irresistible charm, which makes you empress of my thoughts and actions alike, make me afraid for myself. Alas, the interview I ask for is perhaps of more danger to me than you! Afterwards it may be that, chained to my promises, I shall find myself reduced to being consumed by a love that I know will never die, without the right even to implore your help! Ah, Madame, for pity's sake do not abuse your power! But then – if it makes you happier, if it makes me seem worthier of you, that alone will console me for any amount of suffering! Yes, I know. To speak to you again would be to give you more powerful weapons against me; it would be to surrender myself more completely to your will. It is safer to defend myself against your letters; they are of course your own pronouncements, but you are not there to give them authority. Yet the pleasure it will be to hear you speak makes me willing to brave the danger. At least I shall have the satisfaction of having done everything for you, even against my own interest, and my sacrifices shall be part of my homage. I shall be only too fortunate if I can prove to you in the thousand different ways I feel it that, without excepting myself, you are and will always be what is dearest to my heart.

Château de —
23 September 17 —

LETTER 84: *The Vicomte de Valmont to Cécile Volanges*

You saw how everything went against us yesterday. I was unable the whole day to give you the letter I had for you; I do not know whether I shall find it any easier today. I am afraid of compromising you by my efforts, should they be more eager than discreet. I should never forgive myself for an imprudence which would be fatal to you and in making you unhappy forever, throw my friend into despair. I know, none the less, the impatience of love; I know how painful it must be, in your situation, to experience any delay in receiving the only consolation you can hope for at the moment. By dint of constant reflection upon ways and means of removing the obstacles in our path, I have found one which will be easy of execution if you are willing to devote some pains to it.

I seem to have noticed that the key to the door of your room, which gives on to the corridor, is always kept upon your mamma's mantelpiece. With that key in our possession everything would be easy, as you will agree; but even without it, I can procure you a duplicate which will serve just as well. To do so it will be sufficient for me to have the original at my disposal for not longer than an hour or two. You will have no difficulty in finding an opportunity to remove it, and in case it is seen to be missing, I enclose with this a key of mine which resembles it enough for the difference not to be discovered, unless it is tried in the lock: and no one will do that. Only be sure that you attach a faded blue ribbon to it like the one that is tied to yours.

You must try to have the key by tomorrow, or the day after tomorrow at breakfast-time. It will be much easier for you to give it to me then, and you will be able to return it to its place before evening, the time when your mamma is most likely to give it her attention. I shall be able to give it back to you at dinner, if we can come to a suitable understanding about this.

You know that when we leave the drawing-room for the dining-room it is always Madame de Rosemonde who comes last. I shall give her my arm. You have only to be a little longer than usual in putting away your tapestry, or else to drop something, so as to remain behind. You will then find it easy to take the key from me – I shall be careful to hold it behind my back. You must not forget, as soon as you have the key, to go over to my old aunt with some show of affection. If by any chance you drop the key, you will not be disconcerted; I shall pretend that it was I who did so, and you may rely upon me absolutely to carry it off.

This little trick is justified by the small confidence you seem to have in your mamma, and the very severe measures she has taken against you. Apart from that, it is the only means by which you can continue to receive Danceny's letters and send him yours; all others are really too dangerous and might, in betraying you both, leave you without resource, so that my prudence as a friend cannot allow you to make any further use of them.

Once we are in possession of the key, there will still be a few precautions to take against the noise made by the door and the lock: but that will be very easy. Under the same cupboard in which I put your writing paper you will find some oil and a feather. You will, some time when you are alone, go to your room and take the opportunity to oil the lock and hinges. Your only care must be not to leave any stains as evidence against you. You must also wait until nightfall, because, if this is done as cleverly as you are capable of doing it, no traces will appear the following morning.

If, however, anything is noticed, do not hesitate to say that one of the servants was responsible. In this case it will be necessary to specify a time and even what he said to you: as, for example, that he was taking precautions against rust and was attending in this way to all the locks that were not ordinarily in use; for, as you must see, it is not very likely that you would have witnessed the business without asking for an explanation. It is these little details that give verisimilitude to a lie, and verisimilitude that ensures that there will be no consequences, since it deprives people of the desire to verify what they are told.

When you have read this letter, please re-read it and even think about it – in the first place because, to do anything well, one must always be thoroughly prepared; then to make sure that I have left nothing out. I am little accustomed to using cunning on my own behalf, and I am not much practised in it. It has taken nothing less than my keen friendship for Danceny, and the interest you arouse in me, to make me decide upon employing such methods, however innocent they may be. I detest everything which savours of deception: that, in brief, is my character. But I have been so touched by your misfortunes that I will attempt anything to mitigate them.

As you may well imagine, once communication is established between us, it will be much easier for me to arrange, on your and Danceny's behalf, the meeting he desires. Do not, however, tell him anything of this as yet. You will only increase his impatience, and the time to satisfy it has not yet quite come. You owe it to him, I think, to allay rather than to sharpen his anxieties. But in this matter I rely upon your delicacy. Good-bye, my dear pupil: for you are my pupil, you know. I hope you will like your tutor a little, above all that you will be guided by him: you will not regret it. Your happiness is my concern, and you may be certain that in it I shall find my own.

24 September 17 —

LETTER 85: *The Marquise de Merteuil to the Vicomte de Valmont*

Now you may set your mind at rest; now, above all, you may do me justice. Listen, and never again put me on a par with other women. I have brought my adventure with Prévan to a conclusion; *to a conclusion!* Do you quite understand what that means? Now you may judge which of us, he or I, will be able to boast. The story will not be as amusing as was the event, but then it would be unfair if you, who have done nothing in this affair but argue, were to derive as much pleasure from it as I, who have given it all my time and energy.

However, if you are planning some great *coup*, if you have some enterprise in hand in which Prévan is to figure as the dangerous rival, now is the time. He leaves the field to you, for a while at least. He will perhaps never recover at all from the blow I have dealt him.

How lucky you are to have me for a friend! I am the good fairy in your story. You languish far from the beauty who has engaged your heart; I say the word and you are again at her side. You want to be revenged upon a woman who has injured you; I find the weak spot where the blow must fall, and deliver her up to your tender mercies. Finally, when you have to remove a formidable opponent from the lists, it is again I you invoke in your prayers, and I who fulfil your wishes. Indeed, if you do not spend the rest of your life giving me thanks I shall think you ungrateful. But I must return to my adventure and begin from the beginning.

The hint of a rendezvous I had made so loudly at the exit of the Opera[1] was understood, as I had hoped it would be. Prévan was

1. See Letter 74.

there; and when the Maréchale said politely that she congratulated herself upon seeing him twice in succession at one of her evenings, he took care to reply that since Tuesday night he had put off a hundred engagements so as to be free to come. (A word to the wise is enough!) Since, however, I wished to be more certain whether or not I was indeed the object of this flattering impatience, I decided I would force the new suitor to make a choice between me and his ruling passion. I announced that I would not sit down to cards: and, as it happened, he too discovered a hundred excuses for not playing, so that it was over lansquenet[1] that I scored my first triumph.

I took possession of the Bishop of — to talk to, choosing him because of his friendship with the hero of the day, whom I wished to afford every facility of approach. I was, besides, very glad to have a respectable witness to vouch, if need be, for my words and deeds. My plan succeeded.

After the customary generalities Prévan, who soon took control of the conversation, gave it a succession of different turns to see which would please me. I rejected sentiment as having no faith in it; gaiety I checked with gravity because it seemed to me too frivolous for a beginning. He was reduced to tactful friendship, and it was under this faded old flag that we joined battle.

The Bishop did not go down to supper; Prévan accordingly gave me his arm, and was of course placed beside me at table. I must give him his due; with great skill he kept up our private conversation while appearing to give all his attention to the general one, of which indeed he seemed to be bearing the entire burden.

At dessert it was mentioned that a new play was to be performed at the Français the following Monday. I expressed a regret that I had not my box for that night. He offered me his, which to begin with I refused, as one does. To which he replied amusingly enough that I had not understood him; that he would most certainly not have sacrificed his box to someone he did not know, and that he meant simply to inform me that it was at Madame the Maréchale's disposal. She fell in with the joke, and I accepted.

We returned to the drawing-room, whereupon, as you will readily believe, he requested a seat in the box for himself; and since

1. [A card game of chance. *Translator's note.*]

the Maréchale, who is very kindly disposed towards him, promised
him one 'if he were good', he made this an occasion for one of those
conversations with a double meaning, his talent for which you have
yourself extolled. In fact, he went down on his knees like an
obedient child – as he put it – and while ostensibly he was asking
her what she meant and beseeching her to explain, he said a great
many flattering and quite tender things, which I was able without
difficulty to apply to myself. Since several of the company had not
returned to cards after supper, conversation became more general
and less interesting: but our eyes spoke volumes. I say our eyes.
I should have said his, for in mine he could read only one meaning:
surprise. He must have thought he had astounded me and that I
was excessively taken up with the prodigious effect he had wrought
upon me. I left him, I think, very satisfied: I was not less so myself.

The following Monday I went to the Français as arranged. I
know you are interested in literary matters, but I can tell you nothing about the performance except that Prévan is a marvellously
talented flatterer and that the piece was a failure: that is all I was able
to learn. I was sorry to see the evening come to an end, I had
enjoyed it so much, and to prolong it I invited the Maréchale to
supper with me: this provided me with a pretext for putting the
same proposal to my amiable cavalier, who asked only for time
enough to fly to the Comtesses de B——[1] and make his excuses there.
The sound of that name roused all my resentment. I saw clearly
that he was going to begin making confidences. I remembered your
wise advice, and resolved ... to continue the adventure. I was
certain I would cure him of such dangerous indiscretions in future.

A stranger among my friends, of whom there were not many
present that evening, he was obliged to pay me all the customary
attentions; thus, when he went into supper, he offered me his arm.
Accepting it, I was wicked enough to make my hand tremble
lightly in his and, as we walked, to lower my eyes and quicken my
breathing, as if in presentiment of my defeat and awe of my conqueror. He was so quick to notice this that in a trice he had
treacherously changed his tone and demeanour. He had been gallant, he became tender. Not that he changed the substance of his
remarks: circumstances saw to that. But his looks became less

1. See Letter 70.

lively and more caressing, the inflection of his voice more soft; his smile no longer calculated, but contented. Finally, having removed the sting by degrees from his sallies, he turned quips into compliments. I ask you: could you have done better yourself?

As for me, I grew pensive, so much so that the company was obliged to notice it; and when they rallied me I was clever enough to make a very poor excuse, throwing Prévan a quick, but timid and bashful glance calculated to make him believe that it was only he I was afraid might guess the cause of my uneasiness.

After supper the Maréchale began one of the stories she is always telling and I took the opportunity of arranging myself on the ottoman in that attitude of abandon which befits a mood of reverie. I was not averse to Prévan seeing me like this, and in fact he honoured me with his most particular attention. As you may imagine, my timid glances did not dare to seek those of my conqueror; but, directed towards him in a humble way, they soon told me that I had succeeded in the effect I wished to produce. I had still to persuade him that I shared his feelings. Accordingly, when the Maréchale announced that she was leaving, I exclaimed in soft and tender tones: 'Oh, lord! I was so comfortable there!' I got up, all the same; but before we parted I asked the Maréchale what her plans were so that I could tell her mine and make it known that I should be at home not the day after, but the next. After this everyone took their leave.

I then sat down to reflect. I had no doubt that Prévan would make the most of the sort of rendezvous I had given him, that he would arrive early enough to find me alone, and that the attack would be a fierce one. But I was quite sure, too, that, aware of my reputation, he would not treat me with that indifference which men display, if they ever do, only towards adventuresses and boobies; I foresaw certain success if he should so much as pronounce the word 'love' – and, especially if he should make any attempt at obtaining it from me.

How easy it is to deal with your *men of principle*! A muddle-headed lover will sometimes disconcert you with his timidity, or embarrass you with his furious transports; he is in a fever, which like any other has its agues and its ardours and sometimes varies its symptoms. But your well-planned advances are too predictable!

Manner of arrival, behaviour, attitude, choice of language – I knew about them all the evening before. I shall not therefore give you the details of our conversation, which you may easily supply for yourself. Note only that by a pretence of reluctance I did all I could to help him – offering embarrassment to give him time to speak; poor arguments to be refuted; fear and distrust to call up his protestations together with that perpetual refrain of 'I ask for no more than a word'; silence in reply to the latter, which it seemed would have him wait for what he wanted, only to make him desire it the more; and all the while a hand taken a hundred times, and a hundred times withdrawn, but never refused. One could spend a whole day at this: we continued for one mortal hour and would perhaps be at it still were it not for the carriage we heard entering my courtyard. This fortunate accident quite understandably made him more eager in his entreaties; and knowing that I was now safe from surprise, I prepared myself with a long-drawn sigh, and yielded up the precious word. Someone was announced, and shortly afterwards we were in the midst of a fairly numerous company.

Prévan asked whether he could come the following morning, and I agreed: but, with an eye to my defences, I ordered my maid to remain in my bedroom throughout the period of his visit. As you know, everything that happens in my dressing-room is visible from there, and it was in my dressing-room that I received him. We talked frankly, and since we had but one desire in common, soon came to an agreement. But it was necessary to get rid of an unwelcome spectator; and here I was ready for him.

Painting him an imaginary picture of my domestic life, I had no difficulty in persuading him that we should never have a moment's liberty; that the opportunity we had enjoyed the day before could only be regarded as a kind of miracle; and that, even so, the risks involved had been too great, since at any moment anyone could have entered the drawing-room. I did not fail to add that my domestic arrangements were thus established because they had never till now been in my way; at the same time I insisted that it would be impossible to change them without compromising myself in the eyes of my household. He tried to look dejected, to work himself up into a bad temper, to tell me that I could not love him very much; and you can imagine how touched I was by all this! So as to strike the decisive blow, I summoned tears to my support. It was exactly like 'Zaïre, are you weeping?' The power he imagined he had over me, and the hopes he had conceived of ruining me at his pleasure, did duty with him for all Orosmane's love.[1]

This dramatic scene concluded, we returned to business. Daytime being out of the question, we considered the possibilities of night. But my porter proved to be an insurmountable obstacle, and I was not willing that we should try to bribe him. The little garden gate was suggested, but this I had foreseen, and I created a dog which, although docile and quiet during the day, became a veritable demon at night. The readiness with which I supplied all these details was exactly the thing to provoke him to recklessness, and when he came to suggest the most ridiculous expedient possible, it was this that I agreed to.

He said first that his manservant was as trustworthy as he was himself. This was no lie: I trusted one quite as much as the other. I was to give a large supper at my house: he would be there, and would choose a convenient moment to leave by himself. The clever confidant would call his carriage and open the door; and he, Prévan, instead of getting in, would adroitly make away. His coachman would notice nothing. Thus, while everyone would think he had left, he would still be in the house, and it was merely a question of knowing how he might reach my room. I must confess that my difficulty at first was to think of weak enough objections to this plan, so that he could appear to be destroying them. He quoted, in reply, instances of its previous use. To hear him talk, one would have thought nothing was more commonplace. He himself had employed it a great deal, more often indeed – because it was less dangerous – than any other.

Overborne by so much unchallengeable authority, I admitted candidly that I did indeed have a concealed staircase which emerged very near my boudoir. I could leave the key in the door, and he could lock himself in and wait, without much risk, until my women had left me. Then, in order to make my consent more credible, I withdrew it a moment later, and refused to grant it again

1. [Voltaire's tragedy *Zaïre* concerns the ill-fated love of the Sultan Orosmane for his captive Christian princess Zaïre. 'Zaïre, are you weeping?' is a famous set-speech in the play. *Translator's note*.]

except on condition of perfect obedience and discretion. . . . Ah, such discretion! In short I was quite willing to prove my love without satisfying his.

His exit, I have forgotten to tell you, was to be made through the little garden gate. It was simply a question of waiting till daybreak, after which time Cerberus would utter no sound. Not a soul passes by at that hour, and at that hour people are soundest asleep. In case you are surprised at this string of feeble arguments don't forget the nature of the situation between us. What need had we to do better? His whole aim was that everything should be discovered, whereas I was quite certain that it would not. The day was fixed for the next but one.

Note well that the whole affair had been arranged without any-one having seen Prévan alone with me. I meet him at supper at the house of a friend; he offers her his box for a new play, and I accept a place in it. During the performance, and in front of Prévan, I invite this woman to supper: it is almost impossible to avoid sug-gesting that he join us. He accepts, and two days later pays me the visit that custom demands. True, he comes to see me again, the following morning; but, apart from the fact that morning visits are no longer exceptional, it is for no one but me to decide that this one is a little excessive; and in fact I later put him back among that class of people who are less intimate with me by a written invitation to a formal supper. Well might I say with Annette:[1] 'There is no more to it than that, really!'

When the fateful day arrived, the day upon which I was to lose my virtue and my reputation, I gave my faithful Victoire her in-structions, and she carried them out as you shall see.

Evening came. There were already a great many people with me when Prévan was announced. I received him with marked polite-ness, emphasizing the small extent of my intimacy with him, and put him to play at the Maréchale's table, since she was the person through whom I had made his acquaintance. The only incident of the evening concerned a little note which my discreet lover found it possible to put into my hands, and which I immediately burnt as is my custom. In it he declared that I could count on him; this vital phrase was, however, buried in a mass of those parasite words,

1. [Heroine of *Annette et Lubin*, a comic opera by Favart. *Translator's note.*]

love, happiness, etc., which invariably proliferate on this sort of occasion.

At midnight, play having come to an end, I suggested a short *macédoine*.[1] My twofold intention was to provide Prévan with a favourable opportunity to escape, and at the same time to make sure he would be noticed, which could scarcely fail to happen considering his renown as a gambler. I was content, too, to have it remembered when necessary that I had not been anxious to be left alone.

Play lasted longer than I expected. The devil tempted me – and I succumbed to the temptation – to go and console my impatient prisoner. I was thus on the path to destruction when it occurred to me that, once I had completely surrendered, I should no longer have sufficient power over him to keep him to that appearance of decency so necessary to my plans. I found the strength to resist: I turned back and took my place again, not altogether without annoyance, at the endless card-game. Finally, however, it did come to an end and everyone left. I rang for my maids, undressed with all speed, and sent them away too.

Can you see me, Vicomte, in my simple negligee, approaching with timid and circumspect tread, opening the door with an uncertain hand to my conqueror? He saw me. Lightning could not have struck quicker. What more shall I tell you? I was vanquished, utterly vanquished, before I had been able to say a word to stop him or to defend myself. He wanted us next to dispose ourselves more comfortably, and more suitably to the circumstances. He cursed his clothes, which, he said, put him at a disadvantage. He wanted us to fight on equal terms. But my extreme timidity opposed the project, and my tender caresses left him no time to carry it out. He occupied himself with other things.

Possessed now of twice his former rights, he revived his claims. 'Listen,' I said then. 'So far I have given you an amusing enough story to tell the two Comtesses de B— and a thousand others: but I am curious to know what conclusion you will find to put to it.' As I spoke I rang as hard as I could. Now it was I who had the advantage, and my action was more effective than anything he could

1. Some readers may not, perhaps, be aware that a *macédoine* is a medley of several games of chance from among which each player has the right to choose when it is his turn to deal. It is one of the novelties of our day.

say. He had done no more than stammer before I heard Victoire come running, calling to the servants she had kept with her as I had commanded. At this point, raising my voice, and in my most regal tone I continued: 'You will leave, Monsieur, and never appear in my presence again.' At which a crowd of my servants entered the room.

Poor Prévan lost his head, and suspecting an ambush in what was at bottom no more than a joke, resorted to his sword – unfortunately for him, since my brave and vigorous *valet de chambre* seized him bodily and threw him to the floor. This, I must confess, put me into mortal terror. I shouted to them both to stop, and ordered all the servants to let Prévan alone, provided they made sure that he left the house. They obeyed: but there was great wagging of tongues. They were most indignant that anyone should fail in respect to *their virtuous mistress*. They accompanied the unfortunate cavalier out in a body with much noise and crying of scandal, just as I wished. Only Victoire remained behind. We spent the interval in putting my disordered bed to rights.

The servants came up again, still in an uproar, and I, still *very much upset*, asked them by what lucky chance it had happened that they were awake. Victoire told me that she had given supper to two of her friends, that they had spent the evening with her – in short all that had been agreed upon between us. I thanked them all and dismissed them, ordering one of them, however, to fetch my doctor immediately. It seemed to me that I ought to fear for the consequences of the terrible shock I had received; and this was a certain means of ensuring circulation and celebrity for the news.

The doctor at length came, felt very sorry for me, and prescribed rest. I gave further orders to Victoire to go out early in the morning, perambulate the neighbourhood, and talk.

Everything succeeded so well that before midday, as soon in fact as my curtains were drawn, my devoted neighbour was at my bedside to hear the true details of my ghastly adventure. I was obliged to join with her for an hour in deploring the corruption of the age. Shortly after, I received a note from the Maréchale, which I enclose. Lastly, just before five o'clock, to my great astonishment, I saw Monsieur ——[1] arrive. He had come, he said, to offer

1. Commanding Officer of the regiment in which Monsieur de Prévan served.

his excuses for the fact that one of his officers could have behaved so insultingly. It was not till he dined with the Maréchale that he had learnt of the affair, and he had forthwith issued orders for Prévan to be conveyed to prison. I asked for a pardon, but he refused. Then it occurred to me that, as an accomplice, I ought to pass like sentence upon myself, and at least confine myself strictly to quarters. I ordered my doors to be shut and announced that I was unwell.

It is to my solitude that you owe this long letter. I shall now write one to Madame de Volanges, who is sure to read it out in company, whereupon you will hear the story again as adapted for publication.

I was forgetting to tell you that Belleroche is outraged and is absolutely determined to challenge Prévan. Poor fellow! Fortunately there will be time enough to cool him down. Meanwhile I must rest: I am tired out with writing. Good-bye, Vicomte.

Château de —
25 September 17 —, evening

LETTER 86: *The Maréchale de — to the Marquise de Merteuil (note attached to the preceding letter)*

GOOD God! What is this I hear, my dear Madame? Can our little Prévan possibly have committed such abominations? And against you, too! To what dangers one is exposed! One shall never be safe, after all, in one's own home! Truly, such goings-on console me for being old. What nothing could console me for, however, is that I have been in some part the cause of your having received this monster into your house. I assure you that if what I am told is true he shall never again set foot over my threshold; and that is the course all decent people will take with him if they know their duty.

I was told that you were feeling very ill and I am anxious for your health. Please give me better news of yourself, or send one of your maids if you cannot do so yourself. I ask only for a word to set my mind at rest. I would have come immediately to your house this morning were it not for the baths which my doctor will not suffer me to interrupt; and this afternoon I must go back to Versailles on my nephew's business.

Good-bye, my dear Madame. You may always count upon my most sincere friendship.

Paris
25 September 17 —

LETTER 87: *The Marquise de Merteuil to Madame de Volanges*

I AM writing to you from bed, my dear good friend. A most disagreeable and utterly unforeseen incident has made me ill with shock and mortification.

Not, of course, that I have anything upon my conscience: but it is always, for a respectable woman, and one who maintains the modesty becoming to her sex, so painful to have the public eye fixed upon her, that I should give anything in the world to have avoided this unhappy experience, and I am not sure yet whether I shall not remove to the country to wait until it is all forgotten. This is what happened.

At the Maréchale de —'s I met a Monsieur de Prévan, whom you probably know by name and who was not known to me in any other wise. Meeting him where I did, I was quite justified, it seems to me, in believing him to be a man of breeding. He is, as to his person, quite presentable and appeared not to lack a certain wit. By chance, and because I was bored with cards, I found myself alone with him and the Bishop of —, while everybody else was occupied at lansquenet. The three of us talked till supper-time. At table some discussion of a new piece was the occasion for his offering his box to the Maréchale, who accepted it; and it was agreed that I should have a place in it. This was for last Monday, at the Français. Since the Maréchale was coming to supper with me after the performance, I suggested to the gentleman that he accompany her, and he came. Two days later he paid me a visit which passed in polite conversation and gave rise to nothing at all remarkable. The following day he came to see me in the morning, which did indeed appear to me a little untoward: but I thought that instead of making him aware of it by the manner in which I received him, I ought rather to let him know by some act of formality that we were not yet as intimately acquainted as he seemed to think. To this end I sent him, that same day, a very cold and ceremonious invitation to the supper I gave the day before yesterday. I addressed him not four times during the whole evening, and he, on his part, left as soon as play was over. You will agree that nothing so far would seem to have been leading up to an incident. When the tables had broken up we had a *macédoine* which lasted till nearly two o'clcck, and at length I went to bed.

It was at least half an hour after my maids had left me that I heard a noise in my room. I opened the curtains in a great fright, and saw a man come in by the door that led from my boudoir. I uttered a piercing scream. In the glow of my night-light I recognized this Monsieur de Prévan. He had the unspeakable effrontery to tell me not to be alarmed, said he would explain his mysterious behaviour, and begged me to make no noise. As he spoke he lit a candle. I was paralysed to the point of not being able to speak. His air of ease and confidence I think petrified me still more. But he had not said two words before I had penetrated the so-called mystery. My only response was, as you can imagine, to hang upon the bell-rope.

By unbelievable good fortune all my servants were spending the evening with one of my maids and had not yet gone to bed. My chambermaid, having answered my call, and hearing me speak heatedly to someone, took alarm and summoned all the others. I leave you to imagine the outcry! My servants were furious; at one moment I thought my *valet de chambre* would kill Prévan. I confess that, at the time, I was very glad to have my supporters rally round me; thinking of it now, I had rather only my chambermaid had come. She would have served my purpose, and I should perhaps have avoided this distressing scandal.

As it is, the noise awoke my neighbours, the servants have talked, and since yesterday the affair has been the gossip of Paris. Monsieur de Prévan is in prison by order of the commanding officer of his regiment, who was so civil as to call on me, to offer his excuses he said. The imprisonment is going to make even more of a sensation: but I was not able to have it otherwise. Town and court have begun to leave their names at my door, which I have closed to everyone. The few people I see tell me that justice is being done me and that public indignation is running high against Monsieur de Prévan. Of course he deserves it, but that does not make the incident any the less disagreeable.

Moreover, the man surely has friends, friends who are bound to bear malice: who knows, who can possibly know what they will invent to say against me? Heavens, how unfortunate a young woman is! She has achieved nothing when she has put herself beyond criticism; she must protect herself from calumny, too.

Tell me, please, what you would have done, what you would do in my place; in short, all your thoughts on the subject. It is always from you that I have received the sweetest consolation and the best advice; it is from you, too, that I like best to receive it. Good-bye, my dear and good friend. You know the feelings by which I am forever attached to you. My love to your charming daughter.

Paris
26 September 17 —

PART THREE

LETTER 88: *Cécile Volanges to the Vicomte de Valmont*

IN spite of the pleasure it is to me, Monsieur, to receive Monsieur the Chevalier Danceny's letters, and although it is no less my wish than his that we should meet again without any hindrance, I have still not dared to do as you suggest. To begin with, it is too dangerous. The key you wish me to exchange for the other one does indeed look very much like it: but there is still a difference, and Mamma looks at everything and notices everything. What is more, though the key has not been used since we have been here, it would need no more than some slight mischance – and if anything were noticed I should be lost forever. And then, it seems to me, too, that it would be a very bad thing to do; to make a duplicate key like that is really going too far! True, it is you who will be so kind as to be responsible for it; but in spite of that, if it were found out, the fault and the blame would be no less mine than yours, since it would be for me that you had done it. Lastly, on two occasions I did decide to try and remove the key, and I am sure it would have been very easy had it been anything else. But, I don't know why, I began to tremble and never had the courage to do it. I think, therefore, we had better leave things as they are.

If you will kindly continue to be as obliging as you have been up to now, you will certainly always find a means of delivering letters to me. Even the last one, if it had not been for the unfortunate circumstance that obliged you to turn round suddenly just at that moment, would have been very easy for us. I am quite aware that you cannot, as I do, think of nothing else but all this; but I prefer to be patient and not to risk so much. I am sure Monsieur Danceny would say the same, since every time he has wanted something which was too difficult for me, he has always agreed to do without it.

With this letter, Monsieur, I shall return you your own, Monsieur Danceny's, and your key. I am none the less grateful for all your kindness, and I beg you to continue in it towards me. It is quite true that I am very unhappy and that without you I should be much more so. But, after all, she is my mother. One must really be patient. And provided that Monsieur Danceny still loves me and you do not forsake me, perhaps a happier time will come.

I have the honour to be, Monsieur, with the deepest gratitude, your very humble and obedient servant.

———

26 September 17 —

LETTER 89: *The Vicomte de Valmont to the Chevalier Danceny*

IF, my dear fellow, your affairs are still not making as much progress as you would like, it is not I who am entirely to blame. I have more than one obstacle to overcome here. Madame de Volanges' vigilance and strictness are not the only ones; your young friend has also thrown a few in my way. Whether she is not eager enough or merely too timid, she does not always do as I advise, although it seems to me that I know better than she what has to be done.

I had thought of a simple, convenient, and safe method of delivering your letters to her which would have made it easier, too, to arrange the interview you desire. But I was not able to persuade her to make use of it. I am the more sorry because I see no other way of bringing you together, and because, even where your correspondence is concerned, I am in constant fear that all three of us will be compromised. Now, you know that I do not want to expose either myself or you to any risk of that.

I should really, however, be sorry were your little friend's lack of confidence in me to prevent my being useful to you. You would perhaps do well to write to her about it. Think it over. It is for you alone to decide; for it is not enough to help one's friends, one must help them in their own way. This might also be yet another opportunity to make sure of her feelings for you; for the woman who maintains a will of her own is not as much in love as she says she is.

It is not that I suspect your mistress of inconstancy. But she is very young. She is very much afraid of her mother, whose only object, as you know, is to spite you. And perhaps it would be dangerous to let too long a time go by without reminding her of your existence. Do not, however, let what I have said give you any anxiety. I have, at bottom, no grounds for misgiving; this is purely friendly solicitude.

I shall not write at greater length as I have really not a little business of my own to attend to. I have made no further progress than you have: but I am as much in love, and that is some consolation. Should I have no success myself, yet succeed in being useful to you, I shall think my time well spent. Good-bye, my dear fellow.

Château de —
26 September 17 —

LETTER 90: *The Présidente de Tourvel to the Vicomte de Valmont*

I AM very anxious, Monsieur, that this letter should cause you no pain; or, if it must, that your pain will be lessened by that which I feel in writing it. You must know me well enough now to be quite certain that I have no wish to distress you. But then you yourself surely have no wish to plunge me in everlasting despair? I beg you, therefore, in the name of the tender friendship I have promised you, in the name, too, of the feelings, more lively than mine, perhaps, but certainly not more sincere, that you have for me, let us not see each other again. Go away. And until you do, let us avoid those private and excessively dangerous conversations, during which some extraordinary power compels me, without my being able to say what I want to say, to spend my time listening to what I have no business to hear.

Only yesterday, when you came to join me in the park, my sole intention was to tell you what I am telling you now; yet what did I do? Talk about your love . . . your love, to which I ought never to make the slightest response! Ah, for pity's sake, go away from here.

Do not be afraid that absence will ever change my feelings for you. How shall I succeed in overcoming them when I no longer have the courage to fight them? You see, I tell you everything. I am less afraid of admitting my weakness than of surrendering to it. But the power I have lost over my feelings I shall not lose over my actions. No, I shall not, I am resolved, though it cost me my life.

Alas! The time is not long past when I felt quite certain I should never have such battles to fight. I congratulated myself upon my security; I was, perhaps, too vain of it. Heaven has punished, has cruelly punished my pride. But because God is all-merciful at the very moment even of His striking us down, He has given me warning of a fall; and I would be doubly culpable if I continued to be wanting in prudence when I am already aware that I have lost my strength.

You have told me a hundred times that you would not buy your happiness at the price of my tears. Ah, let us not talk of happiness; let me only recover my peace of mind!

Think how much stronger will be the claims you acquire to my heart if you grant me this request: claims founded on virtue, which I shall never have to question. How I shall delight in my gratitude! To you I shall owe the pleasure of enjoying a delicious feeling without fear of remorse. As things are, on the contrary, I am terrified of my feelings and of my thoughts, equally afraid whether I consider you or myself. The very idea of you alarms me. Though I cannot escape it, I fight it. I cannot banish it, but I repel it.

Would it not be better for both of us to bring this state of trouble and anxiety to an end? Will you, who have always had a sensitive nature which even in the midst of a life of error inclined you to virtue, will you not have some consideration for my painful situation, will you not listen to my pleas? These violent emotions will give way to a calmer, though not less tender interest in you: then, restored to well-being by your kindnesses, I shall hold life dear again and shall say with all the joy in my heart: this peace that I feel, I owe to my friend.

In submitting to a few trifling privations, which I do not impose upon but only ask from you, do you think you will be paying too dear for an end to my torments? Oh, if to make you happy I had only to consent to unhappiness for myself, believe me I should not hesitate for a moment. . . . But to be guilty! . . . No, my friend, no, I had rather die a thousand deaths.

Already attacked by shame, the precursor of remorse, I am afraid both of others and of myself. I blush in company, in solitude I tremble. My life offers nothing now but pain. I shall have no peace unless you give me your consent. My most praiseworthy resolutions are not enough to reassure me. I formed one yesterday, yet I spent last night in tears.

You see before you your friend, the one you love, confused, suppliant, asking you for peace and innocence. Ah, God! Were it not for you, would she be reduced to making so humiliating a request? I do not blame you for anything. I know too well from my own experience how difficult it is to resist an imperious feeling. To appeal is not to complain. Do from generosity what I do out of duty, and to all the feelings you have inspired in me will be added my eternal gratitude. Good-bye, Monsieur, good-bye.

27 September 17—

LETTER 91 : *The Vicomte de Valmont to the Présidente de Tourvel*

YOUR letter has so dismayed me, Madame, that I still do not know how I shall be able to reply to it. Of course, if the choice must be between your happiness and mine, it is for me to make the sacrifice and I shall do so without hesitation; but it seems to me that such important matters ought first to be discussed and understood, and how can we do so if we are neither to speak to nor see each other again?

Really! When the noblest of feelings has brought us together, will it do for some foolish fear to separate us, perhaps forever? In vain shall tender friendship, ardent love, demand their rights. Their voices shall not be heard. And why? What is this pressing danger that threatens you? Ah, believe me, your fears, so lightly conceived, are already, it seems to me, strong enough guarantees of your safety.

Permit me to tell you that again I notice traces of the unfavourable impression you were once given of me. No woman trembles before the man she respects. Least of all will she banish from her side one she has judged worthy of her friendship. It is the dangerous man she fears and flies from.

Yet who was ever more respectful and more submissive than I? I am already, as you see, careful what I say. I no longer allow myself those sweet epithets, so dear to my heart, names I shall never cease to call you in secret. I am no longer the faithful and unhappy lover, accepting advice from a tender and sympathetic friend. I am the accused before his judge, the slave before his master. My new roles, of course, impose new duties; I undertake to fulfil them all. Hear what I have to say, and if you condemn me I shall submit and leave. I promise even more; would you rather be the despot who judges without a hearing? Do you feel you have the courage to be unjust? Command, and I shall still obey.

But let me hear your judgement or your orders come from your lips 'Why?' you will perhaps ask in turn. Ah, if you ask that question you understand very little of love or of my heart! Will it mean nothing to me to see you once more? Ah! When you find how despair weighs upon my soul perhaps your look of comfort will keep it from succumbing. And then, if I must renounce love and friendship, for which alone I exist, at least you will see what you have done, and your pity will remain with me: a poor recompense, for which, it seems to me, I am prepared to pay dearly, dearly enough to hope to obtain it even though I do not deserve it.

So you are going to send me away from you? Are you willing, then, that we should become strangers to each other? Willing, did I say? You want it to happen; and while you assure me that my absence will not alter your feelings, you hasten my departure the sooner to set about destroying them.

You already speak of replacing them with gratitude. A feeling that a stranger might obtain from you for some trifling service, an enemy, even, in ceasing to injure you: that is all you have to offer me! And you want my heart to content itself with that! Ask your own: if a lover, if a friend were to come one day to tell you of his gratitude, would you not say indignantly: go away, you are ungrateful?

I shall say no more, but beg your indulgence for what I have said. Forgive the expression of a grief which owes its being to you. It will make no difference to my perfect submission. But I beseech you in my turn, in the name of those sweet feelings which you yourself invoke, do not refuse to hear me; and out of pity, if nothing else, for the mortal agony in which you have plunged me, do not defer the moment of doing so. Good-bye, Madame.

27 September 17 —, evening

LETTER 92: *The Chevalier Danceny to the Vicomte de Valmont*

OH, my dear friend! Your letter has frozen me with terror. Cécile . . . Oh, God! Is it possible? Cécile does not love me any more. Yes, I perceive that frightful truth through the veil your friendship has thrown over it. You meant to prepare me for the fatal blow; I thank you for your care, but is love ever to be deceived? It flies ahead of its interests; it does not learn, but divines its fate. I am no longer in doubt of mine. Speak to me without evasion: you can, and I beg you to do so. Tell me everything: what gave rise to your suspicions, and what confirmed them. The least detail is precious. Try, above all, to recall her words. One word instead of another can change a whole sentence; the same one sometimes has two meanings . . . . You can have been mistaken. Alas! I am still trying to comfort myself. What did she say to you? Does she blame me for anything? Does she not at least make excuses for herself? I should have foreseen this change in the difficulties that she has for some time found in everything. Love does not acknowledge so many obstacles.

What course should I take? What do you advise? Should I try to see her? Is that really impossible? Absence is so cruel, so fatal . . . and she has refused a means of seeing me! You do not tell me what it was. If there was too much danger involved, she knows that I would not want her to run any risks. On the other hand I know your prudence, and I cannot, to my misfortune, have anything but complete faith in it.

What shall I do now? What shall I say to her? If I betray my suspicions they will perhaps distress her, and if they are unjust how shall I ever forgive myself for having distressed her? If I hide them I am deceiving her, and I am incapable of deceiving her.

Oh, if she knew what I suffered, she would be touched by my pain. She is not without feeling, I know. She has an excellent heart, and I have a thousand proofs of her love. She is too timid, too easily embarrassed, but she is so young! And her mother treats her so badly! I shall write to her. I shall keep my head. I shall ask her only to leave everything to you. Even if she refuses again, she cannot at any rate be angry with me for asking; and perhaps she will agree.

To you, my friend, I offer a thousand apologies on her behalf and mine. I assure you she appreciates the value of your efforts, and she is grateful for them. It is not mistrust on her part, but timidity. Be indulgent: friendship can show no fairer face. Your friendship, I need not say, is very precious to me and I do not know how I can ever repay you for all that you are doing in my interest. Good-bye: I am going to write to her immediately.

I feel all my fears return. Who would have said that one day I should find it so difficult to write to her! Alas! Only yesterday it was my greatest joy.

Good-bye, my dear friend. Continue in your efforts for me, and pity my plight.

Paris
27 September 17 —

LETTER 93 : *The Chevalier Danceny to Cécile Volanges*

I CANNOT conceal how distressed I was to learn from Valmont of the lack of confidence you continue to display in him. You are not unaware that he is my friend and that he is the only person who can bring us together again. I should have thought these might have been considerations of sufficient weight with you: I am sorry to find that I was mistaken. May I hope at least that you will explain your motives? You will not discover further difficulties to prevent your doing so? Without your help I cannot solve the mystery of your conduct. I dare not doubt your love; you, too, would surely not dare to betray mine. Ah, Cécile! . . .

Is it really true that you have refused a means of seeing me? A *simple, convenient, and safe method*?[1] This is how you love me! So short an absence has completely changed your feelings. But why deceive me? Why tell me that you love me still, that you love me more than ever? Has your mamma, in robbing you of your love, robbed you of your honesty as well? If she has left you at least with some pity, you will not hear unmoved of the frightful torments you have caused me. Ah, if I were to die I should suffer less.

Tell me, is your heart irrevocably closed against me? Have you utterly forgotten me? Thanks to your refusal, I cannot tell when you will receive my appeals, or when you will reply to them. Valmont's friendship made our correspondence secure. But you, you did not want this. You find writing to me painful; you preferred not to do it often. No, I no longer believe in love, in honesty. Oh! what can I believe in, if Cécile has deceived me?

Answer me then! Is it true that you no longer love me? No, that is not possible. You are deluding yourself. You are maligning your heart. A passing fear, a moment's discouragement perhaps, but quickly banished by love: is that not so, my Cécile? Oh, no doubt I was wrong to accuse you. How happy I should be if I was wrong! How I should like to make you my most tender apologies, to atone for a moment's injustice with a lifetime of love!

Cécile, Cécile, have pity on me! Try to see me, take all the means at hand! See what absence can do! Fears, suspicions, even coldness perhaps! One look, one word, and we shall be happy. But there, how can I still be speaking of happiness, when it may be lost to me forever? Tortured by fear, cruelly hemmed in between unjust suspicions and an even more terrible truth, there is no thought I can take refuge in, I continue my existence only to suffer and to love you. Ah, Cécile! You have the power to make life dear to me; the first word you utter will signify the renewal of my happiness or certain and eternal despair.

Paris
27 September 17 —

1. Danceny does not know what it is. He is merely repeating Valmont's phrase.

LETTER 94: *Cécile Volanges to the Chevalier Danceny*

I CAN understand nothing of your letter, except the pain it gives me. What has Monsieur de Valmont told you, and what can have made you believe that I no longer love you? It would perhaps be very lucky for me if that were so, since I should certainly suffer less; and it is very hard, when I love you as I do, to find that you always think I am wrong, and instead of consoling me are always the cause yourself of the troubles that afflict me most. You think I am deceiving you, telling you what is not true! What a fine idea you must have of me! But if I were the liar you accuse me of being, what would my motives be? There is no doubt that, if I no longer loved you, I should only have to say so for everyone to approve. Unfortunately that is more than I can do – oh, that it should be for the sake of someone who shows me no consideration at all!

What have I done to make you so angry? I lacked the courage to remove the key, because I was afraid Mamma might notice it, and I should then be in even worse trouble than before – you, too, on my account; and then again because it seems to me it would have been wrong. But it was only Monsieur de Valmont who spoke to me about it: I could not possibly know whether you were in favour or not, since you knew nothing about it. Now that I know that you are, do you think I shall refuse to remove the key? I shall remove it tomorrow. Then we shall see what you have to say.

However much of a friend Monsieur de Valmont is to you, I think I love you quite as much as he does, to say the least; yet it is always he who is right and I who am wrong. I assure you I am very angry. It may be of no consequence to you, since you know that I always calm down immediately. But now that I am to have the key, I shall be able to see you whenever I choose to; and I assure you that I shall not choose to if you behave like this. I prefer the troubles I cause myself to those you cause me. Consider what you will do.

If you wanted to, how much we could love one another! And at least we would have to bear only the sufferings that others inflict on us! I assure you that if it were in my power you would never have cause to complain of me: but if you don't believe me, we shall always be unhappy, and it will not be my fault. I hope we shall soon be able to see each other, and then have no further need to plague each other as we do at present.

If I could have foreseen this, I should have removed the key immediately. But I really believed I was doing right. Don't, then, hold it against me, please. Don't be disheartened any longer, continue to love me as much as I love you, and I shall be very happy. Good-bye, my dear.

Château de —
28 September 17 —

LETTER 95: *Cécile Volanges to the Vicomte de Valmont*

PLEASE be so kind, Monsieur, as to send me back the key you gave me to put in the other one's place. Since everyone is in favour of my doing this, I must needs be too.

I do not know why you told Monsieur de Danceny that I no longer loved him. I do not believe I have ever given you occasion to think so; and it has given him great pain, and me too. I am well aware that you are his friend; but that is no reason for distressing him, or me for that matter. You will do me a great favour by telling him that the contrary is the case next time you write, and that you are certain of it; for it is in you that he places most confidence. As for me, when I say something and it is not believed, I do not know what to do next.

About the key you need have no fears. I remember perfectly all you recommended me to do in your letter. If, however, you still have the letter and are willing to give it back to me with the key, I promise you it will have all my attention. If you can do this tomorrow as we go into dinner, I shall give you the other key the day after tomorrow at breakfast, and you will return it to me in the same way as you let me have the first one. I should not like to leave it any later, since there would then be a greater risk of Mamma's noticing something.

Once you have the key, perhaps you will be good enough to make use of it for fetching my letters: in this way Monsieur

Danceny will more often have news of me. It is true that we shall have a much more convenient method than at present, but at first I was too afraid: please forgive me, and I hope you will continue to be no less obliging than you have been in the past. I shall always be very grateful for it.

I have the honour to be, Monsieur, your most humble and obedient servant.

———

28 September 17 —

LETTER 96: *The Vicomte de Valmont to the Marquise de Merteuil*

I DARE say that since your adventure you have daily expected my plaudits and compliments. I don't doubt that you have even been a little out of humour at my long silence. But can you blame me? I have always thought that the moment one no longer has anything but praise for a woman, one may be easy about her and turn to other things. Nevertheless, my thanks on my own account, and congratulations upon yours. To crown your happiness, I am even willing to confess that on this occasion you have surpassed my expectations. After which let us see whether I, in my turn, have not fulfilled yours, at least in part.

It is not Madame de Tourvel I want to tell you about. That affair goes too slowly for you: it is, I know, only the finished work that interests you. Long-drawn-out encounters bore you, whereas I have never tasted such pleasure as I derive from all this apparent procrastination.

Yes, I like watching, contemplating this prudent woman as she takes, without knowing it, a path which allows of no return, which flings her willy-nilly in my wake down its steep and dangerous descent. Frightened of the peril she is courting, she would like to stop but cannot hold back. Care and skill can shorten the steps she takes: nothing can prevent them succeeding each other. Sometimes, unable to face the danger, she closes her eyes and lets herself go, putting her fate in my hands. More often some new fear rouses her to new efforts. In her mortal terror she tries once more to retreat, and exhausts her strength in regaining a little ground; but soon some magic power transplants her yet nearer the danger she has vainly attempted to fly. Then, having no one but me for guidance and support, and unable to blame me any longer for her inevitable fall, she implores me to postpone it. Fervent prayer, humble supplication all that mortal man in his terror offers the Divinity, I receive from her. And you think that I, deaf to her prayers, destroying with my own hands the shrine she has put up around me, will use that same power for her ruin which she invokes for her protection! Ah, let me at least have time to enjoy the touching struggle between love and virtue.

After all, do you think that the spectacle you rush so eagerly to the theatre to see and applaud so furiously is less fascinating in actuality? The sentiments you greet with so much enthusiasm; the feelings of a pure and tender nature that fears the happiness it yearns for, that cannot stop defending itself even when it has given up resisting, are they to have no value for the man who has inspired them? Those, nevertheless, those are the delicious satisfactions this heavenly woman daily offers me. And you blame me for savouring such delights! Ah, the time will all too quickly come when, debased by her fall, she will be no more to me than any other woman.

But I am forgetting, while I speak of her, that I did not intend to speak of her. Some power or other draws me to her, brings me back to her continually even if it is only to insult her. Let us put these dangerous thoughts aside. Let me be myself again and speak of jollier things: your pupil, for instance, who has now become mine. Here I hope you will recognize me in my true colours.

For some days, during which I had been better treated by my tender devotee and was consequently less concerned about her, I had been conscious that the little Volanges was in fact extremely pretty; and that, if it was absurd to be enamoured of her as Danceny is, it was perhaps equally so for me not to look to her for the distraction my solitude compels me to find. It seemed to be only just, too, that I should have some reward for my efforts on her behalf, and I remembered, besides, that you had offered her to me before Danceny had any pretensions in the matter. I decided I could legitimately claim certain rights in a property which was his only because I had refused and relinquished it. The pretty look of the little creature, her fresh little mouth, her childish air, even her gaucherie, confirmed me in these wise determinations. I decided to act upon them, and success has crowned my enterprise.

You are already wondering how I arrived so soon at supplanting the cherished lover, and what method of seduction can have been appropriate to such lack of years and experience. Spare yourself the trouble: I took none at all myself. While, with your skill in handling the weapons of your sex, yours was a triumph of cunning, I, restoring to man his inalienable rights, conquered by force of authority. Sure of seizing my prey if I could come within reach of her, I had no need of strategem, except to secure a means of approach, and the ruse I employed for that purpose was hardly worthy of the name.

I took my opportunity as soon as I received Danceny's next letter to his mistress. Having given her the signal of warning agreed upon between us, I exercised all my ingenuity, not in giving her the letter, but in failing to find a means of doing so. I pretended to share her resulting impatience, and having caused the evil I pointed out the remedy.

The young lady occupies a room, one door to which gives on to the corridor. The mother had, as was to be expected, removed the key, and it was only a question of recovering it. Nothing could have been easier: I asked only to have it at my disposal for two hours whereupon I should be responsible for procuring a duplicate. After that everything, correspondence, meetings, nocturnal rendez-vous, would have become convenient and safe. Yet – would you believe it? – the cautious child took fright and refused. Another man would have been crushed by this: I saw in it no more than an occasion for pleasure of a more piquant kind. I wrote to Danceny complaining of the refusal, and did it so well that the blockhead would not be satisfied till he had obtained, exacted rather, a promise from his timorous mistress to grant my request and leave everything to my discretion.

I was very pleased, I must say, with my change of role, and with the young man's doing for me what he thought I would be doing for him. The idea doubled the worth of the enterprise in my eyes, so that as soon as I had possession of the precious key, I hastened to make use of it. That was last night.

Having made sure that all was quiet throughout the house, armed with my dark lantern and clothed as befitted the hour and the circumstances, I paid my first visit to your pupil. I had everything arranged (she herself had obliged me) so that I could enter without noise. She was in her first sleep, the deep sleep of youth, so that I arrived at her bedside without waking her. I thought at first of proceeding further and attempting to pass myself off as a dream. But, fearing the effect of surprise and the consequent alarms, I decided instead to wake the sleeping beauty with every caution, and eventually succeeded in preventing the outcry I had anticipated.

When I had calmed her initial fears, and since I was not there to chat, I risked a few liberties. There is no doubt she was not taught enough at the convent either about the many different perils to which fearful innocence is exposed, or about all that it has to protect, or be taken by surprise: for, directing her whole attention and all her energies to defending herself from a kiss, which was nothing but a feint, she left everything else defenceless. How could I let my advantage slip? I changed my line of attack and immediately seized a position. At this point we both thought all was lost. The little creature, quite horrified, made in good earnest to cry out: fortunately her voice was strangled in tears. She then threw herself towards the bell-rope, but I had the presence of mind to take hold of her arm in time.

'What are you trying to do?' I said to her. 'Ruin yourself for ever? What will it matter to me if someone comes? How will you convince anyone that I am not here with your permission? Who else but you could have provided me with a means of entering your room? As for the key which I have from you, which I can only have obtained from you, will you undertake to explain its purpose?' This short harangue pacified neither grief nor rage; but it inspired submission. I don't know whether my tones were eloquent; my gestures, at all events, were not. One hand was needed for power, the other for love: where is the orator that could aspire to grace in such a position? If you can picture the circumstances you will agree that they were favourable for attack: but I am a blockhead, and as you say, the simplest woman, a mere convent girl, has me by the leading-strings like a child.

The girl in question, in the midst of her despair, knew that she must find some way of coming to terms with me. Entreaties found me inexorable and she was reduced to making offers. You will suppose I set a high price upon my important position: no, I promised everything away for a kiss. True, once I had taken the kiss I did not keep my promise: but I had good reason not to. Had we agreed that the kiss should be taken or given? After much bargaining we decided upon a second, and this one was to be received. Having guided her timid arms around my body, I clasped her more lovingly in the one of mine that was free, and the sweetest kiss was in fact received: properly, perfectly received: love itself could not have done better.

So much good faith deserved its reward, and I immediately granted the request. The hand was withdrawn; but by some extraordinary chance I found that I myself had taken its place. You imagine me very breathless and busy at this point, don't you? Not at all. I have acquired a taste for dawdling, I tell you. Why hurry when one's destination is in sight?

Seriously, I was glad for once to observe the power of opportunity, deprived in this case of all extraneous aid, with love in combat against it; love, moreover, sustained by modesty and shame, and encouraged by the bad humour I had provoked, which had been given free rein. Opportunity was alone; but it was there, offering itself, continually present, whereas love was not.

To confirm my observations, I was malicious enough to exert no more strength than could easily have been resisted. It was only when my charming enemy, taking advantage of my lenity, seemed about to escape me that I restrained her with the threats of which I had already felt the happy effects. Oh well, to go no further, our sweet inamorata, forgetting her vows, first yielded and then consented: of course, tears and reproaches were resumed at the first opportunity. I don't know whether they were real or pretended, but, as always happens, they ceased the moment I set about giving her reason for more. At length, having proceeded from helplessness to indignation, and from indignation to helplessness, we separated quite satisfied with one another and looking forward with equal pleasure to this evening's rendezvous.

I did not return to my room till daybreak, dying of sleep and fatigue: I sacrificed both, however, to my desire to appear this morning at breakfast. I have a passion for the mien of the morning after. You have no idea of this one. Such embarrassment of gesture, such difficulty of movement! Eyes kept steadily lowered, so large, and so haggard! The little round face so drawn! Nothing was ever so amusing. And for the first time her mother, alarmed at this extreme alteration, displayed some sympathetic interest! The Présidente, too, danced attendance round her. Oh, *her* sympathy is only borrowed, believe me! The day will come for its return, and that day is not far off. Good-bye, my love.

Château de —
1 October 17 —

LETTER 97: *Cécile Volanges to the Marquise de Merteuil*

OH God, Madame, how heavy-hearted, how miserable I am! Who will console me in my distress? Who will advise me in my difficulties? This Monsieur de Valmont . . . and Danceny? No: the very thought of Danceny throws me into despair . . . . How shall I tell you? How shall I say it? . . . I don't know what to do. But my heart is full . . . I must speak to someone, and in you alone can I, dare I confide. You have been so kind to me! What shall I say? I do not want you to be kind. Everyone here has offered me sympathy today . . . they have only increased my wretchedness: I was so very much aware that I did not deserve it! Scold me instead; give me a good scolding, for I am very much to blame. But then save me. If you will not have the kindness to advise me I shall die of grief.

Know then . . . my hand trembles, as you see. I can scarcely write. I feel my cheeks on fire. . . . Oh, it is the very blush of shame. Well, I shall endure it. It shall be the first punishment for my fault. Yes, I shall tell you everything.

You must know, then, that Monsieur de Valmont who hitherto has delivered Monsieur Danceny's letters to me, suddenly found it too difficult to continue in the usual way. He wanted a key to my room. I can certainly assure you that I did not want to give him one: but he went so far as to write to Danceny, and Danceny wanted me to do so. I am always so sorry to refuse him anything, particularly since our separation which has made him so unhappy, that I finally agreed. I had no idea of the misfortune that would follow.

Last night Monsieur de Valmont used the key to come into my room as I slept. I was so little expecting this that he really frightened me when he woke me. But as he immediately began to speak, I recognized him and did not cry out; then, too, it occurred to me at first that he had come to bring me a letter from Danceny. Far from it. Very shortly afterwards he attempted to kiss me; and while I defended myself, as was natural, he cleverly did what I should not have wished for all the world . . . but first he wanted a kiss. I had to: what else could I do? The more so since I had tried to ring, but besides the fact that I could not, he was careful to tell me that if someone came he would easily be able to throw all the blame on me; and, in fact, it would have been easy on account of the key. After this he budged not an inch. He wanted a second kiss; and, I don't know why, but this time I was quite flustered and afterwards it was even worse than before. Oh, really, it was too wicked. Then, after that . . . you will spare my telling you the rest, but I am as unhappy as anyone could possibly be.

What I blame myself for most, and what, nevertheless, I must tell you about, is that I am afraid I did not defend myself as well as I was able. I don't know how that happened. I most certainly am not in love with Monsieur de Valmont, quite the contrary: yet there were moments when it was as if I were. . . . As you may imagine, this did not prevent me from saying no all the time: but I knew quite well that I was not doing as I said: it was as if I could not help it. And then, too, I was so very agitated! If it is always as difficult as this to defend oneself, one needs a good deal of practice! It is true that Monsieur de Valmont has a way of saying things so that one is hard put to it to think of a reply: at all events, would you believe that when he left I was almost sorry, and was weak enough to agree to his returning this evening? That is what horrifies me more than all the rest.

Oh, in spite of all, I promise you I shall stop him coming. He had scarcely left when I knew for certain that I had been very wrong to promise him anything. What is more, I spent the rest of the night in tears. It was Danceny above all who haunted me! Every time I thought of him my tears came twice as fast till they almost suffocated me, and I thought of him all the time. . . . I do even now, and you see the result: my paper quite sodden. No, I shall never be consoled, if only on his account . . . . At length I could cry no more, and yet could not sleep for a minute. And when I woke this morning and looked at myself in the mirror, I frightened myself I was so changed.

Mamma noticed it as soon as she saw me and asked me what was wrong. I began at once to cry. I thought she was going to scold me, and perhaps that would have hurt me less: but quite the contrary. She spoke to me kindly! I scarcely deserved it. She told me not to distress myself like that! She did not know what I had to be distressed about. That I should make myself ill over it! There are moments when I should like to be dead. I could not restrain myself. I threw myself sobbing into her arms, crying 'Oh, Mamma your daughter is very unhappy!' Mamma could not help crying a little herself, and that only increased my misery. Fortunately she did not ask why I was unhappy, or I could not have forborne telling her.

I beseech you, Madame, write to me as soon as you can and tell me what I must do; for I have not the courage to think of anything and can do nothing but suffer. Please address your letter to Monsieur de Valmont; but if you are writing to him at the same time, I beg you not to mention that I have said anything to you.

I have the honour to be, Madame, ever with the most sincere friendship, your very humble and obedient servant. . . . I dare not sign this letter.

Château de —
1 October 17 —

LETTER 98: *Madame de Volanges to the Marquise de Merteuil*

NOT many days ago, my dear friend, it was you who were asking me for comfort and advice: now it is my turn, and I am making the same request of you that you made of me. I am in very great distress indeed, and I am afraid I may not have found the best way out of my troubles.

It is my daughter who is the cause of my anxiety. Since our departure from Paris she has clearly been dejected and unhappy; but I expected that, and had hardened my heart with the severity I judged necessary. I hoped that absence and distraction would soon destroy a love that I regarded rather as a childish aberration than a true passion. Far, however, from having gained anything by coming here to stay, I now observe that the child is surrendering more and more to a dangerous melancholy, and I am seriously afraid that it may injure her health. During the last few days especially there has been a visible change in her appearance. It struck me yesterday in particular, and everybody here was really alarmed.

What further proves to me that she is deeply affected is that she is now obviously capable of overcoming the timidity she has always shown in my presence. Yesterday morning, simply upon my asking her whether she was ill, she flung herself into my arms saying that she was very unhappy, sobbing and weeping. I cannot tell you how painful this was to me. Tears came to my eyes immediately, and I scarcely had time to turn away to prevent her seeing them. Fortunately I was prudent enough not to ask her any questions, and she herself did not dare to say anything further. It is clear, none the less, that it is still this unfortunate passion that torments her.

What course shall I take, however, if this continues? Shall I make my daughter unhappy? Shall I turn to her disadvantage the very qualities of mind and heart in her that are most to be valued, her sensibility and her constancy? Is it for that I am her mother? And were I to stifle the natural feeling that makes us all want the happiness of our children; were I to look upon that as a weakness, which, on the contrary, I believe to be the first and most sacred of our duties; if I force her choice, shall I not be answerable for the dreadful consequences that may ensue? What a way to use the authority of a mother, to offer one's daughter the alternatives of crime and misery!

I shall not, my dear friend, imitate those I have so often condemned. I was capable, certainly, of attempting to choose for my daughter, but by that I was doing no more than help her with my experience. It was not a right that I exercised, but a duty I fulfilled. I should, on the other hand, be neglecting another duty were I to dispose of her without a thought for an attachment I was not able to prevent her forming, and of which neither she nor I can judge the extent or duration. No, I cannot permit her to marry one man and love another. I prefer to compromise my authority rather than her virtue.

I think, therefore, I shall be doing the wisest thing by retracting the promise I have given Monsieur de Gercourt. I have told you my reasons, and it seems to me that they should weigh more with me than promises. I shall go further: in the present state of things, by fulfilling my engagement I should really be violating it. For, after all, if I owe it to my daughter not to betray her secret to Monsieur de Gercourt, I owe it to him, at the least, not to abuse the ignorance in which I leave him, to do for him all that I believe he would do for himself if he knew everything. Am I, instead, when he relies upon my good faith, when he honours me in choosing me for his second mother, to betray him shamefully; am I to deceive him in the choice he wishes to make for the mother of his own children? These ideas, which contain so much truth, and which I cannot refuse to entertain, alarm me more than I can say.

Against the misfortunes they bring me to fear, I compare a daughter happy in a husband who is the choice of her heart, recognizing duty only by the pleasure she finds in fulfilling it; a son-in-law, equally contented, gladder each day of the choice he has made; each finding happiness only in the happiness of the other, and the happiness of both combining to increase mine. Should the hope of so pleasant a future be sacrificed to vain considerations? What are the considerations, after all, that give me pause? Those of advantage only. But to what end was my daughter born rich, if she is, none the less, to be a slave to fortune?

I agree that Monsieur de Gercourt is, perhaps, a better match than I could have expected for my daughter; I shall even admit that

I was extremely flattered when his choice fell upon her. But after all, Danceny comes from as good a family as he; he yields nothing to him in personal qualities; and he has the advantage over Monsieur de Gercourt of loving and being loved. True, he is not rich; but is my daughter not rich enough for the two of them? Oh, why rob her of the satisfaction of bestowing her riches upon the man she loves?

Are not the marriages which are the result of calculation and not of choice, marriages of convenience as they are called, where everything is mutually agreeable except the tastes and characters of the couple concerned, are they not the most common source of these outbreaks of scandal that become daily more and more frequent? I had rather wait: I should at least have time to learn to know a daughter who is now a stranger to me. I should have quite enough courage, I am sure, to cause her a passing disappointment, if she stood to gain a more solid happiness from it: but to risk delivering her up to perpetual despair, that is not in my heart.

These, my dear friend, are the thoughts that torment me, concerning which I beg your advice. Such serious questions are very ill-suited to your gaiety and charm, and seem scarcely less so to your age: but your good judgement is so far in advance of that! Besides, your friendship will come to the aid of your prudence, and I have no fear that either one of them will deny the maternal solicitude that implores their help.

Good-bye, me dear friend. Never doubt the sincerity of my feelings for you.

Château de —
2 October 17 —

LETTER 99: *The Vicomte de Valmont to the Marquise de Merteuil*

FURTHER little incidents, my love; but only dialogue, no action. So compose yourself in patience: in fact, summon as much of it as you can: for while my Présidente proceeds at a snail's pace, your pupil is in retreat, which is a great deal worse. Oh, well, I have wit enough to be amused by these little things. As a matter of fact I am growing quite accustomed to staying here, and can even say that I have experienced not a moment's boredom in this gloomy mansion of my old aunt's. On the contrary, have I not pleasures, privations, hopes, uncertainties? What more has the theatre itself to offer? Spectators? Oh, wait and see. I shall not want those either. If they are not here now to watch me at work, I shall show them my task complete: they will then have only to admire and applaud. Yes, they will applaud: for I can at last predict with certainty the moment of my austere devotee's surrender. I assisted this evening at the death-agony of virtue. A sweet helplessness is going to reign in its place. I have fixed the moment for not later than our next interview: but I can hear you already scoffing at my conceit. Predicting victory, boasting before the event! Oh, dear, dear, calm yourself! To prove my modesty I am going to begin with the history of my defeat.

Truly, your pupil is a very ridiculous little person! She is really a child who ought to be treated as such: and one would be letting her off lightly by putting her in the corner! Would you believe that after what happened between us the day before yesterday, after the friendly farewells we said the next morning, I found, when I returned in the evening as she had agreed to let me do, that the door was locked from the inside? What have you to say to that? One sometimes meets with this sort of puerility the day before: but the day after! Is it not amusing?

I was not, however, disposed to laugh at first. Never had I been more conscious of the force of my character. It was certainly not with any thought of pleasure that I had kept my rendezvous, but solely out of politeness. I was in great need of my bed, which seemed to me at that moment preferable to anyone else's, and I had not left it without regret. Yet I had no sooner found an obstacle in my path than I was on fire to remove it. I was particularly humiliated by the thought that a child had outwitted me. I withdrew, therefore, in high dudgeon: and with the intention of meddling no further with the stupid girl or her affairs, immediately wrote her a note to be delivered to her today, in which I stated my estimate of her true worth. But, as they say, sleep is the best counsellor. This morning I decided that as I am not offered a choice of amusements here, I would have to make the most of this one. So I tore up the offensive note. Having thought about it since, I am unable to conceive how it can have occurred to me to bring an adventure to an end before I had acquired some means of ruining its heroine. To what, however, may one not be provoked by the impulse of the moment? Happy the man, my love, who, like you, has trained himself never to yield to it! My revenge, therefore, I have deferred. I have made the sacrifice in the interests of your designs upon Gercourt.

Now that I am no longer angry, I see your pupil's conduct as merely ridiculous. In fact, I should very much like to know what she hopes to gain by it! I am at a loss to imagine. If it is only self-defence, it must be admitted she has begun a little late. She really will have to give me the clue to the puzzle one day. I am most eager to know. It was perhaps only that she felt tired? Frankly, that is possible; for she very probably does not know that love's arrows carry with them, as did Achilles' spear, the balm that heals the wounds they make. But no, from the wry faces she made all day, I should guess that repentance comes into it somewhere . . . something of the kind . . . something to do with virtue. . . . Virtue! . . . What has virtue to do with her? Ah, let her leave it to the woman who really was born for it, the only one who can make it beautiful, can make it worthy of love! . . . Forgive me, my dear, but it was only this evening that there occurred between Madame de Tourvel and myself the scene that I am about to describe to you, and I am still under the influence of some emotion. I shall have to make a great effort to forget the impression she made; it was precisely to help me do so that I sat down to write to you. You must make some allowances at first.

Madame de Tourvel and I have for some days been in agreement about our feelings; our only dispute now is about words. It had always been, of course, *her friendship* that answered *my love:* but the language of convention did not alter the facts, and even had we remained upon these terms, my progress, though it would perhaps have been slower, would not have been less sure. There was already no longer any question of my leaving, as she had desired at first; and as for our daily meetings, while I took care to offer her opportunities, she took as much care to seize them.

Since it is ordinarily when we are out walking that our little rendezvous take place, the dreadful weather we have had all day today disappointed my hopes: I was even quite annoyed by it. I could not foresee how much the circumstance would be to my advantage.

Walking being out of the question, the ladies sat down to cards after dinner; and since I seldom play, I found myself superfluous. I chose the moment to go up to my room, intending to do no more than wait until they were likely to have finished their game.

I was on my way to rejoin the company when I met the charming creature returning to her room. In a moment of imprudence, or perhaps weakness, she asked in dulcet tones: 'Where are you going? There is nobody in the drawing-room.' I needed no further pretext, as you may imagine, to attempt a sortie into her own room. I met with less resistance than I expected. True, I had taken the precaution of beginning a conversation at the door, and of beginning it upon indifferent topics; but no sooner had it been properly launched when I brought up the real issue and spoke *to my friend of my love*. Her immediate reply, though simple, seemed to me expressive. 'Oh, please!' she said, 'don't speak of that here', and she trembled. Poor woman! She knows her fate is sealed.

She was wrong, nevertheless, to be afraid. I had for some time been confident of achieving success sooner or later, and seeing her exhaust so much of her energy in futile struggles had made me decide to conserve my own strength, to wait without making any effort until she should give in out of fatigue. As you know, the victory must be complete. I shall owe nothing to circumstances. It was precisely with this idea in mind, and in order to show eagerness without committing myself too far, that I returned to the word 'love', so obstinately evaded hitherto. Sure of ardour being taken for granted, I assayed a more tender tone. Evasion no longer disappointed me, it grieved me: did not my sympathetic friend owe me some consolation?

By way of consoling me, a hand was left in mine; the lovely body leant against my arm, and we found ourselves in extremely close proximity. You must surely have observed how, in this sort of situation, as defence weakens, demands and refusals are exchanged at closer and closer quarters; how the head is turned aside and the eyes lowered, while disjointed remarks are delivered in a weak voice at longer and longer intervals. Such are the precious symptoms that in the plainest terms announce the heart's consent: but persuasion will rarely, as yet, have touched the senses, and I am even of the opinion that it is always dangerous at this moment to embark upon too decided a course of action. Since the condition of abandon is never unattended by a certain sweet pleasure, it would be impossible to break new ground without arousing some irritation, and that would infallibly turn to the advantage of the defence.

In the present case prudence was all the more necessary: I had special cause to fear the alarm which her own self-oblivion could not, in the end, fail to arouse in my languorous love. So that I did not even insist that the avowal I demanded be spoken. A look would be enough. A single look, and I should be happy.

My dear, those beautiful eyes were actually raised to mine. That heavenly mouth even pronounced these words: 'Well! yes, I . . .' But suddenly her glance faded, her voice failed, and the adorable woman collapsed in my arms. I had scarcely time to catch her when she disengaged herself with convulsive force and, with a wild look and her arms extended to Heaven, cried 'God . . . oh, my God, save me!'; and straightaway, quicker than lightning, she was upon her knees at ten paces from me. I could see that she was on the point of suffocating, and advanced to her help, but she, taking hold of my hands, bathing them in tears, even at times embracing my knees, said: 'Yes, it is you. It is you who will save me! You don't want me to die. Leave me; save me; leave me; in God's name, leave me!' These frantic exclamations could scarcely escape her lips for the sobbing, which had redoubled in force. Meanwhile she held on to me with a strength which could not in any case have permitted my leaving her; so, summoning my own strength, I raised her up in my arms. At the same instant her tears ceased; she stopped speaking, her limbs stiffened, and violent convulsions succeeded the storm.

I was, I admit, deeply moved, and I think I should have agreed to her demands, even if circumstances had not compelled me to do so. The fact remains that, having administered some practical assistance, I left her as she had begged me to, and am now glad that I did so. I have already almost obtained my reward.

I expected that, as had happened on the day of my first declaration, she would not appear that evening. But at about eight o'clock she came down to the drawing-room, simply announcing to the company that she had felt very unwell. Her face was drawn, her voice feeble, and her bearing composed: but her looks were soft, and they were frequently fixed upon me. When her refusal to join the card table obliged me to take her place, she even sat beside me. During supper she remained behind alone in the drawing-room. At our return I thought I noticed she had been crying. To make certain, I told her it seemed to me that she was still suffering from her indisposition; to which she made the obliging answer: 'It is one of those ailments that does not go as quickly as it comes!' At length, as we retired, I gave her my arm; at the door of her room she squeezed my hand with some force. There seemed to me, it is true, to be something involuntary in the gesture. But so much the better. It is one more proof of my power.

I am sure she is now delighted to have arrived where she is. All the expenses have been paid; nothing further remains for her to do but enjoy herself. Perhaps, as I write, she is already pondering that thought! And even if she is, on the contrary, concocting some new plan of defence, we know, do we not, what becomes of those? I ask you, could any plan outlast our next meeting? I quite expect, of course, there will be some difficulty in reconciling her to the fact: but then! once the first step is taken, are these strait-laced prudes ever able to stop? Their love is a veritable explosion; resistance only increases its force. My fierce ascetic would begin to run after me were I to stop running after her.

In conclusion, my love, I return as always to you, to keep you to your word. You have not, of course, forgotten what you promised me after my success: that little infidelity to your Chevalier? Are you ready? For my part, I long for it so much that we might still be strangers to each other. For that matter, knowing you is perhaps all the more reason for wanting it. I say that:

In justice to you, not in compliment.[1]

This will be my first infidelity to my staid conquest; and I promise you I shall make use of the first available pretext to leave

1. Voltaire: *Nanine*, a comedy.

her for twenty-four hours. That shall be her punishment for keeping me so long away from you! Do you know that this affair has kept me occupied now for more than two months? Yes, two months and three days. I count tomorrow since it is not till then that it will finally be accomplished. Which reminds me that Madame de B — resisted for three whole months. I should be delighted to discover that open coquetry can maintain a defence for longer than the most ascetic virtue.

Good-bye, my love. I must leave you, for it is very late. This letter has taken me further than I intended; but since I am sending to Paris in the morning, I decided to give you an opportunity of sharing the joy of a friend a day in advance.

Château de —
2 October 17 —, evening

LETTER 100: *The Vicomte de Valmont to the Marquise de Merteuil*

My dear, I am deceived, betrayed, ruined. I am in despair. Madame de Tourvel has left. She has left without my knowledge. I was not there to oppose her departure, to arraign her shameful treachery! Ah, don't imagine that I would have let her go. She would have stayed. Yes, she would have stayed, had I been obliged to resort to force. But there you are! In my blind confidence I was peacefully asleep; I was asleep when the lightning struck. No, I had no inkling at all of her departure. I must give up trying to understand women.

When I think of yesterday! Yesterday? It was only last evening! That soft look, that tender tone of voice! And that clasp of the hand! And all the while she was planning her escape! O, women, women! Don't wonder, then, that you are deceived. Yes! Men know no treachery that they have not learnt from you.

What pleasure I shall take in my revenge! I shall find her again, the traitress: I shall recover my dominion over her. If love by itself could do so, what will it not achieve with vengeance at its side? I shall see her again at my knees, trembling, bathed in tears, crying for mercy in that lying voice; and I shall be without pity.

What is she doing now? What is she thinking of? Congratulating herself, perhaps, on having deceived me; and, true to her sex, deciding that this is the sweetest pleasure of them all. What her much-vaunted virtue was unable to do, natural cunning has done without effort. Fool that I am! I feared her discretion: it was her sincerity I should have distrusted.

And to be compelled to swallow my resentment! To dare show nothing but sorrowful concern when I have a heart bursting with rage! To find myself reduced once more to going down upon my knees to a rebellious woman who has escaped my power! Have I deserved to be so humiliated? And by whom? A timid woman who never saw battle before. To what end have I established myself in her heart, have I set her ablaze with all the fires of passion, have I stirred her senses to delirium, if now, secure in her refuge, she can take more pride in her flight than I in my triumph? And shall I endure it? My dear, you don't believe that? You would not think so slightingly of me?

But what is the power that draws me to this woman? Are there not a hundred others who would be glad of my attentions? Would they not hasten to respond? And though this one is worth more than they are, has not the attraction of variety, has not the charm of new conquests, and the glory of their number, pleasures as sweet to offer? Why do we give chase to what eludes us, and ignore what is to hand? Ah, why indeed? . . . I don't know, but I am made to feel it is so.

There is no longer any happiness for me, no longer any peace but in the possession of this woman whom I love and hate with equal fury. I cannot tolerate my life until hers is again mine to dispose of. Then, contented and calm, I shall see her in turn buffeted by the storms that assail me now, and I shall stir up a thousand others too. I want hope and fear, faith and suspicion, all the evils devised by hate and all the blessings conferred by love, to fill her heart and to succeed one another there at my will. That time will come. . . . But what a great deal there is still to do! How near I was yesterday! And today how far! How shall I reach her? I dare risk doing nothing yet. I feel I must be calm before I can make a decision; at the moment, the blood races through my veins.

My torments become twice as painful for the coolness with which everyone here treats my questions about the incident, as to its cause, as to the whole extraordinary aspect it wears. . . .Nobody knows anything; nobody wants to know anything: they should scarcely have talked of it at all, had I been willing to talk of anything else. Madame de Rosemonde, to whom I flew this morning upon hearing the news, replied with the imperturbability of her age, that it was the natural consequence of Madame de Tourvel's indisposition yesterday; that she had been afraid of being taken ill, and had preferred to return home. She finds it quite simple: she would have done the same herself, she told me. As if there could be any comparison between them: between my aunt, who has nothing left to do but die, and the woman who is all the charm and torment of my life!

Madame de Volanges, whom at first I had suspected as an accomplice, appeared not to be affected, except by the fact that she had not been consulted in the proceeding. I am very glad, I must admit, that she was not afforded the pleasure of doing me an ill turn. This proves to me, too, that she is not confided in as much as I had feared she might be: so that is one enemy the less. How pleased she would be if she knew it was I who am responsible for the disappearance! How she would swell with pride had it taken place on her advice! My God, how I hate her! Oh, I shall be seeing her daughter again: I mean to make her dance to my tune. I think therefore, that I shall be staying here some time. At any rate, the little thought I have given the matter inclines me to this course.

Don't you think, after all, that having made so decided a gesture, my ungrateful beloved is bound to be in dread of my reappearance? If, therefore, the thought has struck her that I might follow, she will not have failed to lock her doors; and I am no more anxious for her to make a habit of that than I am to suffer the humiliation of it myself. I should prefer, on the contrary, to announce that I am remaining here. I shall even entreat her to return. And when she is quite convinced that I am staying away, I shall arrive upon her doorstep. We shall see how she takes that meeting. But it must be deferred so as to increase its effect, and I don't yet know whether I shall have the patience. I have opened my mouth twenty times today to call for my horses. However, I shall control myself. I undertake to be here to receive your reply to this. I ask only, my love, that you don't make me wait for it.

More than anything else, it would annoy me not to know what is happening. My valet, however, who is in Paris, has some right of access to the chambermaid. He may be useful. I am sending him money and instructions. I hope you will not object to my enclosing both with this letter, nor to putting yourself to the trouble of sending them to him by one of your servants, with orders to deliver them to him in person. I take this precaution because the odd fellow has a habit of never receiving letters I write him when they contain directions that incommode him in any way; and he does not seem to me, at the moment, to be as taken with his conquest as I should like him to be.

Good-bye, my love; if some happy thought strikes you, some means of hastening my progress, let me know of it. I have more than once acknowledged how useful your friendship can be; I acknowledge it again. I feel calmer since I began writing to you. At least I am speaking to someone who understands me, and not to one of the cabbages in whose midst I have been vegetating since this morning. Truly, the longer I live, the more I am tempted to think that in all the world it is only you and I who are worth anything.

Château de —
3 October 17 —

LETTER 101: *The Vicomte de Valmont to Azolan, his valet*

You must be exceedingly stupid to have left here yesterday morning without knowing that Madame de Tourvel was leaving too; or, if you knew, not to have told me about it. To what purpose do you spend my money getting drunk with footmen; to what purpose do you spend time, which ought to be employed in my service, playing the gallant with chambermaids, if I am not, as a result, to be better informed of what is happening? Such, however, has been your negligence. I warn you that if you make one more mistake in this business, it will be the last that you commit in my service.

It is necessary that you inform me of everything that happens at Madame de Tourvel's: of her health, whether she sleeps or not; whether she is sad or gay; whether she goes out often and to whose house; whether she receives anyone at home, and whom; how she passes her time; whether she is bad-tempered with her maids, particularly with the one she brought here with her; what she does when she is alone; whether, when she reads, she reads uninterruptedly, or breaks off to daydream; what she does when she writes. Remember, too, to make friends with the man who carries her letters to the post. Offer, as often as possible, to run the errand for him; and whenever he accepts, dispatch only those letters that seem to you to be of no consequence, sending me the rest, particularly those addressed to Madame de Volanges, should you find any.

Make arrangements to continue a while longer as your Julie's fond admirer. If she has found another, as you believe, make her agree to share her favours. You are not going to pride yourself on any ridiculous sense of delicacy: you will be in the same situation as a great many others who are your betters. If, however, your colleague makes a nuisance of himself; if you should observe, for instance, that he occupies too much of Julie's time during the day, thereby permitting her to be less often with her mistress, you will find some means of getting rid of him: or you will pick a quarrel with him, Don't be afraid of the consequences: I shall give you my support. Above all, you are not to leave that house. Only the most constant attention will enable you to see everything, and to see true. If it should happen that one of the servants is dismissed, you may even offer yourself in his place, as being no longer employed by me. Say in this case that you have left me to look for a more peaceable and well-regulated household. Try, in other words, to get yourself accepted. I shall keep you, notwithstanding, in my own service during this time. It shall be as it was with the Duchesse de— and in the end Madame de Tourvel will reward you equally well.

Were you well enough supplied with skill and enthusiasm these instructions would suffice; but to make up for what you lack in either respect I am sending you some money. The enclosed note authorizes you, as you will see, to draw twenty-five *louis* from my agent; for I have no doubt you are at present without a sou. You will employ as much of this sum as is necessary in persuading Julie to enter into correspondence with me. The rest will do to provide the servants with drink. Make a point, as far as is possible, of entertaining in the janitor's quarters, so that he will always be glad to see you. But don't forget that it is not your pleasures, but your services that I am paying for.

Encourage in Julie a habit of noticing everything, and of reporting everything, even what might seem to her to be negligible details. Better that she should record ten useless facts, than omit one interesting one; and often what seems to be unimportant is not so. Since I must be told immediately of any occurrence that seems to you to merit my attention, you will, as soon as you receive this letter, send Philippe on the messenger's horse to establish himself at —.[1] He will remain there till further orders, as a relay in case of necessity. For ordinary correspondence the post will do.

Be careful you don't lose this letter. Read it every day, as much to make sure that you still have it as to be certain you have forgotten nothing. Do, in short, all that you must do as being honoured by my confidence. You know that, if I am satisfied with you, you will be no less so with me.

*Château de —
3 October 17 —*

LETTER 102: *The Présidente de Tourvel to Madame de Rosemonde*

YOU will be surprised, Madame, to learn that I am leaving your house so suddenly. It will seem to you a very extraordinary thing to do: but you will be twice as astonished when you know my reasons. You will perhaps think that, in taking you into my confidence, I do not show enough consideration for the equanimity necessary to your age; that I am disregarding, too, those feelings of reverence I owe you on so many grounds! Ah, Madame, forgive me, but my heart is oppressed, and it is only to a friend who is as kind as she is prudent that I can look for relief. Who else but you could I have chosen? Look upon me as your child. Look upon me

1. A village half-way between Paris and Madame de Rosemonde's château.

with a mother's tenderness, I beseech you. My feeling for you gives me, perhaps, some right to it.

Where has the time gone when I was wholly given up to such praiseworthy feelings, when I was ignorant of those others that, afflicting the soul with mortal anguish – the anguish I now suffer – deprive it of strength to resist at the same time that they impose the necessity of resisting? Ah, this fatal visit has ruined me. . . .

What can I say after all? I am in love, yes, I am desperately in love. Alas! For the first time I have written that word, so often demanded and never given, and I should pay with my life for the pleasure of being able just once to let him hear it who has inspired it; yet I must continue to refuse! And he will continue to doubt my feelings, and to think himself ill-used. I am very unhappy! Why is it not as easy for him to read my heart as to rule it? Yes, I should suffer less if he knew how much I suffered. You yourself, to whom I say this, can have as yet but little idea how much that is.

In a few moments I shall have left him and made him unhappy. When he thinks he is still near me, I shall already be far away from him: the hour when I was used to seeing him every day will find me in a place to which he has never been, and where I must never allow him to come. My preparations are already made; everything is here, before my eyes; they can rest on nothing that does not speak of this cruel parting. All is ready: I alone am not! . . . And the more my heart protests, the more it proves how necessary it is to submit.

I shall submit, of course. Better die than live guilty. I am already, I feel, only too guilty; only my good sense remains to me; virtue has disappeared. I must, however, admit to you that what does remain I owe to his generosity. Intoxicated by the pleasure of seeing him, of hearing him speak, by the sweet awareness of his presence near me, by the even greater happiness of being able to make him happy, I lost all strength of mind and will; I had scarcely enough left to struggle, I had none to resist; I trembled with a sense of my danger without being able to escape it. Well then! He saw my distress, and took pity on me. How should I not love him for that? I owe him more than life itself.

Ah, if by staying with him I had only my life to tremble for, do not imagine that I should ever bring myself to leave! What is my life without him? Should I not be only too happy to lose it? Condemned to being the eternal cause of his misery and mine, unable either to pity myself or comfort him; to defending myself each day against him and against myself; to sparing no effort in making him suffer when I wish only to devote my whole care to his happiness: are not a thousand deaths better than such a life? Yet that is going to be my fate. I shall endure it, nevertheless; I must find the courage to do so. O you, whom I have chosen for my mother, bear witness to my vow.

Accept, too, my promise that I shall never conceal from you any one of my actions; accept it, I beg you. I ask this of you as I would ask your help in an extremity. Bound thus to tell you everything, I shall begin to believe myself always in your presence. Your virtue will take the place of mine, for I could certainly never allow myself to blush in your sight: under that powerful restraint I shall, while I cherish in you the kind and reliable support of my weakness, honour you, too, as the guardian angel who will save me from shame.

I have felt shame enough in making you this request. Such are the fatal results of a presumptuous assurance! Why did I not sooner come to fear the inclination that I felt growing in me? Why did I flatter myself upon my ability to control it or conquer it? Imbecile! How little I know about love! Ah, if I had fought it with more decision it would perhaps have acquired less power over me. Perhaps, then, my departure would not have been necessary. Or, though I submitted to so painful a necessity, I need not perhaps have broken off entirely a friendship which it would have been sufficient to enjoy less frequently! But to lose everything at once! And forever! Oh, my friend! . . . But there! Even as I write to you I am betrayed into improper admissions. Ah, let me leave, let me leave; my involuntary sins may, at least, be expiated by my sacrifices.

Good-bye, my worthy friend. Love me as a daughter; adopt me for one of yours; and you may be certain that, in spite of my weakness, I shall rather die than make myself unworthy of your choice.

3 October 17 —, at one o'clock in the morning

LETTER 103: *Madame de Rosemonde to the Présidente de Tourvel*

I was more distressed by your departure, my dear, than surprised at the reason for it. Long experience – and my interest in you – were enough to make clear to me the state of your feelings; and, to tell you the truth, there was nothing, or almost nothing, in your letter that was new to me. Had I only the letter to go by, I should still not know who it is that you love; for, though you speak of 'him' constantly, you do not once write his name. But I do not need to be told: I know quite well who it is. I remark upon it only because I am reminded that this was always the way of love. I see it is still just as it used to be.

I scarcely thought that I should ever be put to recalling memories far removed from me now and totally inappropriate to my age. Since yesterday, however, I have been very preoccupied with them, in the hopes of finding something that might be of use to you. But what can I do except admire you and pity you? I commend the wise decision you have made: but I am alarmed by having to understand that you judged it necessary. When one has reached that point, it is very difficult to keep away from the man towards whom one's heart is constantly drawn.

Do not, however, be discouraged. Nothing is impossible to the noble spirit you have; and if the day should come (God forbid!) when you have the misfortune to succumb, believe me, my dear, you must at least leave yourself the consolation of having fought with all your might. Besides, what is beyond the power of human wisdom must be left to the Divine Grace to perform at its will. Perhaps you are on the point of receiving its succour; and your virtue, put to the proof of the most painful trials, will emerge purer and more resplendent than before. That strength, which is not yours today, you must hope to receive tomorrow. Do not, however, look to it so much for support, as for encouragement to you to use your own strength to the full.

Leaving it to Providence to protect you from a danger against which I can do nothing, I confine myself to supporting and consoling you as far as I possibly can. I cannot relieve your distress, but I shall share it. And with that to justify me, I shall gladly receive your confidences. Your heart, I know, needs to be opened to some-one. I open mine to you: age has not yet chilled it to the point of being insensible to friendship. You will always find it ready to welcome you. This will be little comfort to your sufferings, but at least you will not weep alone; and when your unhappy love, grown too strong for you, compels you to speak of it, it is better that you should do so to me than to *him*. You see how I follow your example: I do not think his name will ever be mentioned between us. For the rest, we understand each other.

I am not sure whether I do well to tell you that he appeared deeply moved by your departure. It would, perhaps, be wiser not to have mentioned it: but I am not fond of that sort of wisdom that distresses one's friends. I am, in any case, obliged to say no more about it. My feeble eyesight and trembling hand do not allow me long letters when I have to write them myself.

Good-bye, then my dear; good-bye, my sweet child. Yes, I am delighted to adopt you for my daughter. You have all that is necessary to a mother's pride and pleasure.

Château de —
3 October 17 —

LETTER 104: *The Marquise de Merteuil to Madame de Volanges*

To be quite honest, my dear and good friend, I could scarcely suppress an impulse of pride when I read your letter. To think that you should honour me with your entire confidence – that you should even go so far as to ask my advice! Oh, I should be so happy to think that I really deserved this mark of your esteem, that I did not owe it merely to the prepossession of a friend. At all events, whatever prompted it, it is most precious to my heart; and having obtained it is in my opinion only one reason more for my trying harder to deserve it. I shall, then (but without any preten-sions to giving you advice) tell you freely what my views are. I hesitate to do so, because they differ from yours: but when I have put forward my arguments you shall be the judge; and if you condemn them, I am converted in advance to your opinion. I shall at least have good sense enough not to imagine I have more of it than you.

If however, for this once, my own opinion proves to be the better one, the reason must be looked for among the illusions of maternal love. This is so praiseworthy a sentiment that it must have found a place in your heart. How plainly, in fact, it betrays itself in the decision you are tempted to make. Thus, if it sometimes happens that you are wrong, it is never but in your choice of virtues.

Prudence is, it seems to me, the virtue which must be preferred above the rest when one is determining the fate of others; and especially when it is a case of sealing that fate with sacred and indissoluble promises, such as those of marriage. It is then that a mother, if she is as wise as she is loving, ought, as you so rightly say, 'to help a daughter with her experience'. How now, I ask you, can she better begin to achieve that purpose than by distinguishing, in her own mind, between what is agreeable and what is proper?

Is it not to debase a mother's authority, is it not to destroy it altogether, to subordinate it to a foolish emotion which maintains an illusory power only over those who are afraid of it, and disappears as soon as it is despised? For my part, I allow, I have never believed in these sweeping and irresistible passions, which seem to have been agreed upon as a convenient general excuse for our misdemeanours. I cannot conceive how any emotion, alive one moment and dead the next, can overpower the unalterable principles of decency, honour, and modesty; any more than I can understand how a woman who has betrayed those principles can be justified by her so-called passion, as though a thief could be justified by a passion for gold, or a murderer by a thirst for revenge.

Ah, who can say he has never experienced a struggle? But I have always tried to persuade myself that to resist it is enough to want to resist; and so far, at any rate, my experience has confirmed that opinion. What would virtue be without the duties it imposes? Its pursuit is in sacrifice; its reward is felt in our hearts. These truths cannot be denied except by those in whose interest it is to disregard them; who, corrupted as they already are, hope to create a temporary illusion for themselves in attempting to justify bad conduct by bad arguments.

But is there anything to be feared from a simple and innocent child – a child of your own, whose pure and decent education can only have strengthened her fortunate heredity? Yet it is to a fear of this kind, a fear, if I may say so, humiliating to your daughter, that you wish to sacrifice the advantageous match your prudence has arranged for her! I like Danceny very much; and for a long time, as you know, I have seen little of Monsieur de Gercourt: but my liking for one and my indifference to the other do not prevent my seeing the enormous difference in their pretensions.

They are equally well-born, I agree. But one has no fortune, while the other's is such that, even without the advantage of birth, it would be sufficient to take him anywhere. I willingly allow that money does not guarantee happiness; but it must also be allowed that it makes happiness a great deal easier to achieve. Mademoiselle de Volanges is, as you say, rich enough for two: nevertheless, the sixty thousand *livres* a year she is going to enjoy will not amount to so very much when she bears the name of Danceny, and must set up and maintain an establishment appropriate to that name. We are no longer in the age of Madame de Sévigné. Luxury nowadays is ruinous. We criticize, but must conform, and superfluities in the end deprive us of necessities.

As to qualities of character, which you make much account of and with good reason, Monsieur de Gercourt's are certainly beyond reproach, and it is to his advantage that they have already been put to the proof. I should like to think, and I do in fact think, that Danceny yields nothing to him here: but can we be as sure of him? It is true that he has till now appeared to be exempt from the usual infirmities of youth, and that in spite of the manners of our age he has shown a taste for good company which makes one argue well of him. But who knows whether or not this apparent good sense is simply the consequence of his mediocre fortune? However little fear there is of a man becoming corrupt or dissolute, he must have money to play the gambler or the libertine: and he may still enjoy the vices which he is chary of carrying to excess. After all, Danceny will not be the first man to have found his way into good company solely for lack of anything better to do.

I am not saying (God forbid!) that I believe all this of him. But there would always be a risk; and how sorry you would be if the consequences were unhappy! How would you answer if your daughter were to say: 'Mother, I was young and inexperienced. I was led astray into an error that was pardonable in one of my age. But Heaven had foreseen my weakness and had provided me with a wise mother to make up for it and to preserve me from it. Why then, forgetting your prudence, did you consent to my unhappiness? Was it for me to choose a husband, when I knew nothing about the married state? Though I were resolved upon it, was it not your duty to oppose me? However, I was never so foolishly insistent. Determined to obey you, I awaited your choice with respectful resignation: never did I swerve from the submission I owed you. Yet the most rebellious of children would suffer no more than I do now. Ah, your weakness has ruined me . . .'? Perhaps her respect for you will silence her complaints. But your mother's love will divine her feelings. And your daughter's tears, for all that they are stifled, will none the less fall scalding upon your heart. Where then will you look for consolation? To this foolish love, against which you should have protected her, but by which, instead, you allowed yourself to be beguiled?

I do not know, my dear, whether I have too strong a distrust of this passion: but I think it is to be feared, even in marriage. It is not that I disapprove of a decent and tender feeling animating the conjugal ties, softening in some sort the duties they impose: but it is not for feeling to form these ties, it is not for the illusion of a moment to govern the choice of a lifetime. After all, in order to choose we have to compare, and how compare when one person alone has all our attention? When that person himself cannot be properly understood, bewitched and infatuated as we are?

I have, as you may suppose, met several women who suffered from this dangerous malady. Some of them received me into their confidence, and not one but made her lover out to be a perfect being. But this chimerical perfection exists only in their imaginations. Out of their heated fancies they produce charms and virtues, with which they adorn the man of their choice according to taste, decking out what is often a very inferior dummy in the vestments of a god. But, whoever he is, they have scarcely dressed him up when, taken in by the illusion of their own creating, they fall to adoring him.

Either your daughter does not love Danceny or she is a victim of the same illusion: if her love is reciprocated, he is its victim too. So that your argument in favour of uniting them forever is reduced to a certainty that in the circumstances they do not and cannot know each other. But, you will say, do Monsieur de Gercourt and my daughter know each other any better? No, of course not; but at least they are only ignorant of, not deceived by each other. What happens between husband and wife in such cases, supposing them to be well-bred? Each studies the other and himself or herself in relation to the other, looks for and quickly finds those inclinations and desires which must be given up in the interests of mutual harmony. Such small sacrifices are made without difficulty because they are reciprocal, and determined upon beforehand: they are the foundation of what soon becomes a mutual regard; and habit, which strengthens all the inclinations it does not destroy, forms by degrees that cordial friendliness and that sympathetic trust in each other, which, together with respect, constitute, it seems to me, the true, the lasting happiness of marriage.

The illusions of love may be sweeter, but who is not aware that they are also less durable? And what dangers threaten at the moment when they die! It is then that the smallest faults begin to seem enormous and insupportable by contrast with the ideal of perfection that has taken possession of our minds. Husband and wife both think that it is the other alone who has changed, that they themselves are still to be appreciated at the value a momentary illusion once set upon them. They are astonished to find that they no longer exert the charm that they themselves no longer feel. Wounded vanity embitters their thoughts, enlarges their wrongs, provokes ill humour, rouses hatred; and frivolous pleasures are at length paid for in lasting misfortune.

That, my dear friend, is my opinion upon the subject that concerns us: I do not defend it, I merely state it: it is for you to decide. But if you stand by your own views, may I ask you to let me know what arguments you have found to put against mine? I should be very glad to know your intentions, and especially to be set at rest concerning the fate of your charming daughter, whose happiness I ardently desire, as much in friendship to her as in the friendship that binds me to you as long as I live.

Paris
4 October 17 —

LETTER 105 : *The Marquise de Merteuil to Cécile Volanges*

WELL, my little one! So you are exceedingly sorry and ashamed! And this Monsieur de Valmont is a wicked man, is he? What! Does he dare treat you as he would treat the woman he loved most of all? Has he taught you what you were dying of anxiety to know? Really, such behaviour is unforgivable. And you, for your part, would like to keep your virtue for your lover (who does not take advantage of it); to cultivate the pains, but not the pleasures of love. What could be better? You would make a marvellous character in a novel. Passion, misfortune, and virtue on top of it all, what an array of splendid things! One is sometimes bored, it is true, during the brilliant display, but it is well done.

There, there, the poor child, how much she is to be pitied! There were shadows under her eyes the next day! What will you say, then, when you see them under your lover's? Come, come, my angel: it will not always be like this: all men are not Valmonts. And then, not to have the courage to raise those eyes! Oh, that indeed you were right not to do: everyone would have seen your adventure written in them. Believe me, though: if that were so, all our women, and even the girls, would wear a much demurer air.

In spite of the compliments I am, as you notice, compelled to pay you, it must still be admitted that you failed to deliver the *coup de grâce*, that is, to tell everything to your mamma. And you had begun so well! You had already thrown yourself into her arms – sobbed – she wept too; what a pathetic scene! And what a pity to have left it incomplete! Your sweet mother, in a rapture of satisfaction and by way of assisting your virtue, would have immured you in a cloister for the rest of your life. There you could have loved Danceny as much as you liked without fear of rivalry or sin. You could have despaired at your leisure, and Valmont would certainly never have disturbed your grief with vexatious pleasures.

Seriously, is it possible at past fifteen years of age to be as much of a child as you are? You are quite right to say that you do not deserve my kindness. I wished, however, to be your friend: and it is not unlikely you need one with the mother you have and the husband she intends to give you! But if you don't grow up a little, what can one do for you? What can one hope for, when what usually brings girls to their senses seems, on the contrary, to have deprived you of yours?

If you could, for a moment, bring yourself to think reasonably you would soon find that you have cause to rejoice rather than complain. But you are ashamed, and that worries you! Oh, you may be at ease on that score: the shame that love brings with it is no different from the pain: it is only felt once. One may make a pretence of it later, but one never feels it again. The pleasure, however, remains, and that is something. I think I have even made out between the lines of your little outburst that you are capable of making a great deal of it. Come now, a little honesty. That agitation that prevented you 'from doing as you said', that made you find it 'so difficult to defend yourself', that made you 'almost sorry' when Valmont left; was it really shame that produced it, or was it pleasure? And 'his way of saying things so that one is hard put to it to think of a reply': was that not a consequence of 'his way of doing things?' Ah, young woman, you are lying, lying to your friend! That is not good enough. But let us say no more about it.

In a situation such as yours, that which for the rest of the world would be a pleasure and no more than a pleasure, becomes a piece of veritable good fortune. After all, since you find yourself between a mother and a lover whose love you will always find necessary, the former's to your interests, the latter's to your happiness, why have you not seen that the only means of achieving these contradictory aims is to pursue a third? In your preoccupation with a new adventure you will seem to your mamma to be sacrificing, for the sake of submitting to her will, an inclination which she does not favour, and at the same time will acquire in your lover's eyes the honour of putting up a defence. While you assure him ceaselessly of your love, you will not offer him the least guarantee of it, and he will not fail to attribute your refusals, which you will hardly find it difficult to make in the circumstances, to your virtue. He will perhaps complain, but will love you the more for it. And the acquisition of this dual merit – on the one hand the sacrifice of love, resistance to it on the other – will cost you no more than the enjoyment of its pleasures. Oh, how many women there are who have lost reputations they might safely have preserved had they been able to carry off a plan of this sort!

Does not the course I am suggesting seem to you to be the most reasonable one to take, as it is certainly the most pleasant? Do you know what you have achieved by the one you have in fact adopted? Your mamma has attributed your access of grief to an access of love; she is beside herself, and is only waiting to be more certain before she punishes you. She has just written to me about it: she will try every means of obtaining a confession from your own lips. She will go so far, she says, as to suggest Danceny to you for a husband, in order to incite you to talk. If you allow yourself to be misled by her pretence of kindness, if you reply according to the dictates of your heart, you will soon suffer a long, perhaps a perpetual imprisonment and will repent your blind credulity at your leisure.

You must meet the ruse she intends to use against you with another. Begin by looking less sorrowful, by making her believe that you are thinking less of Danceny. She will be the more easily convinced in that this is the usual effect of absence. And she will be the more pleased with you in that she will be provided with an excuse to applaud her own prudence in removing you from Paris. But if she still remains doubtful, insists on putting you to the test, and broaches the subject of marriage to you, take cover like a well brought-up girl in your complete obedience. What will you, in point of fact, be risking? As far as husbands are concerned, one is as good as another; and even the most inconvenient is less of a trial than a mother.

As soon as she is more pleased with you, your mamma will have you married. Then, with more freedom of action, you will be able to leave Valmont for Danceny or even to keep them both, just as you choose. For, you must remember, your Danceny is agreeable:

but he is one of those men you may have when you want, and for as long as you want: you may therefore make yourself easy about him. Valmont is quite another matter: difficult to keep, and dangerous to leave. He demands great skill, or, if you have none, great tractability. On the other hand, if you could succeed in attaching him to you as a friend, it would indeed be a piece of good fortune. He would put you immediately in the first rank of our women of fashion. It is thus that one acquires substance in the world, not by blushing and crying, as you used to do when your nuns made you kneel to your dinner.

You will then, if you are wise, try to be reconciled to Valmont, who must be very angry with you; and, since one must always be capable of correcting one's mistakes, don't be afraid of making a few advances to him. You will soon learn that though a man takes the first step, we are nearly always obliged to take the second ourselves. You have a pretext for doing so: for you must not keep this letter: I insist that you return it to Valmont as soon as you have read it. Don't, however, forget to seal it up again before doing so. In the first place you must take all the credit yourself for your proceedings with him: you must not seem to be acting upon advice. And then, you are the only person in the world who is enough my friend to hear me speak as I do.

Good-bye, my angel. Follow my advice and tell me whether you are not the better for it.

P.S. By the way, I was forgetting ... one word more. Take more care of your style. You still write like a child. I can quite see the reason for it: you say what you think, and never what you don't believe. This will do between us who can have nothing to conceal from one another: but with everybody! With your lover above all! You will always be taken for a little ninny. You will agree, I am sure, that when you write to someone it is for his sake and not for yours. You must therefore try to say less what you think than what you think he will be pleased to hear.

Good-bye, my dear heart. I shall kiss you instead of scolding you, in the hope that you will be more reasonable in future.

Paris
4 October 17 —

LETTER 106: *The Marquise de Merteuil to the Vicomte de Valmont*

BRAVO, Vicomte: this time I love you madly! For the rest, the first of your two letters led me to expect the second, which did not astonish me at all. While, proud of your forthcoming success, you were claiming your reward and asking me whether I was ready, I could see quite well that I need be in no very great hurry. Yes, on my honour: as I read your touching account of the tender scene that left you so *deeply moved*, as I noticed you displaying a self-restraint worthy of the finest epoch of our chivalry, I said to myself a dozen times: 'There goes another botched affair.'

But it could not have been otherwise. What do you expect a poor woman to do when she surrenders and is not taken? Upon my word, in such circumstances she must at least save her honour: and that is what your Présidente has done. I may tell you that, having observed that her course of action has proved really not ineffective, I propose to make use of it myself at the first more or less serious opportunity that offers: but I assure you that if the man for whom I go to so much trouble does not take more advantage of it than you, he may certainly renounce me forever.

There you are, then, reduced to absolutely nothing! And by two women one of whom had already passed the point of no return, while the other aspired to nothing better! Well! You will think I am boasting, you will say that it is easy to be wise after the event, but I can swear to you that I expected it. You are really without any genius for your calling; you know what you have learnt but can invent nothing new, so that as soon as circumstances no longer conform to your usual formulas, as soon as you have to deviate from the customary path, you are brought up short like the merest schoolboy. An attack of childishness on the one hand, and on the other a relapse into prudery are enough, because they do not happen every day, to disconcert you; you could neither prevent them nor cure them. Ah, Vicomte, Vicomte! You are teaching me not to judge men by their successes. Soon we shall have to say of you: 'He was once a man of mark.' And when you have perpetrated absurdity after absurdity you come running back to me! It seems I have nothing better to do than to repair the mischief. Doing that, at any rate, would keep me fully occupied.

Be that as it may, one of your two adventures was undertaken without my approbation, and I shall not meddle with it; as for the other, since you have shown some willingness to oblige me in it, I shall make it my concern. The letter I enclose, which you will first read and then deliver to the little Volanges, is more than enough to bring her back to you. But, I beg you, take some pains with the child. Let us work together to make her the despair of her mother and Gercourt. Don't be afraid of increasing the doses. It is quite clear to me that the little creature will not be at all frightened if you do. Our designs upon her once fulfilled, she must continue as best she can.

I am now entirely disinterested where she is concerned. I had some thought of making a kind of assistant in intrigue out of her, of employing her, as it were, for subordinate roles, but I see that the material is lacking. She has a stupid ingenuousness, which did not even yield to the medicine you administered, a medicine that is seldom without effect. It is, in my view, the most dangerous malady from which a woman can suffer. It denotes, in particular, a weakness of character which is nearly always incurable, and is an impediment to everything; so that, while attempting to fit the girl for a life of intrigue, we should only be turning out a woman of easy virtue. Now, I can think of nothing more insipid than the complaisance of stupid women who surrender, knowing neither how nor why, simply because they are attacked and cannot resist. This sort of woman is absolutely nothing but a machine for giving pleasure.

You will say that we have only to turn her into one of these and our plans are suited. Well and good! But don't forget that everyone is soon familiar with the springs and motors of these machines; and that, to make use of this one without danger it will be necessary to do so with all speed, to stop in good time, then to destroy it. In fact we shall not lack the means to get rid of it: Gercourt will always be there to shut it away when we require. And in the end, when he can no longer doubt the fraud, when it is quite public and altogether notorious, what will it matter if he takes his revenge, so long as he can find no consolation? This that I say of the husband you will, no doubt, apply to the mother: so that is that.

Having fixed upon this line of proceeding as the best, I have decided to hurry the girl a little, as you will see from my letter. This makes it very important to leave nothing in her hands that might compromise us, and I beg you to take care of that. Once this precaution has been taken, I shall see to the moral persuasion: the rest is your concern. If, however, you notice in the course of events that the ingenuousness is correcting itself, we shall still have time to change our plans. We should in any case have had sooner or later to do what we are going to do: our efforts will under no circumstances be wasted.

Did you know that my own efforts were in danger of being so, and that Gercourt's lucky star had almost prevailed over my prudence: that Madame de Volanges had a moment of natural weakness and wanted to give her daughter to Danceny? This was the meaning of the more sympathetic interest you noticed being offered *the morning after*. And you again would have been the cause of this fine state of affairs! Fortunately the solicitous mother wrote to me about it, and I hope my reply will turn her against the idea. I spoke so often of virtue, and above all flattered her so much, that she should find, after all, that I am right.

I am sorry not to have had time to copy the letter, so that you might have been edified by the austerity of my moral views. You might have seen how I despise those women who are depraved enough to take a lover! It is so easy to be a bigot in writing! It never harms anyone else, and is no bother to oneself. . . . And then I am not unaware that the good lady has herself, like anyone else, been guilty of some little weaknesses in the days of her youth, and I should not be sorry to humiliate her a little, if only to disturb her conscience: it would console me a little for the compliments I have paid her to the discomfort of my own. It was again, in the same letter, the thought of hurting Gercourt that gave me the courage to speak well of him.

Good-bye, Vicomte. I very much approve of your decision to stay where you are for some time. I can think of no way to hasten your progress, but invite you to relieve your boredom in the company of our pupil. As for me, you must see, in spite of your polite quotation, that it is still necessary to wait; and you will agree, I have no doubt, that it is not my fault.

Paris
4 October 17 —

LETTER 107: *Azolan to the Vicomte de Valmont*

Monsieur,

IN accordance with your instructions I went immediately I received your letter to Monsieur Bertrand, who gave me the twenty-five *louis* as you had commanded. I asked him for two more for Philippe, whom I had told to leave immediately as Monsieur instructed and who had no money; but Monsieur your agent refused, saying he had no instructions from you as to that. So I had to give the money to Philippe myself, and Monsieur will take that into account if he will be so kind.

Philippe left yesterday evening. I strongly advised him not to move from the inn, so that one could be sure of finding him in case of need.

I went immediately to Madame the Présidente's to see Mademoiselle Julie: but she was out and I spoke only to La Fleur, from whom I was not able to learn anything because since he arrived he has been in the house only at mealtimes. It is his assistant who is on duty, and as Monsieur knows, I have no acquaintance with him. But I made a beginning today. I returned this morning to Mademoiselle Julie's, and she seemed very glad to see me. I inquired after the reason for her mistress's return; but she told me she knew nothing, and I think that is true. I called her to account for not letting me know they were leaving, and she assured me she knew nothing about it until the evening before when she attended Madame to bed: indeed she spent the whole night packing and did not have more than two hours' sleep, poor girl. She did not leave her mistress's room that evening until past one o'clock, and when she left, her mistress was just sitting down to write.

In the morning, before she left, Madame de Tourvel gave a letter to the concierge. Mademoiselle Julie does not know for whom it was: she says it was perhaps for Monsieur. But Monsieur has said nothing.

All during the journey Madame wore a great hood over her face, and her face could not therefore be seen: but Mademoiselle Julie is sure that she cried a great deal. She did not say a word all the way, and did not wish to stop at —,[1] as she had done coming – which Mademoiselle Julie was not too pleased about, as she had eaten no breakfast. But, as I said to her, a mistress is a mistress.

On their arrival Madame went to bed: but she only remained there for a few hours. On rising she called the porter and gave him orders to admit nobody. She made no *toilette* at all. She sat down to dinner, but ate only a little soup, and immediately left the table. Coffee was taken to her room, and Mademoiselle Julie went in at the same time. She found her mistress putting papers away in her desk, and distinctly saw that they were letters. I should be willing to stake anything on their being Monsieur's. Of the three that arrived for her in the afternoon, she was still looking at one long into the evening! I am quite sure that this again was one of Monsieur's. Why, then, did she run away like that? It astonishes me, I must say. But Monsieur must surely know the reason, and it is none of my business.

In the afternoon Madame the Présidente went into the library, and removed two books which she carried to her boudoir. Mademoiselle Julie, however, assures me that she read for not more than a quarter of an hour the whole day, and that she did nothing else but examine the letter and dream, resting her head on her hand. Since I thought Monsieur might be very glad to know what books they were, and since Mademoiselle Julie could not tell me, I had myself taken into the library today under the pretext of wanting to look around it. There were only two empty spaces for books, one being for the second volume of *Christian Thoughts*, the other for the first volume of a book entitled *Clarissa*. I write the title as I saw it written: Monsieur will perhaps know what it is.

Last evening Madame took no supper; she only drank some tea.

She rang early this morning, asked for the horses to be ready immediately, and before nine o'clock was at the Cistercian church, where she heard Mass. She wished to make her confession, but her

1. The same village, half-way to Paris.

confessor was away and will not be back for another week or ten days. I thought it would be as well to let Monsieur know this.

Then she came home, took breakfast, and afterwards began writing, continuing until nearly one o'clock. I found an early opportunity of doing what Monsieur was most anxious of all for me to do; it was I who took the letters to the post. There was nothing for Madame de Volanges, but I am sending a letter to Monsieur which was for Monsieur the Président. It seemed to me to be the most interesting. There was also one for Madame de Rosemonde; but I supposed that Monsieur could always see that when he wanted to, and so let it go. As to what remained, Monsieur will soon know everything since Madame the Présidente has written to him too. From now on I shall obtain all the letters he wants, for it is nearly always Mademoiselle Julie who gives them to the servants, and she has assured me that, out of friendship for me and for Monsieur too, she will willingly do what I ask.

She did not even want the money I offered her, but I feel sure Monsieur will wish to make her some little present; and if he so desires, and would like me to do it on his behalf, I could easily find out what she would like.

I hope that Monsieur will not find me negligent in his service, and I am very anxious to clear myself of the accusations he makes against me. If I did not know of Madame the Présidente's departure, it was, on the contrary, my zeal in Monsieur's service that explains it, since it was he who sent me off at three o'clock in the morning: which was why I did not see Mademoiselle Julie the evening before, having slept as usual at the 'Tournebride', so as not to wake anyone in the house.

As to what Monsieur says of my being often without money, in the first place it is because I always like to do the proper thing, as Monsieur knows; and then I must, after all, maintain the honour of the coat I wear.

I know I should, perhaps, save a little for the future, but I put my entire trust in Monsieur's generosity, who is such a good master.

As for going into Madame de Tourvel's service while remaining in Monsieur's, I hope that Monsieur will not insist upon it. It was quite different with Madame the Duchesse; but I shall certainly not wear livery, and a magistrate's livery at that, after having had the honour of being Monsieur's valet. In every other possible way Monsieur may dispose as he likes of one who has the honour to be, with as much affection as respect, his very humble servant.

Roux Azolan, valet

Paris
5 October 17 —, at eleven
o'clock in the evening

LETTER 108: *The Présidente de Tourvel to Madame de Rosemonde*

Oh, my dear kind mother! How I needed your letter, and how thankful I am to you. I read it again and again; I could not tear myself away from it. To it I owe the few moments of relief I have had since my departure. How good you are! Wisdom and virtue have sympathized with weakness! You have taken pity on my sufferings! Ah, if you knew what sufferings . . . they are terrible! I thought I had felt all the pains of love, but the truly unspeakable torment, which one must have experienced to be able to conceive, is to be separated from what one loves, to be separated forever! . . . Yes, the grief that crushes me today will return tomorrow, the day after tomorrow, for the rest of my life. My God, how young I still am, and how long a time remains for suffering! . . .

To be the instrument of one's own misery, to tear out one's heart with one's own hands; and while one suffers insupportable tortures, to feel at every instant that one may end them with a word; and that this word should be a crime! Ah, my dear!...

When I took the painful decision to leave him I hoped that absence would increase my courage and my strength: how wrong I was! It seems, on the contrary, that absence has completed their ruin. I had more to fight against once; but even though I resisted I did not suffer complete privation. At least I saw him sometimes. Often, without daring to lift my eyes to his face, I felt his own fixed upon me. Yes, my dear, I felt them. It was as if they brought warmth to my soul, as if his looks, though they did not meet mine, could still reach my heart. But now, in this dreadful solitude, cut off from all that is dear to me, alone with my misfortunes, every moment of my dreary existence is an occasion for tears and there is nothing to sweeten the bitterness. My sacrifices have brought me no consolation; those I have made hitherto serve only to make the others more painful that I have still to make.

Only yesterday this was brought home to me. Among the letters delivered to me there was one from him. My servant was still two yards away from me when I recognized it among the others. I rose involuntarily from my chair: I was trembling, I could scarcely conceal my emotion, and my state of mind was not entirely disagreeable. A moment later, when I was alone again, the illusory pleasure vanished, and left me only with one more sacrifice to make. Could I, after all, open the letter which I longed to read? The fate that pursues me decrees that when something seems to be offered me as a consolation, it is only, on the contrary, a demand for some new renunciation, which is the more cruel when I think that Monsieur de Valmont must share it.

There it is at last, the name that haunts me continually, the name I have found it so difficult to write. The sort of accusation you made against me about it truly alarmed me. I beseech you to believe that false modesty has in no way affected my confidence in you: and why should I be afraid of naming him? Ah, it is my feelings, and not their object, that I blush for. Who but he could be worthier of inspiring them? Yet, I do not know why, his name does not come naturally to my pen. Even just then I had to think before putting it down.

To return to him, you tell me that he appeared to you to be *deeply moved by my departure*. What then did he do? What did he say? Has he spoken of returning to Paris? Please dissuade him from doing so in so far as you can. If he has properly understood me, he will not bear me a grudge for leaving him: but he must also understand that my decision is irrevocable. One of my worst torments is not knowing what he thinks. I still have his letter here . . . but I am sure you are of my opinion and that I ought not to open it.

It is only because of you, my dear indulgent friend, that I am not entirely separated from him. I do not want to abuse your kindness; I understand perfectly that your letters cannot be long; but you will not refuse your child two words, one to keep up her courage and the other to comfort her. Good-bye, my most worthy friend.

Paris
5 October 17 —

LETTER 109: *Cécile Volanges to the Marquise de Merteuil*

It was only today, Madame, that I gave Monsieur de Valmont the letter you did me the honour of writing to me. I kept it for four days in spite of my frequent fears that someone should find it; but I hid it away very carefully, and whenever the sense of my troubles overcame me I shut myself up to read it again.

I quite see now that what I thought was a great misfortune is scarcely a misfortune at all; and I must admit that there is a great deal of pleasure in it, so much so that I am hardly unhappy at all any more. It is only the thought of Danceny that still torments me at times. But there are already a great many occasions when I don't think of him at all! The fact is, too, that Monsieur de Valmont is very agreeable!

Our reconciliation took place two days ago: it was very easy, since I had scarcely said two words to him when he told me that if I had something to tell him he would come to my room that evening, and I had only to reply that I was willing. And then, as soon as he was there, he seemed to be no more annoyed than he would have been if I had never done anything to him. He only scolded me afterwards, and even then very gently, as if . . . just like you: which proved to me that he is as much of a friend to me as you are.

You cannot imagine how many curious things he has told me, things I should never have believed; especially about Mamma. I should be very glad if you would let me know whether they are all true. At any rate, I could not help laughing at them; so much so that once I laughed out loud, which frightened us both very much. Mamma might have heard, and if she had come to investigate what would have become of me? This time she would certainly have sent me back to the convent!

Since we must be prudent, and since, as Monsieur de Valmont said himself, he would not risk compromising me for anything in the world, we have agreed that from now on he will come only to open the door, after which we shall go into his room. There we have nothing to fear. I have already been there once yesterday, and as I write I am waiting for him to come for me again. I hope, Madame, that you will no longer be able to find fault with me.

There was, however, one thing in your letter that surprised me very much, and that is what you say about Danceny and Monsieur de Valmont after I am married. I seem to remember that one day at the Opera you said the opposite: that once I was married I should have to love no one but my husband, and that I should even have to forget Danceny; but then, perhaps I misunderstood you, and I should much prefer it this way because now I am no longer so afraid of being married. I even want to be, since I shall have more freedom when I am, and I hope I shall then be able to manage my affairs so that I need think of no one but Danceny. I am quite sure that I shall be really happy only with him, for the thought of him still disturbs me, and I can have no peace unless I am able to forget him, which it is very difficult to do. As soon as I think of him I am immediately miserable again.

What comforts me a little is that you assure me he will love me more: but are you quite sure of that? . . . Oh, yes, you would not want to deceive me. Yet how odd that it is Danceny I love, and Monsieur de Valmont . . . But, as you say, it is perhaps a piece of good fortune! Anyhow, we shall see.

I could not entirely understand your remarks on the subject of my style of writing. It seems to me that Danceny likes my letters as they are. I am quite aware, however, that I ought to say nothing to him of what is going on with Monsieur de Valmont; so you have no reason to be afraid.

Mamma has not yet said a word about my marriage; but leave it to me. When she does speak I promise you that, since she will only be doing so to trap me, I shall not hesitate to lie to her.

Good-bye, my very dear friend. Thank you very much. I assure you I shall never forget all your kindness towards me. I must finish here for it is nearly one o'clock and Monsieur de Valmont will be here before long.

Château de —
20 October 17 —

LETTER 110: *The Vicomte de Valmont to the Marquise de Merteuil*

O Heavenly Powers, I had a soul attuned to sorrow; give me one to support felicity![1] It is, I think, the tender-hearted Saint-Preux who says this. Better endowed than he, I am capable of sustaining both emotions at once. Yes, my dear, I am at once very happy and very unhappy; and since you have my entire confidence, a twofold account of my pains and my pleasures is owing to you.

Know, then, that my ungrateful devotee still keeps me under severe restraint. I am at my fourth rejected letter. I am perhaps wrong to say it is the fourth; for having guessed, after the first rejection, that it would be followed by a good many others, and having no desire to waste time in this way, I decided to reduce my complaints to a few platitudes and to omit the date from the letter: since the second dispatch it is the same one that has been travelling to and fro. I have done no more than change the envelope each time. If one day my beauty, as beauties generally do, finally relents out of fatigue if nothing else, she will keep the letter and there will be time enough then to find out what has been happening. As you will understand, I cannot, with this new species of correspondence, keep myself properly informed.

I have, however, discovered that the fickle creature has changed her confidante: at any rate I have confirmed that since her departure from here no letters have arrived from her for Madame de Volanges, whereas two have arrived for old Rosemonde; and since the latter has said nothing, since she has not so much as opened her mouth on the subject of 'her dear, delightful friend', about whom

1. Rousseau, *La Nouvelle Héloïse.*

previously she would never stop talking, I conclude that it is she who has been taken into confidence. I presume that, on the one hand, it is the necessity of talking to someone about me, and, on the other, a slight shame where Madame de Volanges is concerned at reverting to the subject of a feeling long since disavowed, that has produced this great change of tactics. I am afraid, too, I may have lost by it: for the older women grow, the harsher and stricter they become. The one might have said worse things about me: but the other will say worse things about love; and our soft-hearted prude is much more afraid of the feeling than of the person who inspires it.

My sole means of acquiring information is, as you may guess, to intercept their secret correspondence. I have already sent orders to my valet and daily await their execution. Till then I can do nothing, except at a venture; so for the past week I have been turning over in my mind every stratagem known to me, everything I have ever gleaned from novels or my own private experience. I can find nothing which suits either the circumstances of the affair or the character of its heroine. There would be no difficulty in finding my way into her house, even at night, nor yet again in putting her to sleep and making another Clarissa out of her: but to have recourse after more than two months of toil and trouble to methods which are not my own! To crawl slavishly in other's tracks, to triumph without glory! . . . No, I shall not allow her *the pleasures of vice with the honours of virtue.*[1] It is not enough for me to possess her: I want her to give herself up. Now, for that, it is not only essential that I gain access to her, but that I should do so at her bidding; that I should find her alone and prepared to listen to me; and, above all, that I should close her eyes to the danger, because, if she perceives it, she must surmount it or die. But the better I know what has to be done, the more difficult I find it to do; and even if you are going to laugh at me again, I must admit that my embarrassment increases the more I think about it.

I think I should be at my wits' end were it not for the happy distraction our pupil supplies: I owe it to her that I have still something better to do than compose elegies.

Would you believe that the girl was so frightened that three long

1. *La Nouvelle Héloïse.*

days went by before your letter produced its full effect? See how a single wrong idea can spoil the most favourable disposition!

At any rate, it was not till Saturday that she came circling round me to mumble a few words: uttered, however, so softly – so smothered by diffidence – that it was impossible to hear them. But the blush they occasioned gave me a clue to their meaning. Till then I had shown reserve: but touched by so amusing a repentance, I was willing to promise the pretty penitent that I would come and see her the same evening. My forgiveness was received with all the gratitude due to so much condescension.

Since I never lose sight of either your plans or mine, I decided to make the most of the opportunity both to gauge the true potentialities of this child, and to hasten her education. But to accomplish the task in greater freedom, it was necessary to change the place of our rendezvous. A mere closet, which is all that separates your pupil's bedroom from that of her mother, was not enough to inspire in her the security she must feel before she can unfold at her ease. I decided, therefore, that I would quite innocently make some noise which would frighten her enough to make her choose a safer refuge for the future. Once more she spared me the trouble.

The little creature laughs a great deal: and, to encourage her merriment, I had the idea of relating, during our *entr'actes*, all the scandalous stories that came into my head. To give them an added spice, and to make them more interesting I ascribed them all to her mamma; whom it amused me to bedeck with vices and follies.

It was not by accident that I hit upon the idea. It encouraged our timid schoolgirl more than anything else could have done, and at the same time inspired her with the profoundest contempt for her mother. I observed long ago that if it is not always necessary to employ this method in seducing a young girl, it is the indispensable and often the most effective course when one wants to corrupt her. For the girl who does not respect her mother will not respect herself: a moral truth I think so useful, that I was very glad to supply another example in illustration of it.

Meanwhile your pupil, who had no thought of morals, was ready to choke with laughter at any moment; and finally, on one occasion, nearly exploded. I had no difficulty in convincing her that she had made a *frightful noise*, and I pretended great terror, which she was easily persuaded to share. So as to drive the lesson home, I banished all further hopes of pleasure and left her three hours earlier than usual. We agreed, as we parted, that from the next day on we should meet in my room.

I have received her there twice already; and in this short space of time the schoolgirl has learnt nearly as much as her master knows. Yes, I have taught her everything, down to the minor complaisances! I have omitted only the art of taking precautions.

Thus busy the whole night long, I have begun to sleep during a great part of the day; and as there is nothing to attract me in the company now at the house, I spend scarcely more than an hour in the drawing-room each day. I even decided today to eat in my room, and I intend not to leave it henceforth except to take a little walk now and again. This idiosyncratic behaviour will be put down to the state of my health. I have declared myself a victim of *the vapours*, and have also announced a little fever. This puts me to no trouble but that of speaking slowly and faintly. As for the change in my looks, trust your pupil for that. *Love will provide.*[1]

I spend my leisure dreaming of ways in which I can regain my lost advantage over that ungrateful woman; also in composing a sort of debauchee's catechism for the use of my pupil. There is nothing in it that is not called by its technical name, and I am already laughing at the interesting conversation this will afford her and Gercourt on the first night of their marriage. Nothing is more amusing than her ingenuousness in using what little she already knows of the jargon! She has no idea that there is any other way of referring to the same things. The child is really enchanting! The contrast between her naïve candour and the language of insult could not, of course, fail to be striking, and, I don't know why, it is only the unusual that pleases me now.

I am, perhaps, a little too preoccupied with it, since I am compromising both my time and my health. But I hope my pretended illness, besides saving me from the boredom of the drawing-room, will be useful, too, with my austere devotee, whose tigerish virtue is nevertheless allied to a most tender sensibility! I have no doubt she has already heard about this grave indisposition, and I should very much like to know what she thinks of it; the more so because

1. Regnard, *Love's Follies.*

I should be willing to swear she will not fail to attach the credit for it to herself. I shall in future govern the state of my heart according to the impression it makes upon her.

There, my love, you know as much about my affairs as I do myself. I hope soon to have more interesting news to give you; and I beg you to believe that, among the pleasures I anticipate, I set great store by the reward I am expecting from you.

Château de —
11 October 17 —

LETTER 111: *The Comte de Gercourt to Madame de Volanges*

IT seems, Madame, that everything is now quiet in this country, and we are daily expecting permission to return to France. I hope you will not doubt that I am still as anxious to return there and to form the ties which are to unite me with you and Mademoiselle de Volanges. My cousin, however, Monsieur the Duc de —, to whom as you know I am under great obligations, has just informed me of his recall to Naples. He tells me that he expects to travel by way of Rome, and hopes *en route* to see that part of Italy with which he is still unacquainted. He invites me to accompany him on the journey, which will take from six weeks to two months. I cannot deny that I should like to make the most of this opportunity, knowing that once I am married I shall have difficulty in finding time for journeys abroad other than those necessitated by my military service. Perhaps, too, it would be more convenient if the wedding were postponed until the winter, since not before then will all my relations be together in Paris at the same time, in particular Monsieur the Marquis de — to whom it is I owe my hope of an association with you. Despite these considerations, my plans in this respect shall be absolutely subordinated to your wishes. However slightly you may prefer your original arrangements, I am prepared to cancel my own. I beg you only to let me know your intentions in the matter as soon as possible. I shall await your reply here, and that alone will decide what I do.

I am, Madame, with respect, and with all the sentiments fitting in a son, your very humble, etc.

The Comte de Gercourt

Bastia
10 October 17 —

LETTER 112: *Madame de Rosemonde to the Présidente de Tourvel* (*dictated*)

I HAVE only this instant, my dear, received your letter of the eleventh,[1] and the gentle reproaches it contains. You must admit that you would have liked to make many more, and that if you had not remembered you were my daughter, you would really have scolded me. It would, nevertheless, have been very unjust of you. It was because I wished and hoped to reply to you myself that I postponed doing so from day to day; and even now, as you see, I am obliged to do so through my maid, at second hand. My miserable rheumatism has attacked me again and lodged itself this time in my right arm, and I am an utter cripple. This is what comes, young and healthy as you are, of having an aged friend: you suffer for her infirmities.

As soon as my pain gives me a little respite, I promise you we shall have a long talk. In the meanwhile I shall say only that I have received your two letters; that they have increased, if that is possible, my feelings of friendship for you; and that I shall never cease to enter, with the most lively interest, into all that concerns you.

My nephew is also a little unwell, but there is no danger and not the least cause for anxiety: it is a slight indisposition which, so far as I can see, affects his temper more than his health. We scarcely see him now.

His confinement and your departure have not made our little circle any more gay. The little Volanges, especially, feels the want of you terribly and spends the whole day yawning fit to swallow her point-lace. During the past few days in particular she has done

1. This letter has not been found.

us the honour of falling into a profound sleep every afternoon after lunch.

Good-bye, my dear. I am still your very good friend: your mamma, your sister even, were my great age to permit my claiming that title. In short, I am attached to you by all the tenderest feelings.

Signed: Adélaïde, for Madame de Rosemonde

Château de —
14 October 17 —

LETTER 113: *The Marquise de Merteuil to the Vicomte de Valmont*

I THINK I must warn you, Vicomte, that they begin to talk of you in Paris. Your absence is remarked, and the reason for it already guessed at. I was present yesterday at a supper where there were a great many people. It was positively affirmed that you were imprisoned in the country by a romantic and unhappy love. The faces of all those who envy your success and of all the women you have neglected were immediately the picture of joy. If you take my advice, you will not allow these dangerous rumours to acquire further substance, and will return forthwith to destroy them by your presence.

Remember that once you allow the idea to lose credence that you are irresistible, you will soon find that in fact you are being resisted more easily, and that your rivals have also lost their respect for you and are daring to enter the lists against you. For which of them does not believe himself to be a match for virtue? Remember, too, that of the multitudes of women you have flaunted in the public eye the ones you have not had will be trying to disabuse the world, while the others will be doing their utmost to deceive it. In any case you must expect to be rated perhaps as much beneath your true worth as you have till now been rated above it.

Come back then, Vicomte, and don't sacrifice your reputation to a childish caprice. You have done all that we wished to do with the little Volanges. As for your Présidente, it is obviously not by establishing yourself ten leagues away from her that you will rid yourself of your fancies. Do you think she will come looking for you? She perhaps no longer thinks of you, or still thinks of you only to congratulate herself upon having humiliated you. Here at least you may find the opportunity that you need of reappearing with a flourish; and if you persist in continuing your ridiculous adventure, I cannot see that your return will make any difference . . . on the contrary.

After all, if your Présidente *adores you*, as you have so often told me and are so little able to prove, her one consolation, her sole pleasure, must now be to speak of you, to find out what you are doing, what you are saying, what thinking, down to the least thing that concerns you. Every trifle assumes a value because of the privation that is felt in general. They are the crumbs that fall from the rich man's table: the rich man scorns them, but the beggar collects them avidly: they are his nourishment. Now, the poor Présidente is at present receiving all the crumbs she wants: and the more she has, the less inclined she will be to give way to an appetite for other things.

Moreover, since you know who her confidante is, you can be in no doubt that each of that lady's letters contains a little sermon on all she thinks proper 'to the support of wisdom and the fortification of virtue'.[1] Why then leave the one with a resource for her defence, the other with a means of attack?

Not that I am altogether of your opinion when you say that you have lost, you think, by the change of confidante. In the first place Madame de Volanges hates you, and hatred is always more clear-sighted and cunning than friendship. All your old aunt's virtue will not commit her for a single instant to speaking ill of her nephew. Virtue has its weaknesses too. And then your fears are based on an observation which is absolutely false.

It is not true that 'the older women grow, the harsher and stricter they become'. It is between the ages of forty and fifty that, desperate at finding their complexions wither and furious at being obliged to give up pretensions and pleasures to which they are still inclined, nearly all women turn into prudes and shrews. This long interval

1. *One can never think of everything!* : a comedy.

is necessary before their sacrifice is complete: but as soon as it has been consummated, they divide themselves into two classes.

The more numerous one, which comprises those women who have had nothing but youth and beauty to recommend them, falls into a feeble-minded apathy, from which it never emerges except to play cards or practise a few devotions. These women are always boring, often querulous, sometimes a little meddlesome, but they are rarely malicious. One cannot say of them either that they are or that they are not severe. They have neither thought nor being, and merely repeat indifferently and uncomprehendingly everything they hear, retaining within themselves an absolute void.

The other much rarer class, and the really valuable one, contains those women who, having been possessed of a character and having taken care to cultivate their minds, are able to create an identity for themselves when the one provided by nature has failed them. They are able to polish their wits where before they had decked out their figures. Their judgement is generally sane, their intelligence at once solid, gay, and graceful. They replace their more seductive attractions with a more appealing kindness, and moreover with that *joie de vivre*, the charm of which only increases with age. Thus, making themselves loved by the young, they succeed in some sort in recapturing their youth. But then, far from being, as you say, harsh and strict, their customary tolerance, their long experience of human frailty, and, above all, the memories of youth which alone reconcile them to life, incline them rather too much perhaps to the side of lenity.

What I can, at any rate vouch for is that, having always sought after old women, the value of whose suffrage I early recognized, I have met several to whom I was attracted as much by inclination as by self-interest. I shall stop there: seeing that at the moment you take fire so easily and burn so earnestly, I am afraid you might of a sudden fall in love with your old aunt and bury yourself with her for good in the tomb you have already so long inhabited.

To resume: in spite of the enchantment your little schoolgirl seems to have cast over you, I cannot believe that she figures at all seriously in your plans. You found her to hand, you took her: well done! But that was no true pleasure. You cannot even, to tell the truth, be said to have enjoyed her completely: you possess absolutely nothing but her person. I leave her heart out of account – I am sure you can scarcely have been interested in that – but you have not even penetrated her head. I don't know whether you have noticed this, but I have proof of it in the last letter she wrote me.[1] I send it to you so that you may judge. Observe that when she speaks of you it is always *Monsieur de Valmont*, that all her ideas, even the ones you have given her, tend always in the direction of Danceny: and that she does not call him Monsieur, it is always just *Danceny*. She thus sets him apart from all the others, so that even though she gives herself to you she is familiar only with him. If a conquest such as this strikes you as *fascinating*, if the pleasures it affords *attract* you, you are certainly a man of modest and not very fastidious pretensions. Keep her; I don't mind: you will even be falling in with my plans. But it seems to me that the affair is scarcely worth more than another quarter of an hour's inconvenience unless you can acquire some degree of power as well: prevent her, for example, from meeting Danceny until you have made her forget him a little more.

Before I leave off discussing your affairs to begin upon mine, I want still to tell you that the illness scheme you announce your intention of adopting is very well known and very often employed. Really, Vicomte, you are not very inventive! I, too, sometimes repeat myself, as you shall see. But I try to rise above it in my attention to detail, and then my final justification is always success. I am going to attempt it again, to embark upon a new venture. It will not, I confess, have the merit of difficulty, but it will at least be a distraction and I am dying of boredom.

I don't know why, but since the Prévan affair, Belleroche has become insupportable. He has so plied me with attentions, tenderness, *veneration*, that I can bear him no longer. His anger at the beginning I found amusing. I had really however to curb it: I should have compromised myself by letting it continue. And there was no way of making him listen to reason. So as to calm him the more easily, I decided to display an increase of affection. But he took this seriously, and since then his permanent state of infatuation has been too much for me. I am especially conscious of the insulting confidence he has in me, and the complacency with which he re-

1. See Letter 109.

gards me as his forever. It is truly humiliating. He cannot rate me very high if he thinks he is worth my fidelity! He told me recently that I can never have loved anyone but him! Oh, at that instant I needed all the prudence at my command not to undeceive him at once by telling him how matters stood. An odd sort of gentleman, I must say, to claim exclusive rights! True, he has a good figure and quite a handsome face: but, all things considered, he is only a journeyman-lover. Well, the time has now come and we must part.

I have been trying for a fortnight and have in turn employed coldness, caprice, temper, squabbles. But the tenacious creature will not let go for anything. I must, therefore, take more violent action, and am consequently carrying him off with me to my country house. We leave the day after tomorrow. We shall have only a few disinterested and not very perceptive people with us, and almost as much liberty as we should have alone. Once there, I shall so over-burden him with love and caresses, we shall live so exclusively for each other, that I am certain he will long even more than I for the end of the expedition which he regards in prospect as so great a happi-ness. If he does not return more bored with me than I with him, you may tell me, and I shall agree, that I am no cleverer than you are.

My pretext for going into this sort of retirement will be that I must devote some serious attention to my great lawsuit, which, in fact, is finally to be decided at the beginning of the winter. I shall be very glad when it is over: it is really very disagreeable to have one's whole fortune hanging in the balance. Not that I am anxious about the result. In the first place all my lawyers assure me that I am in the right; and, even if I am not, I should be very stupid if I could not win a case in which my only adversaries are minors still in their infancy and an aged guardian! Since, however, I must neglect nothing in so important an affair, I shall, as a matter of fact, be taking two lawyers with me. A jolly excursion this is going to be, don't you think? Still, if I am to win my suit, and be rid of Belle-roche, I shall not regret the time I spend on it.

Now, Vicomte, guess who the successor is to be: I give you a hundred tries. Never mind! I know you have never been good at guessing. Well: it is Danceny. Are you surprised? After all, I am not yet reduced to looking after children, but this one deserves to be made an exception of. He has the graces of youth without its frivolity. His extreme reserve in company is perfectly suited to warding off suspicion, and he is only the more amiable when he puts it off in private. Not that I have spoken to him yet in private: I am still only his confidante. But under the veneer of friendliness I think I discern more lively feelings on his part towards me and am aware of a great many of my own towards him. It would be a great pity if so much spirit and delicacy were to be sacrificed to and blunted by that little idiot of a Volanges! I hope he is mistaken in thinking he loves her: she is very far from deserving it! Not that I am jealous of her: but it would be murder, and I want to save Danceny from that. I beg you then, Vicomte, to do what you can to prevent him meeting *his Cécile* (as he still has the bad habit of calling her). A first penchant is always stronger than one thinks and I could be sure of nothing were he to see her again just now; especially if it were during my absence. When I return I shall take care of and be responsible for everything.

I thought of taking the young fellow with me, but sacrificed the idea to my usual prudence. Besides, I should have been afraid of his noticing something between Belleroche and me, and I should be in despair were he to have the least idea what passes between us. To his imagination, at least, I want to appear pure and stainless: such as I should have to be, in other words, to be really worthy of him.

Paris
15 October 17 —

LETTER 114: *The Présidente de Tourvel to Madame de Rosemonde*

MY dear friend, I do not know whether you are in any condition to reply, but, yielding to my deep disquiet, I cannot help asking you some questions. The state of Monsieur de Valmont's health, which you tell me is attended with *no danger*, does not leave me feeling as confident as you seem to be. It is not unusual for melancholy and disgust with the world to be warning symptoms of some grave illness. The sufferings of the body, like those of the mind, arouse a desire for solitude; and we often accuse a man of ill-humour whom we ought only to pity for his misfortune.

It seems to me that someone should be consulted. How is it that, since you are ill yourself, you have no doctor by you? My own doctor, whom I saw this morning and whom I shall confess I consulted indirectly, is of the opinion that in naturally active persons this sort of sudden apathy is never to be ignored. Sickness, he said moreover, will not yield to treatment unless it is treated in time. Why run such risks with someone who is so dear to you?

What doubly increases my anxiety is that for the past four days I have not heard from him. My God, you would not misinform me about his health? Why should he have stopped writing so suddenly? If it were only my persistence in returning his letters, I think he would have stopped sooner. At all events, though I have no faith in presentiments, I have for the last few days felt so oppressed that it frightens me. Ah, it may be that I am on the brink of the worst of misfortunes!

You would not believe, and I am ashamed to tell you, how painful it is no longer to receive those letters which, none the less, I should still refuse to read. I should be sure, at any rate, that he still thought of me, and I should see something that came from him! I never opened the letters, but the sight of them would make me weep. Tears at least were a relief, and they alone have dispelled to some extent the continual oppression I have been under since my return. I beseech you, my kind friend, write to me yourself as soon as you can; and send me every day meanwhile your news and his.

I see that I have had scarcely a word to say on your own account: but you know my feelings, my unreserved attachment to you, my sincere gratitude for your sympathetic friendship. You will forgive me for the difficulties I am in, the dreadful sufferings, the frightful torments of having evils to fear of which I am myself, perhaps, the cause. Great God, how that desperate thought obsesses me and tears at my heart! But I still had to submit to this new torture, and it seems that I was born to suffer them all.

Good-bye, my dear. Love me: pity me. Shall I have a letter from you today?

Paris
16 October 17 —

LETTER 115: *The Vicomte de Valmont to the Marquise de Merteuil*

IT is incredible, my love, how easily two people, the moment they are separated, cease to understand each other. As long as I was with you, we shared the same ideas, the same point of view; because I have not seen you for nearly three months, we are no longer of the same opinion about anything. Which of us is wrong? You would certainly answer without hesitation, but I, who am wiser or more polite than you, shall not decide. I shall merely reply to your letter and continue giving you an account of my conduct.

Thank you, first, for your advice concerning the rumours current about me. But I have no anxieties on that score. I am sure I shall soon be able to put a stop to them. Rest assured: I shall reappear in society more famous than ever before and worthier still of you.

I hope I shall even be given some credit for my adventure with the little Volanges, of which you seem to make so little. As if it were nothing to lure a girl from her beloved in the space of an evening, and make use of her thereafter as often as I wish with no further difficulty, entirely as though she were my property; to obtain from her what I should never dare demand from women whose business it is to provide it, and this, too, without in the least upsetting her tender love, without obliging her to be inconstant or even unfaithful. After all, I have not so much as penetrated her head! Thus, when my whim has passed, I shall replace her, so to speak, in the arms of her lover, without her having noticed anything. Is this, then, so commonplace an achievement? Besides, believe me, even when she is out of my hands, the ideas I have given her will continue to develop; and I prophesy that soon the shy little school-girl will take wing and soar to such heights as will do honour to her master.

If, however, the public prefer something in the classic style, I shall exhibit my Présidente, that paragon of all the virtues! Respected even by our most depraved libertines. So much so that they gave up considering even the possibility of attack! I shall exhibit her, I say, unmindful of her duty and her virtue, sacrificing her reputation and two years of prudent living to pursue the happiness of giving me pleasure, to intoxicate herself with that of loving me, thinking herself rewarded for so much renunciation by a word, a look, which, even so, she does not always obtain. I shall do more. I shall leave her. And, if I know the woman, I shall have no successor. She will overcome her need of comfort, her habituation to pleasure, even her desire for revenge. After all, she will have existed only for me; and, however long a course she runs, I alone shall have opened and shut the barrier. Once I have achieved my triumph I shall say to my rivals: 'Look on my work, and find, if you can, its parallel in our age!'

Whence, you will ask, comes this sudden access of assurance? It is that for the past week I have been in my beauty's confidence: she does not tell me her secrets, but I find them out. Two letters from her to Madame de Rosemonde have told me all I want to know, and I shall only read the rest out of curiosity. I need absolutely nothing now in order to succeed except access to her, and I have already discovered a means. I am going to make use of it forthwith.

You are curious, I suppose? . . . But no, to punish you for thinking me uninventive, you shall not know what it is. Seriously, you deserve to be deprived of my confidence, at least while this affair lasts; in fact, were it not for the delicious prize you offer for success, I should speak of it no more. I am angry, you see. However, in the hopes that you will mend your ways, I am willing to confine myself to inflicting a light punishment: and now, reverting to clemency I shall forget my own grand designs for a moment to discuss yours with you.

So there you are in the country, as tedious as sentiment, as depressing as fidelity itself! And that poor man Belleroche! Not content with making him drink the waters of oblivion, you put him on the rack! How is he? How does he take his surfeit of love? I should so much like him to become only the more attached to you: I should be curious to see what more efficacious remedy you could find to administer. I pity you really for being compelled to have recourse to this one. I have only once in my life made love in cold blood, and then, to be sure, for a very good reason, since it was with the Comtesse de —. A dozen times in her arms I was tempted to say: 'Madame, I renounce the position I solicited.

Permit me to leave the one I now occupy.' Consequently, of all the women I have had, she is the only one I take real pleasure in tra-ducing.

As for *your* reasons, I find them, to tell you the truth, extra-ordinarily foolish; and you were right in thinking that I should never have guessed the name of Belleroche's successor. What! Is it for Danceny that you are going to all this trouble? Come, come, my dear, leave him to adore *his virtuous Cécile*: don't meddle with the children at play. Leave the housemaids to educate the schoolboys: let them have *their little innocent games* with the convent girls. Why have a novice on your hands who will be incapable either of taking you or of leaving you, and for whom you will have to do everything yourself? I tell you in all seriousness, I disapprove of your choice. However much of a secret you keep it, it will humiliate you – at any rate in my eyes and in your own conscience.

You have, you say, a great inclination for him: well, you are certainly mistaken, and I think I have even discovered the reason for your error. This admirable distaste for Belleroche came over you at a time of dearth, and since Paris offered you no range of choice, your imagination, always a little too lively, seized upon the first object that presented itself. But consider that, when you return there, you will have hundreds to choose from: and if you are afraid of running the risk of inactivity meanwhile, I offer myself for the amusement of your leisure hours.

Between now and your arrival in Paris all my important business will have been accomplished, one way or another. And certainly neither the little Volanges, nor the Présidente herself, will be oc-cupying my time to such an extent that I cannot devote as much of it to you as you wish. Perhaps I shall even, in the meanwhile, have returned the little girl to the arms of her discreet lover. Though I cannot agree, whatever you say, that this affair has no *attractions*, it is true that since I intended her, for the rest of her life, to have an idea of me as being superior to all other men, I assumed a role with her that I could not for long sustain without risk to my health. Since then I have no longer been much interested in her, except for the concern that one owes to family affairs. . . .

You don't understand? . . . I await the coming period for the confirmation of my hopes, and the assurance that I have fully succeeded in my enterprise. Yes, my love, I have already had the first indication that my schoolgirl's husband shall run no risk of dying without posterity, and that the head of the house of Gercourt shall in future be an offshoot of the house of Valmont. But let me finish the enterprise to my own taste that I undertook only at your request. Remember that if you make Danceny unfaithful you will deprive the story of all interest. Consider, too, that having offered myself as his deputy, I have, it seems to me, some right to preference.

Indeed I rely so much upon it, that I have not hesitated to obstruct your plans by helping to increase the discreet lover's tender passion for the first and most worthy object of his choice. Having found your pupil yesterday busy writing to him, and having first disturbed her in this agreeable task to put her to a still more agreeable one, I asked to see the letter; discovering it to be cold and constrained, I made her see that this was not the way to console a lover, and persuaded her to write another to my dictation: in which, imitating her little babblings as best I could, I tried to encourage the young man's love by giving him more certain expectations. The little creature was quite delighted, she told me, to find herself writing so well: from now on, I shall be in charge of her correspondence. What shall I not, in the end, have done for Danceny? I shall have been at once his friend, his confidant, his rival, and his mistress! I am even at the moment doing him the service of removing him from your dangerous clutches. Yes, dangerous without doubt: for to possess you and to love you is to buy a moment's happiness with an eternity of remorse.

Good-bye, my love. Take heart and dispatch Belleroche as soon as you can. Let Danceny go, and prepare to recover—and to restore to me – the delicious pleasures of our first acquaintance.

P.S. My compliments on the impending settlement of your lawsuit. I should be very pleased if the happy event were to occur under my regime.

Château de —
19 October 17 —

LETTER 116: *The Chevalier Danceny to Cécile Volanges*

MADAME DE MERTEUIL left this morning for the country, so that now, my dear Cécile, I am deprived of the one pleasure that remained to me in your absence: that of talking about you to your friend and mine. For some time now she has allowed me to think of her as a friend: and I was the more eager to do so since it seemed a means of bringing you nearer to me. Heavens! How kind a woman she is! And what a flattering charm she contrives to throw over friendship! It is as if her feelings in this respect are strengthened and ennobled by all that she refuses to love. If you knew how fond she is of you, how much she likes to hear me speak of you! . . . That is probably what most attracts me to her. What a joy it would be to live only for you both, to come and go endlessly between the delights of love and the pleasures of friendship, to devote my whole life to them, to be, as it were, the focal point of your mutual attachment, and to feel always that in furthering the happiness of one I should be of equal service to the other. I hope you will love her; I hope you will love her very much, my dear: she is an adorable woman. You will, in sharing them, increase the value of my own feelings for her.

Since I have experienced the charm of friendship, I want you to feel it too. The pleasures I do not share with you seem to me to be only half enjoyed. Yes, my Cécile, I should like to fill your heart with all the sweetest of feelings, so that each of its emotions would be a new happiness to you; I think, even so, that I should never be able to return you more than a fraction of the joy I should have from you.

Why must so delightful a possibility be only a figment of my imagination: why must reality, on the contrary, offer me nothing but painful and perpetual privations? I see clearly that I must abandon the hopes you once gave me that I might see you in the country. I have no comfort but to persuade myself that, after all, it is impossible for you. But you don't tell me so, you don't commiserate with me! I have already made you two complaints on the same score that you have left unanswered. Ah, Cécile, Cécile! I believe that you do love me with all your heart, but your heart is not on fire like mine! If only it were for me to remove the obstacles! Why is it my interests that are at stake, and not yours? I should soon prove to you that there is nothing that love finds impossible.

You don't tell me, either, when this cruel separation is to come to an end. Here, at least, I may be able to see you. Your charming eyes will revive my despondent soul; their sweet regard will reassure my heart, which is at times in need of reassurance. Forgive me, Cécile; my fears are not suspicions. I believe in your love, in your constancy. Ah, I should be too unhappy if I doubted them. But so many obstacles! And new ones all the time! My dear, I feel discouraged, so discouraged. Madame de Merteuil's departure has, it seems, revived the consciousness of all my misfortunes.

Good-bye, my Cécile; good-bye, my dear love. Remember that your lover is suffering, and that you alone can give him back his happiness.

Paris
17 October 17 —

LETTER 117: *Cécile Volanges to the Chevalier Danceny (dictated by Valmont)*

Do you think, my good friend, that I need any reprimanding to make me sorry for you, when I know that you are suffering? And do you doubt that I suffer for your misfortunes as much as you do? I share even the ones I cause you knowingly; and I have more to endure than you because you are not fair to me. Oh, that is not kind of you. I see what it is that annoys you: I have not answered your two requests to come here. But is it so very easy to let you have an answer? Do you think I don't know that what you are asking for is very wrong? Yet, if I have so much difficulty in refusing you at a distance, how would it be if you were here? What is more, for having wanted to give you a moment's consolation, I should have to suffer for the rest of my life.

All the same, I have nothing to hide from you. Here are my reasons. You may judge for yourself. I should perhaps have done what you asked were it not, as I have told you, that Monsieur de Gercourt, who is the cause of all our troubles, is not to arrive here as soon as he was expected; and since Mamma has, for some time, been very much more friendly towards me, since, for my part, I make as much of her as I can, who knows what I may be able to persuade her to? And if we can be happy, without my having anything to be ashamed of, will that not be much the better way? If I can believe what I have often been told, men love their wives less if their wives have loved them too well before marrying them. It is fear of that which holds me back more than anything else. My dear, are you not sure of my heart, and will there not always be time?

Listen; I promise you that if I cannot avoid the misfortune of being married to Monsieur de Gercourt, whom I already heartily detest without ever having met him, nothing will keep me from being as much yours as I can possibly be, even before my marriage. Since I don't wish to be loved by anyone but you, and since, if I do wrong, it will not, as you know, be my fault, the rest is a matter of indifference to me: as long as you promise me that you will always love me as much as you do now. But till then, my dear, leave things as they are: and don't ask me to do what I have good reasons for not doing, especially when you know that I am sorry to have to refuse.

I wish, too, that Monsieur de Valmont were not so eager in your cause. It only makes it the more difficult for me. Oh, you have a good friend in him, I do assure you! He does everything for you that you would do for yourself. But good-bye, my dear. It was very late when I began writing to you, and a part of the night is already gone. I am going to bed to make up for lost time. I embrace you, but don't scold me any more.

Château de —
18 October 17 —

LETTER 118: *The Chevalier Danceny to the Marquise de Merteuil*

If I am to believe my almanack it is only two days, my beloved friend, since you went away; but if I am to believe my heart, it is two centuries. Now – I have it upon your authority – it is always one's heart one should go by; it is therefore high time that you came back. All your business affairs must be more than disposed of. How can you expect me to be interested in your lawsuit when, whether you succeed or fail, I must in any case pay for it with the boredom I suffer in your absence? Oh, I could pick a quarrel with you! How sad it is, with so fine an excuse for ill temper, to have no right to show it!

Is it not, none the less, a genuine breach of faith, an act of base treachery, to leave your friend behind you when you have made him incapable of supporting your absence? You would consult your lawyers in vain: they could find no justification for so wicked a proceeding. Besides, lawyers deal in arguments: and arguments will not do to answer feelings.

As for me, you have told me so often that reason has prescribed this journey of yours that you have put me quite out of humour with reason. I intend to listen to it no longer: even when it tells me to forget you. That would indeed be very reasonable, and not as difficult to do as you might think. I should only have to break myself of the habit of thinking constantly about you; and there is nothing here, you may be sure, that can remind me of you.

Our prettiest women, or, as is generally said, the most agreeable ones, are so far beneath you that they can suggest only the faintest idea of the being you are. I even think that, to a practised eye, the more they resemble you at first, the more the difference is afterwards apparent. Whatever they do, though they use all the arts at their command, there is always something lacking: they are not you, and therein precisely lies the only charm. Unfortunately, when the days are long and one is unoccupied, one daydreams, builds castles in the air, creates an illusion. By degrees one's imagination takes fire: one would like to beautify the picture; one brings together everything that can possibly give pleasure; one arrives, finally, at perfection. When that has happened, the portrait recalls the model, and one is quite astonished to find that one has done nothing but think of you.

At this very moment I am the victim of a more or less similar error. You think, perhaps, that it was because I wanted to express my thoughts concerning you that I began this letter? Not at all: it was to distract me from them. I had a hundred things to tell you which did not concern you, which, as you know, are of the deepest concern to me: it is from them, however, that I have been distracted. Since when has the charm of friendship prevailed over that of love? Ah, if I looked closer I should perhaps find a little reason for self-reproach! But, hush! Let us forget this trifling mistake, lest I commit it again. Let my friend herself be blind to it.

Why are you not here to answer me, to call me back when I go astray, to talk to me of my Cécile, to increase, if that is possible, the happiness I find in loving her by reminding me that it is your friend whom I love? Yes, I must confess, the love I feel for her has become all the more precious to me since you have been so kind as to receive its confidences. It is such a pleasure to open my heart to you, to tell you of my feelings, to express them without reserve! And, it seems, the more you take them to your own heart, the more I value them. I look at you, and say to myself: 'In her is contained all my happiness.'

The situation has not changed, and there is nothing new to tell you. The last letter I received from *her* increased and confirmed my hopes, but puts off their fulfilment still further. However, her motives are so kind and so honourable that I can neither blame her nor complain. Perhaps you do not altogether understand what I am telling you; but why are you not here? Though one is willing to tell a friend everything, one dare not commit it all to paper. The secrets of love, especially, are so delicate that one cannot let them out in that way on their own. If one does sometimes allow it, one should at least not lose sight of them; one must somehow see them safely to their new home. Oh, come back, then, my beloved friend: you see how necessary your return is. Forget the *thousand reasons* that keep you where you are, or else teach me how to live where you are not.

I have the honour to be, etc.

Paris
19 October 17 —

LETTER 119: *Madame de Rosemonde to the Présidente de Tourvel*

ALTHOUGH I am still in great pain, my dear, I am trying to write to you myself so that I may speak to you of your concerns. My nephew continues misanthropic. He sends very regularly every day to ask after me: but he has not once come to inquire for himself, although I have sent a message asking him to do so. So that, for all I see of him, he might as well have stayed in Paris. This morning, however, I met him where I scarcely expected to meet him: in my chapel, where I had gone for the first time since my painful indisposition. Today I learnt that for four days he has been there regularly to hear Mass. God grant that this continues!

As I came in he approached me and very affectionately congratulated me upon the improvement in my health. As Mass was beginning, I broke off the conversation, which I expected to resume later; but he disappeared before I could rejoin him. I shall not conceal the fact that I found him a little altered. But, my dear, do not make me repent of my confidence in your good sense by giving way to excessive anxiety. Rest assured, above all, that I should prefer to distress you than to deceive you.

If my nephew continues to keep me at a distance, I shall, as soon as I am better, have recourse to calling upon him in his room, and shall try to fathom the cause of this singular eccentricity, for which, I am inclined to believe, you are in some part responsible. I shall let you know what I discover. I am leaving you now: I can no longer move my fingers. Besides, if Adélaïde knew that I was writing, she would grumble at me for the rest of the evening. Good-bye, my dear.

Château de —
20 October 17 —

LETTER 120: *The Vicomte de Valmont to Father Anselme* *(of the Cistercian monastery in the rue Saint-Honoré)*

I HAVE not the honour of your acquaintance, Monsieur; but I know that you have the entire confidence of Madame the Présidente de Tourvel, and I know, moreover, how eminently worthy you are of it. I think, then, I may address myself to you without being guilty of an indiscretion, to beg you to do me a very necessary service, one that will be truly worthy of your holy office, and one in which Madame de Tourvel's interest is equally involved with mine.

I have in my possession important documents which concern her, the contents of which may be revealed to no one. I must not, nor do I wish to, deliver them into any but her own hands. I have no means of telling her about them, because there are reasons, which perhaps you know from her – but which I do not think I am permitted to tell you – why she has decided to refuse to correspond with me: a decision which I cannot, I willingly admit, now disapprove, since she was not able to have foreseen incidents which I myself was very far from expecting, and which cannot have been possible but for the supernatural power that one is compelled to acknowledge produced them.

I beg you then, Monsieur, to be so kind as to tell her of my new resolutions, and to ask, on my behalf, for a private interview, at which I can at least offer apologies as partial amends for the wrongs I have committed, and, in exchange for this last sacrifice, demolish the only remaining traces of the error or fault of which I have been guilty in relation to her.

Only after this initial expiation could I dare to lay at your feet the humiliating confession of my past aberrations, and implore your intercession in the interests of a much more important and unhappily more difficult reconciliation. May I hope, Monsieur, that you will not refuse me the aid that is so necessary, so precious to me, and that you will condescend to support me in my weakness and guide my feet in the path that I most ardently desire to follow, but which, I blush to admit, I have never yet found?

I shall await your reply with the impatience of a penitent who is eager to make amends. Please believe that I am, with as much gratitude as reverence

Your very humble, etc.

P.S. You have my permission, Monsieur, supposing you consider it proper, to communicate this letter in its entirety to Madame de Tourvel, whom I shall make it my duty to respect for the rest of my life, and in whom I shall never cease to honour the woman sent from Heaven to recall my soul to virtue by her own inspiring example.

Château de —
22 October 17 —

LETTER 121: *The Marquise de Merteuil to the Chevalier Danceny*

I HAVE received your letter, my too-young friend. But before thanking you I must find fault with you, and I warn you that if you don't mend your ways you will have no more letters from me. Take my advice and renounce this tone of flattery, which is pure cant when it is not the expression of love. Does friendship speak in this vein? No, my friend: every sentiment has the language proper to it: to make use of the wrong one is to disguise the thought one wishes to express. I know that our little ladies understand nothing of what is said to them unless it is translated somehow into the usual jargon; but I thought I deserved, I must admit, to be distinguished from them. I am really sorry – perhaps more than I ought to be – that you judged me so ill.

You will therefore find in my letter only what is lacking in yours: frankness and forthrightness. I might well say, for example, that it would be a great pleasure to see you, and that I am cross to find people around me who bore me, instead of people who amuse me, but you would translate that same sentence into: 'teach me how to live where you are not', so that, I suppose, when you are by your mistress's side you will not know how to live there unless I make a third. What a pity! Then there are the women 'who always lack something; they are not me': will you perhaps find your Cécile wanting too? This is what comes of using a language which nowadays is so abused that it means even less than the jargon of compliment. It has become no more than a set of formulas, and one believes in it no more than one believes in 'your very humble servant'.

When you write to me, my friend, let it be to tell me what you think and feel, and not to send me phrases which I can find, without your help, set forth more or less to advantage in the latest novel. I hope you will not be angry at what I say, even if you find it a little ill-humoured. I don't deny the ill humour but, to avoid even so much as the appearance of the fault I reproach you with, I shall not tell you what is true, that my vexation is perhaps a little increased by my separation from you. It seems to me that, all things considered, you are worth more than a lawsuit and two lawyers, and perhaps more even than the *attentive Belleroche*.

You see that, instead of deploring my absence, you ought to be glad of it: for never have I paid you so fine a compliment. I think I am being swayed by your example. I shall soon be saying flattering things myself. But no, I prefer to stand by my honesty. It is honesty alone, then, that assures you of my sympathetic friendship, and the interest it inspires. It is very agreeable to have a young friend whose heart is engaged elsewhere. This is not every woman's system: but it is mine. It seems to me that one may give oneself up with greater pleasure to a feeling from which one has nothing to fear. Hence for your sake I have come, rather early perhaps, to playing the confidante. But you choose your mistresses so young that you have made me aware for the first time that I am beginning to grow old! You do well, however, thus to prepare for a long life of constancy which with all my heart I wish may be mutual.

You are right to give way before the 'kind and honourable motives' which, from what you tell me, are delaying your happiness. A long defence is the only source of merit remaining to those who are not always used to resist. What I should find unpardonable in anyone but a child like the little Volanges, would be an incapacity to fly from danger of which her own admission of love had given her sufficient warning. You men have no idea what virtue is and what it costs to sacrifice it! But, if a woman reasons at all, she will know that for her, quite apart from the fault she commits, weakness is the worst of misfortunes. I cannot imagine how any woman could ever succumb to it who had opportunity for a moment's reflection.

Don't dispute that truth. It is chiefly because of it that I am attached to you. You will save me from the dangers of love; and although I have till now been quite well able to defend myself from them without you, I shall be grateful to you for saving me, and shall love you the better, and more, for doing so.

Upon which, my dear Chevalier, I pray God to keep you in His holy and venerable protection.

Château de —
22 October 17 —

LETTER 122: *Madame de Rosemonde to the Présidente de Tourvel*

I HAD hoped, my charming daughter, that I would at last be able to calm your anxieties, but now I see, to my chagrin, that I must on the contrary further increase them. Be calm, none the less. My nephew is not in danger. It cannot even be said that he is really ill. But something extraordinary is certainly happening to him. I understand nothing of it: but I left his room with such a feeling of sorrow, perhaps even of fear, that I am loath to make you share it. Yet I cannot help speaking of it to you. Here is an account of what happened. You may be sure that it is a faithful one, for if I should live another eighty years I could never forget the impression that doleful scene made upon me.

Well, this morning I went to my nephew's room. I found him writing, surrounded by various heaps of papers which seemed to be the object of his labours. He was so preoccupied that I was in the middle of the room before he turned around to see who had come in. He rose as soon as he saw me, and I distinctly noticed the effort he made to compose his features. It was that, perhaps, that made me examine him more closely. He was not, it is true, fully dressed and his hair was unpowdered; but I found him looking pale and un-kempt, his face in particular quite changed. His glance, no longer lively and gay as we know it, was sad and downcast. In short, between ourselves, I should not like you to have seen him as he was, for it was a most touching spectacle and would, to my mind, have roused in you that tender compassion which is one of the most dangerous of love's snares.

Though very much struck by what I saw, I began the conversation as though I had noticed nothing. I spoke to him first of his health, and though he did not say it was good, he did not, in so many words, say it was bad. Then I complained of his retirement, which I said appeared a little like wilful eccentricity, and tried to add a touch of gaiety to my little reprimand. But he replied only, in a significant tone: 'That, I admit, is one more crime. But it shall be paid for with the rest.' His manner of saying it, even more than what he said, a little damped my jocularity, and I hastened to tell him that he attached too much importance to what was purely a friendly reproach.

We then resumed our conversation more calmly, and a little later he told me that soon perhaps some business, *the most important concern of his life*, would be recalling him to Paris: but since I was afraid to guess, my dear, and since such a beginning may have led to unwelcome confidences, I asked him no questions, but contented myself with saying that a little amusement would benefit his health. I added that for once I should not persuade him to stay, since my friends were dear to me for their own sakes. It was upon this simple remark that, seizing hold of my hands, he began to speak with a vehemence I cannot describe. 'Yes, my dear aunt,' he said, 'let a nephew who respects, who esteems you, be dear, very dear to you; and, as you say, let it be for his own sake. Don't be anxious for his happiness; don't disturb, with thoughts of regret, the eternal peace he hopes soon to enjoy. Tell me again that you love me, that you will forgive me. Yes, you, I know, will forgive me. I know you are kind. But how can I hope for the same indulgence from those against whom I have so offended?' Then he stooped towards me to hide, I think, the signs of grief which none the less the sound of his voice betrayed.

More moved than I can say, I rose hurriedly. He must have noticed my alarm, for immediately and with more composure he continued: 'Forgive me. Forgive me, Madame. I was beside myself. Please forget what I have said and remember only my profound esteem for you. I shall not fail', he added, 'to renew my respects to you before I leave.' It seemed to me that the last sentence committed me to putting an end to my visit; and, in fact, I left.

But the more I think of it, the less idea I have of what he meant. What is this business, *the most important concern of his life*? For what reason does he ask my forgiveness? Why did he involuntarily give way to emotion when he spoke? I have already asked myself these questions a thousand times without being able to find an answer. I cannot even see what there is in all this that relates to you. However, since the eyes of love see further than those of friendship, I did not wish to leave you in ignorance of anything that passed between my nephew and myself.

I have made four attempts to finish writing this long letter, which I should make longer were it not for the fatigue that overcomes me. Good-bye, my dear.

Château de —
25 October 17 —

LETTER 123: *Father Anselme to the Vicomte de Valmont*

I HAVE, Monsieur le Vicomte, received the letter you did me the honour of writing to me, and called yesterday, as you desired, upon the person in question. I explained the object of and motives for the meeting you propose. Though I found her anxious at first to abide by her former decision, yet, when I had shown her that by refusing she would perhaps risk standing in the way of your happy restoration to the fold and opposing thereby in some sort the merciful designs of Providence, she agreed to receive your visit – on condition, at all events, that it will be the last one – and charged me to tell you that she will be at home next Thursday, the twenty-eighth. If the day does not suit you you will be so kind as to tell her so, and suggest another. Your letter will be received.

Allow me, however, Monsieur le Vicomte, to ask you not to postpone the meeting unless you have strong reasons, so that you may the sooner and the more entirely give yourself up to the praiseworthy inclinations of which you have given me some indication. Remember that he who delays in seizing the opportunity of grace is exposed to the danger of its being withdrawn; that though the Divine Goodness is infinite, its dispensation is yet regulated by justice; and that a moment may come when a merciful God is transformed into a God of vengeance.

Should you continue to honour me with your confidence, I beg you to believe that you have my whole attention whenever you desire it. However busy I may otherwise be, my most important concern shall always be to fulfil the duties of the holy ministry to which I am particularly devoted; the happiest moment of my life will be that of seeing my work progress under the blessing of the Almighty. Weak sinners that we are, we can do nothing by ourselves! But God, who is recalling you, can do everything; and we shall be equally indebted to His goodness, you for the firm desire to return, I for a means of returning you to Him. It is with His help that I hope soon to persuade you that holy religion alone can give you, even in this world, the solid and lasting happiness which is vainly sought in the blindness of human passion.

I have the honour to be with respectful regard, etc.

Paris
25 October 17 —

LETTER 124: *The Présidente de Tourvel to Madame de Rosemonde*

AMID all the astonishment, Madame, into which the news I received yesterday has thrown me, I am not unmindful of the satisfaction it must cause you, and I hasten to inform you of it. Monsieur de Valmont is no longer concerned either with me or with his love, and no longer wants anything but to make amends, by leading a more exemplary life, for the faults, or rather the errors, of his youth. I was informed of this great news by Father Anselme, to whom he applied for guidance in the future – as also for the purpose of arranging an interview with me, the principal object of which I assume to be the return of my letters, which he has kept till now in spite of my request to the contrary.

I can only, of course, approve this happy change of heart, and congratulate myself if, as he says, I have played some part in it. But why should I have been chosen for its instrument, why should my life have been deprived of all peace? Can Monsieur de Valmont's happiness never have been achieved without my misfortune? Oh, my kind friend, forgive these complaints. I know it is not for me to question the Divine decrees: but while I beg Him continually, and always in vain, for the power to conquer my unhappy love, He is prodigal of strength where it has not been asked for, and leaves me a helpless prey to my weakness.

But let me stifle these guilty complaints. Do I not know that the Prodigal Son was received, when he returned, with more favour than his father showed the son who never went away? What account may we demand of One who owes us none? And were it possible for us to have any rights where He is concerned, what rights could I claim? Could I boast of the virtue I owe only to Valmont? He has saved me; could I dare complain of suffering for his sake? No: my sufferings will be dear to me, if his happiness is their reward. Certainly, it was necessary for him to return to the Universal Father. God, who made him, must watch over his creation. He would never have fashioned so charming a creature to make only a reprobate of it. It is for me to endure the consequences of my foolhardy imprudence; ought I not to have known, that since it was forbidden to love him, I should not permit myself to see him?

My crime, or my misfortune, was in refusing for too long to acknowledge that truth. You are my witness, my dear and worthy friend, that I submitted to the sacrifice as soon as I realized the necessity for it, but it was still not complete as long as Monsieur de Valmont did not share it. Shall I confess to you that it is this thought that most torments me now? Insupportable pride that allows the evils we suffer to be mitigated by those we cause others to suffer! Ah, I shall subdue this rebellious heart; I shall teach it humility.

It was with this, especially, in mind that I at length agreed to receive a visit from Monsieur de Valmont next Thursday. I shall hear him tell me himself that I am no longer anything to him, that the feeble and fleeting impression I made upon him has been completely effaced! I shall see him look at me without emotion, while the fear of revealing mine will make me lower my eyes. The same letters he so long refused to return at my repeated requests, he will give back with indifference, as useless objects which no longer have any interest for him. And my trembling hands, receiving the shameful trust, will feel the hands that restore it steady and calm. Then I shall see him leave . . . leave forever, and my eyes as they follow him will not see him turn to glance back!

That so much humiliation should have been reserved for me! Ah, let me at least make use of it to pierce my soul with the consciousness of my frailty. . . . Yes, I shall treasure the letters he no longer cares to keep. I shall condemn myself to reading them every day until my tears have obliterated every word. His own I shall burn for being tainted with the dangerous poison that has eaten into my soul. Oh, what is love if it can make us miss even the dangers to which we have been exposed; can make us afraid of yielding to our feelings, even when they have been deprived of their object? Let us fly this deadly poison, which leaves us to choose only between shame and misery, and frequently imposes both. Let prudence, at least, prevail where virtue cannot.

How long it still is to Thursday! That I could make my painful sacrifice this instant and forget at once both its occasion and its object! This visit unnerves me: I am sorry I gave my promise. What need has he to see me again? What are we now to one another? If he has offended me, he has my pardon. I congratulate him for wishing to make amends for the wrong he has done: I commend him for it. I shall go further and imitate him. I have been led into the same errors, and his example will recall me from them. But if his purpose is to fly from me, why does he begin by seeking me out? Is the most urgent necessity not for us to forget each other? Ah, certainly it is, and that shall be my sole concern from now on.

With your permission, my dear friend, it is by your side that I am going to undertake this difficult task. When I am in need of help, perhaps even of consolation, I want to receive it from no one but you. You alone can understand me and speak the language of my heart. Your precious friendship will fill my whole life. Nothing will be too difficult for me if it is to justify the care you are kind enough to devote to me. I shall owe you my peace, my happiness, my virtue; and the reward of your goodness to me will be to have made me worthy of it at last.

I have been, I think, very incoherent in this letter. I presume so, at any rate, to judge from the continual agitation I have felt while writing it. If you should find sentiments in it of which I ought to be ashamed, draw the veil of your indulgent kindness over them. In that I have entire confidence. From you I cannot wish to conceal a single impulse of my heart.

Good-bye, my most worthy friend. I hope, within a few days, to tell you when you may expect me.

Paris
25 October 17 —

LETTER 125: *The Vicomte de Valmont to the Marquise de Merteuil*

WELL, there she is, defeated, this arrogant woman who dared to think she could resist me! Yes, my dear, she is mine, utterly mine. Since yesterday she has had nothing left to yield me.

I am still too full of my happiness to be able to appreciate it, but I am astonished at the strange charm of what I experienced. Can it then be true that virtue increases the value of a woman, even in the very moment of her weakness? No, let us put that childish idea with the other old wives' tales. Is not a first attempt almost universally met with a more or less well-conducted resistance? And I have nowhere else found the charm of which I speak. It is not the charm of love, either: for if I did at times, beside this astonishing woman, experience sensations of weakness which resembled that pusillanimous passion, I was always able to conquer them and to reassert my principles. Even had yesterday's episode, as I think, carried me further than I expected to go; even though I did, for a moment, share the agitations and intoxications I had provoked, the passing illusion would by now have been dissipated. Yet the same charm subsists. I should even, I admit, feel a rather delicate pleasure in giving way to it, were it not that it causes me some disquiet. Shall I, at my age, be overmastered like a schoolboy by an obscure and involuntary feeling? No: I must, before all else, find it out and fight it.

Perhaps, for the rest, I have already glimpsed its cause. I am, at any rate, pleased with the notion, and should like to think it true.

Of the multitudes of women for whom I have fulfilled the role and functions of a lover I have never, till yesterday, met one who was not at least as eager to give herself as I was to bring her to doing so; I would even put down as prudes the ones who met me only half-way, as against the many others whose provocative defences were never designed wholly to conceal the preliminary advances they were making.

Here, on the other hand, I encountered from the first an unfavourable prejudice, which was later supported by information and advice from an odious but perspicacious woman; natural and extreme timidity strengthened by a cultivated modesty; an attachment to virtue, governed by religion, with two years of triumph already to its credit; lastly, a series of brilliant manoeuvres, inspired by these various feelings, conducted with only one end in view: the avoidance of my pursuit.

This is not, then, as in my other campaigns, a simple capitulation more or less to my advantage, from which it is easier to derive profit than pride. It is total victory, bought with painful endeavour and decided by masterly strategy. It is not, therefore, surprising that such a success, due to me alone, should for that very reason be worth more to me. The access of pleasure I experienced in the moment of triumph, and which I still feel, is nothing but the delicious sensation of glory. I encourage myself in this belief because it spares me the humiliation of thinking that I might in any way have been dependent on the very slave I had subjected to my will; that I might not find in myself alone everything I require for my happiness; and that the capacity to give me enjoyment of it in all its intensity might be the prerogative of any one woman to the exclusion of all others.

These judicious reflections will govern my conduct on this important occasion; and you may be sure I shall not allow myself to become so entrammelled that I cannot break my new ties with ease whenever I wish. But I talk already of breaking: and you don't yet know how I acquired the right to do so. Read on, then, and see to what dangers wisdom is exposed when it comes to the rescue of folly. I was so carefully attentive both to what I said and to the replies I received, that I hope to give my account of the whole with an exactitude that will satisfy you.

You will see, from the two copies of letters attached,[1] whom it was I chose as mediator between myself and my beauty, and how zealously the holy personage devoted his energies to bringing us together. What I have still to tell you – I learnt it from a letter

1. Letters 120 and 122.

intercepted in the usual way – is that the fear and the expected humiliation of being jilted had a little shaken the prudence of our austere devotee, and had filled her head with sentiments and ideas which were none the less interesting for lacking common sense. It was after these preliminaries, which you must know about, that yesterday, Thursday the twenty-eighth, the day chosen and stipulated by the ungrateful creature, I presented myself at her house, a timid and repentant slave – to leave it a garlanded conqueror.

It was six o'clock in the evening when I arrived to see the fair recluse. (Since her return, her doors have been closed to everybody.) She attempted to rise when I was announced; but her trembling knees would not permit her to sustain an upright posture, and she sat down again immediately. The servant who had announced me had some service to perform in the room and this seemed to make her impatient. We filled the interval with the customary compliments. But so as to lose not a moment of time that was precious to me, I carefully examined the locale, and there and then marked down the theatre of my victory. I couldn't have chosen a more convenient one, for there was an ottoman in the room. But I observed that, facing it, hung a portrait of the husband, and I was afraid, I admit, that with so extraordinary a woman, a single look directed by chance in his direction might in a moment destroy the work of so much time and trouble. At length we were left alone, and I came to the point.

Having discovered, in the exchange of a few words, that Father Anselme must have informed her of the motives of my visit, I began to complain of the rigorous treatment I had been subjected to. I emphasized particularly the *contempt* that had been shown me. This was denied, as I expected; and, as you, too, would expect, I cited as proof the fear and distrust I had aroused and the scandalous flight that had ensued, the refusal to reply to my letters, even to receive them, etc., etc. As a justification was then embarked upon which would have been very easy to accomplish, I thought I had better interrupt; and so as to be forgiven for my rudeness I immediately covered it over with flattery. I resumed: 'If your charm could make so profound an impression upon my heart, no less profound was the impression made upon my soul by your virtue. Carried away, I suppose, by a desire to emulate it, I went so far as to believe I was worthy of doing so. I do not blame you for having judged otherwise. I am being punished for my error.' Since an embarrassed silence prevailed, I continued: 'I wished, Madame, either to justify myself in your eyes, or to obtain your forgiveness for the wrongs you imagine I have done you, so that I might at least be able to end, in some peace of mind, a life to which I have attached no further value since the day you deprived it of all its charm.'

Here there was an attempt at a reply. 'My duty did not permit me to . . .' The difficulty, however, of completing the lie demanded by duty cut short the sentence. I therefore resumed in a more tender tone: 'Is it true, then, that it was from me that you fled?'

'My departure was necessary.'

'And is it necessary that you stay away from me?'

'I must.'

'And forever?'

'I must.'

I need not tell you that during this short dialogue our tender-hearted prude spoke in the most dejected tones and never once raised her eyes to mine.

I decided I had better animate the languid scene a little; so, rising, I said with an air of annoyance: 'Your firmness has restored my own. Well then, yes, Madame, we shall be separated. Even further separated than you think. And you will congratulate yourself at your leisure upon what you have done.' A little surprised at the tone of rebuke, she began to answer: 'The decision you have taken . . .'

'Is a consequence of my despair,' I returned with vehemence. 'You wanted me to be unhappy. I shall prove to you that you have succeeded beyond your hopes.'

'I desire only your happiness,' she replied. And the sound of her voice began to betray deep feeling.

So, throwing myself at her feet, and in the dramatic tones you know, I cried: 'Ah, cruel woman! Can any happiness exist for me that you do not share? How can I find it away from you? Ah, never! never!'

I must say that in having recourse to this expedient I had counted very much on the assistance of tears: but whether I was in the wrong mood, or whether, perhaps, it was only the effect of constant and exacting attention to detail, I found it impossible to summon any.

Fortunately I remembered that to subdue a woman one means is as good as another, as long as she can be surprised into strong emotion that leaves a profound and favourable impression upon her. Compassion being out of the question, I appealed to fear. Changing only the inflection of my voice, and remaining in the same posture, I continued: 'Yes, I swear this vow at your feet. I shall possess you or die.' As I uttered these words our eyes met. I don't know what the timid creature saw or thought she saw in mine: but she rose looking terrified, and disengaged herself from the embrace I held her in. I did nothing to restrain her, since I have several times remarked that scenes of despair, when conducted with too much enthusiasm, lapse after any length of time into ludicrousness, from which they can only be saved by real tragedy, and tragedy I was very far from wishing to play. However, while she made her escape, I added in low and sinister tones, but loud enough to be heard: 'Well, then! Let me die!'

Whereupon I rose, and, silent for a moment, threw, as if haphazardly, some wild looks in her direction, which for all their air of distraction were none the less sharply observant. Her hesitant demeanour, heavy breathing, the stiffening of all her muscles, her trembling half-raised arms, were all proof enough of the effect I had intended to produce. But since in the business of love nothing is concluded except at close quarters, and since we were by then at a fair distance from one another, it was necessary above all to effect a re-approach. To this end I assumed, as soon as I could, an air of composure calculated to soothe the effects my violence had produced without effacing the impression it had wrought.

By way of transition I said: 'I am quite wretched. I meant to live for your happiness, and I have destroyed it. I devote myself to your peace of mind, and destroy that too.' I continued with an air of composure, but some constraint: 'Forgive me, Madame. I am little accustomed to storms of passion and have not learned to control them. If I was wrong to give way, remember at least that it has happened for the last time. Ah, calm yourself, I beseech you calm yourself.' As I spoke, I drew insensibly nearer her.

'If you wish me to be calm,' replied my terrified beauty, 'be calmer yourself.'

'Ah, well! Yes. I promise you I will,' I said. 'If the effort is great,' I added in feebler tones, 'it will not, at least, be for long. But', I immediately continued as though distraught, 'I came, did I not, to return your letters? For God's sake, be willing to receive them back. Only this painful sacrifice remains to be made: leave me nothing that may weaken my courage.' I drew the precious collection from my pocket. 'Here they are,' I said, 'your deceitful assurances of friendship. They once reconciled me to life. Take them back. Give me the sign that will part me from you for ever.'

Here my fearful beloved yielded entirely to tender solicitude. 'But, Monsieur de Valmont, what is the matter? What do you mean? Do you not willingly do what you have come to do? Is this not the fruit of your reflections? And have they not brought you, too, to approve the course that my duty has obliged me to take?'

'Well,' I returned, 'your course has decided mine.'

'And what is that?'

'The only one that, in taking me from you, can put an end to my sufferings.'

'But tell me. What is it?'

At this point I took her in my arms without meeting any resistance at all. Judging from this neglect of the proprieties to what extent emotion had gained sway, I said, risking some enthusiasm: 'Adorable woman! You have no idea of the love you inspire. You will never know how I have worshipped you, how much dearer my feelings have been to me than life! May your days be even more peaceful and prosperous: may they be blessed with all the happiness of which you have deprived me! Repay my sincere wishes with one regret, at least, one tear; and please believe that the last of my sacrifices will not have been the most painful. Good-bye!'

As I spoke I heard her heart beat violently. I noticed the change in her face. I saw, above all that she was choked with tears, which yet fell slowly and painfully. It was only then that I decided to pretend to leave. Holding me back by force she said with spirit:

'No. Listen to me.'

'Let me go', I replied.

'You shall listen to me. I insist.'

'I must fly from you. I must!'

'No!' she cried. . . .

And with that last word she threw herself, or rather fell, into my arms in a faint. Since I was still suspicious of so easy a success, I feigned extreme alarm. But even as I expressed it, I took her, or carried her, towards the place previously appointed for the field of glory. In fact she did not return to herself until after she had submitted and surrendered to her happy conqueror.

So far, my love, you will, I think, have been pleased with the orthodoxy of my method: you will have seen that I have in no respect diverged from the true principles of an art that is, as we have often observed, very similar to that of warfare. Judge me, then, as you would Turenne or Frederick. I have been obliged to combat a foe who wished only to temporize. By clever manoeuvring I secured for myself the choice of terrain and dispositions. I succeeded in lulling the enemy into security, so as to fall upon her more easily in her place of refuge. I made sure that security was succeeded by terror before I engaged in the fight. I was risking nothing, since I could look for great advantage in case of success, and was certain of other resources in case of defeat. Lastly, I did not commit myself to action till assured of a safe means of retreat by which I could protect and preserve my previous gains. No man, I think, could have done more, But now I am afraid I have grown soft like Hannibal among the fleshpots of Capua. This is what subsequently happened.

I quite expected that so important an event would not pass off without the usual grief and despair, and if I noticed at first a little more than the customary confusion, and a sort of inner withdrawal, I attributed both to the influence of a prudish disposition. So, without attending to slight irregularities which I judged to be purely local, I simply followed the main course that consolation takes, convinced that, as usually happens, sensation would come to the help of sentiment, and that a single action would accomplish more than any amount of persuasion, which nevertheless I did not neglect to offer. But I met with a truly alarming resistance; not so alarming in its strength as in the form it took.

Imagine a woman seated in stiff immobility with a fixed expression on her face, seeming neither to think nor to listen, nor to understand; from whose staring eyes the tears fall continuously and unchecked. Such was Madame de Tourvel whenever I spoke; and if I tried to recapture her attention with a caress, even of the most innocent kind, her apathy gave way immediately to terror, suffocation, convulsive movements, sobs, from time to time a cry, but never a single articulate word.

These attacks occurred several times, with increasing severity. The last was so violent that it utterly discouraged me, and I feared for a moment that I had won a useless victory. I fell back upon my store of platitudes, among which I found the following: 'And are you in despair because you have made me happy?' At this, the adorable creature turned towards me, and her face, although still a little distraught, had already resumed that heavenly expression. 'Happy?' she said. You may imagine my reply. 'Are you then happy?' I redoubled my protestations. 'And happy because of me!' I added compliments and tender words. While I spoke her limbs relaxed. She fell back limply in her chair and, leaving me the hand I had ventured to take in mine, said: 'That thought, I find, is a solace and a comfort to me.'

As you may imagine, having been put back upon my path, I did not turn from it again; it was really the right one, perhaps the only one. So, when I decided to try for a second success, and met at first with some resistance, what had passed before made me circumspect. But having called the idea of my happiness once again to my assistance, I was soon made to feel once again its favourable effects. 'You are right,' said the tender-hearted creature. 'I can no longer endure my existence unless it is of use in making you happy. I devote myself entirely to that. From this moment on I am yours, and you will hear neither refusals nor regrets from my lips.' With such candour – naïve or sublime – did she give up her person and her charms, increasing my happiness by sharing it. Intoxication was complete and reciprocal and, for the first time with me, outlasted pleasure. I left her arms only to fall at her feet and swear eternal love; and to tell the whole truth, I meant what I said. Even after I had left her, the thought of her was still with me, and I have even now to make an effort to be rid of it.

Ah, why are you not here, to set off, at least, the charm of success with the pleasure of reward? But I lose nothing by waiting, do I?

And I hope I can take for granted between us the happy arrangement I suggested in my last letter. As you see, I am as good as my word: my affairs, as I promised, have made sufficient progress for me to give you a part of my time. Make haste, then, and dispatch your tedious Belleroche: leave your mawkish Danceny to his own devices, so that you may occupy yourself exclusively with me.

But what are you so busy with at your country house that you don't so much as reply to me? Do you know that I could be annoyed with you for less? But happiness makes for indulgence. Besides, I don't forget that in including myself once again among the number of your suitors, I must, once again, submit to your little whims. Remember, however, that this new lover intends to lose none of his former rights as a friend.

Good-bye – as I would say it of old. . . . Yes, *good-bye my angel! I send you all love's kisses.*

P.S. Do you know that Prévan, after a month in prison, has been obliged to leave his regiment? All Paris is talking about it now. So there he is, cruelly punished for a crime he did not commit, and your success is complete.

Paris
29 October 17 —

LETTER 126: *Madame de Rosemonde to the Présidente de Tourvel*

I SHOULD have replied to you earlier, my dear child, had not the fatigue of writing my last letter revived my malady and deprived me, these last few days, of the use of my arm. I was very anxious to thank you for the good news you gave me of my nephew, and no less so to offer you my sincere felicitations on your own account. One is obliged to see this as truly the work of Providence which, in putting one to the test, has saved both. Yes, my dear, God, who wished only to try you, has saved you at the very moment when your strength was exhausted; and, in spite of your little complainings, you have, I think, some thanks to return Him. I am fully aware that it would have been more agreeable, from your point of view, had this resolution been taken in the first place by you, and had Valmont's followed merely as a consequence: it seems to me even that the rights of our sex would thus have been better safe-guarded, and we cannot afford to lose any! But what are these trifling considerations against the important ends that have been achieved? Does the man saved from drowning complain of having had no choice in the matter of a means?

You will soon find, my dear daughter, that the sufferings you so fear will subside of themselves; and even though they were to continue forever at their full strength you would still find them easier to endure than remorse and self-contempt. Useless for me to have spoken to you sooner with this apparent severity: love is an independent feeling, which prudence can help us to avoid, but which it cannot overcome, and which, once born, can die only a natural death or from an absolute want of hope. It is want of hope in your case which gives me the courage, and the right, to speak my opinion freely. It is cruel to frighten the desperately ill, who can benefit only from comfort and palliatives; but it is wise to enlighten the convalescent about the dangers they have courted, so as to inspire in them the prudence they need, and encourage a submission to the advice they may need for the future.

Since you have chosen me for your doctor, I shall speak to you as such, and tell you that the little indispositions you now suffer, which perhaps require some remedy, are nothing in comparison to the frightful infirmity of which you are now safely cured. Then, as your friend, as the friend of a reasonable and virtuous woman, I shall permit myself to add that the passion you were victim to, unfortunate enough in itself, was doubly so by reason of its object. If I can believe what I am told, my nephew, whom I admit it is perhaps a weakness in me to love, and who has in fact, besides a great deal of charm, many praiseworthy qualities, is neither safe with women nor guiltless where they are concerned, and will ruin them as soon as seduce them. I am sure you have converted him. Never was anyone more worthy to do so: but so many others have flattered themselves in the same way whose hopes have been deceived, and I should much prefer you not to suffer the same fate.

Consider now, my dear, that instead of all the dangers you would have had to undergo, you will have, besides a clear conscience and your proper peace of mind, the satisfaction of having been the principal cause of Valmont's reformation. As for me, I have no doubt that it was largely due to your courageous resistance, and that one moment's weakness on your part would perhaps have condemned my nephew to a lifetime of error. I like to think so, and should like you to think so too: in that thought you will find your first consolation, and I new reason for loving you more.

I shall expect you here in a few days, my dear daughter, as you tell me to do. Come and recover your happiness and calm in the place where you lost them; come, especially, to rejoice with a loving mother in your having so faithfully kept the promise you gave her never to do anything that was unworthy of her or of you!

Château de —
30 October 17 —

LETTER 127: *The Marquise de Merteuil to the Vicomte de Valmont*

If I have not replied, Vicomte, to your letter of the nineteenth, it is not because I have not had the time. It is quite simply that it annoyed me with its want of common sense. I thought, therefore, that I could not do better than commit it to oblivion. But since you have returned to it, since you seem to insist upon the proposals it contains, and since you take my silence for consent, I must speak my mind clearly.

I may sometimes have had pretensions to bodying forth a whole seraglio in my person; but I have never been persuaded to belong to one. I thought you knew that. At any rate, now that you can no longer be ignorant of it, you may easily imagine how ridiculous your suggestion appears to me to be. I! I, sacrifice my inclination, and a new one at that, to devote my time to you! And how? In waiting my turn, like a submissive slave, for the sublime favours of your *Highness*. When, for example, you would like a moment's distraction from the *strange charm* that the *adorable*, *heavenly* Madame de Tourvel alone has made you feel, or when you are afraid of compromising the superior idea you are pleased the *attractive* Cécile should have of you; then, descending to my level, you will come in search of less lively pleasures it is true, but then not of the same consequence. And your precious favours, though seldom bestowed, will be more than enough to keep me happy!

You are well endowed, to be sure, with a good opinion of yourself. Not so I, apparently, with modesty: for look at myself as I will I cannot see that I have sunk so low. This is perhaps a fault in me: but I warn you that I have many more. That especially of thinking that the *schoolboy*, the *mawkish* Danceny, who is entirely devoted to me, who has sacrificed for my sake, without making a merit of it, a first passion before it has even been satisfied, who loves me as only at that age one can love, can, in spite of his twenty years, serve my happiness and pleasure more effectually than you. I shall even permit myself to add that, should the whim take me to give him an assistant, it would not be you, at least for the moment.

And what are my reasons, you will ask. In the first place, there may very well be none: for the caprice which favours you may with equal justice ignore you. I am, however, willing, for politeness' sake, to explain my motives. It seems to me that you would have too many sacrifices to make for my sake; while I, instead of expressing the gratitude you would not fail to expect, should be quite capable of thinking that you owed me even more! You will agree that, so far removed from each other in our way of thinking, we have no hope of coming to an understanding; and I am afraid it will be a long time, a very long time, before I change my views. When I do, I shall give you notice of the fact. Till then, believe me, you must make other arrangements and keep your kisses. You have so much opportunity to find better recipients for them!...

'Good-bye – as I would say of old,' you say. But it seems to me that of old you set a somewhat higher value upon me; you had not altogether relegated me to minor roles; above all you were willing to wait until I had said 'yes' before you were sure of my consent. You must be satisfied, then, with my saying good-bye, not as I, too, would have said it of old, but as I am saying it now.

Your servant, Monsieur de Valmont.

Château de —
31 October 17 —

LETTER 128: *The Présidente de Tourvel to Madame de Rosemonde*

It was not until yesterday, Madame, that I received your belated reply. It would have killed me immediately, had my life still belonged to me, but my life is in another's possession: and that other is Monsieur de Valmont. I conceal nothing from you, you see. Though you should find me no longer worthy of your friendship, I am still less afraid of losing it than betraying it. All I can tell you is that, given the choice between the death of Monsieur de Valmont and his happiness, I decided in favour of the latter. I am not boasting, nor accusing myself: I am simply stating a fact.

You may easily imagine the impression your letter, and the harsh truths contained in it, must in the circumstances have made upon me. Do not suppose, however, that it awakened any regrets in me, or that it could ever bring about a change in my feelings or my conduct. It is not that I do not still suffer cruelly; but when my heart is most torn, when I am afraid that I may no longer be able to endure the torment, I tell myself Valmont is happy, and everything disappears before that thought, or rather turns before it into pleasure.

It is to your nephew, then, that my life is devoted; for him that I have been ruined. He has become the sole centre of my thoughts, my feelings, and my actions. As long as my life is necessary to his happiness, my life shall be precious to me, and I shall think it fortunate. If some day he decides otherwise . . . he shall hear neither complaint nor reproach from my lips. I have already dared to confront that fatal moment, and my decision is taken.

You see now how little I can be affected by the apprehensions you seem to be under that Monsieur de Valmont will one day bring about my ruin: for before he can wish to do that he will have ceased to love me, and what will reproaches be to me when I cannot hear them? He alone will be my judge. Since I shall have lived only for him, to him I shall entrust my memory; and if he is compelled to acknowledge that I loved him, I shall have been sufficiently justified.

You have just seen into my heart, Madame. I have preferred, by being honest, the misfortune of losing your respect to that of making myself unworthy of it by stooping to lies. I thought I owed you this entire confidence in return for your former kindness to me. To add one word more might make you suspect that I am still counting upon it, when in fact I judge myself to have forfeited my claims.

I am with all respect, Madame, your very humble and obedient servant.

Paris
ı November ı7 —

LETTER 129: *The Vicomte de Valmont to the Marquise de Merteuil*

TELL me, my love: why the tone of bitterness and irony that pervades your last letter? What is the crime I have committed, unwittingly it seems, which puts you in so bad a temper? You accuse me of assuming your consent before I have obtained it: but I thought that what, with anyone else, might appear as presumption could never between us be taken for anything but confidence; and since when has that sentiment been incompatible with friendship or love? In uniting hope and desire I merely yielded to a natural impulse, the impulse that will have us always take the shortest road to the happiness we seek; and you mistook for a sign of pride what was only the effect of my eagerness. I know quite well that custom in such cases demands a respectful uncertainty; but you know, too, that that is nothing but a formality, a simple matter of protocol; and I was, it seems to me, justified in thinking that this careful punctiliousness was no longer necessary between us.

It seems to me, too, that frankness and freedom, when they are supported by a relationship of long standing, are far preferable to the insipid flattery that so often debases love. Perhaps, for the rest, if I think highly of such ways, it is only because of the value I attach to the past happiness they recall: but for that very reason I should be all the more sorry to have you think otherwise.

This, however, is the only crime I am aware of having committed: for I cannot suppose that you could seriously think another woman existed anywhere in the world that I prefer to you, much less that I have appreciated you as little as you pretend to believe.

You have looked at yourself, you say, and cannot see that you have sunk so low. I can well believe it, and that proves that your looking-glass does not lie. But could you not have arrived more easily and more justly at the conclusion that I certainly cannot have passed any such judgement on you?

I search in vain for an explanation of this strange idea. It seems to me, however, that it derives more or less directly from my having allowed myself to speak in praise of other women. This I infer, at all events, from your affectation of emphasizing the epithets *adorable*, *heavenly*, *attractive*, that I have used in speaking to you of Madame de Tourvel and the little Volanges. But don't you know that these words, chosen more often at random than upon reflection, express not so much an opinion of the persons in question as the mood one is in when one is speaking of them? And if, at the very moment of my being so deeply affected by one or the other, I yet desired you no less ardently; if I gave you a decided preference over both of them, since, after all, I cannot renew our former relationship without prejudice to both, I don't think you have so very much cause for complaint.

It will be no more difficult for me to excuse the *strange charm*, which seems also to have shocked you a little. In the first place, the fact that it is strange does not make it any stronger. Come now, who could improve upon the delicious pleasures that you alone can offer, ever new and ever more lively? I meant only that this one was of a kind I had not yet experienced, but without attempting to set a value upon it. And I added what I shall now repeat: that, whatever it is, I shall fight it and conquer it. And I shall do so with more enthusiasm if I may consider the trifling task as an offer of homage to you.

As for little Cécile, it is no use speaking to you of her. You have not forgotten that it was at your request that I took charge of the child, and I await only your permission to be rid of her. I may have taken notice of her freshness and ingenuousness; I may even have been able, for a moment, to find her *attractive*, because one always takes more or less of a pleasure in one's work, but there is certainly in no respect enough substance in her to claim one's attention for long.

Now, my love, I appeal to your sense of justice, to your former kindness for me, to our long and perfect friendship, to the entire confidence in each other which has since strengthened our ties: have I deserved the harsh tone you adopt with me? But how easy it will be for you to make amends whenever you wish! Say but a word and you will see whether all the charms and attractions in the world can keep me here, not only for a day but even for a minute. I shall fly to your feet and into your arms, and shall prove to you a thousand times and in a thousand ways, that you are and will always be the rightful sovereign of my heart.

Good-bye, my love. I most anxiously await your reply.

Paris
3 November 17 —

LETTER 130: *Madame de Rosemonde to the Présidente de Tourvel*

WHY, my dear, do you no longer wish to be my daughter? Why do you as much as declare that all correspondence will cease between us? Is it to punish me for not having guessed something that was against all probability? Or do you suspect me of having distressed you deliberately? No, I know your heart too well to believe that you could think thus of mine. The pain your letter gave me, therefore, I feel much less on my account than on yours.

Oh, my young friend, it grieves me to say it, but you are much too worthy of love ever to be made happy by it! And, indeed, where is the woman of delicacy and sensitivity who has not found misfortune in the very feeling that promised her so much happiness? Do men ever appreciate the women they possess?

Not that many of them are not honourable in their conduct and constant in their affections: but even among these, how few are also capable of understanding our hearts! Do not imagine, my child, that their love is like ours. They feel, of course, the same delight; often they are more carried away by it; but they are ignorant of that anxious eagerness, that careful solicitude, which provokes us to the constant and tender attentions whose sole object is always the man we love. A man enjoys the happiness he feels, a woman the happiness she gives. This difference, so essential and so little noticed, yet influences the whole of their respective conduct in the most remarkable way. The pleasure of one is to satisfy his desires, of the other it is, above all, to arouse them. Giving pleasure for him is only a means to success; while for her it is success itself. Coquetry, so often held in accusation against woman, is no more than the abuse of their way of feeling, and is itself a proof of the way they feel. Lastly, that exclusive attachment to one person, which is the peculiar characteristic of love, is in a man only a preference, which seems at the most to increase a pleasure that with some other woman might be diminished, but not destroyed; whereas in women, it is a profound feeling, which not only annihilates all other desires, but, stronger than nature and disobedient to her commands, may cause them to derive only repugnance and disgust from the very source of pleasure itself.

Do not be led to believe that the more or less numerous exceptions which may be cited against these universal rules can in any way disprove them. Public opinion is their guarantee, which in the case of men only will distinguish between infidelity and inconstancy. It is a distinction which men make use of when they ought to be humiliated by it; a distinction which, among our sex, is never made except by those depraved women who are a disgrace to it. Any means will serve to spare them the painful consciousness of their degradation.

I thought, my dear, you might find it useful to have these reflections to set against those chimerical fancies of perfect happiness with which love never fails to abuse our imaginations; false hopes that one clings to even when one sees that they must perforce be abandoned; the loss of which, moreover, aggravates and multiplies the griefs, all too real already, that are inseparable from deep feeling! The task of alleviating your sufferings or of reducing their number is the only one that I wish or am able to fulfil at this moment. Where the illness is without remedy, advice can only bear on the regimen. All I ask of you is that you should remember that to pity a sick man is not to cast blame upon him. Indeed, who are we to cast blame upon each other? Let us leave the right to judge to Him who reads our hearts; I should even go so far as to believe that in His paternal sight a host of virtues may redeem a single weakness.

But I beg you, my dear friend, renounce these violent resolutions which are an indication less of strength than of an entire loss of courage. Do not forget that in giving up your life into another's possession, to use your own expression, you cannot, all the same, have deprived your friends of that part of it which already belonged to them and which they shall never cease to claim.

Good-bye, my dear daughter. Think sometimes of your fond mother, and be sure that you will always, above all else, be the object of her kindest thoughts.

Château de —
4 November 17 —

LETTER 131: *The Marquise de Merteuil to the Vicomte de Valmont*

WELL done, Vicomte. I am better pleased with you this time than the last. But now let us talk as good friends, and let me convince you that the arrangement you seem to favour would be, as much for you as for me, absolute folly.

Have you not as yet observed that pleasure, which is undeniably the sole motive force behind the union of the sexes, is nevertheless not enough to form a bond between them? And that, if it is preceded by desire which impels, it is succeeded by disgust which repels? That is a law of nature which love alone can alter: and can love be summoned up at will? Nevertheless, love is necessary, and the necessity would really be very embarrassing had not one perceived that fortunately it will do if love exists on one side only. The difficulty is thus reduced by half without much being lost thereby: in fact one party enjoys the happiness of loving, the other that of pleasing – the latter a little less intense it is true, but to it is added the pleasure of deceiving, which establishes a balance; and so everything is satisfactorily arranged.

But tell me, Vicomte, which of us will be responsible for deceiving the other? You know the story of the two gamblers who recognized each other for card-sharpers even as they played. 'We shall win nothing from each other,' they said, 'let us share the stakes', and they abandoned the game. We must, believe me, follow their prudent example. Let us not waste time together which might otherwise be so profitably employed.

To prove to you that in this I am swayed by your interest as much as mine, and that I am not acting out of annoyance or caprice, I shall not refuse you the reward agreed upon between us. I am perfectly sure that for a single night we shall be more than sufficient for each other; and I don't even doubt that we shall enjoy it too much to see it end without regret. But let us keep in mind that this regret is necessary to happiness. However sweet the illusion, let us not believe that it can last.

As you see, I am quite ready to oblige, even though you have not yet fulfilled your part of the bargain: for, after all, I was to have the first letter written by your Heavenly Prude. But whether you still intend to abide by it, or whether you have forgotten the terms of a contract which perhaps interests you less than you would have me believe, I have as yet received nothing, absolutely nothing. However, if I am not mistaken, the tender devotee writes a great deal. What else can she possibly do when she is alone? She surely has not the good sense to amuse herself. I could therefore, if I wished, find a few little complaints to make against you; but I pass them over in silence to make up for the slight bad temper I may have shown in my last letter.

Now, Vicomte, there remains only a request to make of you, as much for your sake as for mine: and that is to put off for the moment what I desire perhaps as much as you. It seems to me it is better deferred until I return to town. On the one hand we shall not have the necessary freedom here, and on the other it would involve me in some risk; for it requires only a little jealousy to fasten me more firmly than ever to this sad creature Belleroche, who at the moment is attached only by a thread. He is already goading himself on to make love to me: we are at the point where there is as much malice as prudence in the caresses I lavish upon him. But at the same time you can well see that this is not the sacrifice to make for you! A double infidelity will make our meeting so much the more charming.

Do you know that I sometimes regret that we are reduced to such courses. There was a time when we loved each other – for it was, I think, love – and I was happy; and you, Vicomte! . . . But why think now of a happiness which can never return? No; whatever you say, it is impossible that it should. In the first place I should demand sacrifices which you certainly could not or would not make for my sake, and which, it might well be, I should not deserve. And then, how could I ever be sure of you? Oh, no, no! I will not so much as entertain the idea; and in spite of the pleasure I find at this very moment in writing to you, I had much better leave you at once.

Good-bye, Vicomte.

Château de —
6 November 17 —

LETTER 132: *The Présidente de Tourvel to Madame de Rosemonde*

I AM so deeply sensible, Madame, of your kindness towards me that I should open my heart entirely to it were it not, in some sort, held back by a fear of profaning what I accept. Why, when kindness is so precious to me, must I feel at the same time that I am no longer worthy of it? I can at least express my gratitude! I can admire, above all, your indulgent virtue, which sees weakness only to commiserate with it, whose irresistible charm maintains so mild, yet so strong a sway over my heart, in company with the charm of love itself.

But can I still deserve a friendship which is no longer enough to make me happy? I might say the same of your advice: I know its value, but I cannot accept it. And how can I disbelieve in perfect happiness, when I feel it at this very moment? Yes, if men are such as you describe them, they must be shunned: they are detestable. But then how little Valmont is like them! If he is subject, as they are, to that violence of passion you call being carried away, how much is it exceeded in him by his extreme delicacy! Oh, my dear! You tell me to share my sorrows with you: enjoy my happiness instead. I owe it to my love; and the object of my love still further increases its value! It is, you say, perhaps a weakness in you to love your nephew. Ah, if you knew him as I do! I love him to idolatry, and yet much less than he deserves. He may once certainly have been led into error. He admits it himself. But who can know true love as he does? What more can I say? His feelings are equal to the feelings he inspires.

You are going to think that this is one of those 'chimerical fancies, with which love never fails to abuse our imaginations'! In that case why should he have become only more tender, more eager now that he has nothing left to obtain from me? I admit I once found in him a certain deliberation, a reserve, which rarely left him, and which often reminded me, in spite of myself, of the false and cruel impression I had been given of him at first. But since he has been able to give himself up without constraint to the impulses of his heart, he seems to divine all the wishes of my own. Who knows, we may have been born for each other! I may have been destined for the happiness of being necessary to his! Ah, if it is an illusion, let me die before it vanishes. But no: I want to live to cherish it, to worship it. Why should he cease to love me? What other woman could make him happier than I do? And I know from my own experience, the happiness one gives is the strongest bond, the only one that really holds. Yes, it is the delightful consciousness of that which ennobles love, which purifies it, so to speak, and makes it truly worthy of a tender and generous heart such as Valmont's.

Good-bye, my dear, my worthy, my indulgent friend. I could write no more if I tried: it is now time for him to come as he promised, and I can think of nothing else. Forgive me! But you wanted my happiness, and it is so great at this moment, that I am scarcely capable of supporting it.

Paris
7 November 17 —

LETTER 133: *The Vicomte de Valmont to the Marquise de Merteuil*

WHAT then, my love, are these sacrifices which you consider I would not make, for which nevertheless I should be rewarded by giving you pleasure? Let me only know what they are. If I hesitate for a moment before offering them to you, you may refuse that homage. Come, what can you have thought of me lately if, even when you are being indulgent, you doubt my feelings and capacities? Sacrifices which I would not or could not make! Do you then think I am in love? Enslaved? Do you suspect that the value I once set upon victory I now attach to the vanquished? Ah, thank Heaven, I am not yet reduced to that, and I am willing to prove it to you. Yes, I shall prove it to you, even if it must be at Madame de Tourvel's expense. You could scarcely, after that, remain in any doubt.

I may, I suppose, have spent some time, without any risk to myself, on a woman who has at least the merit of belonging to a species one rarely meets. Perhaps, too, my meeting with this adventure during the off-season encouraged me to commit myself further than usual; and even now, when the great world has scarcely yet resumed its whirl, it is not surprising that I am almost entirely preoccupied with it. But remember, too, that I have hardly had a week to enjoy the fruits of three month's labours. I have so often kept for longer what was worth less and has not cost me so much!... and you have never drawn conclusions from that to my discredit.

Besides, do you want to know the real cause of my interest? Here it is. This woman is naturally timid: from the first she doubted her happiness, and that doubt was enough to destroy it, so much so that I have scarcely yet begun to be able to judge how far my own power extends in this respect. This is something, nevertheless, that in general I have always been curious to discover; and opportunities for doing so are not as easily come by as you might think.

In the first place, pleasure, for many women, is simply pleasure and never anything else. For them, whatever the title they bestow upon us, we are never more than servants, mere functionaries whose only merit is industry: the one who does most, does best.

Another class of women, perhaps the most numerous today, are

317

almost exclusively concerned with a lover's prestige, with the pleasure of having snatched him from a rival and the fear of having him snatched in turn from them. We do, it is true, play some part, more or less, in the sort of happiness they enjoy; but it depends more on our circumstances than on our persons. We are its means, but not its instrument.

For my experiment, therefore, I needed a delicate and sensitive woman who made love her only concern, and who, even in love, saw no further than her lover; whose emotions, far from following the usual course, reached her senses through her heart; whom I have, for example, seen (and I don't refer to the first occasion) emerge from pleasure dissolved in tears, yet find it again in the first word that touched her sympathies. In addition she must have a natural candour, become irrepressible from a habit of indulging it, which could not, therefore, allow her to disguise a single one of her feelings. Now, you will agree, such women are rare: and I dare say that, were it not for this one, I should perhaps never have met any.

It is not surprising, therefore, that she should interest me for longer than anyone else; and if my experiment upon her demands my making her happy, perfectly happy, why should I refuse, particularly since her happiness will be useful to me rather than otherwise? But does it follow, from the fact that my mind is occupied, that my heart is enslaved? No, of course not. Hence, the value I cannot help attaching to this adventure will not prevent my engaging in others, or even sacrificing it to more agreeable ones.

I am still so much at liberty, that I have not even neglected the little Volanges, in whom I take so small an interest. Her mother is bringing her back to town in three days' time, and yesterday I established my communications: a little money for the porter, a few compliments to his wife, were enough for the purpose. Can you conceive why Danceny was unable to find so simple a method? And people say that love inspires ingenuity! On the contrary, it stupefies those who are under its sway. And you think I am incapable of resisting it? Ah, depend upon it, in a few days I shall already, by sharing it, have weakened the perhaps too-vivid impression I received; and if sharing it once is not enough, I shall do so again and again.

I shall be none the less ready to return the little convent girl to her discreet lover as soon as you judge proper. You no longer, I think, have any reason to demur; as for me, I am quite willing to render poor Danceny this signal service. It is, to tell the truth, the least I owe him for all that he has done for me. He is, at the moment, in extreme anxiety to know whether he will be received at Madame de Volanges'. I soothe him as much as I can by telling him that, one way or another, I shall effect his happiness at the first opportunity; and meanwhile I continue to be responsible for the correspondence which he wishes to resume as soon as 'his Cécile' arrives. I already have six letters from him and I shall certainly have one or two more before the happy day. That boy must be very idle!

But let us leave this childish pair and return to ourselves. Let me think only of the sweet hopes your letter has given me. Yes, of course you will be sure of me, and I cannot forgive you your doubts. Have I ever ceased to be faithful to you? The ties that bound us were unloosed, not broken. Our supposed rupture was only an illusion of the imagination: in spite of it we have in our feelings, in our interests, remained at one. Like the traveller who returns disillusioned, I shall find that I left true happiness to chase false hopes, and shall say with d'Harcourt:

The more I saw abroad, the more I longed for home[1]

Don't, then, resist the thought, or rather the feeling, that draws you back to me. Having tasted all the pleasures of our separate careers, let us enjoy the happiness of discovering that none of them is comparable to that which we once experienced together, and shall again – to find it more delicious than ever before.

Good-bye, my love. I am willing to await your return: but make it soon, and don't forget how much I long for it.

Paris
8 November 17 —

1. Du Belloi, *Tragedy of the Siege of Calais.*

LETTER 134: *The Marquise de Merteuil to the Vicomte de Valmont*

REALLY, Vicomte, you are like a child in front of whom one can say nothing! And to whom one can show nothing without his wanting to snatch at it! A simple thought occurs to me, which I warn you, too, that I cannot seriously consider, and because I mention it to you, you take advantage of the fact to remind me of what I have said; to hold me to it when I want to forget it; to make me in some sort, and in spite of myself, share your foolhardy desires! Is it generous of you to leave me to support the burden of prudence alone? I tell you again, as I tell myself repeatedly, that the arrangement you propose is absolutely impossible. Even though you bring to it all the generosity you show me at this moment, don't you think that I, too, have my delicacy which will not allow me to accept sacrifices that are detrimental to your happiness?

Now, is it not true, Vicomte, that you are deluding yourself about the feeling that attaches you to Madame de Tourvel? If it is not love, what is love? You deny it in a hundred ways; but you prove it in a thousand. What, for example, is the meaning of this subterfuge you resort to in order to hide from yourself (for I believe you to be sincere with me) that the interest you take in your 'experiment' is, in fact, a desire, which you can neither conceal nor conquer, to keep this woman? One would think you had never made another woman happy, perfectly happy! And, if you have any doubt of that, your memory is a very bad one! No. It is not that. In a word, your heart is playing tricks upon your reason, inducing it to deceive itself with specious arguments. I, however, in whose most intimate interest it is not to be deceived, am not so easily satisfied.

While remarking that, out of politeness, you were careful to avoid the words you imagined had offended me, I noticed all the same that, perhaps unconsciously, you expressed the same ideas. In fact it was no longer the adorable, the heavenly Madame de Tourvel, but *an astonishing woman, a delicate and sensitive woman* – to the exclusion of all others; finally, a *rare woman*, one such as is not likely to be met a second time. It is the same with that strange charm, which is not of the *strongest kind*. Well, maybe: but since you have never experienced it till now, there is reason to believe that you will never experience it again: and your loss is still irreparable. If these, Vicomte, are not certain symptoms of love, it must be denied that there are any.

Rest assured that on this occasion I speak without rancour. I promised myself not to give way to it again, being too well aware that it could become a dangerous pitfall. Believe me, we had better be friends and leave it at that. Be grateful only for my courage in resisting you: yes, my courage: for that is sometimes necessary even in avoiding a decision one knows to be a bad one.

It is therefore only to persuade you to my way of thinking that I am going to reply to your question about the sacrifices I should exact, which you could not make. I use the word 'exact' deliberately, because I am quite sure that in a moment you are, in fact, going to find me too exacting: but so much the better! Far from being offended by your refusal, I shall thank you for it. What is more, I don't want to pretend with you: I shall perhaps need it.

I should demand then – see, what cruelty! – that the rare, the astonishing Madame de Tourvel become no more to you than the ordinary woman that she is: for, let us not deceive ourselves, the charm we think we find in others exists only in ourselves, and it is love alone that confers beauty on the beloved. I know that you would probably make the effort to promise, even to swear, to do what I ask, impossible though it may be; but I must tell you I should believe no empty speeches. I could not be convinced but by the whole of your conduct.

That is not yet all; I should be capricious. About the sacrifice of little Cécile, which you offer me with so good a grace, I should care not at all. I should ask you, on the contrary, to continue in this uncongenial employment until further orders from me; perhaps because I should like thus to abuse my power, perhaps because, out of a sense of kindness or of justice, I could be satisfied with ruling your feelings without wishing to spoil your pleasures. Be that as it may, I should require to be obeyed; and my instructions would be strict!

It is true that I might thereupon think myself obliged to thank you: who knows? Perhaps even to reward you. I should certainly, for example, cut short an absence which would begin to seem intolerable. I should at last see you again, Vicomte, and I should see you again . . . how? . . . But you must remember that this is only a conversation, a simple account of an impossible scheme: I don't want to be the only one to forget about it.

Do you know I am a little anxious about my lawsuit? At any rate, I decided I must know the precise extent of my resources. My lawyers cited a few laws and a great many 'authorities', as they call them: but I could see no more reason than justice in them. I almost regret having refused a settlement out of court. However, it reassures me to remember that the Public Prosecutor is clever, the counsel eloquent, and the plaintiff pretty. If these three qualifications were no longer worth anything, our whole legal procedure would have to be changed, and what would then become of respect for tradition?

The lawsuit is now the only thing that keeps me here. The Belleroche affair is over: case dismissed, costs divided. He is busy regretting this evening's ball: the true regret of the idle man. I shall give him back his entire liberty when I return to town. In making him this grievous sacrifice I shall be consoled by the generosity he finds in it.

Good-bye, Vicomte, write often. The catalogue of your pleasures makes up, at least in part, for the boredom I suffer.

Château de —
11 November 17 —

LETTER 135: *The Présidente de Tourvel to Madame de Rosemonde*

I SHALL try to write to you, but am not sure yet that I can. Ah, God! To think that in my last letter it was excess of happiness that kept me from continuing. Now it is an excess of despair that overwhelms me: that leaves me strength only to feel my sufferings, and deprives me of power to express them.

Valmont . . . Valmont loves me no longer. He has never loved me. Love does not disappear like this. He deceives me, betrays me, insults me. All the miseries, the humiliations there are, I feel them all, and he is the cause of them!

And do not think this is any mere suspicion: I was so far from suspecting anything! I am not so fortunate as to have any doubts. I have seen him: what can he possibly say to excuse himself? But what does it matter him? He will not even try ... Wretched woman! What difference will your tears, your reproaches make to him? It is not you that interest him!...

It is, then, true that he has sacrificed me, indeed delivered me up ... to whom? A vile creature ... vile, do I say? Ah, I have even lost the right to despise her. She has not betrayed so many responsibilities. She is less guilty than I. Oh, how painful is suffering when it springs from remorse! I feel my torments twice as keenly. Goodbye, my dear friend. However unworthy of your pity I have made myself, you will yet feel some for me if you have any conception of what I suffer.

I have just re-read my letter, and realize that it does not tell you anything, so I shall try and find the courage to tell you the dreadful story. It happened yesterday; I was to go out to supper for the first time since my return. Valmont came to see me at five o'clock. Never had he seemed so tender. He gave me to understand that he would prefer me not to go out, and, as you may imagine, I immediately decided to stay at home. Two hours later, however, his manner and tone of voice changed suddenly and quite perceptibly. I do not know whether I could have said anything to annoy him; whatever it was, he pretended, a little while later, to remember some business which obliged him to leave me, and he went off not, however, without expressing the deepest regrets, which appeared to be tender and which I then believed to be sincere.

Left to myself, I though it right not to neglect my former engagements since I was free to fulfil them. I finished my *toilette* and entered my carriage. My coachman, unfortunately, took me past the Opera, and I found myself detained in the traffic at the exit. Four paces ahead, and in the next line of carriages, I saw Valmont's. My heart immediately began to beat fast, but not in fear. My only thought was for my carriage to move forward. It was his instead that was obliged to draw back beside mine. I leant out immediately. Imagine my astonishment at seeing at his side a woman who is well-known for a courtesan! I withdrew, as you may guess. I had seen enough to break my heart. But what you will scarcely believe is that this harlot, with a knowingness apparently derived from unthinkable confidences, neither left the door of the carriage, nor ceased to look at me, shrieking with laughter so as to attract the attention of everyone.

In spite of my state of prostration, I allowed myself to be taken to the house where I was to sup: but it proved impossible for me to stay. I felt at every instant that I was about to faint, and, worst of all, could not hold back my tears.

On returning home I wrote to Monsieur de Valmont, and sent the letter immediately; he was not at home. In my desire to rouse myself at any price from this life-in-death, or end it forever, I dispatched my servant again with orders to wait. But before midnight he returned, saying that Valmont's coachman, who had been sent back, had told him that his master would not be coming home that night. I decided this morning that I could do no more than ask for the return of my letters and request him never to come to my house again. I did in fact give orders accordingly; but they were probably superfluous. It is nearly midday; he has not yet presented himself here, and I have not even received word from him.

Now, my dear friend, I have nothing further to add. You know everything; you know my heart. My only hope is that it will not be for much longer that I remain a burden upon your sympathy and friendship.

Paris
15 November 17 —

LETTER 136: *The Présidente de Tourvel to the Vicomte de Valmont*

AFTER what happened, yesterday, Monsieur, you will, of course, no longer expect to be received at my house, and have doubtless very little wish to be received here. The purpose of this note is, therefore, not so much to ask you never to come here again as to request you to return my letters: letters which ought never to have existed, and which, though they may have interested you moment-arily as proofs of the infatuation you induced in me, can only be a matter of indifference to you now that my eyes are opened and they express only a feeling which you have destroyed.

I realize, and I admit it, that I was wrong to place any confidence in you, a mistake to which many others before me have been victims. For this I blame only myself. But I did not think, all the same, that I deserved to be delivered over by you to insult and contempt. I thought that, in sacrificing everything for you, in losing for your sake not only the esteem of others but my own, I need not, never-theless, expect to be judged by you more harshly than by the pub-lic, in whose opinion there is still an immense difference between a weak woman and a depraved one. These injuries, which anyone would complain of, are the only ones I shall mention. About the injuries to my feelings I have nothing to say: your heart would not understand mine. Good-bye, Monsieur.

Paris
15 November 17 —

LETTER 137: *The Vicomte de Valmont to the Présidente de Tourvel*

YOUR letter, Madame, has only just been delivered to me. I trem-bled as I read it, and it has left me with scarcely strength enough to reply. What a frightful idea you have of me! Ah, of course I have my faults; faults such as I shall never forgive myself for while I live, even though you should in your indulgence draw a veil over them. But how far from my nature are, and have always been, those you accuse me of now! Who, I? Humiliate you! Disgrace you! When I respect you as much as I cherish you; when I have known no pride such as I have felt since the moment you judged me worthy of you. Appearances have deceived you, and I admit they have been against me: but did you not have it in your heart to question them? Was it not the mere idea that you might have been ill-used by me that revolted you? And you gave it credit none the less? Hence, you not only judged me capable of this terrible folly, you were even afraid that your kindness towards me had exposed you to it. Ah, if you think yourself so degraded by your love, how base a creature I myself must be in your eyes!

Oppressed by the painful feelings this thought arouses in me I waste time in dismissing it that I should spend in destroying it. I shall confess everything. Yet another thought still holds me back. Must I then recall an incident which I should like to erase from my memory, fix your attention and my own upon a momentary error which I would willingly redeem with the rest of my life, the reason for which I am unable to discover, the memory of which will always reduce me to humiliation and despair? Ah, if in accusing myself I must excite your anger, you will not have to look far for your revenge: you have only to leave me to my remorse.

Yet, who would believe that the principal cause of this incident was the all-compelling charm you exert over me? It was that which made me too long unmindful of important business I could not postpone. I left you too late. The person I went to meet was no longer there. I hoped to find him at the Opera, but that journey was equally unfruitful. I saw Émilie there: Émilie, whom I first met at a time when I was very far from knowing either you or your love. She was without her carriage, and asked me to take her to her house not ten yards away. I foresaw no consequences, and agreed. But it was then that I met you; and I knew immediately that you would be led to think me guilty.

The fear of displeasing or distressing you is so powerful in me that it was bound to be, and was in fact, very soon noticed. I confess that it even tempted me to make the girl promise not to show herself: but this precaution on the part of delicacy turned to the discomfiture of love. Never certain, as no woman of her class ever is, of the power she has usurped unless she can abuse it, Émilie was very careful not to let slip so splendid an opportunity. The more my embarrassment increased, the greater the delight she took in exposing herself; and her stupid laughter, of which I blush to think that you should for a moment have believed yourself to be the object, was provoked by nothing other than the cruel pain I was suffering, itself the consequence of my respect and my love for you.

Hitherto, of course, I had been more unfortunate than culpable;

and those injuries 'which anyone would complain of, the only ones you mention', having no existence, cannot be held against me. But it is useless for you to say nothing of injuries to your feelings. I shall not preserve the same silence: I have too great an interest in breaking it.

Not that, in my present confusion at so unthinkable an aberration, I can bring myself to recall it, without extreme pain. Deeply conscious of my wrong, I should be quite willing to endure its pain and to hope that time, my undying tenderness, and my repentance would bring forgiveness. But how can I be silent, when what remains to be told is of so much concern to your delicacy?

Do not imagine that I am looking for a way of excusing or palliating my fault: I admit myself guilty, But I do not admit, and I shall never admit that this humiliating mistake could be regarded as a crime against love. Come, what can there be in common between an assault upon the senses, between a moment of self-oblivion, soon followed by shame and regret, and the purest sentiments, which can only take root in a delicate soul, which can only be nourished by respect, whose ultimate fruit is happiness? Ah, do not so profane the name of love. Beware, especially, of profaning yourself by treating as of equal importance what can never be compared. Leave it to base and degraded women to fear a rivalry which, in spite of themselves, they feel they must acknowledge, to experience the torments of a jealousy as cruel as it is humiliating. But you, turn your eyes from things that would offend your sight; and, pure as the Divinity, punish the offence, as He does, without being sensible of it.

But what penance can you impose upon me more painful than the one I now undergo? What can compare with my regret at having displeased you, with my despair at having distressed you, the insupportable idea that I have made myself less worthy of you? You think of punishment – while I, I ask for comfort! Not because I deserve it, but because it is necessary to me, and I may obtain it only from you.

If, of a sudden, forgetting my love and yours, no longer setting any value upon my happiness, you decide, on the contrary, to give me up to everlasting suffering, you have the right to do so. Strike me down. But if, with more indulgence or more compassion, you recall the tender feelings that united our hearts; that intoxication of the soul, ever renewed, ever more deeply felt; those sweet, blessed days we owed to each other; all the myriad gifts of love, which love alone bestows! – if so, perhaps you will prefer to revive than to destroy them. What else can I say? I have lost everything, and lost it through my own fault: but I may recover everything through the goodness of your heart. It is now for you to decide. I shall add but one word more. Only yesterday you swore to me that my happiness was secure while it depended on you! Ah, Madame, will you now give me up to everlasting despair?

Paris
15 November 17 —

LETTER 138: *The Vicomte de Valmont to the Marquise de Merteuil*

I INSIST, my love: I am not in love, and it is not my fault if circumstances compel me to play the part. Be persuaded only and return: you will see for yourself how sincere I am. I gave proof of it yesterday which cannot be contradicted by what is happening today.

I was at the Tender Prude's, for lack of anything else to do, for the little Volanges, in spite of her condition, was to spend the night at Madame de V —'s, who has been beforehand with a ball. Idleness at first encouraged me to prolong my visit. I even, to this end, exacted a little sacrifice. But hardly had it been granted, when my anticipation of pleasure was disturbed by the thought of this love you persist in ascribing to me, or rather accusing me of; so that I was left with no other desire than that of being able at once to assure myself, and to convince you, that it was nothing on your part but pure slander.

I therefore acted decisively: and, under some slight pretext, left my beauty overcome with surprise, and no doubt even more with affliction, while I went calmly to meet Émilie at the Opera. She would confirm to you that, till this morning when we separated, not the smallest regret disturbed our pleasures.

I should, however, have had serious cause for disquiet had not my accustomed nonchalance come to my rescue. I was scarcely four houses away from the Opera, with Émilie in my carriage, when that of the Austere Devotee drew up exactly alongside mine. Whereupon an obstruction in the traffic kept us beside each other for nearly ten minutes. We could not in broad daylight have been more clearly visible to each other, and there was no means of escape.

But that is not all. It occurred to me to tell Émilie that this was the woman of the letter (you will perhaps remember my little joke, when Émilie was my desk).[1] Émilie – who had not forgotten – being of a mirth-loving disposition, would not be satisfied until she had examined *this pillar of virtue*, as she put it, at her leisure, breaking into such scandalous peals of laughter as gave the latter considerable umbrage.

That is not yet all. The jealous woman sent to my house that very evening. I was not there: but, in her obstinacy, she sent a second time, with orders to wait for me. As for me, as soon as I had decided to stay at Émilie's I sent back my carriage, giving my coach-man no other orders than to return for me in the morning. Since, on arriving home, he found Cupid's messenger there, he did not think twice before telling him that I should not be back that night. You may well imagine the effect of this news, and that at my return I found my dismissal awaiting me, pronounced with all the dignity suitable to the occasion!

Thus this adventure, interminable according to you, might well have come to an end this morning: if it is not yet over, that is not, as you are going to think, because I am anxious to prolong it. It is because, on the one hand, I do not think it proper to allow myself to be dismissed, and, on the other, because I want to reserve the honour of a sacrifice for you.

I have therefore replied to the severe little note with a long and sentimental screed. I have offered lengthy arguments, and rely on love for the task of making them acceptable. I have already succeeded. I have just received a second note, still very severe, confirming our perpetual separation just as I expected; no longer, however, in quite the same tone. Above all, I am never again to be seen: this decision is announced four times in the most irrevocable

1. Letters 46 and 47.

manner. I conclude that there is not a moment to lose before presenting myself. I have already sent my valet to secure the hallporter; and I shall follow him myself presently to have my pardon signed. With sins of this kind, there is only one formula which confers absolution, and that must be received in person.

Good-bye, my love; I hasten to meet the great challenge.

Paris
15 November 17 —

LETTER 139: *The Présidente de Tourvel to Madame Rosemonde*

How sorry I am, my dear friend, for having spoken too much and too soon about my passing vexations! It is my fault that you are now distressed; you still have my troubles upon your mind, while I – I am happy. Yes, all is forgotten, forgiven, or rather amends have been made. Grief and anguish have given way to peace and delight. Oh, the joy of my heart! How can I express it? Valmont is innocent: no one could be guilty who loves so much. The terrible, insulting injuries I accused him so bitterly of having done me, he did not commit; and if, on a single point, I was obliged to be indulgent, had I not also injustices to make reparation for?

I shall not give you in detail the facts and arguments that excused him. Perhaps they cannot be properly appreciated by the mind: it is for the heart alone to feel their truth. If, however, you were to suspect me of weakness, I should appeal to your own judgement to support mine. With men, you say yourself, infidelity is not inconstancy.

Not that I feel that this distinction, sanctioned or not by public opinion, is any the less wounding to the pride: but why should I complain of that, when Valmont suffers even more? Do not imagine that he forgives himself or consoles himself for a wrong which I am willing to forget; yet how fully has he made amends for so small a fault in the excess of his love and the extravagance of my happiness!

I am either happier than I was before, or I am more conscious of the value of happiness since I feared I had lost it: but what I can say for certain is that, if I felt I were strong enough to undergo once again sufferings as cruel as those I have just endured, I should not think them too high a price to pay for the extreme happiness I now enjoy. Oh, my dear mother! Scold your inconsiderate daughter for having distressed you in her excessive haste. Scold her for having had the temerity to judge and calumniate a man she ought never to cease from worshipping. But, while you recognize her imprudence, see that she is happy, too, and increase her joy by sharing it.

Paris
16 November 17 —, evening

LETTER 140: *The Vicomte de Valmont to the Marquise de Merteuil*

How is it, my love, that I have received no reply from you? My last letter seems to me, nevertheless, to have deserved one. I should have received it three days ago, and I am still waiting! I am annoyed, to say the least, so shall say nothing to you at all about my most important affairs.

As to whether the attempted reconciliation achieved its full effect; as to whether, instead of distrust and recrimination, it produced only an increase of tenderness; as to whether it is I at present to whom apologies and amends are made for suspicion cast upon my honesty, you will hear not a word. And, were it nor for last night's unexpected incident, I should not be writing to you at all. But since the latter concerns your pupil, and since very probably she will not be in a position to tell you about it, at least for some time, I shall undertake to do so myself.

For reasons which you may or may not guess, Madame de Tourvel has for some days been spared my attentions; and since these reasons cannot apply where the little Volanges is concerned, I have been cultivating her the more assiduously. Thanks to the obliging porter, there were no obstacles to overcome, and your pupil and I have been living a comfortable and regular life. But habit leads to negligence. At first we were never able to take sufficient precau-

331

tions, and would tremble behind locked doors. Yesterday, an incredible piece of inadvertence was the cause of the accident I am going to tell you of; and if, for my part, I was let off with a fright, the little girl has had to pay more dearly for it.

We were not asleep, but in that state of relaxation and repose which follows pleasure, when we suddenly heard the bedroom door open. I immediately leaped to my sword, as much in my own defence as that of our pupil. I advanced to the door and saw no one. It was open however. As we had a lamp with us, I made a search, but found not a living soul. Then I remembered that we had forgotten our usual precautions. Having been merely pushed to, or not properly shut, the door had reopened of its own accord.

Returning to my timid companion to calm her fears, I found her no longer on the bed. She had fallen down, or had attempted to hide herself, between the bed and the wall. At any rate she was stretched there unconscious and motionless except for occasional violent convulsions. Imagine my embarrassment! I succeeded in returning her to the bed, and even in bringing her round: but she had been hurt by her fall and it was not long before she began to feel the effects.

Pains in her back, violent colic, and certain other much less equivocal symptoms soon led me to diagnose her condition: but to tell her about it I had first to tell her what her condition had been to begin with, for she was without the slightest suspicion. Never before, perhaps, has anyone preserved so much innocence while so effectively doing all that is necessary to lose it! Oh, this young lady wastes no time thinking!

She wasted a great deal, however, in feeling sorry for herself and I felt I must come to some decision. I agreed with her, therefore, that I should go to see the family physician and the family surgeon, and that, in addition to warning them that they would be sent for, I should confide everything to them under seal of secrecy; that she, for her part, would ring for her chambermaid, whom she would or would not take into her confidence, as she saw fit; but that in any case she would send for medical assistance, and, above all, forbid anyone to wake Madame de Volanges, a natural and tactful attention on the part of a daughter who is afraid of upsetting her mother.

I made my two visits and my two confessions as quickly as I

could, from thence returned home, and have not been out since. But the surgeon, who was a previous acquaintance of mine, came here at midday to report on the invalid's condition. I was not mistaken, but he hopes that, barring accidents, nothing will be noticed in the house. The chambermaid is in the secret, the physician has put a name to the malady, and the affair will be settled like a thousand others of its kind – unless it is going to be useful to us later to have it talked about.

But is there still any community of interest between us? Your silence makes me doubt it; I should no longer believe it at all, did not my desire to do so make me snatch at any excuse for sustaining my hopes.

Good-bye, my love: I embrace you, even though I bear you a grudge.

Paris
12 November 17 —

LETTER 141 : *The Marquise de Merteuil to the Vicomte de Valmont*

LORD, Vicomte, how irritating your persistence is! What does my silence matter to you? Do you think that, if I say nothing, it is for lack of arguments to put forward in my defence? Ah, would to God it were! No, no; it is only that it would pain me to have to put them to you.

Tell me the truth. Are you deluding yourself, or trying to deceive me? The disparity between what you say and what you do admits of no other explanations: which of these is correct? What do you want me to say, when I don't know myself what to think?

You seem to take great credit upon yourself for your last encounter with the Présidente; but what, after all, does it prove in support of your views or against mine? I certainly never said that you loved this woman so much that you would never deceive her, that you would not seize every opportunity of doing so that appeared to you to be easy and agreeable; I did not even doubt that you would think almost nothing of satisfying the desires she herself had aroused with another woman, the first that crossed your path; and I am not surprised that, with a licentiousness that one would be wrong to deny you, you did for once deliberately what you have done a thousand times merely as the occasion offered. Everyone knows that this is simply the way of the world: the way of all of you, whoever you are, Neros or nobodies. The man who behaves otherwise nowadays is taken for a romantic, and that is not, I think, the fault I find in you.

But what I have said and thought about you, what I still believe, is that you are in love with your Présidente: not, it is true, a very pure or very tender love, but one such as you are capable of feeling; one, that is to say, that leads you to seek qualities and charms in a woman who does not possess them; one that places her in a class apart, and relegates all other women to the second rank; one that keeps you attached to her even while you are insulting her; one, lastly, such as I imagine a Sultan might feel for his favourite Sultana, such as leaves him free to prefer, very often, a simple odalisque. My comparison seems to me to be the more just in that, like the Sultan, you have never been either the lover or the friend of a woman, but always either her tyrant or her slave. Hence I am quite sure that you humiliated and degraded yourself to a degree in order to restore yourself to favour with this fine creature! Then, only too happy to have succeeded, as soon as you thought the moment had come to obtain your pardon, you left me 'to meet the great challenge'.

Again, in your last letter, if you did not talk about this woman to the exclusion of all else, it was because you did not wish to tell me anything of your 'important affairs': they seem so important to you that your silence about them appears to you as a punishment inflicted on me. And it is after these myriad proofs of a decided preference for someone else that you calmly ask me whether 'there is still any community of interest between us!' Beware, Vicomte! Once I reply to that question, my reply will be irrevocable; my hesitating to make it at this moment has already, perhaps, told you too much. So I wish to say absolutely no more about it.

All that I can do is to tell you a story. You will perhaps not have time to read it, or to give it the attention necessary to understanding it – that I leave to you. It will only be, in the last resort, the story of a fallen woman.

A man of my acquaintance entangled himself, as you did, with a woman who did him little credit. He had the good sense, from time to time, to feel that sooner or later this affair must reflect adversely upon him: but though he was ashamed of it, he did not have the courage to break it off. His embarrassment was all the greater for his having boasted to his friends that he was absolutely free, for he was not unaware that our liability to ridicule always increases in proportion as we defend ourselves from it. Thus he spent his life committing one stupidity after another, never failing to say afterwards: 'It was not my fault.' A woman, a friend of this man's, was tempted at one time to throw him to the public in his infatuated state, so as to make him permanently ridiculous. However, being more generous than malicious by nature, or perhaps for some other reason, she decided to try a last resource, so as to be, whatever happened, in a position to say, like her friend: 'It was not my fault.' She therefore sent him – as a remedy, the application of which might be efficacious in his illness – but without further remark, the following letter:

'One is very soon bored with everything, my angel; it is a law of nature. It is not my fault.

'If therefore I am now bored with an adventure which has claimed my attention for four mortal months, it is not my fault.

'If, that is to say, my love was equal to your virtue – and that is certainly saying a great deal – it is not surprising that the one came to an end at the same time as the other. It is not my fault.

'It follows that for some time I have been deceiving you, but then your relentless tenderness forced me in some sort to do so! It is not my fault.

'A woman that I love madly now insists that I give you up for her sake. It is not my fault.

'I quite realize that this is the perfect opportunity to accuse me of perjury: but if, where nature has gifted men with no more than constancy, she has given women obstinacy, it is not my fault.

'Believe me, you should take another lover, as I take another mistress. This is good, very good advice: if you find it bad, it is not my fault.

'Good-bye, my angel. I took you with pleasure: I leave you without regret. I shall come back perhaps. Such is life. It is not my fault.'

This is not the moment, Vicomte, to tell you what effect was achieved by this last attempt, and what followed: but I promise to tell you in my next letter. In it will also be contained my ultimatum on the subject of the treaty you propose to renew. Till then, I shall say good-bye, no more ...

By the way, thank you for your account of the little Volanges; that must be kept for after the wedding, an article for the gossips' gazette. Meanwhile accept my condolences on the loss of your posterity. Good night, Vicomte.

Château de —
24 November 17 —

LETTER 142: *The Vicomte de Valmont to the Marquise de Merteuil*

UPON my word, my love, I don't know whether I misread or misunderstood your letter, the story you told me, and the little specimen of epistolary art included in it, but I may say that the last-named seemed to me to be original and potentially very effective, so I quite simply made a copy of it which I sent off to the Divine Présidente. I did not lose a moment: the tender missive was dispatched last evening. I preferred it this way, because in the first place I had promised to write to her yesterday; and then, too, because I considered the whole night would not be too long for her to collect herself and meditate upon this *great challenge* – to risk for a second time your criticism of that expression.

I was hoping to be able to send you my dearly-beloved's reply this morning: but it is nearly midday, and I have received nothing yet. I shall wait until five o'clock, and if I have no news by then I shall go in search of it; for especially in the matter of challenges it is only the first steps that are difficult.

Now, as you may imagine, I am exceedingly eager to learn the end of the story about this man of your acquaintance who was so

336

strongly suspected of not being able, when necessary, to sacrifice a woman. Did he not mend his ways? And did not his generous friend receive him back into favour?

I am no less anxious to receive your ultimatum, as you so politically call it! I am curious, above all, to know whether you will still attribute my behaviour to love. Ah, certainly there is love, a great deal of love, behind it. But love for whom? However, I am not attempting to assert any claims: I expect everything from your kindness.

Good-bye, my love: I shall not seal this letter until two o'clock in the hopes that by then I shall be able to attach the looked-for reply.

At two o'clock in the afternoon
Still nothing: there is very little time. I have not a moment to add another word: but will you now still refuse love's most tender kisses?

Paris
25 November 17 —

LETTER 143: *The Présidente de Tourvel to Madame de Rosemonde*

THE veil is rent, Madame, on which was pictured the illusion of my happiness. I see by the light of a terrible truth that my path lies between shame and remorse to a certain and none too distant death. I shall follow it ... I shall cherish my torments if they are to shorten my life. I send you the letter I received yesterday; I shall add no comment, it carries its own. This is no longer a time for complaint, but only for suffering. It is not pity I need, but strength.

Please receive, Madame, the only farewell I shall say, and hear my last prayer: which is to leave me to my fate, to forget me entirely, to count me no longer among the living. There is a point reached by misery where even friendship increases suffering and cannot heal it. When the wounds are mortal, all relief is inhumane. There is no feeling in my heart but despair. I look for nothing now but profound darkness in which to bury my shame. There I shall weep for my faults, if I am still capable of tears! For, since yesterday, I have not shed a single one. They no longer flow from my desolate heart.

Good-bye, Madame. Do not reply. On this cruel letter I have vowed never to receive another.

Paris
27 November 17 —

LETTER 144: *The Vicomte de Valmont to the Marquise de Merteuil*

YESTERDAY, my love, at three o'clock in the afternoon, impatient at the want of news, I presented myself at the Forsaken Beauty's: I was told she was out. I interpreted the phrase as a refusal to see me, which neither annoyed nor surprised me; and I left in the hopes that my visit would commit so polite a woman to honouring me with a word of reply. In my desire to receive one I expressly called in at my house about nine o'clock, but found nothing there. Astonished at this silence, which I did not expect, I instructed my valet to make inquiries and to find out whether the sensitive creature were dead or dying. When I finally came home, he told me that Madame de Tourvel had in fact gone out at eleven o'clock in the morning with her maid; that she had been driven to the convent of —, and that at seven o'clock in the evening she had sent back her carriage and her servants, who were to say that she was not to be expected home. Really, she does everything *comme il faut.* Convents are the accepted refuge of widows. If she persists in her praiseworthy resolutions, I shall have to add, to all the obligations I already owe her, the fame that will soon surround this adventure.

As I told you some time ago, I shall, in spite of your anxieties, reappear in society blazing with new glories. Let the stern critics who accuse me of a romantic and unhappy love show me then what they can do; let them effect more prompt, more brilliant ruptures. No, they can do better. Let them offer themselves as consolation: the way is clear. Well then, let them only try to run the course I have covered in its entirety: and if one of them achieves the smallest success, I shall accord him the palm. They will all find out, however, that when I take the trouble the impression I make is ineffaceable. Ah, this time it certainly will be: I shall set all my previous triumphs at naught were this woman ever to prefer a rival to me.

The decision she has taken flatters my vanity, I admit: but I am sorry she has found the strength to disengage herself to such an extent from me. There will now be other obstacles between us than those I have placed there myself! Suppose I wish to return to her, she might no longer want it. But what am I saying? No longer want it, no longer find in it her supreme happiness? Is that any way to love? And do you think, my love, that I ought to allow it? Could I not, for example – would it not be better to try and bring the woman round to the point of foreseeing a possible reconciliation, the reconciliation she must desire as long as she hopes for it? I could attempt this without attaching too much importance to it, and consequently without giving you any offence. On the contrary, it would be a simple exercise for us to perform together; and even if I were to succeed, I should merely have acquired another opportunity to renew, at your bidding, a sacrifice which has been, I think, agreeable to you. Now, my love, it remains for me to receive my reward, and all my thoughts are for your return. Come quickly, then, to claim your lover, your pleasures, your friends, and your share of adventures.

My own adventure with the little Volanges has turned out exceedingly well. Yesterday, when in my anxiety I was incapable of staying in one place, I even called, in the course of my wanderings, on Madame de Volanges. I found your pupil already in the drawing-room, still in invalid's garb, but fully convalescent and all the fresher and more interesting for it. You other women, in a similar position, would have spent a month upon your chaises-longues: upon my word, long live the youngsters! To tell you the truth, she made me decide to find out whether her cure was complete.

I have also to tell you that the little girl's accident has been in a good way to sending your *sentimentalist*, Danceny, out of his mind, at first with grief, now with joy. *His Cécile* was ill! You know how the mind reels under such misfortune. He sent for news three times a day, and not one day passed without his appearing in person. At length, in a beautiful epistle addressed to Mamma, he asked permission to come and congratulate her on the recovery of a possession so precious to her: and Madame de Volanges agreed, so that I found the young man established much as he had been in the past, except for a few little familiarities that he dares not now allow himself.

It was from him that I learnt these details: for I left at the same time as he, and I pumped him. You have no idea the effect this visit made upon him. Impossible to describe the joy, the desires, the transports. I, who love strong emotions, succeeded in turning his head completely by assuring him that in a few days I should put him in a position to see his mistress at even closer quarters.

In fact, I decided to give her back to him as soon as I had made my experiment. I want to devote myself entirely to you. Besides, was it worth the trouble of putting your pupil to school with me merely to deceive her husband? The triumph is in deceiving her lover! And especially her first lover! For, as for me, I have not been guilty of so much as uttering the word 'love'.

Good-bye, my love: come back as soon as you can to enjoy your prerogatives over me, to receive my homage and pay me my reward.

Paris
28 November 17 —

LETTER 145: *The Marquise de Merteuil to the Vicomte de Valmont*

SERIOUSLY, Vicomte, have you left the Présidente? Did you send her the letter I prepared for her? Really, you are charming, and you have exceeded my expectations! I can sincerely say that this triumph flatters me more than any I have achieved till now. You will perhaps think that I am setting a very high value upon the same woman that I once rated so low: not at all. The fact is that it is not over her I have won my triumph: it is over you. That is the amusing thing; that is what is so truly delicious.

Yes, Vicomte, you were very much in love with Madame de Tourvel, and you are still in love with her: you love her to distraction. But because it amused me to make you ashamed of it, you have bravely sacrificed her. You would have sacrificed her a thousand times rather than take a joke. To what lengths will vanity lead us! The sage was indeed right who called it the enemy of happiness.

Where would you be now had I wanted merely to play a trick on you? As you well know, though, I am incapable of deceit; and even if you are to reduce me, in my turn, to despair in a convent, I am willing to run the risk. I give myself up to my conqueror.

However, if I capitulate, it is really out of pure weakness: for, if I wished, how I could still quibble! And you, perhaps, would deserve it. I wonder, for example, at the cunning – or the clumsiness – with which you calmly suggest my letting you renew your relations with the Présidente. It would suit you very well, would it not, to take the credit for breaking with her, without losing the pleasure of enjoying her? And since the apparent sacrifice would thereafter be no sacrifice at all for you, you offer to renew it at my bidding! Were we to go on in this way, the Heavenly Devotee would continue to think herself the sole choice of your heart, while I should plume myself on being the preferred rival. Both of us will have been deceived, but you will be happy, and of what importance is anything else?

It is a pity that you have so much talent for making plans, and so little for putting them into practice; and that by one ill-considered move you have yourself placed an insuperable obstacle between you and what you desire.

Really, how can you, if you had any thought of renewing your relations with Madame de Tourvel, have sent her my letter? You, on your part, must have thought me very clumsy. Ah, believe me Vicomte, when one woman takes aim at the heart of another, she rarely fails to find the vulnerable spot, and the wound she makes is incurable. While taking my aim at this one, or rather while directing yours, I had not forgotten that she was a rival whom you had temporarily preferred to me, and that, in fact, you had considered me beneath her. If my revenge misses the mark, I agree to taking the consequences. Thus, I am quite prepared for you to try everything you can: I even invite you to do so, and promise not to be annoyed when you succeed, if you succeed. I am so easy on this score, that I shall press the point no further. Let us talk of other things.

For example, the little Volanges' health. You will give me confirmation of her recovery when I return, will you? I shall be very pleased to have it. After that, it will be for you to decide whether it would suit you better to give the little creature back to her lover, or to make a second attempt at founding a new branch of the Valmonts, under the name of Gercourt. That idea struck me as quite amusing; in leaving the choice to you, however, I must ask you not to make any definite decision until we have talked matters over between us. This is not to put you off for any length of time, for I shall soon be in Paris. I cannot positively give you a date, but you may be sure that as soon as I arrive, you will be the first to be informed.

Good-bye, Vicomte. In spite of my grudges, my spite, my criticisms, I still love you very much, and I am preparing to prove it to you. *Au revoir*, my dear.

Château de —
29 November 17 —

LETTER 146: *The Marquise de Merteuil to the Chevalier Danceny*

I am leaving at last, my dear young friend. I shall be in Paris to-morrow evening. I shall not be receiving anyone, what with the confusion a removal invariably entails. If, however, you have something urgent to tell me in confidence, I am willing to make you an exception to my rule. But I shall except only you; so I must ask you to keep my arrival a secret. Even Valmont shall not know of it.

If I had been told some time ago that you would one day have my exclusive confidence, I should not have believed it. But yours has attracted mine. I am tempted to believe that you have used your arts, perhaps even your enchantments, upon me. That would, to say the least, have been very wicked of you. However, I am in no danger at present: you have too much else to do! When the heroine is on the stage, one is scarcely interested in the confidante.

You have not so much as found time to tell me of your latest success. When your Cécile was away, my days were not long enough to listen to all your tender plaints. You would have made them to the echoes if I had not been there to hear them. When she was ill and you honoured me again with an account of your anxieties, it was because you needed someone to talk to about them. But now that the one you love is in Paris and is well, now especially that you are able to see her sometimes, she is more than enough. Your friends are no longer anything to you.

I don't blame you for it; it is the fault of your twenty years. Has it not been known since the time of Alcibiades that young men know friendship only when they are in trouble? Happiness provokes them sometimes to indiscretions, but never to confidences. I might say as Socrates did: 'I like my friends to come to me when they are unhappy.'[1] But Socrates, being a philosopher, was quite able to do without his friends when they did not come. In that respect I am not quite as wise as he: I have felt your silence as deeply as only a woman can.

Don't, however, think I am importunate: I am very far from being so! The same feeling that makes me aware of my loss, helps me to support it with courage when it is the proof, or the cause, of my friend's happiness. I don't, therefore, count on seeing you tomorrow evening, unless affairs of love leave you unoccupied and free; and I forbid you to make the least sacrifice on my account.

Good-bye, Chevalier. I am looking forward to seeing you again. Will you come?

Château de —
29 November 17 —

LETTER 147: *Madame de Volanges to Madame de Rosemonde*

YOU will certainly be as sorry as I am, my dear friend, when you learn of the condition Madame de Tourvel is in. She has been ill since yesterday, and her illness came on so suddenly, and manifests itself in symptoms of such gravity that I am really alarmed.

1. Marmontel, *The Moral Tale of Alcibiades.*

343

A burning fever, violent and almost continual delirium, an un-quenchable thirst: that is all there is to be observed. The doctors say they are as yet unable to diagnose. Treatment will be the more difficult because the patient obstinately refuses every remedy, so that she had to be held down by force while she was bled, and twice again while the bandage was refastened which in her delirium she is perpetually trying to tear off.

You who have seen her, as I have, so fragile, so gentle and sweet, can you imagine that four persons are scarcely able to hold her down, and that at the slightest attempt to reason with her, she gives way to unspeakable fury? For my part, I am afraid this may be more than just delirium – I am afraid it may be a real derangement of the mind.

My fears are increased by knowing what happened the day before yesterday.

On that day at about eleven o'clock she arrived with her maid at the convent of —. Since she was educated there, and has been in the habit of returning from time to time, her visit was not regarded as in any way out of the ordinary, and she appeared to everybody to be happy and well. About two hours later she inquired whether the room she had occupied as a schoolgirl was vacant, and on being told that it was, she asked to see it again: the prioress and some other of the nuns accompanied her. It was then that she announced that she was returning to live in this room, which, she said, she ought never to have left, adding that she would not now leave it *until she died*: that was the expression she used.

They did not at first know what to say to her, but when they had recovered from their initial astonishment, they explained to her that her status as a married woman would not allow of her being received into the convent without special permission. Neither this argument nor a thousand others were of any avail; from then on she refused obstinately to leave not only the convent but even her room. At length, at seven o'clock in the evening, the nuns, wearying of the struggle, agreed to her spending the night there. They sent back her carriage and servants and left it to the next day to come to some decision.

I am assured that her looks and manner during the whole even-ing, far from being in the least distraught, were deliberate and composed, except that on four or five occasions she fell into an abstraction so deep that they were unable to say anything to rouse her from it, and that on each occasion, as she emerged, she raised her hands to her forehead, which she seemed to clasp with some force. One of the nuns asked her at this whether she was suffering from a headache. She gazed at her a long time before replying, saying at length: 'The pain is not there!' A moment later she asked to be left alone, and begged that in future she should be asked no more questions.

Everyone withdrew except for her maid, who fortunately had to sleep in the same room for lack of space elsewhere.

According to this girl's report her mistress remained quiet until eleven o'clock in the evening, at which time she said she wished to go to bed. But before she was completely undressed, she began to walk rapidly about the room, gesturing a great deal. Julie, who had been a witness of all that had passed during the day, dared not say anything and waited in silence for nearly an hour. At length, Madame de Tourvel called to her twice in quick succession, and she had scarcely time to run to her before her mistress fell into her arms, saying: 'I am exhausted.' She allowed herself to be taken to bed, but would eat or drink nothing and refused to allow the girl to call for help. She asked only for some water to be put by her, and ordered Julie to go to bed.

The latter assures me that she stayed awake until two o'clock in the morning without hearing, during this time, either sound or movement. But she was wakened at five by the sound of her mistress talking in a loud voice; and having asked her whether she needed anything and received no reply, she took the lamp and went to her bed. Madame de Tourvel did not recognize her, but interrupting her incoherent soliloquy, cried out sharply: 'Leave me alone. Leave me in darkness. It is in darkness that I must live.' I myself noticed yesterday how often this phrase recurs to her.

Julie took advantage of this semblance of a command to leave the room in search of people and help: but Madame de Tourvel refused both with the transports and passions that have so often since recurred.

This state of affairs placed the whole convent in so difficult a situation that yesterday at seven o'clock in the morning the prioress decided to send for me. . . . It was not yet light. I hurried off immediately. When I was announced to Madame de Tourvel, she seemed to recover consciousness and replied: 'Oh, yes! Let her come in.' But when I reached her bedside she looked at me fixedly, and taking my hand suddenly in hers and pressing it she said in a firm but mournful voice: 'I am dying because I did not believe you.' Immediately afterwards, covering her eyes, she reverted to her most commonly recurring cries of: 'Leave me alone,' etc., and lost all consciousness.

The words she spoke to me, and others that escaped her in her delirium, lead me to fear that this cruel malady springs from a cause more cruel still. But let us respect our friend's secrets. Let us be content with pitying her misfortune.

The whole of yesterday was equally disturbed, divided between transports of fearful delirium and periods of lethargic depression, the only times at which she takes or gives any rest. I did not leave her bedside till nine o'clock in the evening, and I am returning this morning to spend the whole day with her. I shall certainly not abandon my unhappy friend: but what is distressing is her persistent refusal of all care and assistance.

I send you last night's bulletin which I have just received and which, as you will see, is anything but comforting. I shall take care to send all the bulletins faithfully on to you.

Good-bye, my dear friend. I am returning to the invalid. My daughter, who is fortunately almost well again, pays you her respects.

Paris
29 November 17 —

LETTER 148: *The Chevalier Danceny to Madame de Merteuil*

O FRIEND that I love! – O mistress that I adore! O you who began my happiness! – O you who are its crown! Kind friend – sweet love – why must the thought of your distress come to disturb my

delight? Ah, Madame, calm yourself: it is friendship that asks –
Oh, dear heart, be happy! It is love that implores.

Come, what have you to reproach yourself for? Believe me, your
delicacy deceives you. The regrets it makes you feel, the wrongs it
accuses me of, are equally illusory. I know in my heart that there
have been no enchantments between us but those of love. Do not
then be afraid to give yourself up to the same feelings that you
inspire, to allow yourself to burn with the same fires you have
kindled. Are our hearts the less pure for having known the truth
so late? No, no. It is on the contrary only the voluptuary, who,
working always according to plan, is able to regulate his progress
and control his resources and foresee the outcome from a distance.
True love does not allow considerations and calculations. It uses
our feelings to distract us from our thoughts; its power is never so
strong as when we are least aware of it; and it is by stealth and in
silence that it entangles us in the web that is as invisible as it is
indestructible.

So it was that only yesterday, in spite of the lively emotion I
felt at the thought of your return, in spite of my extreme pleasure
at seeing you, I still thought it was no more than peaceable friendship that prompted and directed me: or rather, having surrendered
entirely to the feelings of my heart, I was very little concerned to
discover their origin or cause. Like me, my dear, you felt without
knowing it the powerful charm that gave our souls up to sweet
feelings of tenderness; and neither of us recognized the god of love
till we had emerged from the intoxication into which he had
plunged us.

But that in itself justifies rather than condemns us. No: you have
not betrayed our friendship, any more than I have abused your
confidence. Neither of us, it is true, knew our feelings; but though
we were under an illusion, we had not tried to create one. Ah, far
from lamenting our fate, let us think only of the happiness it has
given us. And instead of spoiling that happiness with unjust reproaches, let us try only to increase it with the charm of perfect
trust and çonfidence. Oh, my dear, how I cherish that hope in my
heart! Yes, from now on, free of all fear, you will give yourself up to love; you will share my desires, my transports, the
delirium of my senses, and the intoxication of my soul, and

every instant of each happy day will be the occasion of some new pleasure.

Good-bye, my beloved! I shall see you this evening, but shall I find you alone? I dare not hope so. Ah, you could not long for it as much as I do!

Paris
1 December 17 —

LETTER 149: *Madame de Volanges to*
Madame de Rosemonde

THROUGHOUT almost the whole of yesterday, my dear friend, I hoped that I should be able to give you better news this morning of our poor invalid's condition: but last evening my hopes were destroyed, and I am left only with regret at having lost them. A certain incident, apparently unimportant, but most cruel in its consequences, has left the invalid at least as disturbed as she was at first, if not more so.

I should have understood nothing of this sudden reversal, had not our unhappy friend taken me entirely into her confidence yesterday. As she has not left me unaware that you, too, know of all her misfortunes, I can speak to you freely about the whole sorry situation.

Yesterday morning, when I arrived at the convent, I was told that the invalid had been asleep for more than three hours, and her sleep was so peaceful and profound that I was afraid for a moment that she might be in a coma. Some time later she awoke and opened the bed-curtains herself. She looked at us all with an air of surprise: and as I rose to go to her, she recognized me, called me by name, and asked me to come nearer. She gave me no time to question her, but asked me where she was, what we were doing there, whether she was ill, and why she was not at home. I thought at first that this was yet another delirium, though less unruly than the first: but I saw that she was quite able to understand my replies. She had in fact recovered her senses, but not her memory.

She inquired in great detail about all that had happened to her since her arrival at the convent, to which she did not remember having come. I replied faithfully, omitting only what I thought might frighten her too much: and when, in my turn, I asked her how she felt, she answered that she was not at present in any discomfort, but that she had been very much disturbed during her sleep and felt tired. I made her promise to keep calm and speak little, after which I partly drew the curtains, leaving them open, and sat down beside her bed. At the same time she was offered some soup which she accepted and enjoyed.

She remained thus for about half an hour, during which time she spoke only to thank me for my care of her; and she put into her thanks the grace and charm that are familiar to you. Then, for a while, she kept complete silence, breaking it only to say: 'Ah, yes. I remember now having come here', and a moment later cried out in stricken tones: 'My friend, my friend, pity me. All my misfortunes return.' As I leant towards her, she seized my hand and pressing it to her cheek continued: 'Great God! Why may I not die?' Her expression, more even than her words, moved me to the point of tears; she noticed them in my voice and said: 'You do pity me! Ah, if only you knew!...' And then, interrupting herself, she added: 'Ask them to leave us alone. I shall tell you everything.'

As I think I have pointed out to you, I already had an inkling as to what might be the subject of this confidence; and afraid that our conversation, which I could foresee would be long and cheerless, might perhaps adversely affect our unhappy friend's condition, I at first refused, on the pretext that she was in need of rest. But she insisted, and I gave in to her entreaties. As soon as we were alone she told me all that you already know from her, for which reason I shall not repeat any of it.

At length, having spoken to me of the cruel way in which she had been sacrificed, she added: 'I was quite sure that I would die, and I had the courage to do so: what I cannot endure is that I should survive in misery and shame.' I tried to combat her discouragement, or rather her despair, with the arguments of religion, hitherto of so much weight with her, but I soon became aware that I was not equal to so exalted a task and fell back on suggesting to her that I call Father Anselme, whom I knew to have her complete confidence. She agreed and seemed even to want very much to see him. He was sent for, and came immediately. He stayed a very long while with the invalid, and said on leaving that if the doctors were of the same mind as he, he thought that administration of the Last Sacraments could be deferred, and that he would return the next day.

This was at about three o'clock in the afternoon, and till five our friend remained quiet enough, so much so that we all recovered hope. Unhappily a letter was then brought for her. When it was offered to her she at first refused it, saying that she did not wish to receive letters, and no one insisted. But from that moment on she appeared to be more agitated. Soon after she asked where the letter had come from. There was no postmark. Who had brought it? No one knew. On whose behalf had it been delivered? The portress had not been told. Then she was silent for some time, after which she began again to speak, but her confused utterances told us only that delirium had returned.

There was, however, one lucid interval during which she asked for the letter that had arrived to be given to her. As soon as she set eyes on it she cried out: 'From him! Great God!' and then in firm, but disconsolate tones: 'Take it back. Take it back.' She immediately had the bed-curtains drawn and forbade anyone to come near her; but almost at once we were obliged to return to her side. She was seized with a more violent delirium than ever before, and in addition with truly frightful convulsions. These symptoms did not subside the whole evening, and this morning's bulletin informs me that the night was no less disturbed. In short, her condition is such that I am astonished she has not already collapsed; and I cannot conceal from you that I am left with but very little hope.

I suppose the unfortunate letter was from Monsieur de Valmont: but what can he still have the audacity to say to her? Forgive me, my dear; I shall refrain from comment. But it is very cruel to see a woman, till now so happy and so worthy of being so, perish in such misery.

Paris
2 December 17 —

LETTER 150: *The Chevalier Danceny to the Marquise de Merteuil*

SINCE I must wait for the happiness of seeing you, my sweet friend, I shall allow myself the pleasure of writing to you. It is in thinking of you that I charm away my regret at being parted from you. To describe my feelings to you, to remind myself of yours is so much a delight to my heart, that even a time of privations confers a thousand precious blessings on my love. However, if I am to believe you, I shall receive no reply from you. This very letter will be the last. We are to deny ourselves a correspondence which, according to you, is dangerous and for *which there is no necessity*. Of course I shall believe that, if you insist: for what can you wish for that I do not, for that very reason, wish for too? But before deciding finally, may we not talk about it?

As far as danger is concerned, you must be the sole judge: I cannot foresee anything, and must confine myself to begging you to look after your safety, for I cannot be easy when you are anxious. On this point it is not that both of us are at one: it is you who must decide for both of us.

It is not the same when we come to *necessity*: here we cannot but be of the same mind. And if our opinions differ it can only be for lack of mutual explanation and understanding. Here, then, is what I think.

There did, of course, seem very little necessity for letters when we could see each other freely. What can one say in a letter which a word, a look, or even a silence could not express a hundred times better? This seemed to me so true that when you spoke of our not writing to each other any more the idea slipped easily into my thoughts: it disturbed them a little perhaps, but did not upset them. It was as if, wanting to plant a kiss upon your bosom, I had encountered a piece of ribbon or gauze: I had only to move it aside, I did not regard it as an obstacle.

But since then we have been separated. As soon as you were no longer with me the thought of letters returned to torment me. Why, I asked myself, this extra privation? We are parted, but does that mean we have nothing further to say to each other? Supposing that, circumstances being favourable, we were to spend a whole day together: should we have to waste the hours in talking that we might be enjoying? Yes, enjoying, my sweet friend; for with you even moments of repose afford delicious pleasures. Finally, however long our time together, it must end in separation: and then one is so alone! It is then that a letter is precious! If one does not read it, one may at least look at it. . . . Ah, yes: one may certainly look at a letter without reading it, just as, it seems to me, I can still find pleasure in touching your portrait at night. . . .

Your portrait, did I say? But a letter is a portrait of the heart, and, unlike a picture, it has not that coldness, that fixity which is so alien to love; it reflects all our emotions: it is in turn lively, joyful, at rest. . . . Your feelings are all so precious to me! Will you deprive me of a means of knowing them?

And are you sure that you will never be tormented by a desire to write to me? If in solitude your heart is full or oppressed, if an impulse of joy goes through your whole being, or if an unwelcome melancholy comes to disturb it for a time, will it not be to your friend that you pour out your happiness or your grief? Will you have feelings that he does not share? Will you leave him, pensive and alone, to wander far from you? My dear . . . my sweet friend! But it is for you to say. I wanted only to reason with you, not to sway your feelings. I have offered you only arguments: my entreaties, I venture to think, would have been more effective. If you insist, I shall try not to be disappointed; I shall do what I can to tell myself what you would have written. But you would say it better than I, you know, and what is more I should be more pleased to hear it from you.

Good-bye, my dear. At last the time draws near when I shall be seeing you. I leave you with all speed so as to meet you the sooner.

Paris
3 December 17 —

LETTER 151: *The Vicomte de Valmont to the Marquise de Merteuil*

You don't of course, Marquise, credit me with so little experience as to think I could have been deceived by the *tête-à-tête* I interrupted this evening, or by the *astonishing coincidence* that had brought Danceny to your house! Not that your practised features did not assume a faultless expression of calm and serenity, nor that you gave yourself away in any one of those exclamations that sometimes escape the guilty or remorseful. I shall even admit that the submissive glances you threw me served you to perfection; and if you could have made them believed as effectively as you made them understood, I should – far from admitting or entertaining the least suspicion – I should not for a moment have doubted that you were extremely provoked by the presence of that *inconvenient third party*. But, so as not to have employed your great talents in vain, so as to have achieved the success you hoped for and effected the illusion you sought to produce, you should have taken greater care to prepare your prentice lover in advance.

Since you have set up as an instructress, you might teach your pupils not to blush, not to be disconcerted at the slightest pleasantry; you might teach them not to deny so vehemently, on behalf of one woman, what they would so feebly disclaim on behalf of another; you might teach them, too, to hear a mistress complimented without feeling obliged to congratulate her upon it; and, if you allow them to look at you in company, let them at least learn beforehand how to disguise that proprietary look which is so easily recognized, and which they so stupidly confuse with an expression of love. Then you may allow them to appear at your public displays without their behaviour doing discredit to their accomplished instructress. I myself should be only too delighted to bask in your reflected glory, and promise to have a prospectus for the new college written and published.

But as things are, I am astonished, I must say, that it is I whom you have decided to treat as a schoolboy. Oh, how soon, with another woman, I should take my revenge! And what a pleasure it would be! How far surpassing the pleasure she believed she was denying me! Yes, it is only where you are concerned that I prefer reparation to vengeance: and don't imagine that I am restrained by the slightest doubt, the slightest uncertainty. I know everything.

You have been in Paris for four days. You have seen Danceny every day, and you have seen no one but him. Even today your doors were still shut. I was able to reach you only because your porter lacked an assurance equal to yours. Yet I was not to doubt, you wrote, that I should be the first to be informed of your arrival, of which you could not let me know the date, even though you were writing to me on the eve of your departure. Will you deny these facts or attempt to excuse them? Either would be impossible: yet I keep my temper! From that you may judge the extent of your power. But, I beg you, be satisfied with having proved that power; don't abuse it any longer. We know each other, Marquise: that warning should be enough for you.

You will be out the whole day tomorrow, did you say? Very well – if you are indeed going out; and you may imagine whether I shall find out or not. But, after all, you will be coming home in the evening. Between then and the next morning we shall not have too much time to accomplish our difficult reconciliation. Let me know, then, whether it is at your house, or at *the other place*, that we are to make our many and mutual expiations. Above all, no more of Danceny. Your stubborn head has been filled with thoughts of him, and I can avoid being jealous of the vagaries of your imagination: but remember that, from this moment on, what was a mere caprice will be taken for a decided preference. I don't consider I was made for that sort of humiliation, and I don't expect to receive it at your hands.

I even hope that your sacrifice will not appear to you to be a sacrifice. But if it should cost you something, it seems to me that I have set you a fine enough example, and that a beautiful and sensitive woman, who lived only for me, who at this very moment is perhaps dying of love and longing, is worth at least as much as a little schoolboy, who, if you like, does not want looks or intelligence, but who is still inexperienced and unformed.

Good-bye, Marquise. I shall say nothing of my feelings for you. All I can do at the moment is to keep from examining my heart. I await your reply. Consider when you write it, consider carefully that, easy as it will be for you to make me forget the offence you have given me, a refusal on your part, a mere delay, will engrave it on my heart in ineffaceable characters.

Paris
3 December 17 —, evening

LETTER 152: *The Marquise de Merteuil to the Vicomte de Valmont*

TAKE care, Vicomte; be more considerate of my extreme timidity! How do you expect me to support the crushing prospect of incurring your indignation, much less to keep from succumbing to the fear of your vengeance? The more so because, as you know, if you did me an ill turn it would be impossible for me to requite you. I would talk about you in vain: your life would continue, its brilliance undimmed, its peace undisturbed. What, in fact, would you have to fear? Having to fly the country, if you were allowed enough time to do so? But does not one live as well abroad as here? And, all things considered, provided the French court left you unmolested wherever else you established yourself, you would be doing no more than change the scene of your triumphs. Now that I have made an attempt to restore your sang-froid by offering you moral reflections, let us return to business.

Do you know, Vicomte, why I never married again? It was certainly not for lack of advantageous matches: it was solely so that no one should have the right to object to anything I might do. It was not even for fear that I might no longer be able to have my way, for I should always have succeeded in that in the end: but I should have found it irksome if anyone had had so much as a right to complain. In short, I wished to lie only when I wanted to, not when I had to. And here you are, writing me the most connubial letters possible! You speak of nothing but wrongs on my part and favours on yours! How can one fall short in the eyes of someone to whom one owes nothing? I cannot begin to imagine!

Let us see: what is all this about? You found Danceny in my

house and that annoyed you? Very well: but what conclusions can you have come to? Either it was pure chance, as I said, or my own doing, as I did not say. In the first instance your letter would be unjust, in the second ridiculous. Was it really worth the trouble of writing? But you are jealous, and jealousy will not listen to reason. Oh, well! I shall do your reasoning for you.

Either you have a rival or you don't. If you have one, you must set out to please, so as to be preferred to him; if you don't have one, you must still please so as to obviate the possibility of having one. In either case the same principle is to be followed: so why torment yourself? Why, above all, torment me? Are you no longer the most amiable of men, can you no longer sustain the role? Are you no longer so sure of success? Come, come, Vicomte: you do yourself wrong. But it is not that; the fact is that in your eyes I am not worth so much trouble. You are less anxious to win my favours than to abuse your power over me. For shame, you ungrateful man. (There's feeling for you! If I were to continue in this way, my letter might become most tender: but you don't deserve it.)

You don't deserve that I make you my excuses either. To punish you for your suspicions you shall keep them: so concerning the date of my return, as about Danceny's visits, I shall say nothing. You went to a great deal of trouble to find out about them, did you not? Well, are you any the better for it? I hope your investigations gave you pleasure: they have not spoilt mine.

All that I can say, therefore, in reply to your menacing letter is that it lacked both the charm to please and the power to intimidate me; and that, for the moment, I could not possibly be less disposed to comply with your requests.

Truly, to accept you for what you now appear to be would be to commit a genuine infidelity. I should not be recovering my old lover, I should be taking a new one, who is very far from being his equal. I have not so forgotten the first as to make such a mistake. The Valmont I loved was charming. I am even willing to admit that I have never met a more charming man. Ah, I beg you, Vicomte, if you find him again, bring him to me: he will always be very well received.

Warn him, however, that in no circumstances can it be either today or tomorrow. His Menaechmus[1] has done him a little dis-service. By being in too much haste I should be afraid of making a mistake. Or is it, perhaps, that I have promised these two days to Danceny? Your letter taught me that for you it is no joking matter when one breaks one's word. You see, then, that you must wait.

But what difference does it make to you? You can always be revenged upon your rival. He will not treat your mistress worse than you have treated his; and, after all, is one woman any different from another? Those are your principles. Even the woman who is 'soft-hearted and sensitive, who lives only for you, and who finally dies of love and longing' is none the less sacrificed to the first whim that passes through your head, to a momentary fear that you are being made a mock of. And do you expect us to go out of our way? Ah, that is not fair!

Good-bye, Vicomte: be amiable again. Come, I ask no more than to find you charming: as soon as I am sure that I do, I promise to give you proof of it. Really, I am too kind.

Paris
4 December 17 —

LETTER 153: *The Vicomte de Valmont to the Marquise de Merteuil*

I AM replying immediately to your letter, and I shall try to make myself clear to you – which is not easy once you have decided not to understand.

No lengthy arguments are necessary to establish that each of us is in possession of all that is necessary to ruin the other, and that we have an equal interest in behaving with mutual caution. That, therefore, is not the question. But between the rash course of ruining ourselves and the doubtless better one of remaining friends as we were before, of becoming more so by renewing our former

---

1. The name shared by the twin brothers in Plautus's *Menaechmi*, a comedy of mistaken identities. (*Translator's note.*)

intimacy; between these two courses, I say, there are a thousand others we might take. There was nothing ridiculous, therefore, in telling you, and there is nothing so in repeating, that henceforth I shall be either your lover or your enemy.

I am perfectly aware that you dislike having to make this choice, that it would suit you better to prevaricate; and I know that you have never liked being forced to choose between 'yes' and 'no'. But you must be aware, too, that I cannot let you escape your uncomfortable dilemma without risk of being imposed upon myself; and you must have foreseen that I would never allow it. It is now for you to decide. I can leave the choice to you, but I cannot remain in uncertainty.

I warn you only that your arguments, good or bad, will not deceive me; nor will I be seduced by such flatteries as you might use to trick out your refusal. The moment for candour has come. I could do no better than set you the example, and I declare with pleasure that I should prefer peace and friendship; but if peace is to be disturbed, and friendship broken I believe I have the right and the means to do both.

I might add that the slightest obstacle put forward by you will be taken by me as a genuine declaration of war. You see: the reply I ask for does not require long and beautiful sentences. A word will suffice.

Paris
4 December 17 —

The Marquise de Merteuil's reply, written at the foot of the same letter.

Very well: war.

LETTER 154: *Madame de Volanges to Madame de Rosemonde*

THE bulletins inform you better than I can, my dear friend, of the sad state of our invalid's health. Entirely occupied with nursing her, I can spare the time to write you only because there is news to give you other than that of her illness. Something has happened which I certainly did not expect. I have received a letter from Monsieur de Valmont, who is pleased to choose me for his confidante, and indeed for intermediary between himself and Madame de Tourvel, to whom he sends a letter attached to mine. This I have sent back with my reply to his letter to me, of which I send you a copy. I think you will decide, as I did, that I neither should nor could have done anything he asked. Even had I wished to, our unfortunate friend would have been in no condition to understand me. Her delirium is continuous. But I wonder what you will say to this despair of Monsieur de Valmont's. In the first place, is one to believe him, or does he want only to deceive us all, even to the last?[1] If for once he is sincere, he may well say that he is responsible himself for his own misfortunes. I do not think he will be very satisfied with my reply: but I must say that everything I learn about this unhappy affair turns me more and more against its author.

Good-bye, my dear friend. I must return to my melancholy task, which becomes so much the more so for the little hope I have of seeing it succeed. You know my feelings for you.

Paris
5 December 17 —

LETTER 155: *The Vicomte de Valmont to the Chevalier Danceny*

I HAVE called twice at your house, my dear Chevalier, but since you have abandoned the role of lover for that of Don Juan you have, quite understandably, become elusive. Your valet assured me that you would be at home this evening, and that he had orders to await you: but I, who know your designs, was quite able to guess that you would come home only for a moment to change into the appropriate costume, and would then immediately resume your victorious career. Well done: I can only applaud. But this evening,

1. It was because nothing was found in the ensuing correspondence to resolve this doubt, that it was decided to suppress Monsieur de Valmont's letter.

perhaps, you will be tempted to change its direction. You know as yet only the half of your affairs: I must apprise you of the other half, and then you shall decide. I hope you will spare the time, therefore, to read this letter. It will not be keeping you from your pleasures since, on the contrary, it has no other aim than to provide you with a wider choice.

If I had had your entire confidence, if you had let me into those of your secrets that you left me to guess, I should have known in time; I should have been less clumsy in my eagerness to help you, and should not now be impeding your progress. But let us start from where we are. Whatever you decide, the course you reject will make someone else happy.

You have a rendezvous for tonight, have you not? With a charming woman whom you adore? For, at your age, where is the woman one does not adore, at least for the first week? The scene of the meeting will add to your enjoyment: a delicious *petite maison*, *taken especially for you*, where pleasure will be enhanced by the charm of freedom and the delights of mystery. All is arranged: you are expected; and you are longing to be there! That is what we both of us know, although you have told me nothing. Now for what you don't know, what, therefore, I have to tell you.

Since my return to Paris I have been trying to find a means of your meeting Mademoiselle de Volanges; I promised you I would do so, and even when I last spoke to you about it, I had reason to infer from your replies, I might say your transports of delight, that by doing so I should be making you happy. I could not have succeeded alone in so difficult an enterprise: but, having prepared the way, I left the rest to the zeal of your young mistress. Her love provided her with resources which were wanting to my experience: at all events, to your misfortune, she has succeeded. Two days ago – she told me this evening – all obstacles were removed: your happiness now depends only on you.

For two days, too, she has been hoping to tell you the news herself. Despite her mamma's absence, you would have been received. But you did not so much as present yourself! And to tell you the whole truth the little creature seemed to me to be – whether reasonably or unreasonably – a little cross at this lack of eagerness on your part. She finally found a means of bringing me to see her and made me promise to send you, as soon as possible, the letter I enclose with this. To judge from her warmth, I could swear there is some question of a rendezvous for this evening. Be that as it may, I promised on my honour and on our friendship that you would receive the tender missive in the course of the day, and I cannot and will not break my word.

Now, young man, what line of conduct will you follow? Faced with the alternatives of coquetry and love, pleasure and happiness, which are you going to choose? If I were talking to the Danceny of three months ago, even a week ago, I should, because I was sure of his heart, be sure of his intentions: but the Danceny of today, pursuer of women, adventurer, who has as is the custom turned into a bit of a rascal – will he prefer a very timid young girl, who has nothing to recommend her but her beauty, her innocence, and her love, to the attractions of a woman who is thoroughly *experienced*?

If you were to ask me, my dear fellow, it seems to me that, even with your new principles, which I readily admit are also more or less mine, circumstances would decide me in favour of my young mistress. In the first place you would be adding one to the score; and then there is the novelty, and the danger of your losing the fruit of your labours if you fail to gather it, for after all, from this point of view it would really be a missed opportunity, and they do not always recur, especially where a first lapse is at stake. Often in these cases only a moment's bad temper is necessary, a jealous suspicion, or even less, to prevent the finest triumph. Drowning virtue will clutch at any straw; once rescued, it is on its guard and no longer so easy to take by surprise.

On the other hand what, in respect of the other lady, are you risking? Not even a rupture, at the most a misunderstanding; and you will have the pleasure of a reconciliation at the price of a few attentions. What other course is open to a woman who has already surrendered, but that of indulgence? What would she accomplish by being severe? Loss of pleasure, without increase of glory.

If, as I think you will, you decide in favour of love, and, as it seems to me, in favour of reason, I think it would be prudent in you not to excuse yourself from the rendezvous. Let her simply wait for you. If you risk giving a reason for your absence, she will be tempted to verify it. Women are curious and persistent; they can find anything out. I have myself, as you know, just been made an example of. But if you leave hope to itself, it will not, since it is sustained by vanity, be entirely lost until long after inquiries can decently be made. Tomorrow you will choose the insurmountable obstacle that detained you; you will have been ill, dead if necessary, or something else that put you in equally desperate plight, and all will be forgiven.

For the rest, whatever you decide, I beg you only to let me know. Since I have no interest in the matter, I shall in any case think you have done well. Good-bye, my dear fellow.

I shall add only that I miss Madame de Tourvel. I am in despair at being parted from her. I should gladly sacrifice half my life for the happiness of devoting the other half to her. Ah, believe me! Only love can make one happy.

Paris
5 December 17 —

LETTER 156: *Cécile Volanges to the Chevalier Danceny (attached to the preceding letter)*

How does it happen, my dear, that I no longer see you though I have not stopped wanting to see you? Do you not want to as much as I? Ah, I am really unhappy now! More unhappy than I was when we were completely separated. The pain that others once inflicted now comes from you, and hurts much more.

For some days now Mamma has scarcely ever been at home: you know that quite well. I was hoping that you would try to take advantage of this period of freedom. But you don't even think of me; I am most unhappy! You so often used to say that it was *I* who loved *you* less! I was quite sure the opposite was true, and here is the proof of it. If you had come to see me, you would in fact have seen me, for I am not like you: I think only of what can bring us together again. You don't deserve to be told a word about all I have done to the purpose – and it has given me a great deal of difficulty. But I love you too much, and I want so much to see you that I cannot help telling you. Besides, I shall soon see now whether you really love me!

I have contrived it so that the hall-porter is on our side. He has promised me that every time you come he will let you in without, as it were, seeing you; and we can trust him, for he is a very honest man. It is only a question, then, of your keeping out of sight once you are in the house, and that will be very easy if you come only at night when there is nothing at all to fear. Mamma, you see, because she has been going out every day, goes to bed every evening at eleven o'clock, so that we shall have plenty of time.

The porter tells me that, if you wish, instead of knocking at the door you have only to knock at his window and he will let you in immediately. Then you will easily find the back staircase. Since there will be no light, I shall leave my bedroom door open, which will provide at least a little. You must be very careful not to make any noise, especially as you pass Mamma's back door. It does not matter about the maid's door, because she has promised me not to wake up; and she, too, is a very good girl! It will be the same when you leave. Now, let us see whether you will come.

Dear God, why does my heart beat so fast as I write to you? Is it that some misfortune is to overtake me, or is it the hope of seeing you that agitates me like this? What I do know, is that I have never loved you so much, and never so much wanted to tell you so. Come to me, then, my dear, my very dear, so that I can tell you a hundred times that I love you, adore you, that I shall never love anyone but you.

I found a means of letting Monsieur de Valmont know that I had something to tell him, and since he is my very good friend he will certainly come to see me tomorrow, when I shall ask him to deliver this letter to you immediately. So I shall expect you tomorrow evening, and you will come without fail unless you want to make your Cécile very unhappy.

Good-bye, my dear: I embrace you with all my heart.

Paris
4 December 17 —, evening

LETTER 157: *The Chevalier Danceny to the Vicomte de Valmont*

You need not, my dear Vicomte, doubt either my heart or my intentions. How could I resist a single one of my Cécile's wishes? Ah, it is truly her and her alone that I love, that I shall love forever! Her sweetness, her ingenuousness have a charm for me, from which I may have been weak enough to be distracted, but which nothing will ever destroy. Though I have been engaged in another adventure, without, so to speak, knowing what I was doing, the thought of Cécile has often come to trouble my sweetest pleasures; and perhaps my heart has never paid her more sincere homage than at the very moment of my infidelity. Meanwhile, my friend, let us spare her delicacy. Let us conceal my misdemeanours from her. Not so as to deceive her, but so as not to distress her. Cécile's happiness is my dearest wish: never should I pardon myself for a fault that had cost her a single tear.

I deserved, I know, your mocking at what you call my new principles. But you may be sure that it is not by them that my conduct at the moment is governed. And I have decided that tomorrow I shall prove it. I am going to make my confession to the very woman who has been the cause of my wrongdoing, and who has shared it. I shall say to her: 'Look into my heart. There you will find feelings of the most tender friendship for you. Friendship joined with desire has so much the appearance of love! . . . We have both been deceived: but though I am capable of error, I cannot be insincere.' I know this lady: she is as honourable as she is kind. She will do more than pardon me: she will approve of what I do. She has often reproached herself for betraying our friendship, her delicacy has often discouraged her love. Wiser than I am, she will strengthen those salutary fears in my heart that I have so rashly tried to banish from hers. To her I shall owe my becoming a better man, as to you I owe my becoming a happier. Oh, my friends, you will share my gratitude! The thought of owing my happiness to you increases its value.

Good-bye, my dear Vicomte. My great joy does not prevent my remembering your afflictions and sympathizing with them. That I could be of some use to you! Is Madame de Tourvel still inexorable then? I am told she is very ill. Dear Lord, how I pity you! May she return both to health and to kinder feelings, and make you happy forever! Those are the prayers of friendship: I venture to hope that they will be answered by love.

I should like to spend longer with you, but time is short and Cécile is perhaps already waiting for me.

Paris
5 December 17 —

LETTER 158: *The Vicomte de Valmont to the Marquise de Merteuil (written immediately upon waking)*

WELL, Marquise, how are you after last night's pleasures? Are you not a little tired? You must admit Danceny is charming! He accomplishes prodigies, that boy! You did not expect as much of him, did you? Come, I shall be fair: a rival such as he well deserved my being sacrificed to him. Seriously, he is full of good qualities. But so much capacity for love, especially, such constancy, such delicacy! Ah, if ever you are loved by him as Cécile is, you will have no rivals to fear: he proved that to you last night. By sheer dint of coquetry another woman might take him from you for a moment: a young man is scarcely able to resist provocation. But a single word from the beloved is enough, as you have observed, to dispel the illusion. So you have only to become that beloved to be perfectly happy.

Of course you will not delude yourself. You have too sound a judgement for there to be any fear of that. However, the friendship that unites us, as sincerely offered on my part as it is acknowledged on yours, made me wish, for your sake, for last night's test, which you owe entirely to my zeal. It was a success, but don't thank me. It would not be worth the trouble. Nothing could have been easier.

In fact, what did it cost me? A small sacrifice and a little skill. I allowed the young man a share in his mistress's favours, but, after all, he had as much right to them as I, and I cared so little in my case! True, it was I who dictated the letter the young lady wrote him: but that was only to save time, for which he had better employment. The letter I sent with it was, oh, nothing, nothing at all! A few friendly observations to guide the prentice lover in his choice. But, on my honour, they were superfluous. To tell you the truth, he did not hesitate for a moment.

And then, in his candour, he is to pay you a visit today to tell you everything: and I am certain the little tale will give you great pleasure. He will say to you, 'Look into my heart', or so he informs me, and you must see how that is bound to settle everything. I hope that in finding what he wants you to find there, you will also, perhaps, discover that taking a young lover is attended with its dangers; moreover, that it is better to have me for a friend than an enemy.

Good-bye, Marquise, until we meet again.

Paris
6 December 17 —

LETTER 159: *The Marquise de Merteuil to the Vicomte de Valmont (a note)*

I DON'T like it when bad jokes ensue on bad behaviour. That is no more my practice than it is to my taste. When I bear someone a grudge, I don't indulge in sarcasms. I do better than that. I take my revenge. However satisfied you may feel at the moment, don't forget that this will not be the first time you have applauded yourself in advance, simply in the hope of a triumph which escapes you at the very instant of your congratulating yourself upon it. Good-bye.

Paris
6 December 17 —

LETTER 160: *Madame de Volanges to Madame de Rosemonde*

I WRITE to you from the bedroom of your unhappy friend, whose condition is still very much the same. This afternoon there is to be a consultation between four doctors. Unfortunately that, as you know, is more often a proof of danger than a promise of help.

It appears however that she was partially restored to reason last night. The maid informed me this morning that about midnight her mistress had her called, desired to be left alone with her, and then dictated a fairly long letter. Julie added that, while she was busy preparing the envelope, Madame de Tourvel's delirium returned, so that the girl did not know to whom she should address it. I was at first astonished that the letter itself had left her in any doubt, but upon her replying that she was afraid she might be mistaken, and that, on the other hand, her mistress had especially instructed her to dispatch the letter immediately, I took it upon myself to open it.

I found what is here enclosed: it is, in effect, addressed to no one for its being addressed to too many people. I think, however, that it was to Monsieur de Valmont that our unhappy friend wished at first to write; but that she was finally, without noticing it, overcome by the disorder of her thoughts. Be that as it may, I decided that the letter should not be delivered to anyone. I send it to you because it will tell you better than I can the thoughts that occupy the mind of our poor invalid. As long as she is so deeply affected, I have scarcely any hope. The body is not easily restored to health when the spirit is so disturbed.

Good-bye, my dear and worthy friend. How glad I am that you are far removed from the piteous spectacle that I must continually keep before my eyes.

Paris
6 December 17 —

LETTER 161: *The Présidente de Tourvel to . . . (dictated by her and written by her maid)*

CRUEL and malignant man, will you never cease to persecute me? Is it not enough that you have tortured, debased, degraded me? Will you deprive me even of the peace of the tomb? Even in this abode of shadows where ignominy has driven me to bury myself, is there no release from pain; is hope still a delusion? I beg no favours that I do not deserve: to suffer without complaint I need no more than that my sufferings should not exceed my strength. But do not make my torments insupportable. Leave me to my griefs, but take from me the cruel memory of the happiness I have lost. Now that you have deprived me of it, do not raise its harrowing image again before my eyes. I enjoyed innocence and peace. It was when I saw you that all quiet forsook me, when I listened to you that I became a criminal. Author of my sins, what right have you to punish them?

Where are the friends that loved me, where are they? My misfortune frightens them away. Not one dares come near me. I am crushed, and they leave me helpless! I am dying, and no one weeps for me. All consolation is denied me. Pity pauses at the brink of the abyss into which the criminal has plunged. Remorse tears at her heart, and her cries remain unheard!

And you that I have insulted. You whose esteem adds to my agony. You, who alone would have the right to be revenged upon me, why are you so far away? Return and punish an unfaithful wife. Let me at last suffer torments that I deserve. I should already have submitted to your vengeance: but the courage failed me to tell you of your shame. It was not dissembling but respect. Let this letter, at all events, tell you of my repentance. Heaven has taken up your cause, and God revenges upon your behalf the injury of which you are ignorant. He tied my tongue and kept back my words, fearing that you might overlook the fault He intended to punish. He shielded me from your kindness, which would have thwarted His justice.

Pitiless in His vengeance, He has delivered me over to the very man who was my ruin. It is at once for his sake and at his hands that I suffer. I try in vain to escape him. He follows. He is here. He taunts me unceasingly. But how different he is from what he was! His eyes no longer speak of anything but hatred and contempt. His lips offer only insults and recriminations. He takes me in his arms only to tear me apart. Who shall save me from his barbarous fury?

But look! It is he. . . . There is no mistaking him: it is he I see again. Oh, my beloved! Take me in your arms. Hide me on your breast. Yes, it is you, it is really you! What dreadful delusion made me misunderstand you! How I have suffered in your absence. Let us not be separated again, let us never be separated. Let me breathe again. Feel my heart, how it beats. Ah, that is no longer fear. It is the sweet excitement of love. But why do you refuse my caresses? Will you not look gently upon me again? Why are you preparing those instruments of death? Who can have changed your features so? What are you doing? Let me go. I am trembling. God! Is it that monster again! My friends, do not desert me. You, the one who begged me to fly from him, help me to fight him. You, more kind, who promised to lessen my griefs, come to my side. Where are you both? If I am no longer allowed to see you, reply at least to this letter. Let me know that you love me still.

Leave me alone, cruel man! What new fury possesses you? Are you afraid some tender feeling may penetrate my soul? You redouble my torments: you force me to hate you. Oh, how painful hatred is! How it corrodes the heart that distils it! Why do you persecute me? What can you still have to say to me? Have you not made it as much an impossibility for me to listen to you as to reply? Expect nothing further from me. Good-bye, Monsieur.

Paris
5 December 17 —

LETTER 162: *The Chevalier Danceny to the Vicomte de Valmont*

I HAVE been enlightened, Monsieur, as to your conduct towards me. I know, too, that, not content with having shamefully tricked me, you do not hesitate to boast about it, and to congratulate yourself upon it. I have seen the proof of your treachery written in your own hand. I confess that it cut me to the quick, and I was not a little ashamed at having helped you so much myself to perpetrate your odious abuse of my blind confidence in you. I do not, however, envy you the despicable advantage you have won; I am only curious to know whether you can maintain every other advantage over me. And that I shall soon find out if, as I hope, you are willing to present yourself between eight and nine o'clock in the morning at the gate of the Bois de Vincennes in the village of Saint-Mandé. I shall see to it that all necessary preparations have been made for the explanations that remain to be entered into between us.

The Chevalier Danceny

Paris
6 December 17 — *evening*

LETTER 163: *Monsieur Bertrand to Madame de Rosemonde*

Madame,

It is with great regret that I fulfil the sad duty of telling you news which must cause you the most cruel grief. Permit me first to urge you to that pious resignation, which we have all so often admired in you, and which alone can help us to support the evils with which our miserable existence is strewn.

Monsieur your nephew . . . My God! must I so distress such a worthy lady? Monsieur your nephew has had the misfortune to be fatally injured in a duel he fought this morning with Monsieur the Chevalier Danceny. I am entirely ignorant of the subject of the quarrel, but it appears, from the note I found in Monsieur the Vicomte's pocket, the note which I have the honour to send you herewith, it appears, I say, that he was not the aggressor. Yet it was he whom Heaven permitted to fall!

I was at Monsieur the Vicomte's waiting for him, at the very moment when they brought him back into the house. Imagine my alarm at seeing Monsieur your nephew, carried in by two of his servants, bathed in his own blood. He had received two sword thrusts in the body, and was already very weak. Monsieur Danceny was also there, and indeed was in tears. Ah, no doubt he had good cause to weep: but it is no time to shed tears when one has been the cause of an irreparable disaster.

As for me, I was beside myself. Of little account as I am, I none the less gave Monsieur Danceny a piece of my mind. It was then that Monsieur de Valmont rose to true greatness. He ordered me to be silent, and taking the hand of the very man who was his murderer, called him his friend, embraced him in front of us all and said to us: 'I order you to treat Monsieur with all the regard that is due to a good and gallant gentleman.' He moreover delivered to him in my presence a great mass of papers. I do not know what they are, but I know that he attaches a great deal of importance to them. Then he asked that he and Monsieur Danceny should be left alone together for a moment. Meanwhile I had sent for aid, both spiritual and medical: but alas! there was no remedy. Less than half an hour later Monsieur the Vicomte had lost consciousness. He was just able to receive extreme unction: the ceremony was scarcely over when he breathed his last.

Great God! When at his birth I received into my arms this precious scion of so illustrious a house, could I have foreseen that it would be in my arms that he was to die, and that I should have to lament his death? So untimely and unhappy a death! I cannot hold back my tears. Forgive me, Madame, for being so bold as to mingle my grief with yours: but there are the same hearts and sensibilities in every walk of life. I should be most ungrateful if I did not for the rest of my days regret the loss of an employer who showed me so much kindness and who honoured me with so much of his confidence.

Tomorrow, after the removal of the body, I shall have everything sealed, and you may rely upon me entirely. You will not be un-aware, Madame, that this unfortunate incident terminates the entail and leaves you free to dispose of your property as you please. If I can be of any service to you, please be so kind as to convey your orders to me: I shall do all I can to execute them punctually.

I am, Madame, with the most profound respect, your very humble, etc.

Bertrand

*Paris
7 December 17 —*

LETTER 164: *Madame de Rosemonde to Monsieur Bertrand*

I HAVE just, my dear Bertrand, received your letter telling me of the terrible calamity of which my nephew has been the unfortunate victim. Yes, of course I have orders to give you, and it is only upon that account that I am able to think of anything other than my dreadful bereavement.

Monsieur de Danceny's note, which you sent me, is most convincing proof that it was he who provoked the duel. I should like you to lodge a complaint immediately, and in my name. In pardoning his enemy, his murderer, my nephew was able to indulge his natural generosity; but I must avenge not only his death but at the same time humanity and religion. The severities of the law cannot be too stringently invoked against this relic of barbarism which still infects the age. I do not think that in such cases we are required to pardon our injuries. I expect you, therefore, to pursue this affair with all the determination and all the energy of which you are capable – so much you owe to the memory of my nephew.

You will make a point, especially, of seeing Monsieur the Président de — on my behalf, and consulting him about it. I shall not write to him, wholly preoccupied as I shall now be by my grief. You will make my excuses, and communicate the contents of this letter to him.

Good-bye, my dear Bertrand. I commend you and thank you for your worthy feelings, and am ever yours.

Château de —
8 December 17 —

LETTER 165: *Madame de Volanges to Madame de Rosemonde*

I KNOW that you have already been told, my dear and worthy friend, of the loss you have just suffered. I know of the affection in which you held Monsieur de Valmont and most sincerely share the distress you must feel. I am truly sorry to add my griefs to those you already bear: but alas! even you can no longer offer our un-happy friend anything but your tears. We lost her yesterday at eleven o'clock in the evening. By an accident of the sort that seems to attend her fate, a mockery of all human prudence, the short interval by which she survived Monsieur de Valmont was long enough for her to learn of his death and, as she said herself, not to succumb under the weight of her misfortunes until their number was complete.

In fact, as you know, she was absolutely unconscious for more than two days. Even yesterday morning when her doctor arrived and we approached her bed, she recognized neither of us, and we could get not a word or the smallest sign from her. Well, no sooner had we returned to the fireplace and the doctor begun to tell me of the sad accident of Monsieur de Valmont's death, when the unfortunate woman recovered consciousness, perhaps in the natural course of things, perhaps because the repetition of the words 'Monsieur de Valmont' and 'dead' recalled to her mind the only thoughts that have occupied it for some time.

Whatever the reason, she abruptly drew aside the curtains of her bed, crying out: 'What! What are you saying? Is Monsieur de Valmont dead?' I hoped to make her believe that she was mistaken, and assured her at first that she had misunderstood. But, far from allowing herself to be persuaded, she insisted that the doctor begin the dreadful story again; and when I still tried to dissuade her, she called me to her and said in a low voice: 'Why deceive me? As though, to me, he were not already dead!' So I was obliged to give in.

Our poor friend listened at first with an appearance of calm, but soon after she interrupted the doctor saying: 'Enough. I have heard enough.' She immediately asked for the curtains to be drawn; and when the doctor made some attempt to attend to her, she refused to allow him to come near her.

As soon as he had left, she sent away her nurse and her maid as well. When we were alone she asked me to help her kneel on her bed, and to hold her as she knelt. She remained silent for some time, her face expressionless but for the tears that flowed abundantly. At length, joining her hands together and lifting them towards heaven she said softly but fervently: 'Almighty God, I submit to your justice. But pardon Valmont. Let only my miseries, which I acknowledge I deserve, not be held against him and I shall be ever grateful for your mercy!' I think I am justified, my dear and worthy friend, in entering into such detail upon a subject which I am very sensible must reawaken and aggravate your griefs, because, on the other hand, I am sure that this prayer of Madame de Tourvel's must bring great comfort to your heart.

After our friend had offered up these few words she fell back in my arms; and scarcely had she been put back to bed when a faintness overcame her, which lasted a long time but which yielded at length to the ordinary remedies. As soon as she recovered consciousness she asked that Father Anselme be sent for and added: 'He is the only doctor I need now. I know that my ills will soon be at an end.' She complained a great deal of a feeling of oppression, and spoke with difficulty.

A little later she had her maid give me the little casket I am sending you, which, she said, contained papers of hers, and instructed me to let you have it immediately after her death.[1] Then – as much as her condition allowed – she spoke with great feeling of you and of your friendship for her.

Father Anselme arrived at about four o'clock and stayed alone with her for nearly an hour. When we returned to the room her face was calm and serene, but it was plain that Father Anselme had been weeping a great deal. He remained to perform the last rites of the Church. That sight – always so impressive and so painful – was still more so for the contrast between the peaceful resignation of the sick woman and the profound grief of her venerable confessor, dissolved in tears at her side. Everyone was moved; the only one who did not weep was the one who was wept for.

The remainder of the day was spent in saying the customary prayers, interrupted only by the invalid's spells of weakness. At length, towards eleven at night, there seemed to be an increase of oppression and suffering. I put out my hand to her arm; she still had strength enough to take it and place it on her heart. I could no longer feel it beating; and in fact our unhappy friend expired at that very moment.

1. This casket contained all the letters relating to her affair with Monsieur de Valmont.

Do you remember, my dear, that at your last visit here less than a year ago, while we were talking of sundry people whose happiness seemed to us more or less assured, we paused with no little complacency to consider the lot of this very woman whose misfortunes, whose death we have now to mourn? So many virtues, graces, so many praiseworthy qualities; so sweet, so gentle a disposition; a husband whom she loved and who adored her; a circle of friends she enjoyed and whose whole delight she was; beauty, youth, fortune: a combination of so many advantages lost through a single imprudence! Oh, Providence! Doubtless we must bow to your decrees, but how incomprehensible they are! I must stop. I am afraid I may increase your own grief by giving way to mine.

I leave you to go and see my daughter who is a little indisposed. Having learned from me this morning of the sudden death of two persons of her acquaintance, naturally she felt unwell and I sent her to bed. I hope, however, that this slight indisposition will have no consequences. At that age one is not yet used to sorrow and its impression is therefore deeper and stronger. So lively a sensibility is no doubt a praiseworthy thing; but how soon what we see day by day of the world teaches us to fear it! Good-bye, my dear and worthy friend.

> *Paris*
> *9 December 17 —*

LETTER 166: *Monsieur Bertrand to Madame de Rosemonde*

Madame,

IN consequence of the orders you were pleased to give me, I have had the honour of seeing Monsieur the Président de —, and have communicated the contents of your letter to him, informing him that, in accordance with your wishes, I would do nothing without his advice. The worthy magistrate has instructed me to call your attention to the fact that the complaint you intend to lodge against Monsieur the Chevalier Danceny would be equally injurious to the memory of Monsieur your nephew and that a court sentence would inevitably reflect upon his honour – which would of course be a great misfortune. His opinion is therefore that it is essential to avoid taking proceedings; and that, if there is anything to be done, it is, on the contrary, to attempt to keep all knowledge of the unhappy affair, which is already only too much of a public scandal, from the Public Prosecutor.

These observations seem to me to be full of wisdom, and I have decided to await further instructions from you.

Allow me to beg you, Madame, to be so kind, when you send them to me, as to add a word on the subject of your health: I am extremely anxious as to the effect upon it of so much grief. I hope my attachment to you and my zeal in your service will excuse this liberty.

I am respectfully, Madame, your, etc.

Paris
10 December 17 —

LETTER 167: *Anonymous to Monsieur the Chevalier Danceny*

Monsieur,

I HAVE the honour to inform you that the question of your recent affair with Monsieur the Vicomte de Valmont was discussed this morning among Messieurs His Majesty's servants at the Public Prosecutor's office, and it is to be feared that proceedings may be taken against you. I thought this warning might be of service to you, either so that you might use your influence to forestall disagreeable consequences, or, in case you are not able to do that, so as to put you in a position to look after your personal safety.

If you will even allow me a word of advice, I think you would do well in the immediate future to appear in public less often than you have been doing for the past few days. Although this sort of affair is normally looked upon with indulgence, there is always, none the less, a certain respect due to the law.

This precaution will be all the more necessary in that it has come to my ears that a certain Madame de Rosemonde, who I am told is

Monsieur de Valmont's aunt, intends to lodge a complaint against you, whereupon the Public Prosecutor could not refuse her demand. It might perhaps be to the purpose if you were able to communicate with this lady.

Private considerations will not allow my signing this letter. But I hope, though you do not know from whom it comes, that you will do justice none the less to the sentiment that has dictated it.

I have the honour to be, etc.

Paris
20 December 17 —

LETTER 168: *Madame de Volanges to Madame de Rosemonde*

THE most astounding and distressing rumours, my dear and worthy friend, are being spread about here concerning Madame de Merteuil. Of course I am very far from believing them, and I am certain that it is all frightful calumny: but I know too well how the most implausible slanders can acquire credit, and how difficult it is to efface their impression once formed, not to be most alarmed at these stories, easy though I know they would be to disprove. I should particularly like to see them stopped in good time before they spread any further. But it was not till very late yesterday that I came to know of the horrors that were just beginning to be put about. And when I sent this morning to Madame de Merteuil's, she had just left for the country where she is to spend the next two days. No one was able to tell me to whose house she had gone. Her under-maid, whom I sent for to speak to, told me that her mistress had merely given orders to expect her next Thursday, and none of the other servants she has left behind are better informed. I cannot myself imagine where she can be; I can think of no one of her acquaintance who stays so late in the country.

Be that as it may, you will, between now and her return, be able, I hope, to provide me with information which may be useful to her. These hateful stories are based on certain circumstances relating to Monsieur de Valmont's death, of which, if they are true, you will clearly have heard; the truth of which, at any rate, you may easily confirm. I beg you to do so as a favour to me. This is what is being bruited abroad, or rather what is still being whispered, but will certainly be proclaimed more loudly before long.

It is said that the quarrel that occurred between Monsieur de Valmont and the Chevalier Danceny was the work of Madame de Merteuil, and that she deceived them both equally; that, as nearly always happens, the two rivals began by fighting and did not arrive at explanations until afterwards; that explanations in this case brought about a sincere reconciliation; and that Monsieur de Valmont, in order to complete the Chevalier Danceny's knowledge of Madame de Merteuil, and also to clear himself entirely, produced, in confirmation of what he said, a mass of letters constituting a regular correspondence he had maintained with Madame de Merteuil, in which she tells the most scandalous anecdotes against herself in the most abandoned style.

It is added that Danceny, in his first indignation showed the letters to anyone that wished to see them, and that now they are going the rounds of Paris. Two in particular are much-quoted:[1] one in which she tells the whole story of her life and principles, which is said to be the height of infamy; the other which entirely clears Monsieur de Prévan, whose story you remember, by affording proof that he did no more than yield to very definite advances on her part, and that the rendezvous was agreed upon with her.

I have, fortunately, the strongest reasons to believe that these imputations are as false as they are odious. First, we both know that Monsieur de Valmont was certainly not interested in Madame de Merteuil, and I have every reason to believe that Danceny was no more so: thus it seems clear to me that she can have been neither the subject nor the author of their quarrel. I cannot see either how it could have been in Madame de Merteuil's interest – supposing her to have reached an understanding with Monsieur de Prévan – to have made a scene which can only have had disagreeable and scandalous consequences, and which might have proved very dangerous for her, since she was thereby making an irreconcilable enemy of a man who was in possession of her secrets, and who at

1. Letters 81 and 85 in this collection.

that time had supporters in plenty. It is remarkable, however, that since that affair not a single voice has been raised in Prévan's favour, and that even he himself has made no protest.

Such considerations might lead me to suspect him as the author of the rumours now current, and to regard these slanders as the work of hatred in a man who, finding himself ruined, hopes in this way at least to spread doubts, and perhaps bring about a useful change of opinion. But from whatever quarter these villainous rumours spring, the most urgent necessity is to destroy them. They would die of themselves were it found, as is likely, that Messieurs de Valmont and Danceny did not speak to each other at all after their encounter, and that no papers exchanged hands.

In my impatience to verify these facts, I sent this morning to Monsieur Danceny. He is not in Paris either. His servants told my footman that he left last night after receiving a warning letter yesterday, and that his destination was secret. Evidently he fears the consequences of this duel. It is therefore only from you, my dear and worthy friend, that I can obtain the details that interest me, and that may become so necessary to Madame de Merteuil. May I ask you again to let me have them as soon as possible?

P.S. My daughter's indisposition was attended with no after-effects. She presents her respects to you.

*Paris
11 December 17 —*

LETTER 169: *The Chevalier Danceny to Madame Rosemonde*

Madame,
You will perhaps find what I propose to do today very strange, but hear me out, I beseech you, before you pass judgement upon me, and do not take for insolence and temerity what is done only in respect and trust. I cannot disguise from myself the wrongs I have done you; and I should not forgive myself for as long as I lived could I for a moment suppose that they might have been avoided.

Rest assured too, Madame, that however free I am from blame, I am not so from regret; and I might add in all sincerity that the regret I cause you has not a little to do with the regret I feel. To believe these sentiments that I am so bold as to assure you of, you have only to do yourself justice: and you have only to learn that, though I have not the honour of being known to you, I have the honour of knowing you.

However, while I deplore the calamity that has caused both your grief and my misfortune, I have been brought to fear that, wholly determined upon revenge, you will, in your efforts to accomplish it, invoke even the severities of the law.

Allow me first to point out to you that on this point your grief deceives you, since my interest in this matter is essentially bound up with that of Monsieur de Valmont, and since he himself would be involved in the obloquy you call down upon me. I might therefore suppose, Madame, that I could count rather on help than on hindrance from you in such efforts as I might be obliged to make to see this unhappy affair consigned to oblivion.

But my pride will not countenance my taking refuge in complicity, which is the resource of innocent and guilty alike: though I reject you as my opponent, I claim you for my judge. The esteem of the people one respects is so precious that I cannot allow myself to be deprived of yours without making some attempt to preserve it: and I think I have a means of doing so.

After all, if you agree that revenge is permissible – or more, that it is a duty – when one has been betrayed in love, friendship, or, above all, in one's confidences; if you agree, my culpability in your eyes is going to disappear. Do not take my word for this: simply read, if you have the courage, the correspondence I am putting into your hands.[1] The number of letters it contains in the original would seem to prove the authenticity of those which are merely copies. For the rest, I received these documents, which I have the honour of forwarding to you, at the hands of Monsieur de Valmont

1. It is from this collection of letters, from the one that was delivered into the same hands at the death of Madame de Tourvel, and from certain letters entrusted, also to Madame de Rosemonde, by Madame de Volanges, that the present collection has been formed. The originals remain in the hands of Madame de Rosemonde's heirs.

himself. I have added nothing to them, and have extracted only two letters which I have taken the liberty of making public.

One was necessary to the accomplishment of Monsieur de Valmont's revenge and mine, to which we both had a right and with which he had expressly charged me. I thought, moreover, that it would be doing a service to society to unmask a woman as truly dangerous as Madame de Merteuil, who, as you will see, is the only and the real cause of all that passed between Monsieur de Valmont and myself.

My sense of justice prompted me to make the contents of the other known so as to clear Monsieur de Prévan, with whom I am scarcely at all acquainted, but who has by no means deserved either the harsh treatment he recently received, or the severe and even more formidable public condemnation he has suffered since then without being in any way able to defend himself.

Of these two letters, therefore, you will only find copies: the originals it is my duty to keep. As for the rest, I could not, I think, commend to safer keeping what I should not, perhaps, like to see destroyed, but should be ashamed to take advantage of. I believe, Madame, that in entrusting these documents to you I am doing as great a service to the persons concerned as I could do by returning them directly; and I am sparing them the embarrassment of receiving the documents from me, and of knowing that I am aware of certain occurrences which no doubt they would prefer to keep a secret from the world.

I think I ought to warn you, by the way, that the attached correspondence is only a portion of a much more voluminous collection of letters, from which it was selected by Monsieur de Valmont in my presence. The rest you will find, when the seals are removed, under the label (which I have seen): 'Account opened between the Marquise de Merteuil and the Vicomte de Valmont.' You will, of course, decide on this matter as your prudence suggests.

P.S. On receiving certain warnings, and upon the advice of my friends, I have decided to stay away from Paris for some time. My place of refuge has been kept secret from everybody else, but shall not be so from you. If you will honour me with a reply, kindly address it to the Commanderie de —, near P—, under cover to Monsieur the Commandeur de —. It is from his house that I have the honour of writing to you.

Paris
12 December 17 —

LETTER 170: *Madame de Volanges to Madame de Rosemonde*

I PROCEED, my dear, from surprise to surprise, and from sorrow to sorrow. You would have to be a mother to form any idea of how I suffered all yesterday morning: and if my most cruel anxieties have since been allayed, I have still to support a very keen affliction the end of which I cannot yet foresee.

Yesterday, at about ten o'clock in the morning, astonished that I had not yet seen my daughter, I sent my maid to find out what could have occasioned the delay. She returned the moment after very frightened, and frightened me a good deal more by announcing that my daughter was not in her room, and that her maid had not seen her there at all that morning. Imagine my state of mind! I summoned all my servants and questioned the hall-porter in particular: all swore that they knew nothing and could tell me nothing about the matter. I proceeded immediately to my daughter's bedroom. The disorder that prevailed indicated that she had obviously left only that morning, but I could find no explanation anywhere. I examined her wardrobes, her writing-desk; I found everything in its place. All her clothes were there with the exception of the dress she was wearing when she left. She had not so much as taken the small sum of money she had in her possession.

Since it was only yesterday that she heard what is being said about Madame de Merteuil, and since she is very much attached to her, so much so that she did nothing but cry all evening; since, too, as I remembered, she did not know that Madame de Merteuil was in the country, my first thought was that she had decided to see her friend and had been foolish enough to go out alone. But as time elapsed and she did not return, all my anxieties were renewed. Every moment increased my uneasiness, and though I longed to know everything, I dared make no inquiries for fear of giving publicity to a happening which later, perhaps, I might wish to conceal from everyone. Really, I have never been so distressed in my life.

At all events, it was not until two hours later that I received, simultaneously, a letter from my daughter and one from the Superior of the convent of —. My daughter's letter said only that she had been afraid I might oppose her vocation to become a nun, and that she had not dared to speak to me about it: the rest consisted merely of apologies for having made this decision without my permission, a decision, she added, which I should certainly not disapprove if I knew what her motives were. She begged me, however, not to ask her.

The Superior informed me that, seeing a young woman arrive at the convent alone, she had at first refused to admit her; but that, having questioned her and learnt who she was, she thought she would be doing me a service by giving my daughter temporary asylum instead of permitting her to venture further afield, which, it seems, she was bent upon doing. The Superior, while she naturally offers to return my daughter to me if I ask for her, urges me, as her profession requires, not to oppose a vocation which she calls 'so pronounced'. She tells me, too, that she was unable to let me know sooner what had happened because she had great difficulty in persuading my daughter to write to me, my daughter's intention being that no one should know where she had gone. What a cruel thing is the thoughtlessness of one's children!

I went immediately to the convent. Having met the Superior I asked her whether I could speak to my daughter, who came only reluctantly and in great fear and trembling to meet me. I spoke to her in front of the nuns, and I spoke to her alone: all I could obtain from her, amidst floods of tears, was that she could be happy only in a convent. I decided to let her stay, but not as a postulant as she wanted. I am afraid the death of Madame de Tourvel and Monsieur de Valmont have made too deep an impression on her young mind. Much as I respect the religious vocation, it is not without pain and even fear that I could see my daughter embrace that condition. It seems to me that we already have enough duties to fulfil without creating new ones; besides, at that age, we are scarcely capable of knowing what is best for us.

What increases my difficulties is that Monsieur de Gercourt is very soon expected back. Must so advantageous a match be broken off? How can one, then, achieve the happiness of one's children, if it is not enough merely to want to do so and to devote all one's energies to the task? You would be doing me a great kindness by telling me what you would do in my place. I cannot fix upon any one course. I find nothing so frightening as having to decide the fate of others, and I am as much afraid on this occasion of yielding to the severity of a judge as I am of giving way to the weakness of a mother.

I reproach myself constantly for increasing your sufferings by telling you of mine. But I know your heart. The comfort you are able to give others will be for you the greatest comfort you are able to receive yourself.

Good-bye, my dear and worthy friend. I await your two replies with great impatience.

Paris
13 December 17 —

LETTER 171: *Madame de Rosemonde to the Chevalier Danceny*

AFTER what you have brought to my knowledge, Monsieur, there is nothing to do but weep and be silent. One is sorry to be still alive when one learns of such horrors; one is ashamed of being a woman when one hears of one capable of such excesses.

I shall be very glad, Monsieur, to join with you, as far as I am able, in committing to silence and oblivion everything that may concern, and everything that may ensue from, this lamentable affair. I even wish it may cause you no other distress than that which is inseparable from the unhappy triumph you were able to achieve at my nephew's expense. In spite of his misdeeds, which I am obliged to acknowledge, I feel that I shall never be consoled for his loss. But my inconsolable affliction shall be the only revenge I take upon you: it is for your heart to calculate its extent.

If you will allow me, at my age, a reflection that is scarcely ever made at yours, I must say that if one only knew where one's true happiness lay one would never look for it outside the limits prescribed by the law and by religion.

You may be sure that I shall willingly and faithfully keep the letters you have entrusted to me. But I must ask you to authorize me to refuse to give them up to anyone, even to you, Monsieur, unless they become necessary to a justification of your conduct. I dare say you will not refuse, and that it is no longer necessary to make you feel how dearly one must pay for giving way even to the justest revenge.

I shall not stop there in my requests, convinced as I am of your generosity and delicacy: it would be most worthy of both to deliver into my hands Mademoiselle de Volanges' letters as well, which apparently you have kept, and which no doubt are of no further interest to you. I know that this young lady has done you great wrongs. But I cannot think that you contemplate punishing them; if only out of respect for yourself, you will not disgrace the person you once loved so much. I need not add that the regard which the daughter does not merit is due at least to the mother, that worthy woman to whom you owe not inconsiderable amends. For after all, whatever excuses are made on behalf of a so-called sincerity of feeling, he who first seduces a still innocent and simple heart becomes thereby the first abettor of its corruption and must forever be responsible for the excesses and aberrations that follow.

Do not be surprised, Monsieur, at so much sincerity on my part. It is the surest proof I can give you of my perfect esteem: to that you will acquire still further claim if you will connive, as I wish, at the safety of a secret, the disclosure of which would be to your own detriment and would bring death to the mother's heart that you have already wounded. At all events, Monsieur, I wish to do my friend this service; and were I afraid that you might deny me such a consolation, I should ask you to remember first that you have left me no other.

I have the honour to be, etc.

Château de ——
15 December 17 ——

LETTER 172: *Madame de Rosemonde to Madame de Volanges*

HAD I been obliged, my dear, to wait while I sent to Paris for the information you require concerning Madame de Merteuil, it would not yet have been possible to give it to you; and no doubt I should have received none but vague and dubious reports. But certain other intelligence has reached my ears that I did not expect and had no reason to expect, and which has only too much foundation. Oh, my dear, how deceived you have been in this woman!

I recoil from entering into the least detail concerning this pack of horrors, but you may be sure that whatever is being repeated falls far short of the truth. I hope, my dear, that you know me well enough to take me at my word, and that you will demand no proof: be content to know that proof exists in abundance, and that I have it at this very moment in my hands.

It is not without extreme reluctance that I make you another, and similar, request: do not oblige me to explain my motives for the advice concerning Mademoiselle de Volanges which you have asked for, and which I am now to give you. I urge you not to oppose the vocation she displays. Of course no argument can justify the coercion of any person into this way of life who is not called to it. But it is sometimes a piece of great good fortune when someone is so called. And as you have observed, your daughter herself tells you that you would not disapprove of her if you knew her motives. He who inspires our inclinations knows better than we do, in our vain wisdom, what is fitting for each one of us; and often what seems an act, on His part, of great severity proceeds, on the contrary, from His clemency.

At all events, my opinion, which I know very well must distress you — and you must judge from that how thoroughly I have considered it before offering it to you — is that you should leave Mademoiselle de Volanges in the convent, since the decision is her own; that you should encourage rather than obstruct the plan she seems to have formed; and that, in anticipation of its being carried out, you should not hesitate to break off the match you have arranged.

Having fulfilled the painful duties of friendship, and being powerless to add any consolations to them, I have only one favour left to ask you, my dear, and that is that you will not question me upon anything relating to this sad affair. Let us leave it in its proper obscurity. Without looking for useless and distressing explanations, let us submit to the decrees of Providence. Let us believe in the wisdom of its ways even though it is not permitted us to understand them. Good-bye, my dear.

Château de —
15 December 17 —

LETTER 173: *Madame de Volanges to Madame de Rosemonde*

Oh, my dear! What a frightful veil you throw over the fate of my daughter! And you seem to be in dread of my trying to lift it! What does it hide from me that can possibly give more pain to a mother's heart than the terrible suspicions to which you have made me a prey? The more conscious I am of your affection, your kindness, the more my torments increase. Since yesterday I have decided twenty times to be rid of these cruel uncertainties, to ask you to tell me everything without evasion and without reserve; and each time I trembled with fear, remembering your request to me not to question you. I have at length reached a decision which leaves me with some hope; and I expect it of your friendship that you will not deny me what I wish: that you will tell me whether I have more or less understood what you might have had to say; and that you will not be afraid to reveal everything to me that a mother's indulgence can excuse and that it is not impossible to make amends for. If my misfortune exceeds this measure, then I shall agree after all to leave you with no other explanation to make than that of your silence. Here then is what I already know, and the utmost extent of what I fear.

My daughter once showed some inclination for the Chevalier Danceny and I was informed that she had gone so far as to receive letters from him, even to reply to them. But I thought I had succeeded in preventing this childish error from having any dangerous consequences. Now that I fear everything, I imagine it might have been possible for my daughter to have escaped my surveillance, and I am very much afraid that, once led into error, she may have taken her indiscretions to an extreme.

I remember several circumstances which might go to strengthen this suspicion. I wrote telling you that my daughter had been taken ill at the news of the accident that befell Monsieur de Valmont: but perhaps it was only the thought of the risk Monsieur Danceny had run in fighting a duel that affected her sensibilities. When, later, she wept so much upon hearing of all that was being said about Madame de Merteuil, what I thought was the sorrow of a friend may only have been the effect of jealousy, or regret at finding her lover unfaithful. Her latest proceeding too, it seems to me, may be explained in the same way. One often feels called to God simply because one is disgusted with man. At all events, supposing these facts to be true, and supposing you to be aware of them, they would, no doubt, have been sufficient in your eyes to justify the harsh advice you give me.

If, however, this were the case, though I could not excuse my daughter, I should still think I owed it to her to try every means of saving her from the dangers and torments of an illusory and short-lived vocation. If Monsieur Danceny has not lost every feeling of decency, he will not refuse to repair a wrong for which he alone is responsible, and I dare say, after all, that my daughter would be an advantageous enough match to gratify him and his family too.

This, my dear and worthy friend, is the sole hope that remains to me. Lose no time in confirming it, if that is at all possible. You may imagine how much I want you to reply, and what a dreadful blow your silence will be.[1]

I was about to seal my letter when a gentleman of my acquaintance came to see me and told me of the cruel humiliation inflicted on Madame de Merteuil the day before yesterday. As I have seen no one these last few days I had heard nothing of the affair. Here is the account of an eye-witness.

Madame de Merteuil, returning from the country the day before

1. This letter remained unanswered.

yesterday, that is Thursday, had herself set down at the Comédie Italienne where she has a box. She was alone in it, and, what must have seemed extraordinary to her, not a single man presented himself to her during the entire performance. When it was over, she proceeded, as she usually does, into the small salon, which was already full of people. A murmur immediately went around, of which, however, she apparently did not suppose herself to be the object. She saw an empty place on one of the benches and sat down; whereupon the other women already sitting there rose immediately, as of one accord, and left her absolutely alone. This very marked display of indignation was applauded by all the men, and the hubbub increased to the extent, it is said, of hooting.

So that nothing should be wanting to her humiliation, it was her ill fortune that Monsieur de Prévan, who has been seen nowhere since his adventure, entered the same salon at that very moment. As soon as he was seen, everyone, men and women alike, gathered round him and applauded him. He found himself, so to speak, carried before Madame de Merteuil by the company, who then made a circle round them both. The latter, I am assured, maintained an air of neither seeing nor hearing anything, and did not so much as change her expression! But I think this is exaggerated. However that may be, this scene – a truly ignominious one for her – lasted until her carriage was announced. As she left, the scandalous jeering was redoubled. It is frightful to be in the position of a relation to this woman. Monsieur de Prévan was warmly welcomed the same evening by the officers of his regiment who were present, and there is no doubt that he will be restored to his official position and rank.

The same person who gave me these details told me that Madame de Merteuil was attacked the following night by a very violent fever, which, it was thought at first, must be the effect of the terrible predicament in which she had found herself; but since last night it has become known that confluent smallpox of a particularly malignant type has declared itself. It would really, I think, be fortunate for her if she died of it. It is said, too, that this whole affair will go very much against her in her lawsuit which is soon to be tried, and for which, it is claimed, she would have needed all her standing.

Good-bye, my dear and worthy friend. I see in all this that the wicked are punished: but I can find in it no consolation for their unhappy victims.

Paris
18 December 17 —

LETTER 174: *The Chevalier Danceny to Madame de Rosemonde*

You are right, Madame, and I shall refuse you nothing that is in my power, since you seem to attach some importance to my compliance. The packet which I have the honour to send you contains all Mademoiselle de Volanges' letters. If you read them you will perhaps be a little astonished that so much ingenuousness can be found together with so much perfidy. That, at any rate, is what struck me most just now when I read them myself for the last time.

But how, especially, can one help feeling the most intense indignation against Madame de Merteuil when one recalls the frightful pleasure with which she devoted all her care to perverting so much innocence and sincerity?

No: I have no love in me. I have nothing left of a sentiment that has been so shamefully betrayed: and it is not love that makes me seek to justify Mademoiselle de Volanges. Yet could not so simple a heart, so sweet and soft a character, have been inclined towards good even more readily than they were allowed to lapse into evil? What young girl, just out of her convent, without experience and almost completely without ideas, taking with her into society, as nearly always happens, an equal ignorance of good and evil; what young girl, I say, could have offered a firmer resistance to such wicked designs? Ah, to be indulgent, it is enough to consider how many circumstances, quite independent of ourselves, maintain the terrifying balance between decency and corruption in our hearts. You did me justice then, Madame, in thinking that the wrongs Mademoiselle Volanges has done me, though I feel them deeply, do not inspire in me any thought of vengeance. It is quite enough to be compelled to cease loving her! It would cost me too much to hate her.

I had no need of reflection to form the hope that all that is of concern to her and may injure her will forever remain a secret from the world. If I seem to have put off for some time my fulfilment of your wishes in this respect, I do not think I need conceal my motives from you: I wished first to be certain that I would not be troubled by the consequences of this unfortunate affair. At a time when I was asking for your indulgence, when I even thought I had some right to it, I should have been afraid of seeming to buy it, so to speak, by doing you a favour. Certain myself of the purity of my motives, I was so proud, I confess, as to wish to leave you in no doubt of them either. I hope you will forgive this perhaps over-fastidious delicacy in view of the respect in which I hold you, and the importance I attach to your esteem.

The same feelings prompt me to ask you, as a last favour, to be so kind as to tell me, whether you think I have fulfilled all the duties that have been imposed upon me by the unhappy situation I have found myself in. Once set at rest on this point, my decision is made: I shall leave for Malta. There I shall gladly make, and religiously keep, the vows that will shut me off from a world which, though I am still young, I have so much reason to abhor. There, under strange skies, I shall try to forget this accumulation of horrors, the memory of which could only sadden and deaden my soul.

I am most respectfully, Madame, your very humble, etc.

Paris
26 December 17 —

LETTER 175: *Madame de Volanges to Madame de Rosemonde*

MADAME de Merteuil's destiny seems at last, my dear and worthy friend, to have been fulfilled. It is such that her worst enemies are divided between the indignation she merits and the pity she inspires. I was quite right to say that it would perhaps be fortunate for her if she died of the smallpox. She has recovered, it is true, but horribly disfigured; more than anything by the loss of an eye. As you may imagine, I have not seen her again; but I am told that she looks truly hideous.

The Marquis de —, who never loses an opportunity to be spiteful, said yesterday in speaking of her 'that the disease has turned her inside out, and that her soul is now visible on her face'. Unfortunately everyone thought the observation very just.

Another incident has recently added still further to her disgrace and misfortune. Her lawsuit was tried the day before yesterday, and the verdict went unanimously against her on every count. Costs, damages, restitution of profits have all been awarded to the minors: so that the small part of her fortune that was not forfeited in the proceedings has been exhausted, and more than exhausted, in expenses.

Immediately she heard the news, though she was still ill, she made her arrangements and left during the night by herself taking the post-coach. Her servants said today that none of them wished to go with her. It is thought that she has taken the road for Holland.

Her flight has been the subject of more outcry than everything else put together, seeing that she has carried off her diamonds – a collection of very considerable value – which should have formed part of her husband's estate; her silver, her jewels; in short, all that she was able to take with her; and has left almost 50,000 *livres* in debts behind her. It is a complete bankruptcy.

The family is to foregather tomorrow to see about accommodating the creditors. Though I am a very distant relation I have offered to make one of the number: but before I attend that meeting, I shall be present at a much more melancholy ceremony. My daughter assumes the postulant's habit tomorrow. I hope you do not forget, my dear, that I make this great sacrifice thinking myself compelled to it for no other reason than that you have preserved your silence since receiving my letter.

Monsieur Danceny left Paris nearly a fortnight ago. It is said that he is going to Malta with the intention of establishing himself there. There may still be time to bring him back!... My dear!... Is my daughter so very guilty?... You will no doubt forgive a mother for the difficulty she finds in admitting so dreadful a truth.

What disasters have of late dogged my footsteps, striking at me through the persons nearest to my heart! My daughter and my friend!

Who would not shudder to think of the misery that may be caused by a single dangerous intimacy? And how much suffering could be avoided if it were more often thought of! What woman would not fly the seducer's first approach? What mother could, without trembling, see anyone but herself in conversation with her daughter? But we never reflect until after the event, when it is too late; and one of the most important of truths, as also, perhaps, one of the most generally acknowledged, is cast aside and forgotten amid the inconsequential bustle of our lives.

Good-bye, my dear and worthy friend; I am now discovering that reason, unable in the first place to prevent our misfortunes, is even less equal to consoling us for them.[1]

Paris
14 January 17 —

1. For motives of our own – and certain other considerations which we shall always consider it our duty to respect – we are compelled to stop here.

We can, at the present moment, give the reader neither the subsequent adventures of Mademoiselle de Volanges, nor any account of the sinister occurrences which crowned the misfortunes and accomplished the punishment of Madame de Merteuil.

Some day, perhaps, we shall be permitted to complete this work. But we cannot commit ourselves on this point: and if it were possible, we should still think ourselves obliged in the first place to consult the public taste, since the public and we have not the same motives for being interested in the book. (*Publisher's note.*)

APPENDIX

THESE letters appear in the manuscript of *Les Liaisons Dangereuses*, but were not included in the editions published during the author's lifetime.

1. *Deleted and replaced by the note to Letter 154.*

The Vicomte de Valmont to Madame de Volanges

I KNOW, Madame, that you do not like me at all; I am no less aware that you have always spoken ill of me to Madame de Tourvel; and I do not doubt either that you are now more than ever confirmed in your opinions. I am even willing to admit that you may have reason to think them well-founded. Nevertheless, it is to you I write, and I have no hesitation in asking you not only to deliver to Madame de Tourvel the letter I enclose for her, but also to make her promise to read it; to induce her to do so by persuading her of my repentance, my regrets, above all of my love. I am aware that my request may appear strange to you. I am myself astonished at it. But despair seizes its opportunities without stopping to think. Besides, the great and intimate interests we have in common override all other considerations. Madame de Tourvel is dying, Madame de Tourvel is unhappy: life, health, and happiness must be restored to her. That is the end to be attained, and any means is good which may ensure or hasten its attainment. If you reject the ones I offer, you will be responsible for the outcome: her death, your regrets, my eternal despair. It will all be your doing.

I know that I have shamefully insulted a woman worthy of all my admiration; I know that it is my fearful misdeeds alone which have caused all her miseries. I am not attempting to disguise my faults, or to excuse them. But you, Madame, beware lest you become an accomplice to them in preventing me from making my amends. I have buried a dagger in the heart of your friend: but I alone can remove the blade from the wound, I alone know how to cure it.

What matter that I am guilty, if I may be useful? Save your friend! Save her! She is in need of your help, not of your vengeance.

Paris
5 December 17—

2. *Added at the end of the manuscript as a letter lost and later recovered. Replaced by the final note.*

The Présidente de Tourvel to the Vicomte de Valmont

O H, my dear, how troubled I have been since the moment you left me: and how I should welcome some peace of mind! Why is it that I am overcome by so intense an agitation that it amounts almost to pain and causes me real alarm? Would you believe it? I feel that even in order to write to you I have to summon all my strength and recall myself to reason. I tell myself, I repeat over and over again that you are happy. But this thought – so dear to my heart, and so happily described by you as the sweet solace of love – has, on the contrary, thrown my feelings into a ferment, overwhelming me with too violent a happiness; while, if I try to banish it from my mind, I succumb immediately to that most cruel anguish which I have promised you so often to avoid and which I ought, after all, to be so careful to avoid since it affects your happiness. My dear, you have taught me to live only for you; teach me now to live without you . . . No, that is not what I mean; it is rather that, without you, I want not to live at all, or at least to forget my existence. Left to myself I can support neither my happiness nor my grief. I feel I must rest, and no rest is possible. I summon sleep in vain: all sleep has fled. I can neither occupy myself nor remain idle. I am in turn devoured by raging fires and numbed by deathly chills. Every movement tires me, yet I cannot stay in one place. In short, what can I say? I should suffer less in the throes of the most violent fever; yet, without being able to explain or imagine why, I am very well aware that my suffering springs only from my powerlessness to restrain or control a profusion of feelings, to whose charm, all the same, I could be quite happy to surrender my whole being.

At the precise moment when you left I felt less tormented; there was indeed some agitation mixed with my regrets, but I attributed it to impatience at the presence of my maids, who entered the room at that instant. They are always slower than I should like at the performance of their duties, and it seemed to me then that they were a thousand times slower than usual. I wanted more than anything to be alone: I had no doubt that, amid so many sweet memories, I should find in solitude the only pleasure to which your absence has left me susceptible. How could I have foreseen that though I had been strong enough in your presence to sustain the shock of so many different feelings experienced in such rapid succession, I should not when alone be able to support them in retrospect? I was very soon cruelly undeceived. . . . Now, my dearest, I hesitate to tell you everything. . . . However, am I not yours, entirely yours? Ought I to conceal a single one of my thoughts from you? Ah, that would be quite impossible! I only claim your indulgence for faults committed unwillingly, faults in which my heart had no share. I had, as usual, dismissed my maids before going to bed. . . .

*Some other French classics
are described on the
following pages*

LA ROCHEFOUCAULD

Maxims · L95

TRANSLATED BY L. W. TANCOCK

In the fashionable manner of his time La Roche-
foucauld, friend of Mme de la Fayette and Mme de
Sévigné, put his reflections on human nature into
proverb-like form. His unflattering assertions do
not merely expose the corruption of the seven-
teenth-century élite in whose midst he lived. These
cruel, wise, and disturbing sayings prick the bal-
loon of conceit and self-deception which many of
us take for our real self. Although there may be no
spiritual uplift in them, they make us look inwards
to discover the true mainspring of our actions,
which is often no more than *amour-propre*, self-
regard, and vanity.

MOLIÈRE

Five Plays · L 36

The Misanthrope and Other Plays · L 89

BOTH TRANSLATED BY JOHN WOOD

A new translation of Molière was overdue: the version most familiar to English readers dates from the early eighteenth century and its idiom is far removed from contemporary English. Lack of effective translations may account, in part, for the neglect of Molière which has long been a reproach and a loss to the English theatre. There are signs that the tide may have turned. If so, it will be to our pleasure and advantage for his is, above all, a comedy which, in George Meredith's words, 'Springs to vindicate reason, common sense, rightness, and justice'.

Five Plays includes *The Would-be Gentleman*, *The Miser*, *Don Juan*, *That Scoundrel Scapin*, and *Love's the Best Doctor*, while besides *The Misanthrope* the other volume contains *The Sicilian*, *Tartuffe*, *A Doctor in Spite of Himself*, and *The Imaginary Invalid*.

The translation keeps close to the original and seeks to retain something of the vigour and felicity of Molière's language in an English which is at once readable and actable.